About the Author

Trish Devine grew up at the foot of the mountain in Taranaki, New Zealand, with a love of books and an inexplicable fascination for Japan.

Teaching in multicultural communities and gaining a degree in social anthropology formalised her cultural interests, cementing skills for researching and writing historic fiction. While living in Hiroshima, Japan, she learned how a new future can emerge from a soul-destroying past.

Trish lives with her partner on the spectacular Hibiscus Coast, north of Auckland, New Zealand.

Rising Sun Falling Rain

Trish Devine

Rising Sun Falling Rain

Olympia Publishers
London

www.olympiapublishers.com
OLYMPIA PAPERBACK EDITION

A CIP catalogue record for this title is
available from the British Library.

ISBN: 978-1-80439-857-9

First Published in 2025

Olympia Publishers
Tallis House
2 Tallis Street
London
EC4Y 0AB

Printed in Great Britain

Dedication

I dedicate this book to the memory of my parents, Mavis and Jack Hinz. Their strong values, the determination to do right by others and an unwavering love for family form the foundations of this story.

Acknowledgements

Thank you to my Hibiscus Coast Writers' Group – Jane Beckenham, Maureen Green, Julie Duffy, Carine Malherb and Monica Judge – for your friendship, expertise and encouragement. And for the lovely long lunch meetings which we will do till we die. Thank you to my Japanese friend Naoe, 'Hatch', for advising on aspects of cultural authenticity, sometimes accompanied by sushi and saké. Thank you to my long-time friend, Editor Susan Williams, for your time and skilled scrutiny. I am so grateful. Thank you to my beta readers for your dedication, time and honesty, allowing me to see my book through readers' eyes. Finally, to Olympia Publishers – thank you for believing in my story and for making my dream come true.

PART ONE

JAPAN 1946

*World peace must develop
from inner peace.
Peace is not just mere
absence of violence.
Peace is the manifestation
of human compassion.
–14th Dalai Lama*

Chapter One

Listen to the whispers of your heart.
– Ancient Wisdom

Mick Mitchell sat uneasy. He'd been gripping the sides of his seat since their army truck, with Buster Daniels at the wheel, had careered out of camp at daybreak.

Now, in the fading light of day, tiredness taking over his stability, Mick found himself reaching for the support of the dusty dashboard or stamping on imaginary brakes. He hoped Buster didn't notice his nervous reactions.

Buster did notice. But he didn't care. 'They don't call me Buster for nothing!' he boasted, taking his eyes off the road to throw a sideways grin at his companion.

Mick didn't respond but slapped a hand on the dashboard. 'Good old Chevy, eh? Damn tough machines. Need to be, on these roads.'

Buster laughed. 'Yeah, never breaks down. Wish it would, bloody rattle-trap. Replace it with something decent. Must be one of the ugliest trucks ever made. Got the nose of a crocodile.'

Tomorrow this would be Mick's truck. Mick's job.

This morning, they'd negotiated a convoluted route, ferrying day volunteers from their village homes in the inland hills to a makeshift hospital in Hiroshima. Now, as dusk descended on the return journey, a refreshing vista of countryside opened up before them, providing relief from the heat and annihilation of the once-city areas behind them.

Not for the first time today, Mick thought about their passengers under the canvas canopy in the back: their bench seat a hard, unpadded plank, providing no protection from the severely pot-holed roads and Buster's gung-ho driving.

They rumbled through cart-width village lanes and hurtled along narrow causeways beside flooded rice fields, rather like giant paddling pools.

'Rice'll be planted any day,' Buster announced, as they bumped along a ridge that dropped away sharply to paddy fields on each side. 'Soon you'll see straight rows of sharp green spikes down there.'

Food from the land, age-old systems, prevailing despite the surrounding chaos.

Mick keenly anticipated being the driver, taking his time, observing how this unfamiliar patchwork of watery plots produced food for its people. He saw optimism in that. A small promise of normality alongside the moonscape of destruction.

His mind wandered back to the rubble-littered land behind them, the once built-up city areas where salvaged building materials were stacked neatly in piles at the roadside.

Pockmarked buildings here and there remained resolute survivors – sentinel over what once was. Makeshift huts put together with remnants and debris – hope for what could be again.

How could anyone here keep a grip on hope? Men in tattered tunics and trousers, sifting through remains as if trying to piece together something – anything – useful. Hollow-cheeked women, hunched, with a small child bundled on their back or toddling beside them, wandering, eyes to the ground, searching for food. Children sitting in the wreckage, engrossed in games from their imaginations, the world their playground.

Mick wondered if Buster, after his time in Japan, still reacted to the desperation. Or had it become an irrelevant background to everyday life, like faded etchings on wallpaper?

He didn't ask, wanting to experience that – and everything else – for himself. Three days since his arrival he was ready to get out and make a difference. The image of dusty, displaced people was already fixed in his mind, powerless to rebuild their lives. If it was him, what would he do? Where would he start? No answers came.

They just need help, the poor beggars – and lots of it.

'We've been trained for combat,' he ventured. 'But these people seem too desperate to cause trouble. It's pretty quiet.'

'Too quiet.' Buster slapped a hand on the steering wheel. 'Two months of driving this heap, back and forth every day. I'm looking forward to my next posting. Done my time in this old jalopy. Happy to hand over the ropes to you, my son.'

Mick nodded. 'Your past, my future.' He wondered how he would find his way tomorrow. It would have been good for Buster to ride with him on his first day driving, to remind him of the route. But he would be on his own, and left to himself to find something to pass the time during the middle of the day.

'Thanks for the tiki-tour today. What do you usually do while you're waiting to drive the villager's home? It's too far to go back to base.'

'You wanna know?' Buster grinned. 'I've got a straw mat rolled up back there.' He indicated behind him. 'Park the truck under a big old shade tree outta town, roll out my mat, and it's good night Buster.'

Mick raised his eyebrows. 'That's it? No other duty?'

'Long as the main job's done. Keep your head down and no-one will notice.'

Mick gave a short laugh. 'I see why it's too quiet. I'd be looking for something worthwhile to fill up the day.'

Buster turned to him, brow lowered, flicked his eyes to the road and back to Mick. They jolted through a series of deep potholes, but he made little effort to avoid them or slow down. Mick glanced behind him, wondering how the villagers were managing, sitting side-on, squashed in with nothing to grip. Words fell out of his mouth. 'Good idea to take it easy on bits like this.'

'Nah,' Buster retorted, missing Mick's point. 'This old Chev can take it. So, can the jeeps. It's the staff cars that break an axle.' The truck lurched and rocked from one pothole to the next. 'What'd you do back home?' Buster shouted over the road noise, unfazed by coming dangerously close to the crumbling edge of the causeway.

'Farm,' Mick said, hoping a brief answer would give Buster no more reason to take his eyes off the road. It made no difference, so he elaborated, more out of nervousness than good manners. 'Farming family, so the draft bypassed us on the land. I didn't get called-up for Europe. Was old enough to go, but essential workers and all that.'

'So how come you're here now?'

Mick shrugged. 'Farming's not really my thing. But Dad needed a hand during the war, all the pressure to produce more food. My younger brother, Sam, is more into farming. He's old enough to help now, so my parents couldn't really object to me going this time. I was keen to get away at last. Glad to get accepted for the occupation forces.'

'I hear you. Me too. Had to get out of that house.' Buster chuckled. 'The call-up for peace keepers played right into my hands. Had no idea what to expect, though. Just knew there'd be destruction on the ground, since the bombings.'

Mick nodded. 'Same. Heard the stories, you know, heroes and horrors on distant shores. Didn't put anyone off, though. Made it all the more exciting really. And the thought of helping this country get back on its feet, a pretty worthwhile cause, I reckon.' He wondered if Buster had a similar humanitarian motivation. 'You volunteer?'

'Yep. Only the blokes who were already away in Europe got shipped here against their wishes. They reckoned they'd done their time. And back home we got more volunteers than needed. Keen bastards, us Kiwis.' He laughed. 'Otherwise you don't go overseas. Stuck in the home country for life. Find a girl, settle down, have kids, work your life away… that's as exciting as it gets. I was ready for a challenge, something different. Prove myself.'

'Would you have volunteered for Europe, if you had been old enough?'

'Prob'ly. Or lied about my age. Heaps of blokes did. Wanted to, but the war ended. Thought I'd lost my chance. Then the Jayforce call-up came along.'

Buster slowed a little as they approached a cluster of children standing on the edge of the road. Their smudged faces and ragged clothes of no concern. Wide smiles and cheerful waving said it all.

Life is simple.

Mick waved back as they rolled past, the giant vehicle dwarfing the little group. 'You like it here? Generally?' Mick asked.

'Mixed feelings.' Buster rubbed a grubby hand over his stubbly chin. 'Don't get me wrong – it's a good experience. The Japs are great. Especially the women.'

'Really?'

'I don't mean like *that*. They're just good sorts. Easy to get along with. The men can be a bit stand-offish. Can't blame them, though. They're not in charge in their own country.'

'What about the volunteers?' Mick asked.

'This lot?' Buster tipped his head towards the passengers in the back of the truck. 'They just think themselves fortunate to live far enough away. No Bomb injuries or fall-out that far out of town. So, they give their time to help those who got clobbered.' He hissed out a breath. 'God knows what it's like in that hospital, what they're dealing with each day.'

On board ship he'd had plenty of briefings, but Mick knew nothing would prepare him for the harsh realities. Now, almost a year after the bombings, it seemed so many were still struggling, dependent on their wits and the scant care of a pieced-together hospital. Most of them would suffer for life, those who didn't have their life cut short.

He was thankful to be in the transport division and not with the medics.

'Hard workers,' Buster continued. 'Guess the women are used to that, following orders. Not sure about these,' he tipped his head again towards the volunteers. 'But the ones at camp – you'll see. Different to home – our sheilas really have more say. Jap women are kind of – servants.'

'What?' Mick's voice rose in disbelief. 'Like slaves?'

'Not exactly. They seem happy enough. They're just not used to having any say. They do what they're told. Keep their heads down.'

'Since the bombings? The war?'

'Can't say. Wasn't here before then. Get the feeling they've always been like that – seems traditional.' He changed gears roughly as they started up the hill, the winding road narrowing even more as bushes closed in on both sides.

Mick hoped anything or anyone on the road ahead would be able to get out of their way.

Buster continued. 'You'll get to know them. Some work at the base, house girls, cooks and the like. Happy to do anything that brings home some money or food for the kids.'

He swung on the steering wheel, careening around several sharp corners. 'Some of the blokes have got something going on with their house girl.'

'Not you?'

'Nah. Nothing against it but it can get complicated. If things don't work out, you still have to face each other every day.' He turned to Mick with a lopsided grin. 'Better to find someone in town…'

'The volunteers…' Mick ventured, tipping his head to the back. 'Do they – socialize?'

Buster shot him a look. 'You mean *the princess*.' His voice was sharp. He glanced at the road, then fixed back on Mick.

Their eyes locked for a moment. Mick knew they were thinking about the same girl. 'Get it straight – this is work. They are our passengers, we're here to provide transport. That's all.'

'I don't see the difference…'

'You know the non-fraternisation rules?'

Mick nodded. 'But I heard they don't really apply any more.'

'They do. You gotta know the boundaries. House girls, the other ones working in camp, they work for us. So, we can suggest something social after hours – or girls around town if you're off duty. With these,' he tipped his head back. 'It's our job. End of story.'

The bushes cleared as the terrain levelled off. Tilled earth edged the road and neat rows of seedlings stretched away into the shadows. The first houses of the village came into view, steep-roofed wooden cabins with dark-stained frames, illuminated by the early evening glow of lanterns hanging at each door, fringing the narrow lane.

Mick wanted to walk through that lane, to peek into those tiny dwellings, to learn about the lifestyle of these people, so radically different from his own.

Suddenly Buster swung into a track that semi-circled around, facing back onto the road.

Mick recognised the bus stop, the pick-up place from the morning.

The day had been overloaded with new information and tomorrow he must remember the route single-handedly. Maybe he could get one of the volunteers to ride up front, point directions.

Mick jumped down as soon as the truck stopped and headed around the back. The first, most able, volunteers were already climbing down, but it wasn't easy to get onto the ladder, as it was fixed under the edge of the platform. Some of them struggled to find the top rung, looking as though they could do with a hand. Mick reached up and offered his. The reactions were mixed. The young women and girls shyly pulled away and persisted unaided.

An apron-wrapped older woman stood at the edge of the platform, squinting down at him, before her face blossomed into a brilliant, gold-flecked smile. She reached for his hand, managed the ladder with surprising grace, then turned to him, saying something that caused the others to laugh. They stopped to watch as she reached up to pat his cheeks, cupping his face between her hands. Still beaming she walked away, throwing another quip into the cluster as they all laughed, chattered and faded into the evening, homeward bound.

Buster appeared at his shoulder. 'That the one you're interested in?' He nodded towards the grandmother and villagers, exhaling a spiral of smoke through his smirk. 'Or this one.' He held up his cigarette gripped between two fingers, pointing it towards the one passenger remaining on the truck platform. 'The princess.'

Mick swung around. There she was. Her skin luminescent, glowing like those village lanterns in the rising moonlight.

She wore a kimono. He'd noticed it this morning – dark blue, like the midnight sky. Bright flowers in red and yellow, on leafy stems growing up from the hem. He knew about embroidery – his mother used to do it. Maybe those flowers were embroidered. The other women wore shorter, plainer jackets and wide-legged pants – more practical for a working day, and certainly more practical for climbing down a ladder.

Buster drew on his cigarette, watching her, squinting through his smoke.

Mick moved forward, stretched up and held out his hand. She turned to look at him, expressionless. Then she stepped to the edge of the platform, smoothly folding into a sitting position without disturbing the wrap of her kimono. In one graceful movement she turned and lowered herself till her feet reached the ground. Lifting the edge of her robe off the dirt, she looked towards them, nodded to Buster, to Mick, and glided away over the stony ground.

Mick gazed after her. He felt his mouth drop open, but he was powerless to change that. He stood there, his eyes following as shadows enveloped the colours of her robe. Even as the truck engine roared and a burst of exhaust fumes engulfed him, he stayed in place until she had drifted out of sight. Still he watched where she had been.

The truck jerking forwards broke the spell and he ran to grab the door handle, pulling himself up into his seat as Buster accelerated away.

They were some distance down the road before Buster said anything. 'Off limits,' he barked, wrenching the wheel, throwing the truck around the darkening track. 'Don't waste your time.'

'Did you?' Mick turned to him. 'Waste some time?'

Buster drew on his cigarette. 'Who wouldn't?' he said, almost to himself, letting out a slow stream of smoke with his words. 'The crown jewels.'

'Who is she?'

'Hard to know. Her father's a big businessman. Has factories in several places out of the city – so he didn't get bombed like most of them. Big employer, he's the local hero. Something like the mayor of this region, over the inland hills and down the other side. A number of towns and villages.'

'Does she live there, in the village?' Mick pointed behind them, remembering the inviting lane, the lanterns leading the way like a string of giant Christmas lights, casting their glow on the honey-toned dwellings.

'Got a big house on a property out the other side.'

'She got a name?'

'No idea. Princess. That's what I call her.' Buster slowed as they came to the base of the incline and began along the causeway, more difficult now that daylight was fast receding.

'Does she mix with them? The others seem to stick together.'

'Doesn't need anyone.' He pushed up the tip of his nose with a finger. 'She's a cut above.'

Mick raised his eyebrows. 'Tough being the big boss's daughter.'

Buster cranked the window handle, grabbed the stub of cigarette from the corner of his mouth. 'Something like that,' he said, launching flying sparks into the night.

Chapter Two

No road is too long
in the company of a friend.
– Japanese Proverb

Mick stepped outside the barracks, pausing briefly to greet the day, cool and refreshing at the early hour. He wondered why Japan was referred to as the land of the rising sun. Surely every country on earth could boast an affiliation with sunrise. As if on cue, the fiery orb silently glided into view over the treetops; creating a blush in the dawn sky that forewarned another sweltering day.

'And it gets hotter,' he'd been told. 'Temperature goes up ten degrees a week.'

'Can't wait,' he muttered, determined not to let the heat get the better of him today as it had done yesterday.

For now, while the air was vibrant and energising, Mick had a plan, involving the ferreting of equipment before anyone saw him. The convoluted army practice of writing for permission and waiting for a reply was something he had no time nor patience for. He wasn't sure of the protocol of the camp yet but guessed he would find out soon enough.

He let himself into the spacious workshop, organised with military precision as expected, and soon found what he was looking for – a hammer, a saw and a few dozen long nails which he scooped into an empty tin can.

Pulling the door shut behind him he headed to his truck, lined up with the other vehicles at the side of the compound.

'What have you got there, Soldier?'

Mick swung around to face a senior rank. He'd heard no footsteps. 'Ladder needs altering, sir.'

The Officer raised his eyebrows, pressed his lips and nodded thoughtfully. 'You're new?'

'Yes, sir. First day driving, today.'

'Whose truck you taking over?'

'Buster Daniels, sir.'

'And the ladder needs fixing?'

Mick didn't want this to rebound on Buster. 'Not actually fixing, sir. The ladder is fine. I've just got an idea – to make it easier to use.'

'We have a workshop – carpenters.'

'Yes, sir, but I'll have time between runs.'

The senior nodded thoughtfully. 'What's your name?'

'Mick Mitchell, sir.'

'Well done, Driver Mitchell. I'll be keen to see your invention.'

'Yes, sir.'

Mick waited for him to turn away before continuing across the stony yard to his truck. He secured the tools under the passenger seat and did a quick readiness check in the back. Finding a broom under the bench he started sweeping the seats and floorboards.

Foremost in his thoughts, breaking Buster's pattern, was Mick's desire to make a real connection with his passengers. He denied any ulterior motive, any favouritism towards any specific passenger. It was his way of doing business – getting things onto a fair and even keel from the get-go.

However, he couldn't deny that '*the princess*' had made an impression on him and that he had lost sleep trying to figure out what it was about her that had made such an impact. To say she looked amazing was an understatement. He couldn't find the words. It was more than that. So much more.

She was very different from any other girl he had come across, not just because of her clothes. Girls at home would clamour for his attention, unlike the cool encounter yesterday.

Buster was right on that score, about reasons for getting away overseas. What did he say? *Find a girl, settle down – your life's over...* Something like that.

Mick chuckled to himself. He'd never thought about settling down. It just didn't interest him.

What did interest him was finding out about life beyond New Zealand. He was keen to learn about all sorts of places. His mother was from another country, the Cook Islands. Maybe that was why he was curious about the world.

Japan couldn't be more different from his peaceful home. For a start, how had these people survived having their security and safety shattered?

What hopes did they have now?

Mick had hundreds of questions. He knew he would have to be patient – build up some rapport. He wanted to win the respect of the older woman, the grandmother, from the village. She stood out as a leader among the passengers, the matriarch – the 'camp mother' as she'd be called in New Zealand. She had a sense of humour and that would be a good bridge for communication.

Meanwhile he tucked the broom under the bench-seat and jumped down from the truck, heading towards the mess hall for an early breakfast.

He'd heard the mess hall had been a tent only a year or so ago, before the carpentry corps replaced the makeshift canvas with a more solid construction.

Tomoko and Yoshi, two local women employed at the camp, were serving breakfast. Mick had got to know them during the weekend language lessons. Tomoko wore her usual head scarf wrapped around like a turban. Mick guessed her to be in her thirties, Yoshi, maybe in her teens.

They greeted him with nodding and smiles.

'You early today, Mick-san? Nobody else so early,' Tomoko ventured.

'I am driving today. I go to the village, just me.' He mimed driving the truck, and looking puzzled about which way to go.

The women found his actions humorous, each holding a hand to cover her laughing mouth.

'Tell me,' Mick ventured. 'What word for older lady?'

'*Oooh?*' The two looked at each other, in confusion.

'Woman?' Tomoko repeated to him.

'Yes, older than you both.' He used his hands, trying to indicate an age beyond theirs.

'Big?' Yoshi asked, her short, smooth hair bobbing as she spoke. She stretched an arm above her head.

'No,' Mick laughed, waving his hands to delete that line of thought.

'She friendly?' Tomoko asked sharply, looking askance.

Mick hesitated, picking up on her suspicions, wondering how to distinguish between various interpretations of the word 'friendly'. He hunched over and walked slowly as if leaning on a walking stick.

'Ah, grandmother!' Yoshi guessed, jumping with excitement, clearly enjoying the game.

'Your grandmother?' Tomoko asked.

'No. In the village.' He pointed across the valley. Then mimed driving the truck and again pointed in the general direction of the villagers he would be picking up soon.

'Friendly lady?' Tomoko persisted.

Mick nodded carefully, gave what he hoped was a motherly smile while he mimed gathering people towards him.

'Ah, ah, *okahsan!* Mother!' Yoshi jumped in.

'*O-kah-san?*' Mick repeated.

'No.' Tomoko lifted her chin and gave Yoshi a sharp look. '*Obasan,*' she announced with unmistakable authority.

Yoshi stepped back, her hair falling like a curtain in front of her face.

'*Obasan,*' the older one repeated to Mick. 'Good name for aunty-woman.'

'*Obasan*,' Mick said, satisfied with the outcome.

He thanked her and turned to her junior, her face still concealed. 'Yoshi-san, thank you for your help.'

Yoshi peered through her hair, eyes flicking from one person to the other like a startled animal before she broke into a brilliant smile.

'Now,' Tomoko said, with a wave of her hand. 'Breakfast!'

Having been too tired to eat much dinner the night before, Mick tucked into his scrambled eggs on toast. After weeks of army food, he was quite used to powdered egg as a substitute for the home-grown version. He knocked-back his mug of tea, wrapped up some toast for later, called his thanks to Tomoko and Yoshi, who were now busy serving a growing queue, and headed out to start his day.

The first part of the route was the easiest to remember. The road down from the army base at one edge of the valley connected very soon with the main causeway road, continuing directly through the paddy fields until the climb up to the village on the other side. It was further on towards the city area where he expected to lose his way, while attempting to navigate the labyrinth of rubble with no street markers.

He'd left earlier than Buster would have done, to allow time for careful driving, indecision and wrong turnings.

Having learned to drive a truck at home on the farm where the terrain was never flat, he was used to negotiating ruts and potholes, often with precious cargo on the back. Today would be no different.

He completed the snaky incline and coasted towards the village, pulling into the turnaround and cutting the engine.

His gaze fixed on the lane between the cottages, finding himself pulled into a silent welcome, into its secrets. Lanterns now extinguished, were replaced by the peachy hue of early sunlight reaching into every detail like an artist's paintbrush, outlining every silhouette with the glow of daybreak.

Voices alerted his attention and he focussed, noticing one, then another of his passengers hurrying along the lane, calling to others as they scurried by the line of dwellings, some still slipping into shoes and pulling on jackets as they rushed and shuffled towards the truck, clearly caught unawares by his early arrival. He jumped down and signalled for them not to hurry, indicating that there was no rush.

Two of the villagers waited outside the first cottage. Then the older woman, *Obasan*, came out and joined them, linking her arms in theirs, all three heading his way.

As they drew nearer, *Obasan* stopped and looked behind her before continuing, chattering to her companions. Again, she stopped and all three turned to look back. What were they waiting for?

Realising his early arrival was causing concern, he wondered about *her* – the princess.

If she lived beyond the village, as Buster said, she would not see the truck.

He would wait. He wanted to see her again, to find out her name and forget the nickname Buster used, maybe to exchange a word or two, to find out if she spoke any English.

Then another figure appeared from *Obasan*'s house, a teenage boy maybe. Slipping into footwear as he scuffled forwards with the clumsiness of youth. *Obasan* raised her voice and the other two laughed at her comment. He ran towards them, then ambled alongside in his loose-limbed gait, seeming to join their conversation with good-humour.

The first arrivals approached the truck, bowing to Mick before scrambling up into the back and taking a seat on the benches along the sides.

Obasan and her friends came closer. The lad, his long legs outgrowing patched trousers and gangly arms extending beyond the cuffs of his long-sleeved shirt, had not been on the truck the previous day. He wore oversized black-rimmed glasses which he frequently pushed back onto his nose as he walked.

They drew closer and Mick became aware they were heading directly for him, rather than the ladder at the back. *Obasan* signalled towards Mick and gave the lad a nod. He stepped forward, bowing to Mick before speaking in carefully rehearsed English.

'This is my grandmother.' He held an open hand towards *Obasan*. 'She say – I go in truck.' He paused, his face reflecting various thought processes. Then he jumped forwards and indicated the passenger seat in the cab. 'This one,' he said. 'I know how to go hospital. I show you.'

Mick's relief was tangible. Without asking he had been given a navigator.

'Yes! Yes, please. *Arigato*.' He found himself nodding repeatedly. *Obasan* and the others beamed with satisfaction, then headed around the back and helped each other up the ladder, taking their seats on the benches.

Mick's navigator scrambled into the cab with some difficulty, losing a shoe in the process, having to climb down and start all over again. Mick checked the passengers in the back.

'Okay?' he asked.

'*Hai!* Okay.' They chorused.

While wanting to allow maximum time to negotiate the rutted roads comfortably, he also wanted to wait for just one more passenger.

He jumped behind the wheel and turned to face his navigator. 'What is your name?'

'My name Hashimoto Kazuya.'

'*Hashi-mo Kaz-wah*?'

'Kazuya.'

Mick tried again. '*Kazu-yar?*'

'It is difficult for you, I think. Maybe say *Kazu*?'

'*Kazu-san?*' Mick offered, remembering that adding *-san* to a name was the polite equivalent of Mr or Mrs.

Kazu smiled at Mick. 'Thank you.' He nodded enthusiastically and pushed his glasses back onto his nose. Then, with textbook English, 'May I ask, what is your name?'

'Mick.'

'Mick-san,' he said with a sense of achievement, then suddenly he turned away and, making noises of urgency, dove a hand into his pocket and withdrew a folded sheet of paper, passing it to Mick.

The paper, like none Mick had seen before, had fine threads running through it.

Unfolding it carefully, he could feel its delicate texture between his fingers. Pink blossoms clustered on the top edge and single petals floated down the page – so exotic – even compared to the fancy letter paper his mother treasured.

Carefully crafted English handwriting formed a short message.

Dear New Driver-san,
I not help at hospital today.
My help days Monday Wednesday Friday.
Thank you for your consideration.
Yours sincerely,
Emiko Tanazawa.

Mick read the letter again and traced the falling petals with his finger to see if they were hand painted. How could such a formal letter seem so intimate?

Remembering Kazu beside him, he took his eyes off the page and turned. 'How did you get this letter?'

'Grandmother – help at garden, big house – *Tanazawa-san*.' He tapped his nose to indicate himself. 'I help too. Help Grandmother. Yesterday, in garden, Emiko-san give me this.' He pointed to the letter.

'Her name is Emiko? The girl on the truck yesterday?'

How else could he be sure it was the same girl? 'Kimono?' He crossed his hands over his front, as if fastening a dressing-gown.

'*Hai*, yes. Emiko-san, always have kimono.' Kazu nodded, smiling. 'It's her family way. She not have…' He screwed his face and mimed the apron-style, tie-at-the-back working overall like his grandmother wore over her tunic and loose trousers. 'She not have that one.'

'How do you know her?'

Kazu whistled-out a breath and shrugged, as if stating the obvious. 'Always, we know. I, since small child, visit Grandmother many, many times. Village very small. Almost same age – Emiko-san eighteen now, I seventeen. We play together, since,' he stretched out a hand to indicate the height of a small child. 'Grandmother long time help garden, big house, *Tanazawa-san*.'

'Thank you.' Mick nodded, grateful to his new companion for being so forthcoming, despite his struggles speaking English.

Mick took a last look at the letter before folding it and tucking it into his chest pocket.

He would have to wait another day.

Starting the engine, he let the truck roll forwards onto the road while Kazu gripped his seat, sitting motionless, staring nervously ahead.

Mick carefully negotiated the spiralling downhill road and levelled onto the first causeway between the watery fields, concentrating on avoiding potholes along the way.

'Your grandmother asked you to come? On the truck.'

'She say – new driver. He kind.' He tapped himself on the nose. 'She say, I must help.

Last driver – not kind. Old lady – not happy.' He shook his head sadly and ran his hands under his seat and down his thighs, pulling a face as if in pain.

Mick nodded, laughed. 'I'll do my best. But these roads are very bad.'

'Road bad, yes. But I see – you very good driver. Old lady – she happy.' He nodded, satisfied.

'You live with your grandmother?' Mick pointed up the hill in the direction of the village.

Kazu nodded. 'When grandfather die, I go live village, with grandmother all the time…'

Mick skirted around the death of the grandfather, not sure about the customs of expressing sympathy. 'When did you start living in the village?'

'Two years, I live village.'

'And before that? With your parents?'

Kazu tipped his head forward. His glasses fell off. He caught them in his hands and held them there. 'Mother, Father, family home – Hiroshima,' he said quietly with finality, nodding to the flattened wasteland ahead.

'Oh, no. I'm really sorry.'

Suddenly Kazu looked up, then quickly repositioned his glasses, blinking into focus. 'Go this way,' he said, indicating a left turn with his hand.

Mick slowed, checked the way was clear and turned onto the adjoining causeway, aware he would have missed that turning without Kazu's prompt.

'I'm glad you are here to help me,' he said, again avoiding the subject of personal loss, the massive tragedy of so many citizens at the hands of his army's allies.

'It is my honour,' Kazu replied. 'And also, my hope…'

'Your hope?'

'When I go live grandmother, I leave school. My school in city.' He took a moment.

Mick glanced his way, saw lips pressed together, saw the determination in holding back emotions that bubbled just below the surface. 'Now – nothing.'

Mick took in Kazu's incomprehensible situation – his family, school, friends, entire past – destroyed.

Kazu rallied. 'But I lucky. I safe. My hope – to be teacher. I hope you help me, Mick-san. I want good English.'

'Of course!' Relief surged. In all this devastation, a seventeen-year-old could accept the past and plan a future.

Kazu smiled. 'Yes?'

'Happy to help.'

Again, Mick wondered about Emiko, if she spoke English. Her handwriting looked practiced and her letter was easy to understand, if not in perfect English. Even still, it could have required extensive use of the dictionary.

'This way.' Kazu indicated another approaching turn.

Passing the last of the sunken paddy fields, they were getting close to the streets of rubble, the raised land that once was homes, schools, shops, playgrounds. Life.

Kazu continued to give directions, navigating a route which differed from Buster's careering through narrow village lanes, leaving dwellings trembling in his wake.

Soon enough Mick recognised the reconstructed hospital building just ahead.

He pulled up, cut the engine and headed around the back to help the passengers climb down.

'Very good ride, good driver, I happy, good ride, *domo arigato* – thank you – thank you…' Kazu translated, as comments were delivered with repeated nods, bows and smiles of appreciation.

Kazu's grandmother climbed down last, accepting her grandson's steadying hand before wrapping her arm around his as she spoke to him sternly, demanding he listen.

Kazu called over his shoulder. 'Mick-san, *Chotto matte* – wait! I come with you?'

'I'll wait.' Mick relied on his young assistant for the project he planned today. He turned away, aware of the tense conversation developing between grandmother and grandson.

Eventually Kazu returned to the cab and jumped into his seat, saying nothing, but looking tense and fidgeting.

'I have a job to do,' Mick announced. 'You can be my translator.'

Kazu brightened. 'I – help?'

'Translator. English – Japanese. You can talk for me.' The lad beamed.

Mick started the engine and they headed back to an area he'd noticed on arrival, where the rubble had been cleared away and building fragments were stacked into piles at the roadside. Workmen with brooms, rakes and spades were sifting through the adjoining lot.

Mick pulled off the road and signalled for Kazu to follow him as he jumped down from the cab. At the back, beside the ladder, Mick explained his idea of creating a portable stairway up to the truck floor. Seeing Kazu's bewildered expression, he mimed a rising zigzag shape, starting at the ground and stepping up to the level of the truck tray. 'Steps,' he said, giving the ladder a shake and sweeping his arms away, to indicate it a failure.

Kazu's eyes lit up. He moved his hands as if they were feet stepping up, one after the other, on Mick's imaginary steps.

'Yes!' Mick shouted. 'You got it.'

Kazu looked pleased with himself. 'My grandmother – and all of others, very happy to have…' he paused to think of the word, but gave up and mimed his stepping hands again.

'Steps,' Mick said. 'Now, we need wood.' He indicated the collection of broken planks beside the road, then pointed towards the workers on the empty lot.

'Ah, you want?' Kazu looked incredulous, pointing to the pile of shattered boards. 'Make – steps?'

Mick sorted through the wood, choosing pieces too small to be of use in rebuilding houses but good enough for a huge improvement on the awkward ladder.

'How much?' he asked Kazu, nodding towards the workers, pulling a small leather coin purse from his pocket.

The lad frowned. 'Not pay, Mick-san. This free.'

Mick fumbled the tinny coins, examining their value. 'Ten?'

'Ten yen,' Kazu answered. 'But not pay men.'

'It's for the steps. Your grandmother and the villagers need better steps.' Mick repeated the stepping mime.

Kazu's voice dropped in pitch. 'Maybe – these are poor men.'

'And maybe they have families to feed.'

Kazu adjusted his glasses and squinted across at them. 'Maybe,' he agreed.

They headed over the rutted ground to where the workmen, insignificant figures in the vast plateau of rubble, were raking and digging. The men looked up, stopped work and stared motionless at the approaching pair.

'Konnichiwa,' Kazu greeted them, bowing and speaking again. Faces closed with suspicion, the men bobbed heads.

Kazu introduced Mick, as he indicated the truck, the inland hills and the direction of the village, then to the hospital still within sight. He motioned to the wood they had put aside by the truck, demonstrating the length and number of pieces they had chosen.

The faces of the men didn't change. They listened, eyes flicking from Kazu to Mick and back. Kazu continued, then turned to Mick and pointed to the pocket that held the coins. Mick pulled out the purse.

The men took notice, their posture shifted, their expressions opened up, their eyes flitted with animation.

Mick began counting. 'Ten yen, twenty, thirty…' He glanced up. Two of the men were smiling. The other three looked at him in disbelief.

'Thirty yen – a lot of money for these men.' Kazu shook his head. 'Too much.'

'But they can't share three coins between five of them. What if I give them ten each? It's less than a dollar.'

'Ten yen each! That's fifty-yen, Mick-san! Too much.' The head shaking continued.

Mick stepped forward, passing one coin to each of the men. They laughed and nodded and bowed and said words of thanks and bowed and laughed again, as if they had won the lottery.

Kazu couldn't keep his smile hidden as they turned back to the truck.

'Doesn't that feel good?' Mick asked.

The five men, suddenly energised, rushed up behind them, chattering and laughing, enquiring which pile of boards they wanted.

Kore wa? This one? And this one? *Kore mo?* This one, as well?

Three stacks of wood were quickly lifted onto the back of the truck, and another few planks, for good measure.

Kazu took time for a final bow while Mick nodded briefly and jumped into the truck. 'Quick, Kazu-san!' he instructed. 'Before we have a truck-load.'

They drove off laughing, looking back at the five men who continued waving as if farewelling dear friends, their arms full-length like windmills until out of sight.

Several miles from the centre, they came to a settlement where more buildings remained, some damaged and repaired, yet people were living here, going about their business. Trees stood tall and green and tidy vegetable plots flourished on any spare land around the homes.

Here, life continued.

Beyond the settlement, Mick pulled into a shady area beside a stream, wondering if this was where Buster took his daily siesta – an unbelievably inviting spot in the increasing intensity of sticky, dust-clinging heat.

He cut the engine and climbed down, Kazu meeting him at the back of the truck, eagerly following his lead, unloading the wood and carrying it into the shade.

Mick pulled the tools from under the seat and started to sort through the planks with the eye of an experienced handyman, assessing and planning, grouping and pencil-marking where lengths needed to be cut.

Kazu picked up the saw, holding it proudly, silently volunteering for the most strenuous task. Mick created a saw-bench with a stack of surplus boards and Kazu began cutting. He persevered when the saw jammed. He persevered when the makeshift bench fell over. He persevered even when his glasses would stay no longer on his sweaty nose.

The steps began to take shape, Mick hammering in nails as fast as Kazu produced cut lengths.

When they could no longer see through their sweat-stinging eyes, Mick signalled towards the stream. They downed tools and sat on the grassy bank, pulling off shoes, boots and socks, rolling up trousers and slowly sinking their feet into the breath-taking water. Mick drank from his army canteen bottle and passed it to his apprentice. Kazu drank and passed it back.

They exchanged a look, sharing workload and water, a simple ritual forming a bond.

Now, they were mates.

'What does your grandmother do at the hospital?' Mick ventured.

Kazu froze. Mick waited, taking another swig from his bottle, offering it again. Kazu reached for it absentmindedly, then feeling its weight – almost empty, passed it back without drinking.

Mick reached into the fast-running stream, cupped his hand and carried dripping water to his mouth, taking a tentative sip, then more, swilling it around, assessing it. He dipped again and swallowed, nodding. 'It's okay.' He submerged the canteen into the clear water until bubbles stopped rising, then placed it on the ground between them.

Mick broke the silence with a long shot. 'Does she do the gardens?'

'*Iie* – no. She help.'

'Do you go with her sometimes? To help…'

Kazu cut in. 'No. I don't like.'

Mick nodded. 'Can understand. Not my thing, either.'

'Grandmother want me go. Today, she tries make me go with her. I want…' He shook his head sadly. 'I can't.' His face screwed up.

Mick recalled the stern words from the grandmother on arrival at the hospital, her arm gripping Kazu, restraining him against his will, and then his request to continue on the truck with Mick.

'*Imohto* – my sister,' Kazu said quietly. 'Everyday, Grandmother go help sister. She very sick.'

'Your sister…?' The thought knocked Mick sideways. It had not occurred to him that any of Kazu's family might have survived.

Kazu allowed his glasses to fall off. He shook his head, his voice coming from somewhere distant. 'She…' He chopped at both elbows with his hands. 'She – no hands.' His voice caught and he coughed.

Mick reached across, offering the canteen again. The lad took a drink.

'I'm so sorry, Mate.' Mick dropped a hand on Kazu's shoulder and lifted it straight away as the skeletal sensation shocked him, his hand too heavy on such a frail frame.

Kazu swiped his hand across his cheek. 'Her face…' he gulped again. 'Very bad. Very burn. Side of face.'

Mick blew out a slow breath. What should he say? What could he say? Nothing!

Nothing would make it better – no explanations of the past or hopes for the future would make any difference.

'So sorry, Mate.' He let the words out, into the air, into the world.

Chapter Three

We learn little from victory,
Much from defeat.
– Japanese Proverb

In silence, they sat side by side, thoughts flowing with the stream.

Mick realised any or all of the villagers on his truck might be visiting loved ones in that hospital, not just volunteering because they had personally escaped the bombings un-scathed. All those happy, chatty, laughing people, grateful for a hard ride in an ugly army truck, may be grieving and suffering, as they go to help desperately, brutally wounded – disfigured and maimed – loved ones.

What have we done?

The insidious long arm of war.

Innocent people at home were also victims – not just those on the front line. Families left to scratch for food while its nation's wealth got poured into grand military plans – achievements and losses.

Suddenly, Mick felt heavy. Suddenly, his work as an army driver seemed less humanitarian and more like a futile gesture to compensate for a massive assault.

Attacks on enemy military bases he could understand, but the citizens – children going to school, women and men struggling for mere existence? Why them?

Had he made the right decision? Was he really cut-out for this job, this situation?

The posters he had seen at home, the request for personnel to sign-up, to volunteer for this great benevolent project, the glory of serving your country, the honour of wearing a soldier's uniform, the chance to go abroad at the expense of your government, the adventure of it all…

Mick looked down at the khaki uniform, remembering how proud he'd been.

So proud.

So ignorant.

Now, the shirt, buttoned-up, was suddenly far too hot, the coarse weave suddenly scratchy and irritating – suffocating.

He grabbed the shirt front in both hands and wrenched it away from his skin. Buttons flew off. He watched one spiral through the air and land in the water, sinking to the stony riverbed.

This is no honour. It's a bloody sham!

The *war* might be over, but this was still war. As long as people had no home or livelihood, no health or happiness, no security or future hopes, as long as people grieved and suffered, it was still war.

Bloody godforsaken war.

***

Mick shook himself and blew out an angry breath. He was here now and committed to the army for a year. What could a year possibly achieve in a situation like this?

What could *he* possibly achieve?

His gaze followed the river, hurrying along as if it had a sense of purpose, no matter what it had confronted upstream.

His grandma came to mind, as she tended to do, when he floundered, her insight, foresight and wisdom always timely.

'Be patient. Don't try to push the river. It will flow of its own accord.'

He cast his eyes upward, offered a smile to the heavens. *Thanks, Grandma.*

Be patient. He was not good at that, but he knew its importance. Things happen in their own time.

Don't be pushy. That certainly had relevance – in a country where ancient ways gently held people together, even after their world had been blown apart.

Let it flow. Accept the status quo. Watch and learn. Observation before action.

Eyes misting, he recalled how the special relationship with his grandma had stood him in good stead. She lived in town and understood that farm life was not his thing. She took him in when the arrivals of his younger siblings left him out.

His grandma had been the glue that held young Mick together. '*What should I do, Grandma?'*

'You're a good boy, Mick', she'd said whenever his world became confusing. '*Don't think too hard. Just do what's right.'*

Do what's right. Be a decent person.

He reached into the flowing water, feeling its pressure against his palm as it rushed away, leaving him to his thoughts.

He cupped a handful and splashed his face and neck. His breath caught.

'Do what's right.'

He knew his mission. To help these people find their way again.

Mick pulled his gaping shirt front together and glanced at his young friend. Kazu's sentence would be for life. He might never escape this legacy. But maybe he would create a better future, speak English well and eventually follow his dreams, if he could learn to deal with the horrors and injustices of his past.

Kazu was right. He *was* lucky. If he had been a year older, he would have surely been conscripted into a military mission with no future. If his grandmother hadn't needed him in the village, he would have been on his way to school in Hiroshima City that fateful morning.

Now he represented a population of young men which had become very thin on the ground. He was a precious member of the next generation and therefore valuable to society. Did he realise the responsibility and opportunity that sat squarely on his youthful shoulders?

Mick's thoughts drifted back to the letter in his pocket. Did Emiko have a loved one in that hospital?

Now was not the time to ask Kazu. Now was the time to regroup – the time for a change of focus and some positive action.

'Steps to make. Let's go.' Mick lifted his feet out of the water, shook them dry, pulled on socks and laced up his boots. Kazu stood up, stomped on the grass and slipped back into his oversized shoes.

Before they picked up tools again, Mick returned his canteen to the truck cab and reached for the surplus toast from his breakfast, wrapped in a cloth.

The frailty of Kazu's shoulder had come as a shock, sign of a hungry lad out-growing his food supply, the harsh truth concealed by loose clothing and the exuberant energy of youth. Added to that, his hair still sticking up like a lopsided mohawk, Kazu had likely jumped out of bed at his grandmother's command, managing to find clothes but not food as he scrambled out the door and headed towards the truck.

Mick handed the package to his helper, indicating for him to eat.

The lad unwrapped the cloth and looked up at Mick in surprise. Mick signalled it was all his and turned away to nail the last step in place.

A bit more securing and the stairway was complete. Stomping on each level, up and down again, Mick tested it for stability and bracing.

Kazu followed, wiping crumbs from his mouth. 'Grandmother be very glad.' He reached the top step, turned around with an arrogant tilt to his chin. 'She be like – queen.' He stepped down with regal grace.

Mick laughed, but was thinking about another pseudo royal. He wondered why it mattered so much what Emiko would think of his creation. He wanted to see her face when she arrived at the truck the next day. Maybe it would mean nothing to her. After all, she had refused his offer to help her down, then managed perfectly without the ladder at all. What if she thought the steps were unnecessary, a waste of wood that could have housed a family?

'Too bad,' he muttered. 'The queen will be happy, and all the others.'

Kazu grinned. 'Yes, happy queen.' He nodded then repositioned his glasses.

'Now for the hard part.' Mick started dragging the steps across the long grass towards the back of the truck, Kazu rushing to help. Mick had measured for the top step to finish just above the height of the truck tray, making it easier to lift the weighty construction by resting the top edge on the tray while levering the stairway up and pushing it back onto the truck floor, where it would ride. A final push and it settled heavily in its travelling position.

Mick gave it a tug, testing its security in place. It held fast. That meant both good and bad. The good – it wouldn't slide off the moving truck. The bad – it would be a devil to pull down when needed and push back when finished with.

'It would be easier to move on and off the truck if it had skids along the back edge.'

Kazu looked baffled.

'Like sled runners.'

No connection.

Mick waved a hand to dismiss the idea. 'That'll be for another day.'

They stacked the surplus boards under the bench seats and motored slowly back through the settlement, Kazu naming each business, goods sold or created, in the open-fronted shops and workshops facing the street.

As they drew level with the last building in the block Kazu announced, 'Tatami maker.'

Mick pulled the truck over. 'Tatami?' He checked. 'For the floor?'

Kazu leant forwards and ran a hand beside his feet.

'Sit on?' Mick asked.

'Yes. Sleep too,' Kazu answered.

'Come,' Mick said, cutting the engine and jumping down from the cab. When Kazu reached his side, he said, 'Ask the tatami maker if he can make tatami mats for the seats.' He turned and pointed to the back of the truck and put his hands underneath him, as if to sit down.

'For seat, in truck? Kazu checked.

'You got it.'

A long work bench on high wooden legs stood in the centre of the open-fronted shop.

The back wall supported shelves holding sheaths of straw and rolls of woven matting, a variety of cutting tools and small trays containing what Mick would call sail-makers needles. There was no sign of work in progress and no response to their greetings.

Kazu calling out to announce their presence, he and Mick ventured along a narrow path to a small dwelling behind the workshop.

'He lives here?' Mick asked.

'Maybe so.'

A small, stooped woman appeared from an adjoining vegetable patch, cradling earthy vegetables against her faded navy kimono.

Kazu made noises of surprise, bowed deeply and spoke to her. She nodded and carried her harvest inside.

'She get him,' Kazu explained.

Then an even more stooped, kimono-clad woman, grey hair twisted into a topknot, came from the house. She stopped to stare for some moments before lowering herself onto a garden bench, eyes fixed on Mick, her face crinkled into frowning folds.

Kazu bowed deeply.

Mick less so. 'All this bowing,' he muttered. 'I'm getting dizzy.'

Kazu completed the ritual and turned to Mick. 'Important for old people. We show respect because we learn many thing from older one.'

Mick felt the stare of the elder, his lack of respect ricocheting back at him, until the tatami maker finally appeared. More bowing and introductions. Kazu's explanation and gestures again included the village in the inland hills, the hospital towards ground zero and the hard seats in the truck.

Tatami-san launched into a lengthy and dramatic monologue, with animation indicating bombings and explosions, damage to his house, his very unhappy elderly mother and his wife getting bossy and talk, talk, talk to him. He clapped his hands over his ears, his wife laughed heartily and his mother muttered something under her breath.

Kazu turned to Mick. 'The bomb damage his house. Mother bedroom very bad.' Kazu shook his head sadly. 'His wife say, no more tatami make, but fix house. Mother say no sleep, her room broke. He say no wood. All wood broken from bombs.'

Mick pointed to the truck. 'We have wood. He can have our wood.' Kazu translated and Tatami-san suddenly looked interested.

The three of them started towards the truck. Kazu jumped up onto the tray and picked up one of the boards, holding it up for Tatami-san to see. The craftsman nodded enthusiastically, then his expression dropped and he spoke to Kazu.

'He has no money to pay for wood,' Kazu translated for Mick.

'Ask him if he would exchange tatami for wood – fair trade?'

Kazu explained and Tatami-san brightened up and nodded. 'Hai.' Yes.

'Then ask him if *we* can fix his house while he makes tatami mats for our seats.' Mick reached up and slapped a hand on the bench seat near him.

Kazu looked disbelieving. 'Can you fix house, Mick-san?'

'I lived on a farm. I can fix anything.' He indicated the steps as an example.

Kazu thought for a moment and jumped down, launching into an explanation with indications towards Mick, the steps, and the broken house.

'Can he show us the house?' Mick suggested.

Kazu translated and Tatami-san turned and led the way back along the path, kicked off his shoes at the door and went in, signalling for them to follow.

Mick stooped through the doorway and looked around. Clutter and confusion filled the tiny room, not the neat, minimalist interior he expected. A wood-burning cooker and its stack of logs dominated the area with a few bowls and cookpots piled onto a low central table.

Walls were covered with hanging utensils. Shelves held jars and containers. On the floor boxes and bins allowed only a narrow path to walk through the room.

They followed him into the adjoining space – no more than an alcove, the three of them hardly fitting side-by-side. This room, in contrast, was devoid of anything but the thick straw tatami mat that gave a slight spongy feel to the floor. Tatami-san slid open a full-height cupboard door, indicating folded bedding which would be pulled out to create a sleeping space – before the bomb.

The dominating feature was a gaping hole in the far wall, affording an unprotected view of the outdoors. Mick stepped closer to the shattered remains and assessed for structural damage. The strong corner posts held fast. It appeared only the light framing and exterior cladding had been destroyed. A relatively superficial problem.

'We can do this.' Mick held up his fingers to Kazu. 'One – two day's work.' Kazu repeated the assessment to Tatami-san.

'How long to make tatami mats for the truck seats?' Mick asked. Kazu translated and relayed the answer – a few days.

'Okay. We start tomorrow?'

Kazu paused, looked hesitant then turned to Tatami-san, launching into a prolonged speech that appeared to sum up the whole process, creating a dialogue equivalent to a paper contract, Tatami-san occasionally nodding in agreement.

Mick realised the very basic level of his Japanese language skills. How long would it take before he could recognise more than the words *hai* – yes and *tatami* in conversations such as these?

He thought again about Emiko's letter in his pocket with its practised handwriting and incomplete yet adequate English. Did that reflect her spoken English too or would it be difficult for them to understand each other? His mind drifted over the possibilities. But he was jumping ahead of himself…

He looked up. Kazu and Tatami-san were looking at him, waiting.

Tatami-san said something. Kazu spluttered, snorted a short laugh then clapped a hand over his errant mouth.

Mick turned to him. 'Did I miss something?'

Kazu looked at his feet and reluctantly answered. 'Tatami maker say you look like in love, Mick-san.' Then he continued. 'Tatami maker say he happy, we fix house, he make tatami for seat. Very good tatami,' he added with emphasis.

The deal was sealed with bowing and smiles.

The three of them unloaded the wood, stacking it neatly outside the workshop. Mick and Kazu were about to leave when Tatami-san's wife called them to the outside table, where she placed a tray holding a china tea-set, not much bigger than the one Mick's sister, Jessica, used to play with at home.

The mother shuffled out through the door carrying an earthen cookpot. Mick thought of beef stew. Her weathered face crinkled into a toothless smile as she placed the pot on the table and lifted the lid. Round, white dumplings floated in broth.

Kazu gasped. 'Suiton!'

The mother nodded, still smiling. It looked like the dumplings Mick's mother would drop into a meaty stew. Doughboys, they called them at home. Here they were floating in soup.

Tatami-san's wife ladled some out for each of them, Kazu's eyes wide in anticipation as she passed the bowls around – with chopsticks to catch the floating dumplings. They nodded their thanks and tucked in.

Kazu wasted no time, drinking the soup directly from the bowl and efficiently gripping the dumplings with his chopsticks, chewing and swallowing, his eyes closed in rapture. Mick understood why. The delicious combination of flavours surprised him, not what he expected from doughboys.

As soon as Kazu's bowl was empty, another serving was ladled. Mick declined seconds, more out of politeness than preference.

Kazu paused, mid-bite and turned to Mick. 'Mick-san, you must have. Not polite to say no thank you.'

Embarrassment combined with anticipation, Mick accepted another serving, offering thanks – *domo*, and apologies – *sumi-masen*, from his scrambled memory of new vocabulary.

Kazu finished chewing and swallowed. 'That a good word, Mick-san, *sumi-masen*.' His cheeky smile was an expression Mick hadn't seen before. 'You maybe need that word *sumi-masen* every day,' Kazu added.

Mick threw him a sideways look. There was more spark to Kazu than Mick had realised.

Kazu raised a curious eyebrow before turning his attention to the last of his soup.

Tatami-san looked particularly pleased as he ate, and Mick wondered if he had not been fed well while his wife and mother waited for him to find a solution to the hole in the wall.

Tea followed, served in cups slightly larger than an eggcup. A farm boy having tea without milk – Mick imagined his father's disapproval, but he had no trouble showing his appreciation by accepting several top-ups, each a little more than a mouthful.

With hosts and guests immensely satisfied with the amount consumed, Mick and Kazu stood to leave, doing justice to the farewell formalities and confirming their return tomorrow.

Kazu settled into his truck seat comfortably, stretched out and crossed one ankle over the other. 'Grandmother, and all other, very happy, new steps,' he said, as they drove towards the hospital.

More than the sentiments Kazu expressed, Mick heard a new-found confidence in speaking English, recognised the satisfaction of a job well done and the fulfilment of a good feed with the likelihood of more, resulting in the surprising spark of cheekiness.

When they pulled up outside the hospital, Kazu jumped down before the engine died and raced Mick to the back. They both pulled on the steps, out and down, positioning them on the ground adjoining the truck floor – like a red carpet.

Kazu fussed around the steps, looking repeatedly over his shoulder along the path to the hospital while pulling aside weeds and kicking away stones that might impede smooth progress to the first step.

Mick stood aside, entertained by Kazu taking ownership with his fussing and preparation.

Voices came within hearing and the villagers appeared around the corner of the bamboo fence. Kazu stiffened, then proudly stepped to the side of the steps like a chauffeur, his open palm indicating the stairway.

When the villagers saw what Kazu was presenting, they froze in amazement, their voices trailing off. Hands clamped over surprised expressions, eyes danced to Mick and back to Kazu, and settled on the stairway. Kazu held up a hand to halt them. He said something.

They nodded and stepped back a pace, looking behind them, waiting.

Soon *Obasan* appeared, face down, shoulders burdened. Kazu jumped forwards to meet her. She looked up at him. Her face brightened. He took her hand and lifted it to shoulder- height, stepping aside so she could see the steps. Her face softened and she shot Mick a look.

With an air of importance, Kazu made an announcement. The villagers laughed. Then he turned to Mick and proclaimed 'The Queen!' as he led his grandmother to the first step.

The villagers clapping, bowing, enjoyed the ceremony, as Kazu walked *Obasan* up the steps, her face reflecting the fun of it all. Step by step, they reached the truck floor, then turned and bowed to their delighted audience.

Obasan fixed her eyes on Mick. She said words he could not understand. But he understood the expression of gratitude on her face.

For Mick, that was the first stage in his mission. He imagined a notch in his belt.

Kazu stepped down, relaying comments to Mick as the other passengers followed up the steps, chattering, laughing, showing each other how easy it was, how clever they felt, how simple to get up to the truck floor. With the last on board, both Mick and Kazu put a shoulder to the stairway and pushed it up onto the truck. Kazu checked on his grandmother, sitting among the others. 'Queen very happy,' he said to Mick, bobbing his head for emphasis.

Kazu's face said it all and they spoke little on the ride home – a day well spent, stomachs fed and tomorrow promising so much more.

Chapter Four

Learn from yesterday,
live for today,
hope for tomorrow.
– Japanese Proverb

'*Ohayoo gozaimasu* – good morning, Mick-san. Early again,' Tomoko observed as Mick arrived for breakfast, his collection of building supplies for the day already procured from the workshop and stowed in the truck.

'Big day. I have a house to fix.'

'House? Fix?' Yoshi looked puzzled.

'Hole in wall.' He spread his arms wide to show the size of the damage. 'From the bomb.' He demonstrated an explosion with sound effects.

'Oooo!' both women responded wide-eyed.

Tomoko narrowed her focus. 'You can fix house, Mick-san?'

'Will do what I can.'

'*Dare no*? – who house?'

'Tatami-san.'

The women laughed. '*Tatami-san* not name,' Yoshi corrected.

'I know,' he laughed with them. 'The tatami maker's house.'

Tomoko tilted her head, assessing. 'You fix house good?'

'I plan to.'

'*Soo desu ka?* – really…?' Her voice faded away and both women settled their gaze on him.

Mick took his breakfast tray. He sat and ate without thinking about the food, responding to offers of top-ups without considering if he actually wanted more. He finished quickly and headed out the door, leaving the leftover toast behind this time, anticipating Tatami-san's womenfolk would again ply them with ample food.

At first push on the starter, the Chevy roared to life. It was still too soon to head directly to the village. Mick didn't want to startle the passengers with an early arrival again.

Keen to get moving, he rolled out of the compound and turned left instead of right, onto the road which traversed the valley higher up. Here, elevated terraces of smaller, odd-shaped paddy fields juxtaposed to fit the lie of the land, fanning out from the lush folds of forested hillsides, descending into the wide, watery patchwork of the valley floor.

Pulling up, he stuck his head out the window, breathing in the fresh moistness of rainforest, the earthy aromas he didn't know he had missed since leaving the farm.

The evergreen forest reminded him of home, except he didn't see any feathery ferns and cabbage trees – which looked nothing like a cabbage and a lot like a spiky palm. And here the birdsong sounded different.

Slipping the truck into gear, he coasted along the road, scanning the pools for signs of the newly planted rice seedlings Buster had predicted. Further ahead, a coolie-hatted worker and an ox-like beast pulling a wooden cart ambled along a side track. Mick cut the engine back to a walking pace, watching them on their way to work.

If he didn't have plans for the day, he would have been happy to walk along here – to experience the day coming to life in a land that was in some ways familiar and yet strangely new.

For Mick, New Zealand and Japan resembled geographical twins, one as far north of the equator as the other was south – two island nations reflecting each other on the map like elongated wings of a global butterfly, stretching along the Pacific Ocean's western rim.

He negotiated a zigzag route down the slopes and onto the main causeway, arriving at the village in good time. Pulling into the turnaround, he cut the engine and waited.

From the village lane another ox cart emerged, guided by a small, hunched person leading the beast on a rope. Several barrels stacked up gave the impression of a heavy load, the large wheels scrunching into the stony road, yet the ox made steady progress as it plodded away from the village.

Mick's gaze was averted by voices as a group of people emerged from the lane, walking towards the truck. He recognised *Obasan*, Kazu and some of the others, who were becoming familiar faces to him. And there *she* was, Emiko-san, a little behind the group.

Mick jumped down from the cab, and Kazu ran ahead to join him at the back of the truck. Simultaneously they reached for the steps, hauled them to the edge of the truck floor and lowered them to the ground.

The first arrivals greeted Mick and made their way to their seats, without the Queen's ceremony of the previous day, even though Kazu stood on guard beside the steps, looking full of pride as he offered assistance.

After the last villager had taken a seat, Emiko appeared. 'Emiko-san,' Kazu said, giving a quick bow.

She returned the bow and turned to Mick.

'Thank you for the letter,' he blurted.

She bowed without comment and turned to face the steps. Lifting the hem of her kimono, she made her way up, taking a seat.

The steps stowed, Mick and Kazu settled into the cab.

'Does Emiko-san speak English?' Having built so much into seeing her again, he was annoyed at his clumsy attempt at conversation and disappointed she had not responded.

'*Hai* – yes, she speak English, some.' Kazu pivoted his hand in a so-so gesture. 'English like me. *Sukoshi desu* – a little bit.'

'Did you learn English at school?'

'*Hai* – yes. All student learn English at school but in war time, it not happen. I think Emiko-san want to learn English more, like me, so study with dictionary and writing practice. Maybe she has teacher. Her father – Tanazawa-san,' Kazu dropped his tone and shook his head slowly, emphasising the respect he felt. 'V-e-r-y important man.' He settled back into his seat and continued, matter-of-fact. 'Emiko-san do what father say. Family custom – very important family.'

Mick blew out a breath. Family status carried little power at home. A farmer's son may become a doctor and a doctor's son may be a drop-out. Especially since the war – even women ran farms, managed factories and ran businesses. You just had to make your own way.

He couldn't get his head around all these social customs and the formalities required to show respect. *This* was going to be a little more complicated than asking a Kiwi girl out to the local dance.

Kicking the engine to life, the truck bumped towards the road, slowing to edge around the ox cart, which had come to a standstill beside the rows of crops.

'What's in the barrels?' Mick asked. 'Water for gardens?'

'*Gesui*,' Kazu replied.

Mick shook his head. 'What's that?'

'English word is honey pot.'

'Honey?'

'*Iie* – not *honey*, Mick-san,' Kazu said emphatically. 'You know honey cart?'

'No idea.'

Kazu laughed 'I teach you English, Mick-san?'

'Seems like it.' Mick grinned.

'Honey pot. Pot from latrine. Every night, honey cart come to house – *Kumitori-sha*. Take away honey pot for garden.'

Mick blinked. *Was he hearing right?* 'Latrine? Lavatory?'

'*Hai, soo desu* – that's right, Mick-san. Good for garden. Make good vegetable grow.'

Culture shock hit Mick in the stomach like an unexpected punch. He shuddered, desperate to shake off the clash of disbelief and nausea.

Human waste on the vegetable garden! Was he on Mars?

Mick shifted his concentration to the road ahead and the bizarre gradually gave way to the familiar as the route to the hospital unfolded. Soon they were pulling down the steps for their passengers to dismount.

Again, Emiko was the last to leave, and again she nodded to them without a word, serenely gliding away in her kimono.

Back in the truck, Mick held onto his questions about her, ignoring the urgency he felt to know more. Instead he turned his curiosity to the day ahead.

'Does Tatami-san have enough straw to make our seat mats?'

'Maybe. I think – tatami straw – cut from field, one year – two year before. Tatami maker keep straw to dry.'

Mick nodded. He knew about hay making, letting the cut grass dry in the sun before bundling it together to store for winter feed. The tatami straw was not that different.

Tatami-san stood on the roadside as they approached, eagerness evident in his stance. He ushered them to the outdoor table where his womenfolk fussed over cloth-covered food bowls and cups of steaming tea.

Mick glanced at Kazu, recalling his voracious appetite at yesterday's visit. 'It would not be polite to refuse,' he said, repeating Kazu's words.

Kazu focussed on the offerings, barely acknowledging Mick's quip. 'Too much food to give away,' he whispered. 'Since war start, little food for family. And many ration.'

Mick was confronted with a dilemma. Having learned the previous day how impolite it would be to refuse such offerings, Kazu had just turned the tables with a new reality – acceptance would mean taking food from a needy family.

Then the reason for his change of heart became clear. 'Grandmother say – not eat.' Kazu turned to Tatami-san's wife, and although Mick could not understand the words, he certainly caught the meaning as Kazu smoothed over the contradiction by expressing his enthusiasm and effusive thanks for a miniature cup of tea for each of them.

The warm, grassy taste still lingering, Mick stood and bowed. Kazu followed and they turned away to start work.

'I tell them we eat big food at army camp,' Kazu said simply, as they pulled the tools from the truck.

Mick blew out a sigh. Tomorrow he would bring the spare toast, just in case.

The two of them lowered the steps for Tatami-san to access the back of the truck and then settled into a rhythm, carrying the planks of wood from behind the workshop to the gaping hole in the house wall. Mick eyed the damage and cut away the jagged ends, creating a neat rectangular opening, before measuring and marking thin timbers for the inside framing.

Kazu sawed the lengths and held them firm while Mick nailed them into place.

Visits from Tatami-san's womenfolk didn't slow their progress as they paused on the inside of the room to inspect the developing lattice of framework.

Mick and Kazu ventured to the workshop from time to time, observing Tatami-san's progress, as he bundled bales of straw, compacting it in a giant press and stitching it with string.

The day's work drew to a close with the wall framework ready for cladding, and the inside core of four thick tatami mats stitched in readiness for covering.

Mick and Kazu bowed farewell before they jumped into the truck, under pressure to reach the hospital and on to the village before dark.

The army camp had been quiet since Tuesday; Buster and his comrades had transferred to Yamaguchi Base to set up another outpost.

Most of Mick's shipmates were there at Yamaguchi – the main base for New Zealand troops. Only Mick had been singled out, as the truck driver to replace Buster, so he'd been sent straight to the outpost in the inland hills.

Above his bunk, the woven ceiling panels played tricks with his eyes, as he analysed the day.

It would certainly be good to have some of his mates around. Or anyone. Even Buster.

Mick laughed at himself. 'I must be desperate.'

On the plus side, the house repair and the seat mats should be finished in another day or so.

On the negative, Kazu had gone hungry. Mick shuddered, remembering the honey cart, in the context of a village struggling to grow its own food and feed others.

Having grown up on a farm that supplied ample food to the community, Mick had never experienced the needs of a hungry society.

He realised now the bags and baskets the villagers carried to the hospital daily must contain contributions of food.

The generosity of Tatami-san's family demonstrated how traditional hospitality over-rode their own needs. And Kazu's grandmother, in forbidding him to eat their offerings, knew he would go hungry as a result.

Mick thought of home. His mother would never let them leave the house without a wholesome breakfast, especially if it was to be a long day. How would *she* feel if there just wasn't enough food for the family? How would *he* feel if he went hungry like Kazu?

In his head, he planned tomorrow's breakfast-time conversation with Tomoko and Yoshi – his request for a *bento box* – a lunchbox for his helper.

The other negative, the elephant in the room – he was no further along in making a connection with Emiko.

He hadn't come to Japan with the intention of finding a girl. Why was he so impatient?

The idea of Japanese women had been a vague curiosity.

Until now.

He ran a hand over his chest pocket and felt the crinkle of delicate paper. Her letter was still there.

Mick's eyes followed the shadows above his head, the patterns shifting with the flicker of the lamp.

How could he justify his fascination with a girl when the likes of Kazu went hungry? He shook himself. *Get your priorities right!*

The next day at breakfast, negotiating for the lunch box was surprisingly easy, once Mick explained it was for his Japanese assistant.

Camp personnel seemed to turn a blind eye as local staff bundled food into the folds of their tunic, heading home to the family. Who could rationalise the excesses of the mess hall while beyond its walls, food restrictions and shortages left the locals in survival mode?

The narrow road familiar now, Mick coasted along, enjoying the freshness of the morning and scanning for signs of progress in the rice paddies.

Emiko wouldn't be on the truck today. In some way, that was a relief, giving him space to review the protocol. He'd come to realise the truck steps on the way to and from the hospital was no place to strike up a conversation. He would have to find a better, more private opportunity.

The villagers were already at the truck stop and they had hauled the steps down before Mick reached the back of the truck.

Kazu relaxed into his seat, ready for the English – Japanese language exchange they had begun to play en-route, like a game of verbal ping pong.

'Honey pots,' Mick said as they edged around the ox cart.

'*Bakyumu-ka,*' Kazu supplied.

Mick attempted the repetition and gave up with a shudder. 'Disgusting.'

Kazu laughed. 'No, Mick-san. Garden need plant food.'

'Okay,' Mick conceded. 'I'll get used to it.'

'Feed all people in *Hinode-mura.*'

'What's that – *hinode…*?'

'Village name.' Kazu pointed behind them. '*Hinode.* Mean sunrise.'

'Sunrise?' Mick responded. 'That's the perfect name for a village on a hill facing East.'

Kazu looked pleased. '*Hai* – yes. *Hinode* – sunrise. *Mura* – village. *Hinode-mura.*'

'The first place to see the sun.' Mick nodded, the apricot glow of dawn on the tiny wooden dwellings etched forever in his memory.

Kazu changed the subject. 'What is difference – steps, stairs?'

'Same thing really. But steps, outside. Stairs, inside.'

Kazu thought about that. 'But – I take steps.' He lifted one foot, followed by the other, as if walking. 'Steps, walk. Same thing?'

Mick laughed and pulled in a breath while choosing his words. 'Step, only one or two times. Walk, is for a long way.'

Kazu shook his head. 'English – very difficult – *muzukashi desu.*'

'What's that?'

Kazu blew out a sigh and spoke with a touch of frustration. 'Mean – very difficult, Mick-san.'

Mick shifted gears as they came to the bottom of the hill, levelled off and started along the causeway. 'Yep. Not easy.'

He searched again in the water. 'When do they plant rice?'

'Maybe two weeks. Maybe three.'

'I thought it was sooner.'

'Usually June. Weather hot and wet.'

'Wet?' Mick was used to a hot, dry mid-summer. Sometimes even a drought. He couldn't imagine rain with the heat. It sounded refreshing. 'I guess that's good for the land, the gardens.'

'Yes. Garden grow very fast.'

The hospital stop went smoothly. Again Tatami-san was waiting beside the road, when they pulled up in front of his workshop. As soon as they jumped down, he bowed and began speaking. Kazu stood motionless, giving the stop – start monologue due attention.

Eventually Tatami-san concluded with a few staccato words, a bow and then silence.

Kazu took a deep breath and turned to Mick. 'Tatami maker very happy to see us. He say *Ohayoo gozaimasu* – good morning.'

Mick nodded good morning and Tatami-san bowed.

Kazu continued. 'Tatami maker say very sorry yesterday, we not accept food. Wife and mother very sad not show suitable welcome. Today, tatami maker say wife and mother make food – different food. Not from ration shop, not from *yami-ichi*.'

'What's that?'

'*Yami-ichi* – English say black market. Not usual shop.' He shook his head solemnly. 'Very expensive. But some people must buy.'

'Why's that?' The idea of a black-market racket was alien to Mick, especially for food.

'Ration – very little food. Many people – not enough. Wait long time at shop. Often nothing left. Go away empty.' He rubbed his stomach to emphasise.

Mick shook his head. This food shortage was worse than he thought. And rationing! With food already in short supply!

Kazu carried on. 'Tatami maker say very important – wife and mother show welcome. They have food from garden. Not buy from shop.'

Mick glanced at Tatami-san, wondering what hardship he knew. Tatami-san nodded, bowed.

'They make special food for summer. Very special.' Kazu's persuasive tone told Mick they could not refuse today. He lowered his voice to little more than a whisper. 'But very secret. All food from garden must be ration. Government say – nobody have more food.'

'Even their own garden is rationed?'

'*Hai* – yes. Everything, must share.' Kazu said, nodding.

Tatami-san took that as an acceptance of his offer and ushered them along the path to the outdoor table, indicating for them to sit on the low stools.

The women appeared from the house, smiling and nodding. Tatami-san's wife placed a large tray on the table, her mother-in-law following up with the teapot.

The wife turned and addressed Mick.

Kazu relayed her message. 'Today, special day for fix house, husband make tatami seat for hospital helpers. Food – say thank you.'

The mother interjected, her voice raspy but strong. Kazu concentrated then conveyed her message. '*Obasan* – grandmother, say very, very big thank you, fix her room. She very happy. She give you special gift.'

The older woman turned to a flat, wide box on the end of the table, stooped to pick it up and shuffled forward. Her face twinkling with mischief, she spoke again as she trundled towards Mick.

Tatami-san's wife exploded with laughter. Tatami-san rumbled a low bark of reprimand.

Kazu looked perplexed, then swallowed hard and translated her words. 'This her wedding kimono. Very old, very special. She want give you, until one day you marry.' Kazu looked at his feet, then repositioned his glasses and continued in a muffled voice. 'She hope you choose her. She like how you look.'

Mick managed to maintain composure, aware her gesture would not go down well – giving away a valuable possession to a stranger. Like yesterday's turned-down breakfast, he faced the conundrum of whether to accept or refuse. Either way, someone would be offended.

He responded with a smile, aware of the generosity from the old lady, despite her frivolous spirit, and began fumbling with the ribbon which held the box closed.

Kazu ended his discomfort. 'In Japan, we not open gift. Just put down.'

Mick sighed with relief. He would ask Kazu later how to return the kimono to the family.

Tatami-san's wife called their attention back to the table. Removing the cloth cover, she revealed a large, segmented tray, its glossy black compartments framing the delicately arranged rainbow of fruity segments, as a picture frame enhances the artwork within.

Kazu's eyes widened as they were each handed a bowl and invited to make their own selection. Mick thought it would be a shame to spoil the display, but Kazu wasted no time approaching the table, deftly manipulating the serving chopsticks, filling his bowl to capacity within moments.

Mick could only admire such dexterity with chopsticks, as he fumbled and dropped his selected portions, before Tatami-san's mother came forwards with a china spoon and a twinkle in her eye.

As much as Mick appreciated her acceptance of him as a foreigner, a *gaijin*, and enjoyed the food, he became more uncomfortable with her attention. Emptying his bowl and teacup quickly, he stood and bowed. Reassuring Kazu to stay as long as he wanted, Mick headed off to collect things from the truck.

Before long, Kazu joined him at the work site and they launched into the project. Wider boards were needed today but finding a colour match with the age-old cladding covering the rest of the wall would not be easy. The patina, the width and texture of the boards varied considerably. The end result would be weatherproof, but it wouldn't be pretty.

As Mick pondered how to make the best of the materials available, he explained the issue to Kazu, who nodded, studied the various planks and stood back to examine the house wall, but offered no input. Mick realised Kazu understood as much about this work as Mick did about using chopsticks.

By noon they had the wall covered in, which was a relief in two ways. The room was weather-proof and the mother's too frequent promenades through the interior room were now hidden from view. Mick had ignored her attempts to communicate and Kazu had showed no wish to translate.

Tatami-san called them to the outside table where a steaming teapot and vegetable chunks served in individual bowls awaited them.

'*Oyatsu*,' their host announced, smiling.

'Snack with fingers,' Kazu translated. 'Not need chopsticks, Mick-san,' he added with a grin.

Mick laughed. 'Hah! *Domo arigato* – thank you,' he replied, appreciating the elimination of chopsticks – and noticing another break in ritual he suspected to be for his benefit. The women were nowhere in sight.

Mick imagined Tatami-san's wife had hustled her in-disgrace mother-in-law off down the road on some phantom errand, avoiding further embarrassment for them all.

Kazu pointed to creamy-coloured slices with purple skin. 'This one *satsumaimo* – sweet potato. This one, orange colour, *kabocha* – pumpkin squash. And this? What you think is this, Mick-san?' He picked up a crisp-looking, white slice. 'Japanese important food,' he added enticingly, popping it in his mouth, chewing and swallowing.

'*Daikon* – white radish?' Mick guessed.

Kazu shook his head. Tatami-san laughed and continued to watch the interaction.

'Important food?' Mick checked.

Kazu nodded and waited for the next guess. Tatami-san had a smile fixed on his face as he looked from one to the other.

'Bamboo shoots!' Mick said.

'Hai! – yes. *Takenoko*, Mick-san.'

Tatami-san clapped his hands and laughed heartily.

Mick enjoyed the unpretentious, bloke-ish silence of smoko, free of formalities. Just three men absorbed in refuelling their energy levels, and for Mick at least, thoughts about how to tackle the job ahead.

Then the idea came to him; create a feature in front of the patched wall, an embellishment, a support for plants to grow up, screening the variation of cladding materials behind.

Back to work, using the narrow slats left over from the framing, they pieced together the trellis and fixed it in place.

Mick and Kazu stood back for a final inspection of their work. Kazu tidied the ground around the wall, pulling away weeds, kicking aside stones, just as he had done when the steps were ready to be used for the first time.

They headed to the workshop to fetch Tatami-san. He raced ahead of them like a child going for ice cream. The three stood and admired the completed project. Tatami-san said right away he would grow beans there.

Mick and Kazu gathered up their tools, stowed them under the truck seat and followed Tatami-san, who beckoned them into his workshop.

The tatami seat mats were stacked four-high on the workbench, the bundled straw now covered with smooth, woven matting, like the rattan beach mats Mick's mother spread on the grass for family picnics. Mick couldn't resist running his hand along the grain of the fibres, its surface as silky as finely sanded wood. The fresh greenish tone surprised him, he expected dry straw would be the colour of hay.

The only thing yet to complete was the fabric binding. Mick had seen how the edges of tatami mats were wrapped, covering the cut ends with a strip of braid, dividing the flooring into juxtaposed, patchworked panels, like a giant puzzle.

But Tatami-san's cheeks sagged like a hound dog and he lowered his gaze as he explained something worrying. Mick waited for Kazu's translation.

'Tatami maker very sorry. He has no—' Kazu stepped forwards and ran his hand over the raw edges, miming the missing braid. 'Can not finish. This' – he mimed again – 'nowhere. Tatami maker go all places. Nobody have it. Not even *yami-ichi.* He very sorry.'

The last thing Mick wanted was to add anxiety to the already desperate situation of shortages. One glance at the craftsman revealed how intensely he felt the shame, especially as Mick and Kazu had held up their side of the bargain.

'Tell Tatami-san not to worry. Tell him the army camp has some braid.' Mick copied Kazu's action, indicating the edging trim. 'Tell him he would be helping us if he would try out army braid. We want to know if army braid is good for tatami making.' A little white lie, and Mick had no idea how he would locate such an item, but it just might save the day.

Kazu made noises of urgency and bowed quickly to Mick, before rattling off the explanation to the distraught man. Tatami-san straightened, looking at Mick and Kazu, as an aura of grateful calm descended over him.

Kazu translated Mick's message that he would try to bring some braid tomorrow, before the three bowed farewell.

Chapter Five

A great man
is one who has not lost his child's heart.
– Ancient Wisdom

Mick got back to camp in good time and, keen to return the tools before being accused of stealing, he pulled them out from under the truck seat and headed straight to the workshop. He opened the door and it banged behind him before he realised he'd already blown his cover.

On the other side of the workshop, in a recessed alcove separate from the working area, a wooden rocking chair clunked back and forth, its occupant only visible by the top of his tawny head, the rest of him enveloped in a misty cloud of smoke curling from the tobacco pipe in his hand.

He looked around at the bang of the door. A crooked smile crossed his freckled face. '*Gidday*,' he said, jumping up and reaching out his hand, gripping Mick's firmly.

'Mick Mitchell, the new driver.'

'Croc Bateman, the old carpenter.'

'Croc! Thought I picked up an Aussie accent.'

'Yep. True Blue. A name like Croc – a bit of a clue.'

Mick laughed. 'You don't find crocodiles in New Zealand.'

'Not much of *anything* there. Not with sharp teeth, anyhow!' Croc nodded towards Mick's armful of tools. 'What you got there, Mick?'

'Just returning a few things I helped myself to a couple days ago. Thought I'd get them back without being found out.'

'Yeah.' Croc grinned. 'Did notice a few things missing. Quite the norm around here. Is a bit unusual for them to come back, though.' He squinted at Mick as if making an assessment.

Mick dropped the tools on the workbench. 'I'll stick these back where I found them.'

'Nah. Just dump them there. I'll get the lads onto it in the morning.'

Croc drew on his pipe. 'Pull up a pew,' he said, indicating a sawhorse under the workbench as he returned to his chair.

Mick dragged his seat over and stopped to look out through a wall of glass panels to a view of the entire terraced valley, right up to the fringe of the forest and down to the main causeway, as far as the last of the paddy fields.

'Not bad, eh?' Croc said.

This was the first time Mick had been able to view the entire valley without having his hands on a steering wheel. He sat down, taking in the vista.

'So, what's your story, Mick? I take it you been here just a few days.'

'Almost a week. I've taken over Buster Daniels' run, ferrying the villagers to the hospital.'

'Buster Daniels, eh! Now there's a bloke and a half!'

Not sure exactly what that meant, Mick guessed it had something to do with Buster being a bit of a hard-case.

'What about you, Croc? How long have you been here?'

'Me?' Croc shifted in his chair and settled into a rocking rhythm, suggesting it could be a long story. 'Got shipped here with my team of builders last September. This place was just tent city then. We had to turn it into something more substantial for you Kiwis.' Croc drew on his pipe and blew smoke rings, 'The rest of my team buggered off to another camp as soon as the job was done.' His gaze followed the swirls towards the ceiling. 'Not me. Why would you want to leave here? Go another place and start all over again? I'm getting a bit long in the tooth for the nomadic life. Thirty next month! Going home in September. Getting married. Time to settle down.' He nodded, agreeing with himself.

'So, you set up this workshop? It's well laid out.' Mick grinned. 'Easy to find things.'

Croc shot him a wry smile. 'Can't work in a mess. But I do love wood.' He slapped a hand on the armrest of his chair. 'Made this. Just for that view.' He waved his pipe towards the windows. 'Not a bad outlook from the office.'

'Yeah,' Mick agreed. 'It's good driving through there too. Every morning, the thought of it gets me out of bed early.'

'Had some time to spare after my old crew left, so added this on.' Croc waved a hand around the alcove. 'The place just seemed to need a picture window. And a decent space for the chair. Contemplation, I call it.'

Mick couldn't take his eyes away – the expanse of the valley, the reflection of the surrounding trees in the water terraces, the distant figures of farmers and animals making their way along the tracks.

With a rush of nostalgia, he remembered his toy farm, the plastic animals and people, fences and gates, the way he loved to create a miniature landscape in the dirt.

'Got a new crew now.' Croc continued. 'Bunch of guys learning the trade. Not much to do around here, but if I can teach them a few woodworking skills, it's better than being useless.'

'Yeah not much happening, especially since Buster and his lot went. The mess is practically empty.' Mick wondered why he hadn't seen Croc at mealtimes. But for now, he had more pressing questions. 'What do you do here in the weekends?'

'Anything we like. It's pretty lax. Some of them sign-out a vehicle and go for a daytrip or even away for the weekend. Get a group together. Blokes and girls from camp, or pick up mates from another outpost.'

'You can do that? Sign out a vehicle?'

'Sure. *You* can easy. You're a driver. You got a truck. All they might ask is you pay for some fuel if you go too far.' He drew on his pipe and watched the smoke swirls. 'Generally, you do what you like in the weekend, long as you stay out of trouble. It's all fairly casual.'

'Can't believe there's no fieldwork, no parades, no training – or the like.'

'That got me too, when I first came. But at first it was just me and my building team. Since the Kiwi military order turned up, things are more regulated. You'll see. The biggest problem is boredom! Like your job – driving there and back, nothing to do in-between. Buster used to head off for a kip in the middle of the day.'

'He did. But I've found things to do so far. Lend a hand to these poor bastards. Fixed a hole in a house wall last couple days.'

'You did?' Croc turned to face Mick, squinting through one eye. 'You can swing a hammer, then?'

Mick shrugged. 'Do what I can. Raised on a farm – and you know what they say about Kiwi ingenuity.' His mouth twisted into a wry smile, not in the habit of blowing his own trumpet. 'The house I fixed is the tatami maker's. He's doing mats for the truck seats in exchange, but he can't access the fabric tape to finish the edges. I told him I'd try to find some webbing straps or something. Any ideas?'

Croc gave a knowing laugh and slapped his palm on the armrest, as if he had just achieved something. 'You need to talk to the Quartermaster, my son!'

'Quartermaster? There's a quartermaster in camp?'

'Well, Chief of Stores, to be exact. But he likes to be called Quartermaster – That's QM in my lingo. You'll see.'

'Where's his store, his supply hut – whatever it's called?'

'Seen that stand-alone building at the other end of the main barracks? He's away from the rest so no-one can sneak in and help themselves. He's like a watchman – got surveillance on all sides. Even his bunkroom's adjoining the stores – on duty day and night!'

'He's there now, then?'

Croc leaned over. Still focussed on the view, he dropped his voice. 'Let me give you a tip, Mick, old son. The old QM gets pretty cranky if you turn up at closing time.'

Mick did a double-take, turning to Croc for clarification. 'When's closing time?'

Croc lifted his arm, squinted at his wristwatch. 'Yep, about now. Give him an hour or so to unwind and get comfortable, then pay him a visit. Great bloke. He's good for socialising after hours, if you feel like sticking your head around his door. Loves a chat. You'll see.'

Mick took a quick shower – army style. Not the unhurried process of home where frequent rain ensured an ample water supply. He dressed, patting his chest pocket then laughed at himself.

Her letter was still there, but he was no further along in solving the puzzle – the Emiko enigma.

At the mess hall Mick filled his plate before turning to survey the seated few. Right away he saw Croc and took a seat near him.

'Bloody awful stew again,' Croc said, in greeting. 'What the hell is this meat? Can't tell if its camel or goanna.'

Mick laughed. 'Damn! I took a double serving.'

'You're gonna regret that, Mate. Mark my words! You'll be chewing 'till breakfast time.'

Mick spun his plate around and started on the mash. 'Spud?' he asked, trying to get the flavour.

'*Nup*,' Croc answered. 'Rice. Boiled to within an inch of its life, then whipped to death.'

Mick persevered with it. 'At least its salty – prevent dehydration.' Croc shook his head defiantly and continued chewing.

Someone across the room shouted, 'There's pudding! Steam pudding. And some sort of custard.'

'Sounds like me,' Croc said, getting to his feet, picking up his near-full plate of stew, returning it to the servery and bringing back a heaped bowl of pudding. 'There's a line-up of a dozen rejected dinners up there, Mate. Don't be ashamed to add to it. Feed the neighbourhood.'

'You mean people will actually eat this?'

'Yeah. Must be bloody hungry, poor beggars.'

Mick followed suit, returning with his pudding bowl laden. 'Think I'll head over to the QM later. You want to come along?'

'Nah, you're on your own with that, Mate. A visit to the QM is not to be taken lightly. He'll want to know all about you. You'll see.' Croc scooped the last from his bowl, licked the spoon clean and stood. 'I'm gonna write to my girl. Good talking, Mick.'

Croc had exaggerated somewhat the surveillance at the QM's hut. A couple of mangy street dogs on long leads lay low around the building, ears twitching. Their growls announced Mick's approach. A flick of the curtain at a small window and a voice from inside calling 'Come on in,' told Mick he'd been approved.

The dogs relaxed down and Mick stepped up into the entrance.

The door flung open and Mick froze.

Before him stood a smooth-headed man, about forty. Round, wire-rimmed spectacles perched on his nose and red lipstick covered his mouth. He wore a kimono. Not the standard navy and white cotton robe that's often worn by women and men at the public baths, but a floor-length, elaborate, silky version with violet irises and a wide, red sash holding the edges together around the middle.

Mick's voice came out in squeaks. 'Ah – err – *hmm*, – I'm looking for the QM?'

'You're looking for the Quartermaster, lad,' boomed a voice, so unfitting the image. 'And you've found him. Rodney Bonhommie, at your service. Come in, come in.'

He stepped back and Mick tentatively entered, wondering if Croc was hiding in the shadows behind him, grinning like a jackass.

'Let me get you a drink.' The QM turned to a kitchen bench, set up with enough equipment to cook his own meals. That explained why Mick had not yet come across him at the communal mealtimes. The QM was not an image he would forget.

Along one side of the room hung a full-length drape, woven into an ancient battle scene, Samurai warriors in flight. Spanning wall to wall, it screened off what could be the sleeping area.

'Take a seat.' The QM indicated a couple of low-slung lounge chairs draped in gaudy velvet.

Mick gawped. *Only in a brothel* – his grandma would have said.

'Came across those pieces in a market in Singapore,' the QM said, in response to Mick's fixed stare. 'Couldn't leave them behind.'

'Thanks.' Mick sank into a chair until his knees were higher than his shoulders.

The QM carried two army-issue enamel mugs, placing one on the low table in front of Mick and balancing the other as he lowered himself into the second chair, the kimono falling open to reveal his army boots and fishnet stockings.

What was going on? Was it dress-up night at the mess? Was he expecting someone else to visit – Oh God! Was he preparing to... socialize? Did he mistake Mick for an arranged caller?

'I'm Mick Mitchell,' he blurted. 'The new driver in camp. Taking over from Buster Daniels. Doing the hospital run…'

'Slow down,' laughed his host. 'Mick – is it?'

Mick nodded and picked up the mug, burning his fingers on the enamel and quickly rotating it to grab the handle. *What was in it?* Hot as tea – but clear like water.

'What do you think of the saké?' The QM nodded towards the mug.

Mick stared. 'Saké? A mug full?'

'I know!' the QM laughed. 'They usually serve it in silly little egg cups, but I say – a drink's a drink. Don't want to do things half-pie. What do you think?'

Mick blew into his mug and took a swig, and quickly a second, to wash down the first, hoping to gulp back the threatening cough. He cleared his throat. 'Don't know much about saké,' he rasped.

'Make my own,' the QM offered proudly. 'Even with *my* buying powers, can't get decent saké these days. The black market has it all tied up. What do you think, eh?'

Mick gulped air. 'Don't know much about it.' He repeated, placing the mug back on the table and changing the subject. 'Croc said you might be able to help me find some tape, or webbing straps – suitable as edging for tatami mats. I'm helping the tatami maker in town. He can't get the fabric stuff any more.'

'Tatami edging tape…' the QM said slowly. 'Never had that request before.' He sipped from his mug and looked thoughtfully into the distance. 'Music?' he asked suddenly.

Without waiting for Mick's reply, he launched himself to his feet and crossed the room to a wooden gramophone cabinet, clicking the hinged lid open and moving the arm across to start the record spinning.

'I am the very model of a modern Major-General,' the QM sang along in his rich baritone, *'I know the kings of England, and I quote the fights historical.'*

He turned back to Mick, raising his voice over the melody. 'Tatami edging? There is something – wait here. Sorry you can't join me, old chap,' he called, disappearing around the dividing curtain. 'No mortal being, other than myself, can set foot into the hallowed halls of the Quartermaster's Store.' And he sung on from behind the curtain. *'I'm very well acquainted, too, with matters mathematical, I understand equations, both the simple and quadratical…'*

Above the operatic tones, Mick heard the rattle of keys, the click of a lock and the slide of an opening door.

He grabbed his mug and headed outside, tipping a good amount of saké onto the ground.

'Can't handle the saké, Mate?' came a voice from the shadows.

Mick let his eyes adjust to the dark and saw the faint image of a rocking chair. 'Jeez, Croc! What the hell are you doing there?'

'Too dark to admire the view. Thought I'd head over here for some entertainment.' He paused to drink from the bottle in his hand. 'Take a tip from me, old son. Fill that mug with water, or he'll be topping it up with moonshine again, as quick as a wink.'

'Why don't you come in?' Mick said, turning to look for water. 'Instead of skulking out here in the shadows.'

'Nah,' Croc said getting to his feet and hefting the rocking chair onto his shoulder. 'Reckon I've seen enough for one day.'

'I see what you mean about boredom,' Mick quipped over his shoulder, heading inside for the water jug.

He'd just sunk back into his seat when the QM returned carrying a bundle of khaki webbing.

'This might do you.' He dropped it in a pile beside Mick. 'We used it for webbing straps when we made our own safari stretchers. Got a better system with the bunks now, so this is redundant.'

'Looks good.' Mick measured the width against his hand. 'Six inches? That'd be about right. Got any more of this?'

'Got a mountain of the stuff. Be glad to get rid of it. It's taking up space.'

'I'm happy to take it off your hands. Probably more than enough for the truck seats, but I'm sure Tatami-san will put it all to good use.'

The QM disappeared around the curtain again and returned with a large canvas bag stuffed full.

Mick stood, finished his drink in a few gulps and returned the empty mug to the bench. 'Thanks for the saké. Good brew.'

The QM fixed his eyes on the mug and shot an astounded look at Mick.

'By the way, if your dogs aren't too fussy, there's a heap of leftover rubbery stew in the mess. It'll give them jaw ache, but might taste okay.'

'Ah, thanks,' said the QM, still looking dumbfounded.

Mick scooped up the spaghetti of canvas and shouldered the bag. 'This'll be just the ticket. Many thanks.'

'Call again,' the QM invited, as Mick headed away.

Chapter Six

Tell me and I'll forget.
Show me and I may remember.
Involve me and I'll understand.
– Ancient Wisdom

Kazu pushed the kitbag and the pile of canvas tape off his truck seat without comment. 'Grandmother not come today,' he said, trying to find room for his feet. 'She do garden – *Tanazawa-san*.'

Mick nodded, noticing the bulging carry-bag Kazu was holding, the one his grandmother usually carried to the hospital. 'Will your sister be okay without *Obasan*?'

Kazu fell silent, clutching the food bag, eyes fixed ahead. The language game didn't happen on that ride.

At the hospital, as the villagers stepped down from the truck, Kazu turned to Mick. 'I go see sister. Grandmother say so.' He turned and spoke to the villagers. They reached out, smiles on their faces, as they drew Kazu into their group, chattering as they headed towards the rickety bamboo fence.

Mick watched them disappear around the corner, remembered the blundering teen only a few days earlier, his hesitancy and anxiety, refusing to visit his sister – even at the grandmother's side.

Mick blew out a sigh, nodded and pressed his lips into a smile. Kazu, in a few short days, had stepped up – he had become a different person.

Mick took the familiar route to Tatami-san's, grabbed the bag full of straps and bundled the loose straps into his arms, heading towards the workshop.

He wondered how today would go, without Kazu as translator. And he wondered how Kazu would manage in the hospital, how he would face his sister.

Tatami-san rushed out when he saw Mick approaching. Reaching out he gathered the canvas straps into his arms and hurried to his workbench, where he dropped the bundle and immediately began an inspection – rubbing his fingers on the texture, pulling it lengthways to test for strength and stretch, bending it widthways to check for flexibility.

Finally, he nodded to Mick. '*Hai,*' – yes, he said. '*Totemo yoi.*'

Mick took that to mean it was satisfactory because Tatami-san had a big smile on his face, as he measured the length of the straps against the sides of the unfinished mats.

'*Hai,*' – yes, he said again, on his final inspection.

Mick lifted the bag to show him the rest of the supply. Tatami-san threw his arms in the air and spoke very excitedly. Mick took it to mean, 'Now I can make more tatami for other people because you have given me so much braid'.

With the speed of a competent craftsman, Tatami-san cut a strap to length and pinned it against the first mat. With tiny, almost invisible stitches he secured it, tapping the long needle through the thick matting with a small wooden block tucked into the palm of his hand.

Mick stood by, watching the process, getting involved when it was time to flip the mat and stitch on the other side.

Tatami-san spent some time bending the strap around the open edge, muttering to himself. Mick guessed the canvas to be a thicker, stiffer material than he would normally work with and therefore it required some persuasion to bend the right way. Mick stepped in, holding the strap in place, ahead of Tatami-san's stitching.

With the first mat completed, they examined and admired the effect.

Tatami-san commented, apparently, on the effect of the canvas, in lieu of his usual edging tape – he thought it looked okay.

Mick nodded, feeling he got the gist of his meaning and added, 'This canvas will be good and durable on the truck seats and it will be sturdy enough to be sat on along those bumpy roads.' He added some mimed action, and Tatami-san laughed and nodded.

They began on the second mat, Mick holding the strap in place and sometimes picking up the block, hammering the needle through. With the first side of stitching complete, they flipped the mat. Tatami-san passed the needle to Mick, his weathered face crinkling into a smile. 'Hai,' – yes, he said, picking up the hammering block and indicating for Mick to have a go at stitching.

Under the regimentation of Tatami-san's tutorship, Mick forced the needle through the stiff, resisting straw pad. Every stitch had to be exact, and Mick lost count of the number of times he was pushed aside by the shoulder-height tatami master, impatiently hammering the needle back out again because it didn't go through the mat straight, the stitch was too big or too small, or not in a straight line.

Taking his time and being meticulous, Mick eventually had fewer interruptions and Tatami-san stepped back a little, relaxing somewhat. They settled into a tempo with Mick exacting the needle work, his master grunting approval and wielding the hammering block.

Mick thought about his father, how they worked together on the farm, his father instructing him on the judgements and processes needed for a satisfactory outcome.

Feeling a heaviness in his chest, Mick let out a sigh. Was he homesick? Of course, he missed his family, but not enough to feel he must return to them. He glanced up and Tatami-san met his eye, a look of total understanding on his wizened face. Mick pressed his lips into a knowing smile. If anyone could understand the pull of home, surely Tatami-san would, in this homeland of hardship.

They completed the third and the forth mat, language no barrier, companionship crossing boundaries. Mick pulled down the steps and they carried the mats up. Tatami-san fiddled and fussed over them until they sat evenly, edge to edge on the wooden benches. The two men stood back and looked at the transformation. The empty, hard benches actually looked inviting.

'Shall we?' Mick suggested, keen to see what the seats felt like.

Tatami-san nodded. 'Hai.' They both turned and lowered themselves carefully, as if half expecting the mats to collapse under their weight.

How could strength and cushioning be as one? For Mick, it felt like sitting on a densely grassed lawn, with the underlying solidity of packed earth beneath the accommodating softness of the surface.

The two men sat there, nodding and grinning like fools. Mick's thoughts focussed on what might be the reaction of Kazu, the villagers and, of course, Emiko.

By the air of pride around Tatami-san, Mick picked up that the master, in being reunited with his trade, had regained his purpose and an overwhelming sense of satisfaction.

Tatami-san stood and moved to another seat, nodding and trying the next, and then the final mat, giving them all a generous nod of approval.

Mick went back to the workshop, bringing a bundle of braid and a cutting tool.

Together they cut lengths and tied the mats in place on the wooden benches.

Before Mick left for the hospital, Tatami-san called his attention and spoke. Mick concentrated on the words. At first, he could understand nothing. Then he picked up '*Kazuya*'.

'Kazu-san?' Mick asked.

Tatami-san nodded. '*Hai, Kazu-san.*' He gestured from the truck to his workshop. 'Bring Kazu-san?' Mick asked.

The tatami master headed into his workshop, picked up the long needle and hammering block, and mimed stitching, repeating Kazu's name. It became apparent he wanted to teach Kazu tatami-making skills, as he had with Mick today.

Both men took time over their farewell bow. '*Domo arigato*,' Mick said, with heartfelt appreciation.

Tatami-san's face mirrored the same sentiments. Mick instinctively went to shake hands then pulled his hand back and let his face express the camaraderie he felt.

What a day! He had never expected he would have a chance to try his hand at one of Japan's oldest crafts. The feeling was mighty.

Mick pulled up at the hospital just as the villagers, Kazu in their midst, wandered out.

Kazu ran ahead to help pull down the steps. His stance told Mick that all had gone well regarding the reunion with his sister. Then Kazu looked into the back of the truck and his eyes widened, taking in the effect of the new seat mats.

'Mick-san! *Tatami*...! Finish!'

Mick grinned. Kazu turned to the villagers and called them forward, ushering them up the steps, enjoying their reactions. Lastly, Emiko paused at the bottom of the steps and nodded formally to Mick. He reciprocated. *Leave it at that for now*. She made her way up and took a seat.

The villagers sat carefully and ran their fingers over the smooth matting. They studied and discussed the unusual braid. They bounced up and down on their seat to test it for cushioning quality and they smiled at Mick. Their expressions said it all.

With the passengers all on the truck, Mick bent to lift the steps.

'*Chotto* – wait, Mick-san.' Kazu headed up the steps and from the truck floor bent over to help pull the steps up. Then he joined the villagers, taking a seat and giving Mick a nod.

'*Ikimasho* – let's go, Mick-san!' Kazu called from among his neighbours. Mick laughed, and headed to the driver's seat.

Kazu had made a huge leap today, taking over his grandmother's role, joining the villagers and visiting his sister.

Mick's day had had been similarly filled with achievement. Tatami-san honoured him with his tutoring in tatami-making.

With Kazu riding in the back, leaving Mick to drive solo, it seemed strange but felt good to be independent behind the wheel.

As they approached the cooler air near the paddy fields, Mick heard singing. He strained to listen. It came from his truck – the village chorus. People along the road turned to look, some laughing and waving, some joining in the song, as the chorus headed home – a satisfactory end to a very surprising first week on the job.

***

Saturday dawned. With no hospital visiting, Mick lacked a sense of purpose, so headed off to breakfast hatching a plan.

Kazu had said he and *Obasan* would be working in the Tanazawa garden all weekend. As Mick understood, some of the lawn areas were being converted to vegetable gardens, to help produce more food. Mick wanted to be a part of that project.

All week he'd bottled his curiosity about the village *Hinode-mura*. Now he would go there.

He also wanted to see where Emiko lived. What was it like – the place Kazu described as *big house, big garden, Tanazawa* family?

But more than that – he wanted to see *Emiko*. He was getting edgy about approaching her and he didn't want to end up feeling shut-out, thinking about her as a lost cause, as Buster had – *the princess, the crown jewels, off limits.*

He needed a strategy.

Mick found Croc at breakfast and asked for details about the vehicle sign-out process. Then he got the nod to borrow a few garden tools from the workshop.

On the road soon after and having no idea how to find the Tanazawa property, Mick hoped he would catch Kazu before he left *Obasan's* house.

Pulling up at the village bus stop, he felt like an intruder. The village seemed quiet, but he was sure there would be activity in and around the dwellings – the residents enjoying a more leisurely start to the day, maybe with time to do the things they usually had to leave behind.

Mick slung the spade and pickaxe over his shoulder and headed across the rough ground, eyes fixed on the settlement which had allured him every morning and evening in the past week.

He heard distant voices but saw no-one. The peachy glow of daybreak had long since merged into full daylight and the heat was rising – although less steamy here in the inland hills, with the highlands breeze.

The gravel road, which bordered the vegetable plantation, curved into the village, narrowing to cart width and smoothing to well-trodden pebbles as it meandered between the dwellings, linking one to the other like leaves along a branch.

Obasan's house, the first in line, showed no signs of life. Mick continued on past, absorbed as he ventured along the path, almost forgetting his plan to join the gardening team, as his fascination lead him forward like an invisible lure.

The walls of the houses, clad with overlapping boards, had their doors and windows screened with sliding panels of lashed-together bamboo and thin wooden lath, some in an open basket-weave, allowing air to flow in and out. *Obasan's* house reflected all the others with its tone-on-tone warm shades of weathered timbers, rather like a chocolate-coated gingerbread house.

Mick had expected to see cultivated gardens around the homes, miniature versions of nature with bonsai, pebbled dry-streams and stone lanterns, so he was surprised by the rough grass edges and unkempt borders. Practical people lived here, busy with the necessities of life, not given to aesthetics.

He noticed here and there the remnants of a garden wall, plants that appeared to have been once strategically placed but since left to follow their will, or a feature of stones now over-shadowed by the exuberance of unchecked nature.

Lanky saplings stretched up from shady spaces where they'd happened to take root, some bending their trunk around the roof edge in search of sunlight. Smaller, scraggly bushes flowered abundantly, all the more vibrant for being free-spirited and unmanicured.

The fragrance of blossom drifted Mick's way, mingling with the good, homely smell of wood smoke. He recalled the cooking fire at Tatami-san's and wondered if these families, like his own back home, gathered around the fire in winter to share food and drink, warmth and laughter?

Strong, square posts supported the lean-to veranda roofs fronting the path, the ground underneath paved with a hotchpotch of stones fitted together like a child's puzzle, trampled into place by generations of footsteps.

Between some posts, ropes of small flags inked with writing and drawings, fluttered in the breeze, like fairground bunting. Mick stood underneath and looked up but found the flapping graphics too intricate to decipher.

Giant bamboo poles, served as downpipes and when split in half became roof guttering, ready to catch the overflow of seasonal downpours.

Doorsteps created by large, flat rocks or thick cross-sections of once-mighty trees stepped up into entrance porches, some screens open enough for a passer-by to see in. Mick paused just long enough for a quick look, but not so long as to feel intrusive.

Long fabric flags hung down in front of some buildings where others had a solid wooden slab sitting upright on a platform, sign-written with the trade or some other relevance about those living within, no doubt.

Mick turned to look back. *Obasan's* house still appeared to be sleeping.

Then he noticed movement at her entrance porch and Kazu appeared, slipping into shoes as he shuffled over the stone step, under the veranda roof and onto the path, looking ahead.

'Mick-san!' he called 'Why you here?'

Mick laughed, lifting the spade and pickaxe off his shoulder. 'I come to help in the garden.'

'You help, Mick-san? But you drive truck. Not do garden,' Kazu said, closing the distance between them.

'I drive truck, make steps, fix house and do garden. No problem.' He handed Kazu the bento-box that Tomoko had made up.

Kazu pushed his glasses into place and fixed a smile on his face, nodding at Mick.

‘Thank you,’ he said. ‘Good to see you, Mick-san. But I late. I go Tanazawa-san garden. Grandmother already work, I think.’

Mick settled the tools back onto his shoulder and turned to walk. ‘Show me the way.’

Kazu started alongside him. ‘Mick-san,’ he protested. ‘You not work Tanazawa-san garden.’

‘If I can help, then that’s good, isn’t it?’

‘Thank you for tools,’ Kazu said, grabbing the spade handle from behind Mick. ‘I take now.’

Mick kept his grip, laughing over the tug-of-war.

‘Mick-san!’ Kazu let go of the handles and blocked the path in front of Mick to make his point. ‘Tanazawa-san not let you work. You, *gaijin* soldier – foreigner, not work for Japanese important man. Very sorry, Mick-san.’ Kazu shook his head slowly, dramatically.

Mick stopped walking. Kazu was right. This was not socially informal New Zealand, where everyone would pitch in for a community working bee – haymaking, decorating the village hall for an event or cutting firewood for someone who didn’t own a chainsaw.

Saturday mornings spent blackberry picking with school mates on the overgrown riverbanks, getting the makings for jam for the school fete, returning with near empty buckets and purple mouths. That was the world he came from.

Mick could accept that here, protocol and procedure formed everyday life. He could not, however, accept the finality of Kazu’s decision. He understood the reasoning but he couldn’t believe it had to be that way.

Sometimes things have to change and he would not stop until he found a way through. This was not about him getting his way. It was about moving forward, finding solutions for the benefit of all.

Every nation in the world had been rocketed into accepting change in order to move forward, especially since wars forced new ideas into everyday thinking. Mick, as a Kiwi visitor, had so much to learn about this place but he also had something to contribute, and he’d be damned if he was going to be turned away so easily.

Besides, if he couldn’t connect with Emiko during the week, it must happen in the weekend.

For now, he conceded. ‘I understand.’ He blew out a breath, deciding to go along with his companion’s request until a better plan arose. ‘I’ll walk with you a bit – show me the village. When we get to Tanazawa-san's place, you can take the tools.'

Kazu considered. 'You not come Tanazawa-san garden?' he checked.

'I'll go to the gate. See what happens then.'

'Why you go to gate?'

Mick side-stepped the question. 'I want to see the rest of your village – *Hinode-mura.* You can tell me what the signs say.' Mick pointed to a wooden slab, fixed upright like a totem pole.

'I read?'

Mick nodded.

'This one, medicine maker, like doctor.'

They walked on, Kazu's steps somewhat cautious, as if he didn't quite trust Mick to keep to his word.

'And this?' Mick asked at the next sign, a worn fabric flag hanging from a curving bamboo pole.

'This – maker for roof.' Kazu pointed to the thick reed thatching. 'Like big tatami,' he added. 'Not many house have this roof. Now roof maker very old man. Not make this roof again.' Mick looked at the other cottages. Many of them had multi-layered wooden shingles or split bamboo tiles.

Kazu relaxed as they walked and talked, Mick observant and curious, Kazu confident and knowledgeable.

When the houses became more spaced out, rows of crops took advantage of any vacant land. Soon, dense forest pressed in on both sides of the path, the air smelling of damp earth and vibrating with the deafening chorus of cicadas, making conversation impossible.

When the noise abated somewhat Mick passed on the message from Tatami-san.

'He want me?' Kazu responded, looking disbelieving.

'*Hai* – yes. He wants to teach you how to make tatami. I think he needs a helper.'

'Me? Make tatami? No Mick-san. I don't do that.'

'Why not? I did.'

Kazu shot Mick a look. 'You make tatami? No.' He laughed.

'Tatami-san showed me how to stitch.' Mick mimed pushing the needle down and up through the matting. 'I helped sew the seat mats.' He grinned at Kazu, feeling proud of the part he'd played and the connections he'd made with Tatami-san.

Kazu, still not convinced, left the idea hanging. 'Soon, Tanazawa-san gate,' he announced. They rounded a corner and the path opened out into a triangular clearing with wide steps radiating out and down, like the folds of a giant paper fan.

Before them stood a small building with a pair of elaborately carved, full-height gates at its centre and a steep pitched roof offering shelter or shade to those coming and going, like a stand-alone porch. Small compartments bordered each side of the gates, like outdoor cupboards.

At first Mick assumed them to be garden sheds, taking advantage of the gate roof to create undercover storage for equipment. Then he noticed well-concealed sliding panels, at a peephole height.

'What are these for?' Mick asked.

'Samurai,' Kazu answered simply. 'Not now, but Tanazawa-san ancestors protect family – from warlord and bandit.'

Mick smiled. 'Samurai gate-keepers.' He shook his head in fascination.

A low bamboo fence marked the front boundary, indicating security was not an issue any more.

Kazu turned to Mick, his face apologetic. 'Mick-san, I can't bring visitor. Sorry. Not my place.'

A scuffle of activity inside the fence some distance away caught their attention. Partly concealed by draping greenery, Obasan scraped away fallen leaves with a cane rake.

'O – o, grandmother!' Kazu whispered, his face a confusion of surprise and anxiety. The raking stopped and the old lady called out.

Kazu replied. '*Ohayoo, Okahsan,*' – hello Grandmother. Then turned to Mick and whispered 'Mick-san, you must go!'

Mick passed the tools to Kazu, then hesitated, wondering how Obasan would react to his presence.

Mick turned to her and bowed. '*Ohayoo, Obasan,*' – hello Aunty, he said, copying Kazu's style of greeting, but right away he could see from the angst on his companion's face that *his* choice of words did not meet approval.

Surprisingly less worried about formalities than her grandson, Obasan beamed her gold-flecked smile and hurried to the gatehouse, clicking the latch and pulling both doors open.

"Mick-san! *Yokoso*,' she exclaimed bowing, stepping back to usher Mick in, with a welcoming sweep of her hand.

Kazu looked perplexed. 'Grandmother say welcome – come in.'

Obasan turned to a garden worker who had just stepped into view carrying a basket of trimmings. She called an instruction.

'*Hai, hai,*' – yes, responded the worker, rushing away out of sight.

'Someone coming,' Kazu said quietly.

Mick looked around. He could neither see nor hear an arrival. 'Who?'

'Servant come soon.' Kazu's head dipped forward. 'Grandmother sent message. You will visit Tanazawa family.' The flatness in his voice sounded a warning. Or was it shame at having been so resistant to Mick coming here; while Obasan was so welcoming.

Mick felt sure there would be only one chance to make a good impression on Emiko and her family. He had intended to quiz Kazu about visitor protocols as they walked – before Kazu advised him so strongly against it.

Mick's original intention to join the gardeners in a worthwhile project would have enabled him to have a discreet presence on the property, under the chaperone of Kazu and his grandmother, and at least a chance to assess how to go about meeting Emiko. Now, rather than being culturally informed or discreet he was about to fall rather clumsily into her world.

'What shall I do?' Mick asked, more to himself than to anyone else. He sensed Kazu just behind him, edging him forward, urging him now to accept the grandmother's invitation to enter.

Obasan seemed to carry some authority and she knew the family well, if only as an employee. If he couldn't trust her guidance, who could he trust?

He stepped through the gates and into the domain of the Tanazawa lineage.

A man approached, his age indeterminable, his footsteps steady and measured, his expression all-seeing, all-knowing.

He wore navy and grey attire, similar in style to the warriors on the quartermaster's curtain. The top wrapped taught across his chest, like a steel breastplate, not fabric. Wide-legged breeches fell in overlapping folds, long enough to hide his feet, wide enough to allow fluid movement in all directions. A short over-kimono hung loosely from his shoulders and a cummerbund knotted stiffly around the middle, its rigid ties jutted downwards like scimitar swords.

Mick noticed two smooth bamboo handles tucked into the waistband, angled at-the-ready. He imagined the out-of-sight blades and how lightning-quick their owner would be, with a flick of the wrist, to bring them into play.

The guard didn't slow his pace until he was just a few steps in front of Mick. There he stopped, bowed quickly and stood upright. Looking Mick in the eye, he spoke directly to him in Japanese, making no concession, showing no concern for Mick's obvious lack of understanding.

Kazu moved silently in behind Mick. 'You go, Mick-san,' he whispered urgently. 'Follow the guide. Tanazawa-san wait for you now.'

Mick swallowed hard. As much as he wanted to accept the invitation to see more of Emiko's life, he didn't want to tumble in head first.

Chapter Seven

If a man has no tea in him,
he is incapable of understanding
truth and beauty.
– Japanese Proverb

With another quick bow, the guard turned and walked away.

Obasan ushered Mick forward, signalling for him to follow; her encouraging smile providing some reassurance. Then she said something, and Kazu translated.

'Grandmother say, "to please the girl, you first must please the father."'

How did Obasan know? Was it that obvious? He had thought he was being discrete and controlled. *Above all he wanted to maintain privacy. How much did Emiko know? Did everyone on the truck and in the village know...? Her father?*

Suddenly, this didn't feel like an invitation. It felt like a summons and there appeared no option – no turning back.

With the escort already several paces ahead, Mick started along the path with no choice but to swallow his pride and accept his fate. He breathed deeply, anticipating the best possible outcome for his visit, while allowing the garden to hold his gaze.

Like theatre curtains opening only partway, glimpses of the scenery beyond were revealed in tantalising segments. Narrow vistas ran away into the distance – along a path, over a bridge, beside a stony stream, around a corner, behind a tree – enticing him onward, like an evocative garden sprite beckoning him to places unknown.

His thoughts drifted back to the events of the past week. What had led him to this place, this time?

On first meeting Obasan, Mick had the gut feeling that she would be a significant go-between, allowing him into the world of the village and the lives of its people – even before he became determined to meet Emiko on territory other than the hospital trips, even before Kazu turned up as his navigator and translator.

At that point, Mick bypassed Obasan, realising the lack of a common language would make any communication too difficult. He took on Kazu as his interpreter and social advisor, but in spite of the language barrier Obasan seemed to have read his mind, while Kazu's youthfulness had not always given him the greatest insight. He just hoped Obasan had his best interests at heart – he must trust.

Mick returned his focus to the garden. The vista from the path at times closing in, suggesting that he was coming to the end of the walk, then opening out around the next corner with surprising depth – huge trees then dwarf trees, giving the impression of greater distance. It seemed as if the entire countryside spread before him and he thought back to the farm, the boundless spaces of his childhood playgrounds made by nature.

A small pond fringed with irises reminded him of his mother's fascination with purple flowers. *Purple and blue attract the bees,* he recalled her saying.

A dry, stony stream bed had a single board as a bridge like the wobbly planks crossing streams at home. And a cluster of rocks almost completely engulfed by moss, resembled round hills and deep valleys in miniature.

The hand-of-man was nowhere in sight – each aspect, every plant and feature appeared as they would in the wilderness, yet Mick knew these effects were created by the fastidious coaching of nature, positioned like a posed family photograph, everything in place, every individual in their Sunday-best no matter which angle you looked from.

Mick recalled the unkempt edges around the village dwellings, indicating residents like Obasan gave their time to practical matters, community needs.

The immensity of these gardens represented people from a very different social hierarchy. Kazu's deference when he mentioned Tanazawa-san started to make sense to Mick, as the 'big house' was not in view, yet.

He wondered if it was madness to pursue Emiko. Was Buster right? Was she really off limits to a lowly occidental soldier with a face of the enemy?

Mick tried to calm his heartbeat, to concentrate on positive thoughts.

What's the worst that can happen? I fail. I fall on my face and get a big NO! I can handle that. I'm a soldier, for God's sake.

And then the house appeared. Mick stood in his tracks, pausing to take it all in. He looked from left to right and back again.

With grand dimensions, the homestead sat low yet delicate on the land, wide verandas and wooden railings making it almost boat-like as it floated over the edge of a lake-sized lily pond.

The shield of weathered-black timbers and shuttered screens conveyed an intimidatingly secretive aura, as if the occupants' eyes could see out, while he, from the outside, could see nothing. Mick imagined samurai stationed in the outer rooms, peering through inconspicuous peepholes, along the verandas and out to the world in all directions.

His escort walked up the wide veranda steps to an entrance porch which separated the outside from the interior.

He turned and indicated a low bench for Mick to sit and remove his shoes. '*Chotto matte, kudasai.*' Mick understood he had to wait there. The escort slipped off his footwear and smoothly stepped inside, out of sight.

In socked feet Mick turned to the hollowed-out stone basin in the corner of the porch. Catching water from the trickling bamboo pipe, he allowed the coolness to splash over his hands, cupping some to his mouth for a sip. It tasted good. He took a mouthful and swilled it around while waiting.

Was Obasan really on his side? This unexpected introduction to Tanazawa-san was not of his asking – or wanting. He had hoped for a chance to talk with Emiko, that's all. Not a grand reception, where he might be lucky for a glance, a formal greeting, and small talk with her father.

The sound of approaching footsteps caught Mick's attention. He turned to see a man emerging from the dark interior, his style of dress similar to the escort, but more striking, more formal, in black. On reaching the doorway, he paused, bowed slowly and stood to face Mick. His dark hair and healthy complexion gave the image of a man much younger than Mick expected for the grand master – the man who would have been the warlord for the region in previous times.

Mick returned the bow. 'Mick Mitchell, New Zealand Jayforce,' he said formally. 'Pleased to meet you – *hajimemashite*,' he attempted.

'Hiroto Tanazawa. Hajimemashite, Mitchell-san.' He bowed again and ushered Mick along the veranda, indicating seats and a low table at the far corner. They sat opposite each other.

'You are the new driver, Mitchell-san.' The host spoke with a soft but confident tone.

Mick was relieved that he spoke English so comfortably.

Mick nodded. 'Yes. I have been here a week.'

'I hear good things you have done. Steps and tatami mats for the truck, and you helped repair the house wall for a citizen.'

'I'm doing what I can.' Mick wondered who had told him these things. Did Emiko report back to her father on the details of her day? But she would not know about the house repair at Tatami-san's unless Kazu had spoken of it. Or was Obasan, as the elder and likely chaperone on the truck, in the habit of providing feedback to her employer?

'My daughter tells me some things,' the host volunteered, 'but not everything.' He laughed and Mick saw the crinkles of fondness on his face. 'But I have my ear to the ground – as you say in English.'

'You speak English very well. Where did you learn?' Mick asked.

'I have a lot of business contacts now from the western world. I am fortunate to learn more than English from them. I am learning about new ways. It is good to move forward, I think.'

Mick nodded, was about to say something when movement along the veranda caught his eye.

Carrying a tray of tea things, Emiko glided towards them. His hope to see her alone was complicated by the restricted surroundings as always – bitter sweet.

Her kimono the colour of peaches with splashes of turquoise, seemed less formal – the fabric silkier than the ones she wore to work at the hospital. Her hair, usually pulled back tightly, now gathered softly around her face, fixed loosely at the back.

She approached the table, lowered the tray and bowed, her eyes flicking sideways to Mick under her veil of hair.

'*Irasshaimase*,' – welcome, she said in a clear voice, lowering to her knees beside the table.

Her fingertips resting like a butterfly on a flower, she placed a teacup before Mick, her eyes lingering on his just enough to make his heart leap. Then she drifted away, turning to her father and placing his tea before him, bowing, silently setting the teapot in the centre of the table, lifting the tray and smoothly rocking back onto her feet, stood, gave a further bow, turned and slipped away.

Mick watched her go. He didn't mind if her father saw the direction of his gaze. He understood that it was expected to admire the beauty of service – the chinaware, the offerings, the setting – and the elegance of presentation.

After she had gone from view, Mick turned to her father, pressed his lips into a smile and nodded – in open appreciation of the hospitality.

'You come from New Zealand, Mitchell-san. I know very little about your country.'

'It's a lot like Japan, in geography. If you take a map of the world and fold it along the equator,' Mick mimed the action, trying to pace his speech, word by word, 'Japan and New Zealand reflect each other. Both long Pacific islands, almost in a direct line from north to south.'

He stopped, realising he had just rattled off a lot of detail for someone who might find English hard to follow.

Tanazawa-san nodded, showing comprehension. 'So, Japan is north of equator and Nyujirando – New Zealand, is south, same distance. Same shape, same volcanoes, same earthquakes?'

Mick laughed. 'Yes, we have those too.'

Tanazawa-san rubbed his fingers over his chin thoughtfully. 'Ah, so.' He nodded. 'Did you live in a city, Mitchell-san?'

'On a farm. Dairy farm.' He paused. 'Cows?'

Tanazawa-san looked uncertain.

'Cows. Cattle. *Moo-oo*,' Mick said and his host laughed spontaneously.

'Moo,' the host repeated, nodding his understanding. '*Miruku?*'

'*Miruku*?' Mick asked. 'Milk! *Hai* – yes, milk. And cheese, and butter. And beef.'

'*Hai, bifu.*'

They sipped their tea in silence, Mick feigning interest in the garden and the house, while hoping Emiko would appear again.

Tanazawa-san pressed his lips together, saying no more, his head nodding almost imperceptibly – absentmindedly, and Mick picked up the indication that his visit had run its course.

He felt as though he was in a stage play, where each character had an expected role, scripted by someone from afar. But for some reason, he hadn't got the script in time. He wanted to stay longer, to see more of Emiko, but like a puppet on a string, he must follow the plan. And now his show was over.

At home it would be simple. 'Hello Mr Tanazawa. Is Emiko in?'

'Sure, wait here, Mick. I'll tell her you're here. Have a good time, you kids.' The father would leave, the daughter would appear. And that would be it. Simple!

Mick finished his tea and nodded. 'Thank you, Tanazawa-san, for your hospitality.'

The two men stood and walked side by side back along the veranda.

'I have enjoyed your visit, Mitchell-san. I hope you will call again.'

The bowing repeated and Tanazawa-san spoke into the inside room.

Mick had managed to get his shoes on as Emiko appeared in the doorway.

'My daughter can walk with you to the gate. She can practice her English now, for mine is tired. I'm sure you will be happy with the substitute.'

Mick turned to acknowledge his host on the veranda, an unreadable undertone to his expression as he graciously, inscrutably, farewelled his guest.

Following Emiko down the steps, Mick caught up with her and they started along the path, side by side.

A short distance away, the samurai guard appeared, ready to follow them, his hand relaxed on a bamboo handle at his waist.

He'll know what's in my head and my heart, Mick thought, feeling completely transparent under the penetrating stare.

The guard fell in behind. Mick gripped his hands behind his back and walked at Emiko's pace, keeping a substantial distance between them. He had the feeling that if he so much as tapped Emiko on the arm, his shoulder would be at risk of dislocation within seconds.

Chapter Eight

The outline of your future path already exists,
for you created its pattern by your past.
– *Sai Baba*

Even with a bodyguard in tow, walking beside Emiko felt as natural as breathing. 'Takeda-san will follow us,' she said in a lowered voice.

Mick breathed out. She spoke near perfect English. He tipped his head towards the guard behind them, grateful for a neutral subject to start their conversation. 'He is Takeda-san?'

'Yes, he is a samurai guard.' Emiko flicked a glance at Mick.

'Does Takeda-san understand English?'

'He does not speak English. Only we speak English.' She quickly glanced at Mick again.

'That's good.' It felt as though they did have some privacy, despite the supervision. Her mouth pressed into a small smile, a restrained agreement.

'But I think he can hear when we say his name. Or any Japanese words.' The humour in her expression softened the alert to Mick.

He nodded, making a mental note to avoid the few Japanese words he had learnt. 'Does he follow you everywhere?

'He watches me mostly here. At home.'

'What about on the truck? Does Obasan look out for you then?'

Emiko laughed, her hand rushing to cover her mouth. 'Obasan not bodyguard. But maybe like mother-guard.' She paused to pick a sprig from a shrub, holding the leaves to her nose. While appearing to inhale, she cupped her hand around her mouth, controlling the direction of her voice. 'You know Yodo-san, on the truck?' she whispered.

Mick shook his head. 'Can't say I do. Which one is she?'

'She has short kimono, wide pants like…' she tipped her head towards the guard following them. 'And always a scarf tied over her hair.'

Mick nodded, remembering the woman who had scaled the ladder with the least trouble, and often seemed to hang aside from the others, almost as if watching Emiko. He wondered how to describe a woman who moved like a man. 'She is very strong.'

'Yes.' She continued in a whisper, 'She is *onna-musha*,'

'What's that – *onna*…?'

Emiko smiled at him. 'You learn Japanese like I learn English. Very difficult to say new words.' She watched his response to her jest, before adding, 'It means woman samurai.'

Mick raised his eyebrows. 'Woman? I didn't know women could be samurai.'

She nodded. 'Not surprising you don't know. Japan is a nation of many secrets.' Her voice took on a mysterious tone. 'For centuries, women had important spy and samurai roles. They make a good spy, and very fast. Maybe sneaky.'

'I'm surprised there are still women samurai, these days?'

She nodded. 'Not many. But to guard a woman, like myself, *onna-musha* is best, I think. Man samurai cannot go all the places a woman must go, and Yodo-san can… how you say – not be seen? She looks like other women? How you say this?'

'Do you mean – she can fit in?'

'*Hai*, Yodo-san fits in. Yodo-san is my bodyguard on the truck.' Emiko watched for his response. 'You did not know this, I think?'

'That's true. I thought she was a villager.'

'She is a villager too, so she fits in. Nobody thinks she's anything else…'

Mick watched her process further thoughts, waited for her to choose the words.

Eventually, she continued. 'I think it's important you know, she is employed by my father. If there is trouble, she keeps me safe. That's her responsible job. Like you, responsible driver and soldier – your job to keep your passengers safe.' She turned to look at Mick. 'I can trust you, too, I think.'

'You can,' he responded, holding her with his eyes, hoping to show just how much she could trust him.

'But I don't talk on the truck,' she continued. 'Everything I say, she hears. She even understands little English, so I must be careful. Maybe she tells my father. Maybe not.' She shrugged, as if it was easy to live under such scrutiny.

Mick digested that, grateful to understand why Emiko had been so formal. Also, he picked up a hint of rebellion. Like young people worldwide, she didn't want her father to know everything she said or did, and that despite such supervision she was still able to have some secrets. It gave him a glimmer of hope that they could possibly meet privately sometime soon.

He wondered to what degree, how much of her life, the father was privy to. Over tea, Tanazawa-san had happily admitted to Mick that his daughter didn't tell him everything.

Mick considered that a surprisingly candid admission from a father to another male, especially a comparative stranger, and a foreigner at that.

Although he was curious, Mick knew not to ask direct questions about the subtleties of the father daughter connection. At home he would have launched in – *'So, what's your old man like? How do the two of you get on?'*

With the flow of their conversation so far, it would have been easy to assume too much, too soon. Here in Japan, he knew a subtler approach was called for.

'So, your father approves of you helping at the hospital?'

She smiled. 'Now he does. At first, he was against it. But I tell him – war changes what women do.' She shook her head defiantly. 'Very different now. Many women have to be in charge because the men are away at war. Some men not come back. Never.' She squared her shoulders and lifted her chin. 'Women have new skills. We have opinions. And we can look after ourselves.'

'Wow! You have said all that to your father?'

She gave a short laugh. 'Some of it. And some things he does not know. He would not agree.'

'Do young people in Japan think like you do?'

'Some do. Like me, many want changes and better roles for women. But some older ones are traditional and don't mind being like a servant.'

Mick glanced at her. 'And you're not like that.' He saw the determined set of her jaw.

At their first meetings, she had portrayed the epitome of Japanese femininity. But in a few minutes of conversation, he saw a very different side to her.

'No, I am not.'

'Do you often talk about these things, with your friends?'

She shook her head and gave a quick laugh. 'Some friends think the same way, like me. But at home, we keep our ideas to ourselves.' She shot a glance at Mick. 'I can see you have different ideas too. You come from a different place. You show respect to people, even women.' She lowered her voice, as if confiding. 'Kazuya-san likes you. Obasan likes you. All women on the truck – they like you. You are kind and helpful.'

'What about you?' Mick said, before thinking it through, and immediately wondered if he was being too forward.

He saw her lips press together, not understanding what that expression meant. 'You don't have to answer that,' he added quickly.

Her honesty and easy conversation had encouraged him to be spontaneous. Just because she spoke openly about her ideas didn't mean she would speak about her feelings. But he couldn't back down now. He had to follow through.

He stopped walking and turned to her. 'I would like to spend more time with you,' he added. 'I'd like to get to know you.' Now he was in boots-and-all. 'Is it possible that we could walk and talk like this another time?' He had to ask, because they were nearly at the gate and Takeda-san, not slowing his pace as they had, was closing the gap.

There she was again – the demure girl, head bowed slightly, smile pursed into a subtle pout, eyes flicking towards him but not quite meeting his gaze.

Eventually she spoke, the formal tone reflecting her upbringing. 'Maybe we can talk again, Mitchell-san. I would also like to learn about the world you come from.' Her eyes connecting with his, and quickly sliding away.

Mick studied her face. *What did that mean? – the way her eyes danced. Teasing? Suggesting? Evading?*

Her answer too indefinite for Mick – he wanted more than a *maybe*. 'When would be a good time?' He was aware his impatience might backfire.

She pursed her lips and Mick thought he had pushed too hard, that she was going to evade his question. Then she spoke, almost in a whisper. 'Maybe – I'll send a message.'

With that she bowed and straightened, her face unreadable, masked with enough formality to please her father when Takeda-san reported back to him.

Mick waited for her to turn away and start back. He watched her unhurried walk until the bend in the path took her out of sight.

Now it didn't matter so much about her father or the guard. Emiko had explained her independent ideas, her willingness to find her own way, albeit in parallel to traditional expectations.

Mick had an answer, although still guarded with a *maybe*, she seemed keen to meet again. And she had taken control – *she* might send *him* a message.

He must wait.

Takeda-san had walked ahead and now stood at the gate, his impatience noticeable, despite his closed expression, as he waited for Mick to exit the property, clicking the gate closed after him and securing the lock.

Mick took the steps two at a time and quickly reached a high point on the forest track, peering through a narrow opening to overlook the expansive garden he had just walked through, his eyes searching for the path as it wound and curved in and out of sight.

There she was – Emiko, making her way home, taking her time, showing no concern for the guard, who had now closed the distance and was not far behind her. She paused to gaze ahead as if taking in the view. Then she spun around and looked directly to where Mick stood at his lookout.

He waved; She didn't respond. He couldn't determine if she was looking at him or if she just sensed he would be there somewhere. It was too distant to decipher her expression before she turned slowly and continued out of sight.

Chapter Nine

Silence is sometimes the best answer.
– 14th Dalai Lama

Mick headed along the track, back to the village, his thoughts reliving the morning. He felt as if he had just taken two licks of his ice cream before it tumbled off the cone and rolled away down the path.

He headed through the village, not paying much attention to the dwellings and their surroundings that had fascinated him earlier. Jumping into his truck, he sat for some time, eyes unfocussed.

In some ways Emiko felt much nearer – he knew more about her – but she was still so far away – untouchable, under surveillance.

He blew out a breath. This was never going to be easy.

Trust you, Mick old son, to go for the highest prize – the one that's just out of reach!

He kicked the truck to life, coasted onto the road and negotiated the winding decline to the causeway. Absentmindedly he motored along the route which, now so familiar, only a week ago had been so foreign.

Instead of heading back to camp, he took a left turn, as he had done every day in the past week, and drove towards the plateau of rubble – the background of continuing life – a scene he had initially found so disturbing.

He didn't turn into the road leading towards the hospital, but kept on straight ahead, travelling through unending streets of nothingness, here and there punctuated with a collection of small buildings that represented an attempt to recreate some sense of community.

Eventually the evidence of destruction lessened, more buildings stood as they always had, the smell of salt in the air assured Mick the coast was near. He travelled north for some time, seeing glimpses of ocean and clusters of coastal buildings, some on stilts, perched over the water's edge.

Finally, he pulled up at a vacant site, got out and ventured into the narrow lane of a fishing village, resisting the urge to clamp a hand over his mouth in response to the overwhelmingly strong fishy smell.

Weathered two-storey buildings huddled side-by-side, festooned with rope nets strung out to dry, their colourful floats dangling in neat rows like ripe fruit. Larger glass balls in their knotted twine baskets lay on the ground amid coils of heavy rope, dominating the narrow spaces between the dwellings. No attempt at gardening here – housing and fishing work taking priority on the precious coastal land.

Mick reached the end of the lane and made his way along the sand, trudging around beached boats, spread-out fishing paraphernalia and children playing in and out of the bubbling waves. They paused to watch him approach and exchanged greetings before returning to their games.

Further along, the beach became deserted, giving him time and space.

He rehashed the morning, his thoughts seeking clarity but resulting in more questions than answers.

Time to talk alone with Emiko was exactly what he had hoped for. Their conversation had flowed, almost like established friends, with little of the awkwardness and hesitancies he would expect with a new acquaintance.

And her laughter – Mick recalled her laughter – *sounding like bells, and how it bubbled so spontaneously that she rushed a hand to cover her mouth.*

Then she had ducked behind the screen of tradition again when he turned the conversation to a more personal level.

Used to being in control of his life, Mick didn't take well to restrictions. He couldn't see the point of such obedience, especially when it seemed outdated formalities were getting in the way of progress – in this case, his progress.

Why had Tanazawa-san, as a protective father, initiated his daughter's stroll with a foreign soldier, albeit chaperoned, on the pretext of her practicing English?

Surely, he could not be receptive to her having a foreign suitor. Although he shared with Mick his enthusiasm for western ways, it seemed unlikely he would think so liberally when it came to his daughter. Especially since Emiko had admitted she didn't reveal her modern attitude to her father as he would not approve.

Mick wondered if supervised freedom could be a father's way of ascertaining whether or not the soldier was a cause for concern, knowing that every nuance of their body language would have been observed. A flick of the eye between them. A glance while waiting for a reaction or an answer. And of course, the sneaked observations – the longer looks, the assessments, the realisation that up close her skin really did glow like the moon, that her hair shone like ripe cherries in the sunlight and her footsteps were silent, as if she floated beside him.

Mick considered that if he was deemed a threat to anyone's equilibrium, he would be frog-marched away if he came within calling distance again. Maybe the samurai guard would be at the gate to send him back up the path whenever he happened that way. Or perhaps a more persuasive deterrent – a life-threatening display of martial arts.

He heaved a sigh, feeling like the donkey with a carrot dangling just out of reach. The carrot had just become a lot more tempting, but the reach had become greater.

The sun sank low and he turned back to see more vessels coming ashore, the fisherman's day coming to an end. Women and children came down to meet the boats, lugging woven baskets of fish back to the village, destined for hungry mouths.

When he arrived back at camp with a combination of hunger and adrenalin grumbling in his stomach, he headed to the mess hall. Rice with slivers of vegetable for Saturday night dinner, and hopefully, the life-saver pudding would follow.

Croc was there, sitting with a group of personnel. Mick joined them.

'The QM has invited anyone who's keen to call in tonight,' Croc announced, with a nod to Mick. 'Apparently he's just bottled a new brew. Wants some opinions.'

A chorus of refusals reverberated around the group, followed by trumped-up alibis and unlikely previous engagements.

'Well, Mick, looks like it's just you and me, son.' Croc eyed Mick across the table.

'You set me up with the QM once before,' Mick replied with a laugh. 'Not falling for the same trick twice.'

'Nah, no tricks, Mate. God's honour.' Croc made a sloppy attempt to cross himself, finishing the gesture by pressing his fingertips to his lips and throwing a kiss into the air, Italian-style.

Comments erupted from the group. 'That's not how you do it,' someone laughed. 'It's clear you don't go to church.'

'The Pope's Italian, ain't he?' Croc shot back.

'Does he drink saké? Mick interjected.

'Funny you should ask.' Croc pointed his fork at Mick. 'I saw the army chaplain heading this way earlier in the day, doing his monthly rounds to this heathen outpost, no doubt.'

'But he don't drink saké no more,' someone added. 'Not since the last time.'

'Who can blame him?' Croc said. 'But he knows where a ready supply of his favourite whisky can be found in these parts, and our quartermaster does like to pay his holy dues.'

Croc finished the last of his rice and pushed the plate away, pulling a laden bowl of pudding towards him. 'Dare say Chaplain'll be dropping in on the QM this evening.'

'Oh, that's okay then,' Mick laughed. 'I'll be in hallowed company this time.'

'I'll be there too, don't forget.' Croc jumped in. 'And didn't I save your bacon last time with the mug-of-water advice?'

Mick stood to get his helping of pudding from the servery. 'Saved my bacon and my liver, dare say.'

The camaraderie of the mess hall was just what he needed to get some relief from analysing his meeting with Emiko. It was time to think ahead.

You're getting too impatient, Mick, old son, he told himself. *Today you made great strides. Don't push the river.*

'Nothing like a bowl of caramel pudding to make you feel pleased with your day,' he said, as he re-joined the group.

'And that's nothing like caramel pudding,' someone quipped.

'More like – soap pudding,' someone else added.

'Flowers,' one of the women suggested. 'I think they pick the flowers along the roadside and mash them in. It tastes like that scented yellow climber.'

'Honeysuckle?'

'I'm eating honeysuckle pudding?' Croc asked.

'Caramel,' Mick insisted. 'I'm thinking about caramel.'

'That's enough flower garden for one day.' Croc stood, picking up his half-empty plates. 'I'll give you a call when I'm heading over to the house of pleasure, Kiwi.'

'What's the dress code?' Mick asked with a grin.

'Ah, the usual. Kimono and fishnets. Don't worry about the lipstick. The QM can supply that.' Croc gave a wink and left.

Keen for some blokes' company and homely conversation, Mick

showered quickly, dressed in mufti khakis and pulled out some paper to write a letter home. While acknowledging how far he had come from the conventional normality of his upbringing, putting it into writing for the family was entirely another matter.

'You ready, Micko?' Croc called from outside.

Happy to leave the letter writing for another day, Mick headed out, grabbing his topped-up water canteen on the way.

He did a double-take. 'What are you wearing, Croc?'

'Hawaiian shirt.' Croc spread his arms like a clothes hanger, to fully display the red and green hibiscus print. 'Cool and comfortable, ideal for such an event. You'll see.'

'Shame I haven't had a chance to get my costume wardrobe organised yet.'

'Yeah, have to take you shopping.'

'Rather go with you than the QM.'

'I hear ya', mate. I hear ya'.'

The dogs pricked up their ears and rumbled their warning growl. The QM shouted a greeting from inside and flung the door wide.

'Come in, lovely lads.' He was sporting a different kimono, a subtle flowery number in cream and beige, the *obi*-sash chocolate brown, fishnets and army boots as before. No lipstick tonight.

'Evening, QM.' Mick and Croc stepped in.

'Take a seat and help yourselves to hors d'oeuvres. I'll pour drinks.' Mick sat on a two-seater sofa that hadn't been there on his previous visit.

'Saw Chaplain this morning,' Croc said, sinking into one of the low chairs, grabbing a savoury from the coffee table on the way down. 'He calling in tonight?'

'Hope so,' the QM replied. 'I need to run a couple of things past him.'

'You?' Croc said. 'What've you been up to, QM?'

'*Ahrrgg*.' QM groaned, dragging a hand over his smooth head. 'I got into some hot water, and I'm not talking *onsen* public baths.'

'I'm sure *we* can help you out with confession,' Croc offered.

'Maybe we could all do confession tonight,' QM suggested, cheering up. 'That's just the sort of party game I'm in the mood for.' He gave a hearty chuckle, then turned to finish pouring saké into mugs.

'Just a half mug for me, thanks.' Mick called. 'I've gotta walk home.'

The quartermaster paid no attention, bursting into a few bars of song.

'*Pack up your troubles in your old kit bag and smile, smile, smile.* It would be good for me to hear what sort of a mess you are all making of your lives. Confession time, it is.' He passed their drinks and sank into the other chair. '*Kampai!*' He raised his mug into the air, then drank.

'*Kampai,*' they echoed.

'What do you think?' QM asked. 'How's the brew?'

'It's great, QM. Best saké I've ever had,' Croc responded.

'Yeah, good,' Mick nodded, putting his mug down after a second tentative sip.

'Let's start with you, Kiwi,' Croc said. 'You're new here. There's gotta be some major stuff-ups this week.'

Mick laughed and quickly defended himself. 'Nup. I've had a perfect week, haven't put a foot wrong. I'm the definitive role model for the New Zealand army.'

Croc spluttered into his saké. 'Jeez, Kiwi. Where's ya' bloody halo?'

'It's confession time,' the QM persisted. 'We won't give up until we have unearthed your deepest secrets. Let me see – any language faux-pas?'

Mick rubbed his chin. 'Not that I can think of.'

'Got the truck stuck or lost your way?' Croc quizzed, helping himself to something from the tray.

'Not so far. Had a good navigator in young Kazu.'

'By the way.' The quartermaster took a swig and swallowed appreciatively. 'How did the tatami mats go?'

'Really good. That webbing was exactly right. Have a look in the back of the truck sometime. The Tatami maker did a great job, and was very pleased with the extra supply, too.'

The quartermaster nodded.

'He got any daughters?' Croc squinted an eye at Mick. 'You could be in with a chance, since you're the blue-eyed boy. Fixed his house up too, didn't you?'

Mick nodded then answered. 'No daughters that I saw, but his old mother gave me her wedding kimono. Thought I might be interested.'

QM chortled.

Croc gave a snort of laughter. 'Not tempted, I take it.'

'Well!' QM swept a hand dramatically across his own robe. 'Where is it? Why aren't you modelling it tonight?'

'Found a way to tactfully return it. They're as poor as church mice.

They could sell it if the old lady doesn't want it any more.'

'I would buy it,' The quartermaster added.

Mick shook his head and laughed. 'Not your size.'

'So,' Croc continued. 'Any other daughters catch your eye this week?'

Mick hesitated, reached for the snack tray, took his time chewing, as if analysing the taste.

'That's a "Yes",' Croc shouted. 'You bloody beauty, Kiwi. You're hot on the trail of some exotic specimen.'

After the events of the morning, Mick felt sure that something in his appearance must indicate what dominated his thoughts, as if he had "hopeful" or "impatient" tattooed on his forehead.

He needed to get some balance in his thinking, like scratching a persistent itch for relief.

He figured some macho talk with the blokes might scratch the itch. He was used to that way of dealing with things. Back home, nothing was secret – everything got discussed openly.

'Yeah,' he began. 'A girl on the truck, one of the passengers.'

'And?'

'Her old man's the big boss – like the mayor of the village, employer of most of them. An aristocrat sort of bloke.'

'You found yourself a ripe cherry,' Croc teased.

'I'm not in for that – don't want to stuff things up.' Mick sipped from his mug, wondering how to get Croc's mind out of the gutter. 'She has interesting ideas about human rights. I guess she represents a new generation here.'

'You are attracted to her intellect,' the QM deducted, 'and that is honourable, I must say, lad.'

'Don't be wet, QM. Who appointed you the Officer of Moral High Ground?' Croc chipped in. 'That's just what blokes say to mask their real intentions.'

'If that's what I was doing, I wouldn't be telling you lot,' Mick laughed. 'I could sow my own wild oats, thanks very much.'

The QM leaned in Mick's direction, his expression earnest, his voice conspiratorial. 'And you have found a girl who's worth more than that. Well done, young Mick.'

'I haven't *found* her. I mean – she's got bodyguards and a father with his finger on the pulse. Welcoming enough, but you wouldn't know what he really thinks.'

The QM tilted his head and looked through his spectacle lenses. 'Inscrutable, that's what they say.'

'Hang on a minute.' Croc put his mug down. 'You've met him already? The old man? You've laid your cards on the paternal table?'

'I didn't set out to meet him. I got sort of escorted…'

'What? You were snooping around and the old man pulled you out of the wood pile?' Croc slapped a hand on his knee and gave a whoop of laughter.

'Something like that.' Mick skimmed over the details of his gardening intentions, his summons to the big house, meeting the father over a cuppa – then the walk with Emiko and the ever-present samurai guard.

'Jeez, son! Sounds like you're in boots and all.'

'Yeah, up to my neck!' Mick gave a short laugh and blew out a long breath. 'What I don't know is – what I'm not sure about is – the protocol. You know? How do you date, here? Do you ask the father? Or do you ask her, direct? That sort of stuff. And where do you go? I don't see any movie theatres.'

Thoughtful expressions set, the other two said nothing. Croc had his sideways squint assessing Mick. The QM dropped his head back and looked down his nose, eyeing Mick through his glasses again, looking perplexed, as you might if a person is speaking a completely foreign language – or a subject you know little about.

The growl of the dogs broke the tension and a voice from outside bid them quiet.

'That'll be the Chaplain,' the QM announced. 'Come on in,' he called, launching himself to his feet.

The visitor poked his head around the door, beamed a smile and stepped in, looking every bit like a clergyman should, right down to the comb-over hairstyle and wire-framed spectacles not unlike the QM's.

'Welcome, welcome, Chaplain,' QM boomed.

'Evenin', Quartermaster,' Chaplain replied, stepping into the centre of the room. He nodded towards Croc. 'Evenin', Croc. How ya' doin' there?'

'Forgive me Father, for I have sinned,' Croc answered, by way of a greeting.

'Good, Croc. Good.' Chaplain rocked on his heels, rubbing his hands together. 'I love a challenge.'

'Chaplain, meet Mick Mitchell,' the QM said, sweeping an arm in Mick's direction.

'Mick, is it?'

Mick got to his feet. 'Yep, Mick Mitchell, new in camp.' They shook hands.

'Declan Delaney – in case you're still uncertain about the Irish accent. Pleased to meet ya', Mick.' The Chaplain shot a glance at Croc and the QM, then back to Mick. 'I'm sorry to see it hasn't taken ya' long to sink to these lowly depths. P'raps we should have a wee talk sometime, and I could guide you to a higher path of companionship.'

Mick laughed. 'That might be a good idea.'

'Now, now, Chaplain,' the QM responded. 'No need to belittle your hosts. Croc and I always give you a good time.' He turned to the kitchen bench, unlocked a high cupboard and grabbed down a bottle of whisky. 'Right where you left it, Chaplain,' he said, pouring into a cut-glass tumbler and handing it to the cleric.

'Thanks, Quartermaster. Pleased to see you're keepin' my Torys safe n' sound.' The chaplain joined Mick on the two-seater.

QM slid the food tray across the table towards him. 'Help yourself, Chaplain.'

The clergyman picked up two savouries, dropping one after the other into his mouth. 'So, Mick, how long have you been here?' he said while chewing.

'Just a week.'

'And he's already in trouble,' Croc quipped.

'Really?' The chaplain looked hopeful.

'Deep trouble,' Croc added, shaking his head solemnly.

'And I'm afraid we are ill-equipped to help,' the QM said. 'What was your question, Mick?'

Mick blew out a breath. 'I think we should change the subject. Chaplain has just arrived. Let him settle in, a bit.'

'Mick's right,' the chaplain agreed, looking at the nearly full mug of saké by Mick's feet. 'We both haven't knocked back our first drink yet, Mick and I. Don't rush us. We need some time to get in the mood.' He raised his glass. 'Anyway, here's cheers to y'all.' He took a taste of his whisky and gave an appreciative sigh. 'I always find I operate a little better after a couple of these.' He studied the amber diamond-pattern on the side of his glass.

'Not taking any of that crap – *Go easy on us 'cause we're new here,'* Croc complained. 'What do you think this is? Sunday school?'

'I'm afraid Croc's right,' QM added. 'Life's too short to beat around the bush, and I want to get to my turn at confession before midnight.'

The chaplain raised his glass again. 'Here, here!' He took another sip, closed his eyes and let the whisky settle in.

Mick sipped his saké again. It went down easier this time. 'This stuff's starting to grow on me.'

'Yeah, an acquired taste,' Croc said, then added in response to the QM's affronted expression, 'for the discerning. No saké in the same calibre as yours, QM.' He took a swig, to reinforce his words and turned back to Mick. 'Get on with it, Kiwi.'

'It's no big deal, really,' Mick continued. 'And I've already decided something. I'm not asking the father, 'cause if he says "no", then I'm stuffed.' He took another sip. 'Besides, she said she'd see me again, so that's good enough for me. It's just a question of where to go.'

'Try a shrine,' the chaplain suggested. 'There's shrines everywhere, and sometimes they come with a garden to wander around – or they're tucked into the forest.' He noticed the doubtful expressions in the room. 'I'm not pushing the Godly barrow here,' he added in defence. 'There seems to be a sort of holy protection attitude to shrines. People see them as a safe place – not to be desecrated, if y' see what I mean. Protected by the gods.'

'Yeah, yeah, I get that,' said Croc, rubbing a hand thoughtfully over his chin. 'Like how you don't fool around in the choir dressing room.'

The QM shot him a look. 'But you did? Heaven help you.'

'Well,' Croc continued with a grin. 'Sally Mason was the only reason I joined the choir.'

The others responded with a mixture of laughs, coughs and head-shaking.

'I hope y've already confessed that,' the chaplain said. 'I'm not inclined to go back that far and hear all about your sordid youth, Croc.'

'You're safe, Padré. That decadent stage of my life is done and dusted. I'm a one-girl man, these days.'

'Pleased to hear that, Croc.' He raised his glass. 'To the happy couple!' Then he turned to Mick, gave him a nod and raised his glass again. 'To them all.'

Chapter Ten

Experience nature.
In doing so
Learn about yourself.
– Japanese Proverb

A silvery moon hung in the midnight sky when Mick and Croc left the QM's and ambled back in the general direction of the barracks.

Croc stopped at the workshop door. 'Goodnight, son,' he called. 'My bedtime ritual – some contemplation from my favourite chair. When the moon's like this, makes the paddy fields shine.' He pulled his pipe and tobacco from a pocket and let the door swing shut behind him.

Mick turned to take in the moon. *The locals reckon there's a rabbit up there.*

The ground under his feet seemed a little uneven so he shuffled sideways to sit on the barracks steps. 'A rabbit, eh?' He studied the shadows and splotches, trying to un-see the man-in-the-moon he knew so well, imagining rabbit's ears and a fluffy tail instead.

His concentration wavered when the sound of whispering drifted from somewhere behind him. He wondered if Croc had sneaked back outside to play a late-night trick on him. Without turning to look, he strained to hear what was being said. Something like '*Chusan…*' And it repeated. '*Chusan…*'

That meant nothing to him. He decided a couple of locals had found some surplus saké and were taking care of it behind the barracks.

He refocussed on the moon.

The whispering continued and became more insistent. Curiosity getting the better of him, Mick got to his feet and wandered around the back of the building. Long vertical poles supported the barracks floor as the ground sloped away, giving a cave-like space in the foundations.

He squinted into the sub-floor shadows, waiting for his eyes to adjust. 'Who's there?'

'*Michusan*?'

'Who are you? What's Michusan…' He attempted to brace himself, in readiness for the unknown. 'Come out so I can see you.'

Soon he could make out the clothing – a tunic top, long baggy pants and a headscarf.

The figure moved easily, stealthily, through the structure and came into view.

Mick recognised her, a woman from the truck – maybe the one Emiko described as her daytime bodyguard. *What was the name? Yoko-san? No, not Yoko. Was it Toko-san? No… Yodo!*

'Yodo-san?'

She came out of the shadows and stood some distance away. '*Hai, Michusan…*'

'*Michusan…*? I have no idea what that means.'

'*Michusan*,' she repeated, taking a few quick steps to close the gap between them, poking a strong finger into the front of his shoulder. 'You, *Michusan…*'

Should he understand? He focussed, and puzzled, tried to think laterally and regretted the saké haze in his brain.

'Are you saying Mitchell-san?' He pointed to himself.

'*Hai*. Emiko-san say – get *Michusan*.'

'Emiko sent you?'

She had said something about sending him a message, but he wasn't expecting it so soon, and not in the middle of the night. As much as he hoped to see her, this all seemed rather strange.

'Come.' Yodo-san turned and scurried along the uneven ground, skirting inside the edge of shadow where moonlight didn't reach, where eyes struggled to see.

Mick stood and watched. 'What is this about?' He certainly wanted to see Emiko, but how could he be sure of the guard's intentions?

Yodo-san stopped and turned, to see he was still rooted to the spot. '*Michusan,*' she repeated with some impatience. 'Come!' With a full-arm gesture, she signalled him forward, as if commanding a charge into battle. She continued on and faded out of sight.

Mick realised he was not going to get an answer in words. His only option was to follow.

Holding on to the foundation poles, he made his way across the uneven ground, stooping to avoid hitting his head on the floor beams – something that had not slowed the diminutive guard.

He didn't consider himself to be drunk, but he guessed he wouldn't pass as sober. It was a good thing Croc would be gazing out the other way over the paddy fields, not being privy to Mick's clumsy, sake-fuelled escapade behind the barracks.

When he reached the end of the building, he found Yodo-san waiting in the shadow of the trees which edged up to the camp's back boundary. Then she turned and disappeared into the forest before Mick reached her.

'Shit! She's like Wonder Woman. Where the hell is she now?'

Luckily it was easy to see the way – the trees had been trimmed to create an opening to the sky and the midnight moon shone directly onto the path, illuminating it like a yellow brick road.

He hurried on, trying to catch up, his senses on alert. Only an occasional bird call and the sound of trickling water interrupted the silence of the night.

As the effects of saké began to burn off, Buster's warnings bounced back on him – *off limits, untouchable, don't risk it, she's trouble...*

So why was he following her bodyguard into the forest?

He had no answer, other than a blindly optimistic hope to see Emiko.

Daring battled with caution as waves of doubt engulfed him. Emiko had told him Yodo-san was employed by her father. That made it highly likely he could be heading into a trap.

He stopped in his tracks. 'This is ridiculous!' He spun around to scan behind, then searched ahead.

Where is this leading? To Emiko? Or into danger?

Already shadow crossed the path where the moonlight didn't reach. In darkness it would be almost impossible to find the way back.

Stupidity!

His mind raced with frightening possibilities and he turned, running, retracing his steps, mouth so dry he couldn't swallow, heart thumping in his chest.

Footsteps drummed up behind him.

Shit! Don't stop. Don't look back. No time... push yourself... faster, man!

'*Michusan*?' his pursuer called.

Mick spun around, breath rasping, ready to defend himself, ready to use any hand-to-hand combat skills he could muster.

Yodo-san came to a halt, a look of confusion on her face, outstretched arms emphasising her shrug. '*Michusan*… come. Emiko-san.' She pointed further down the track. 'Come.'

Mick pulled in a breath, willing his pulse to settle, his panic to waver.

The mention of Emiko didn't guarantee a thing, but it did tie in with her suggestion of getting in touch again, and it refreshed his hopes of finding her at the end of this crazy venture.

Yodo-san faced him, expression clouded with concern.

If Emiko had arranged this meeting and he didn't follow through, it would reflect badly, and possibly ruin his chances of connecting with her again.

I've got to see this through.

He shrugged and nodded towards the path ahead. Yodo-san spun around and lead the way forward.

Soon the path widened. The sky brightened. Mist rose where treetops opened into a clearing, the moon round and pure overhead.

Around the next turn in the track Mick stopped. The path ended at a roofed gateway – a simpler version of the Tanazawa garden entrance, but here a high, solid fence curved away on both sides, forming a strong barricade.

Extracting a bangle-sized keyring from the folds of her jacket, Yodo-san stepped up to the entrance. She selected a long, black key and clicked open the heavy lock. Pushing the gate inward, she stepped aside to usher Mick through.

He stood in place. 'Where is Emiko-san?' he demanded, reluctant to enter such a fortress for no good reason.

Yodo-san tipped her head towards the opening, giving him a knowing nod.

Mick stepped up and peered through – to steamy water, an onsen – a natural thermal pool, in the forest.

He scanned the high-fenced enclosure before walking in, crossing the deck to the edge of the pool where steps entered the water.

Yodo-san secured the gate behind.

Senses alert, Mick strained for a sign of Emiko. Rising steam carried the astringent smell of sulphur, reminding him of childhood holidays in Rotorua. Those memories combined with this reality created the hope for adventures entirely new.

'Where is Emiko-san?'

She must be here. Somewhere.

Shaped irregularly by nature, mossy rocks and overhanging plants softly screened the shadowy recesses of the pool's perimeter as it curved in and out of sight.

Mick peered into the nooks and hollows.

Yodo-san interrupted, drawing attention to the deck area behind him where a partition jutted out from the fence. On a bench seat attached to the screen lay folded fabric in soft peachy shades – Emiko's kimono.

She is here.

He struggled to concentrate as Yodo-san instructed him, miming the removal of his shirt and trousers, tapping a space on the clothes bench with the palm of her hand, and then showing him behind the screen to a concealed alcove. A low stool made from a tree stump, smoothed and shiny, sat under a bamboo spout. She pulled on a wooden handle and water spurted from the hollow cane before she shut it off.

'Wash,' she said, swiping her hands under her armpits, between her legs from front and back, then pointing to the corresponding areas on Mick. 'All,' she said, before turning and striding away, disappearing into the leafy shadows on the far edge of the deck.

Mick stared after her, sensing where she stood, feeling her all-seeing gaze as if he was already naked.

He'd heard about onsen – showering before the communal bath. The explanations normalised the experience of public nudity – a ritual for cleanliness and relaxation. Very different from his home life, taking individual turns behind a closed door in the family bathroom.

But no onsen story mentioned a female sentinel in the undergrowth. Nobody discussed a romantic aspect to the communal bathing ritual. And nobody had explained the protocol around a private onsen and a first date, at midnight.

Removing his shoes and stuffing his socks inside, he pushed them under the bench, dwarfing the dainty shoes already there. Unbuttoning his shirt, slipping it off and folding it quickly, he dropped it on the bench beside Emiko's tidy pile, following with his trousers. He paused and turned his back to the pool and the general direction of the guard.

He looked down. His body betrayed him. The major was standing at attention. How on earth could he enter the water without the cover of swimming shorts?

It wouldn't be the first time his boxer shorts had doubled as a swimming costume, but he would need to remove them first to shower. Putting the shorts back on as swimwear could be considered hygienically and culturally wrong.

As would stepping into the pool starkers, right now.

He pressed his lips and mustered his thoughts while trying to exercise control. He hoped Emiko wasn't peering through the poolside undergrowth, wondering why he was taking so long.

Yodo-san reappeared suddenly and reached out as if to grab at his shorts. He jumped aside, clasped hands pressed against him where needed. Her face broke into a wide smile. She stepped forwards to the bench and patted his pile of clothes. '*Koko ni*,' – here. Then she pointed at him, to the shower area and to the steps down into the pool.

Reaching into a pocket, she pulled out a scarf-like piece of fabric the size of a hand towel and held it flat at her waist, letting it drape towards her knees. She gave him a nod, an unreadable little smile and passed the fabric to him.

This was it? The privacy screen?

He nodded thanks, waited for her to turn back before stepping out of his boxers and diving behind the screen.

If it was his rugby team at the end of a muddy game, the communal shower would be nothing more than a chance to rehash the tactics and look forward to a beer.

This was different. This was about a girl. And he didn't need his enthusiasm to be so damn obvious.

Mick sat on the stool and pulled the handle. A gush of warm water hit him between the shoulder blades.

Not just any girl. One who – for some reason – really mattered.

Thinking how helpful cold water would be, he stood and did a quick turnaround under the spout. Having showered earlier in the evening, he didn't want to waste time now.

Flicking the tap off, he gave his head a shake, swiped a hand over his face and grabbed the cloth to his front.

It hardly covered everything. It hardly covered *anything*. It didn't cover what he most needed to conceal right now.

He clamped an arm diagonally across his front, holding the inadequate cloth against himself and made a dash for the pool. Onsen etiquette the least of his concerns, he jumped over the steps and dropped into the waist-deep water, kicking off to the far side before turning around.

There she was.

Emiko.

Across the pool.

Moonlight crowned her ebony hair with a silvery-blue halo. Her shoulders, curving from the water's indigo surface like a sculpture in alabaster, her face lustrous, surreal, flickering with fragments of iridescent jade.

Their eyes met. Their lips smiled.

Mick had no idea what to expect, what to do.

At home the next step would be a given – a naked girl and a naked guy, a bit of privacy, and whatever naturally followed.

Here, no such thing could be taken for granted. For a start, they weren't alone. He glanced around. No sign of Yodo-san but he knew she was there. Watching.

Turning back to Emiko, he wondered what to say. It seemed to be much too late for hello. They were naked in a pool at midnight, for heaven's sake.

Emiko moved a delicate hand across her mouth, at first appearing to brush her fingertips over her lips, but something in her eyes said more. He studied her, watched her mouth move as if to speak then settling into a soft pout. Her hand glided across again, the forefinger outstretched brushing her top lip, pausing imperceptibly in the centre, the other fingers curling slightly away.

The universal gesture of '*shhh*'.

Mick gave a slow nod and settled into the water.

He blew out a gentle breath and moonbeams danced across the surface to Emiko. After moment's hesitation, he followed them, floating to sit on the ledge beside her.

Emiko flicked her eyes to his, an expression flitting across her face. Her mouth opened as if to speak, then her lips settled together softly, a moist shimmer drawing his gaze.

The breeze picked up and a tendril of hair floated free, settling across her brow. Silky threads of ebony. Mick reached out, brushed it aside, fingertips lingering.

The touch. The first touch.

She flinched, blinked, then stilled, her eyes locking on his, her breath tremulous.

In one move, his mouth met hers, lips melting, brushing softly, wanting – needing more.

So much more.

The sound of footsteps dragged his attention aside as Yodo-san stepped into view. Emiko pulled away, fingers speeding to her mouth.

Mick could not let her leave without a further plan. 'Can we meet somewhere –' he ventured – 'just us two?' The thought of another week of formal nodded greetings and farewells at the truck steps was not acceptable.

Yodo-san called her name.

She whispered to him. 'I must go.'

He nodded, understanding, but still his eyes held hers. 'Is there a shrine, where we can meet?'

'*Hai* – yes.' She pointed over the treetops, across the valley. 'Near the village.'

'When? Monday afternoon?'

'*Hai.*'

'And Tuesday, Wednesday, Thursday, Friday?'

Her laugh tinkled like bells.

Yodo-san began unlocking the gate.

He leaned close, inhaling her fragrance, one moment more – a sharp sound broke the spell.

Yodo-san, at the top of the steps, had clapped her hands together.

Emiko promptly moved towards the steps – as if still an obedient child, pausing to glance over her shoulder at him, eyes dancing – now very much a woman.

He turned away, letting her leave the onsen in privacy. He would wait.

In stillness and silence, their togetherness had been complete.

Mick Michell, you have won the lottery.

PART TWO

JAPAN 1946

To love is nothing.
To be loved is something.
But to love and be loved
is everything.
–Japanese Proverb

Chapter Eleven

The moon watched over our first kiss
and bound us together
with a thousand threads of silver.
Forever.
– Emiko

The rabbit in the moon was so big, so bright, over the onsen. I knew in my heart that it was a special moon, with a special message. The rabbit means kindness and good things coming soon.

Coming to me? What good things?

My breath caught and I hardly dared to imagine.

Sunday, a quiet day in my family, I managed to sleep a little later than usual and walk in the gardens a little longer, following the path Mick-san had walked with me just the day before.

Was it only one day ago? It seemed much longer. So much had happened since his visit.

Change was in the air.

Big change.

***

I stood at our entrance gate for some time. Mick-san had walked through that gate. I brushed my fingers over the latch. His fingers had touched that latch.

When he was leaving, he had run up the steps on the other side and turned to wave, before going out of sight along the shady forest track.

I hadn't waved back. Takeda-san had been watching.

I waved now, pretending Mick-san was standing there again.

Turning back, I put my hands together, holding his touch of the gate between my fingers.

I picked leaves from the bush, the one I had picked from and smelt yesterday, when I was telling him about Yodo-san being *onna-musha.*

He had tried to say the words – *What is that, onna…?* – and I teased him about saying Japanese words, same as my trouble saying English words.

I warmed the leaves in my palms and inhaled their aroma, as I had the day before, remembering his smile, the way he looked at me, directly, with honesty.

He did not mind when I teased him. He laughed. He liked open talking. Not many people I know enjoy open talking. In my family, and all the places I go, there are old rules about respect and being silent.

It's not easy for the younger ones like me to try new ways.

So, I think, for my family, speaking Japanese is the tradition. For me, speaking English is my freedom.

I allowed my thoughts to drift to the onsen at midnight. My heart leapt at the memories still vivid in my mind, in my soul. I had to control my reactions because my knees turned to jelly and I found it difficult to walk.

At the onsen, Mick-san asked about the nearest shrine. How lucky for me there is a shrine near my home, near the village where he comes in the truck every day.

Also, lucky, the rest of my family go to the shrine every morning. But me, I am too sleepy in the morning. I go to the shrine in the late afternoon – some days after hospital work, other days after my job at father's factory, and sometimes it's just before dark.

'Monday,' Mick-san had said. 'And all other days.'

My heart jumped a little when I thought of how he had smiled, a little sideways, a little shy. He had pretended it was a joke to meet at the shrine *every* day. But I could see in his eyes, he was saying his truth.

Then he had leaned to me. My breath had stopped – his lips moved close to mine and I was ready for his kiss this time – but a noise made me jump.

Yodo-san had clapped her hands. We had to leave the onsen.

***

On Monday morning, Kazu-san joined me, walking to the truck. 'Mick-san will take me to visit the tatami maker again,' he said. 'Tatami maker is like grandfather.'

When we got home to the village late afternoon, Mick-san said with a big voice, 'Kazu, where is the shrine?'

Kazu-san pointed to the beginning of the path, not far from the truck.

Mick-san nodded and his eyes jumped to me. His silent message said, 'Meet me?'

The village glowed and shadows grew longer in the late sunshine, as families returned home to prepare their meal.

Noisy *hiyo-dori* – bulbuls, squawked overhead, flying home to their forest perches. I walked on, as if I was returning home too, but beyond the houses, away from village eyes, I turned into a different path and made my way up the hill to the shrine.

I took my time, although my insides were very impatient. I remembered mother would have said '*slowly, slowly. Be calm. Arrive serene.*'

Before the *tori* – the gateway with its big red posts and overhead carvings – Mick-san waited for me. I was pleased.

Once, some other foreign soldiers had walked right into the shrine, not stopping to bow.

Everyone in the village talked about their mistake, their ignorance.

Mick-san was going to say something but I held a finger to my lips.

'Must do shrine visit first. Ritual is important.' I moved up to the *tori.* 'Stand this side, not in middle. Middle is for spirit world.'

I bowed and he did too. We walked together along the path towards the tiny shrine where bamboo bells dangled on coloured ropes.

His hand brushed mine. Did he mean to touch me? Yes!

It happened again.

I had to concentrate. I needed to teach him the shrine tradition.

We approached the water basin, carved out of a giant stone by many years of patient trickling from a bamboo spout.

'Even soft water can shape a giant boulder over long time.'

He turned to me, his mouth a little open, his eyes showing surprise. It seemed he had never heard that before.

'Never give up,' he whispered.

I watched the ripples on the pool. 'It continues flowing and overflowing with mountain rain. It won't stop, in case its work gets undone.' I bowed thanks for the water and reached for one of the bamboo ladles hooked above the basin.

Mick-san followed my actions. One at a time we tipped water over our left hand, then our right, cupping a handful to cleanse our mouths, finally tipping out the last water, running it down the long bamboo handle, to wash away our touch.

Our hands brushed again, as he put his ladle back right beside mine.

I turned and walked towards the shrine. Reaching into my pocket for two offering coins, I gave Mick-san one and showed him where to put it in the box.

'Now ready to say wish or prayer.' I bowed two times, clapped my hands two times, pulled on the bell ropes and closed my eyes, listening to the echo of the bamboo chimes.

I felt him move close beside me, not showing respectful distance. I stepped away a little and his hand caught mine.

'Do we say our wish out loud?'

'This is a sacred place,' I said, a little breathless.

He didn't let my hand go. 'What does that mean for us?'

'All my life, I understand shrine rules say "no-touching". Everywhere, it is not polite to show feelings.' He still held my hand. I didn't pull away, it felt exciting but it also felt wrong.

He glanced around. 'What if no-one is here to see us?'

I thought about that. 'Gods see us. They are in the trees and in the air all around.'

He looked at the ground, as if praying, talking in a low voice. 'When we walked in the garden at your home, you told me you have new ideas that your father or grandmother may not agree with. Does that mean traditional ways can bend to allow new ways that might suit better?'

I looked at him, letting the idea settle. I had heard that before, but in different words, Japanese words. 'The bamboo that bends is stronger than the oak that resists.' A playful breeze tickled the bamboo leaves overhead, catching my eye. 'Now I understand a new rule.'

He reached for my other hand and pulled me to face him, his expression kind. 'It's not really a rule – I mean, it doesn't need to be a rule, not like the law. It just means – it might be all right to try new ways, if it doesn't bother anyone.'

'I think…' my voice came out quietly, 'my Japanese life, everything same, always. My English life, everything new.'

He tugged playfully on my hands, making me smile. He smiled too, bending a little to look right into my eyes, giving me courage to continue.

'What's your English life?'

'You are my English life – you and English talk, and new ideas, makes me think different. It's like freedom thinking. Like I never thought I could think or feel.'

His kiss surprised me, but I didn't stop him. I was lost in the feelings, the racing feelings, both strong and helpless feelings, stirred up like sweet and sour.

With a leap inside me, my heart and my mind joined together, like lightning and thunder, followed by summer rain to wash the world clean.

Suddenly, my world became clearer.

***

Lucky for me I knew the pathway well, from the shrine back to my house. My late-in-the-day visits here often extended into darkness, especially after my mother had passed – surprisingly I felt closer to her at the shrine than at home.

Mick-san may have had more difficulty on his path back to the truck, as the sunset glow had already faded from the western sky.

Yodo-san was waiting for me beside the path halfway to my home. 'Did you see me at the shrine?' I asked her.

She shot a look at me and nodded.

'Did you see someone else there?'

'Mitchell-san,' she replied, turning to lead us along the darkening track.

Yodo-san had been my overseer for many years. We communicated when necessary. Not a warm relationship, but a practical one.

'What are you thinking?' I asked, needing to find out where her loyalty sat.

She stopped and turned to face me, considering the answer with a crease on her brow. 'Is he a good man?'

I blew out a breath.

How much, really, did I know about him?

I shrugged. 'I think so.'

'Think?' she repeated and pressed a closed fist to her chest. 'What about here – your heart? What does this tell you?'

I smiled, my defences escaping, giving way to all the excitement surging through my body.

Her eyebrows shot up. 'I see heart feeling,' she said. 'I see your face.' She turned and continued down the path. 'You will marry that man,' she threw over her shoulder.

'Marry! I don't know him that well.'

'Know!' she repeated, turning to fire her words at me. 'Knowing does not matter. Only heart feeling matters.' She pressed a fist to her heart again and continued walking.

Who was I to argue? As *onna-musha,* she lived on her instincts and understood things on a level way beyond my comprehension.

My imagination flew away from me in wildly exciting spirals, leaping into the twilight sky like festival fireworks.

Marry a foreigner?

Over the past week, the magical feelings of falling in love had dominated my being – my waking, sleeping, dreaming, emotional existence – all focussing around every moment we spent together.

My thoughts into the future went no further than the next time we would meet.

But to marry him?

I hadn't dared think that far ahead. My heart raced at the prospect.

There were so many differences. And my family – although my father seemed open-minded and willing to let new ideas into his world, I suspected that did not stretch as far as marriage traditions for me, his only child.

I stumbled along behind Yodo-san, grappling with this new possibility.

'You worry about your father,' she said into the dark. 'What is your future? What is anybody's future?' She spun around to face me. 'I tell you what is your future. Anything you want it to be. You can make your own destiny. Not wait for it to come to you.'

I stared at her as she walked on.

Could I really make my own decisions? Although I fantasised about freedom of choice, I had grown up believing everyone had a pre-determined path, and that they – especially women – had no option but to follow that path; just as we were following the forest track to get home in the dark.

In my experience, there was no other way.

But Yodo-san, I now suspected, knew of other ways.

I had the sense of following not only her footsteps, but her thinking – while coming into contact with my heart feeling.

All the years of having Yodo-san at my side, I had thought of her as nothing but my bodyguard. I had never had a deep conversation with her, never considered she could be my guide on a higher level. She had kept to her thoughts, and I kept mine.

Through the screen of blackened trees glimmered lights from my garden.

'Yodo-san,' I whispered, anxious to tie up the loose ends of our conversation while still some distance from the big house.

She stopped and turned to me.

From my mouth came words I could not yet believe. 'I can choose who I marry?' The silence of darkness crowded in around us.

Her hushed voice floated to me like the deepest secret – but also like the voice of the gods, echoing from the heavens, around the hilltops, for all to hear.

'Traditions are invisible ties. You can accept – or you can walk away. Hard part is trying to walk down the middle. Traditions don't like freedom. Freedom doesn't like traditions. Choose either one. Not both.'

She faced me a little longer, like punctuation at the end of her words, before turning and leading us into the glow of lanterns along the garden pathway, to the back entrance of my home.

***

How could I sleep? Love and marriage. Two separate things. Or were they?

If Mick-san loved me, did that mean he wanted to marry me? Or would it be different for him?

How could I tell if he loved me? Should I ask him – or wait for him to say?

Questions, questions!

No answers.

Only sticky, humid darkness, and my hair wrapping around my neck in a strangle-hold. Finally falling asleep, only to dream that my father had cast a spell to punish me, turning my hair into sharp-tongued snakes spitting out words of betrayal, so that no man, no person, would ever come near me.

Daylight ended the torment.

I rolled my futon away and splashed cold water on my face and neck, twisted my hair roughly into a topknot, before kneeling at the *tokonoma* – the altar. Its vase of summer hydrangeas softly perfumed my aura as I prayed for guidance.

Preparing for my morning bath, the hot water spray soothed my tense shoulders. I washed and sank deep into the tub until its water lapped my earlobes.

Mick-san dominated my mind. I stilled, breathed, and waited for my head to clear.

Waking rituals accompanied daybreak as always, but this would be no ordinary day.

I would not see Mick-san today, for Tuesdays and Thursdays I helped at my father's clothing factory, overseeing the workers and teaching sewing to the trainees.

Not seeing Mick-san did not mean he would be less in my thoughts. Yodo-san's words bounced around in my head – *marry that man – traditions are invisible ties – you choose your destiny...*

***

My father waited on the veranda as I hurried out, nodding 'good morning' while fixing the tie on my *haori* – my over-kimono.

'This is not a good *haori* for today.' He reached out and tugged at the wide sleeve, as if it was dish rags to throw away. 'I will wait while you change to your new *haori*. You must make a good impression at the factory.'

'It's just the factory,' I protested. 'The same as every other day.'

'I'm thinking of a new role for you. Maybe a step up.' He turned to head down the veranda stairs, throwing his words decisively over his shoulder. 'It's important for you to dress well today.'

I stared at his back. 'What new role?'

'Change. Quickly!'

When I returned to the veranda, Takeda-san stood at the bottom of the steps, ready to escort us by automobile along the rough road, which began at the back of our garden and descended to the factory in a valley town, further inland from *Hinode-mura* village, further away from Hiroshima.

I wanted to ask again about the new role. I hoped it would give me more decision-making with the clothing designs. For some time, I had been keen to develop more European-style fashion.

Father's face remained stern for the duration of our journey, and I knew better than to pursue the matter.

The staff were lined up outside the factory, ready to bow their greetings and gratitude to Father, as they did every morning, before they scuttled inside to start work.

Only the factory custodian remained, addressing Father. 'Sato-san and Sato-san Junior are waiting in your office.'

Without any sign of surprise, Father nodded and indicated me to follow him.

'What can Sato-san want at this time?' I hissed, annoyed at this unpleasant interruption to my morning. 'We have already dealt with distribution for next season. We can't make clothes any faster. And that son…' My voice trailed off, more in irritation than any concern of being overheard.

Father waved a hand to silence me and hurried on inside. I trailed after him, wondering what on earth this had to do with me.

Sato Junior, dragging in a breath, launched to his feet on our arrival, even more eagerly than his portly father. They both stooped into slow, respectful bows, Father reciprocating – showing uncharacteristic warmth towards his long-time adversary.

My eyes darted to Father. 'What is this?' I demanded.

He signalled for us all to be seated and waited painstakingly for everyone to settle, before speaking. 'Sato-san and I have been discussing the future of our business connections.' Father turned to the outer office, signalling his assistant to bring tea. 'As two old men, we can plan only so far into the future.'

The two seniors laughed companionably, as they had never before.

'The real future of our businesses,' Father continued, 'lies with the next generation.' Sato Junior nodded knowingly, his thick neck wobbling like jelly.

Father turned to me. 'Sato-san has made a proposal.'

My heart lurched.

Sato Junior breathed noisily and both visitors displayed smug, all-knowing smiles.

Father paused as his assistant entered carrying a tray, bending over the low table to place the cups and pour the tea.

She provided the pause I desperately needed, so I made my move – took my chance to intercept this festering nightmare.

'Excuse me!' I jumped to my feet. 'I have work to do,' I blurted as I scrambled from the room.

Father knew better than to seek me out. His staff thought of him as an honourable man, and, maybe even more so, considered me affectionately as one of them, albeit the boss's daughter.

I knew and he knew it would be a mistake to bring family matters to the factory floor, so he left me alone.

I didn't emerge, ensconced in the factory workshop, surrounded by the comforting hum of industry.

All day his image loomed in my head like a tiger waiting for the cornered rabbit to emerge from the burrow, ready to pounce when the time was right.

I couldn't believe my world had turned around so much in a day, so suddenly upside-down.

Only yesterday I chanced upon the radical idea of marrying Mick-san and had promptly set my heart on it.

I knew my father would have initially opposed my marrying Mick-san, but I believed he would have eventually seen it my way – a mere mosquito bite on the face of my love-soaked dream.

But now he expected me to marry Sato Junior. Having entered into a business-like agreement, he would not, could not, back down. He had already bartered me off.

Today, the invisible ties of tradition had developed into the knotweed vine, reaching out its snagging thorns to entrap me.

Our dreaded journey home began with Father's same stern expression he had maintained on the way to the factory in the morning.

The bumping of the vehicle over the rough road raked at my bad temper and my insides threatened to explode.

Soon I realised my situation would not improve while locked in silence and I would be no better off at the journey's end than I was at its beginning.

'Father,' I began, staring straight ahead. 'I cannot marry Sato Junior.'

He gave a chuckle, as if the matter was above discussion. 'Of course, you can. And you will!'

I drew in a breath, trying to steady my racing heart. 'Father, he is not my type. I want to marry someone with an open mind, someone who has a future beyond our own narrow business connections.'

He didn't stop me talking, but I knew he wasn't considering my words.

His face was closed.

Not knowing what else to do, I continued. 'These are different times. Daughters can choose who to marry. Women now can vote in elections. They can manage a business.' I glanced at him, and threw in my final pitch. 'Sato Junior is not a good person. I have no respect for him.'

'Then you can make him into a good person,' he responded. 'You will learn to respect him. It's your duty.'

I shuddered at the thought.

His tone changed. 'Your mother made a good person out of me.' He tried a quick smile. I saw it as insincere.

He continued. 'She worked very hard to be a good wife. She knew her place.'

The words erupted from my mouth. 'And she died because of it.'

A loud crack startled me and my head jerked aside as if my neck would break. My hand raced to my stinging cheek. I swung to my father in disbelief, his assaulting hand still raised, threatening to strike me again.

Hatred boiled in his eyes.

I swung on the handle beside me, throwing all my weight at the door as it released, catapulting me out onto the ground and rolling me away from the moving vehicle. At once I was on my feet, fearing he, or worse, Takeda-san, would be taking up the chase.

Tears streaming unchecked, astounded by the attack and the dizzying speed of my escape, I scrambled to get balance and ducked away into the thick of the forest.

As a child I had often escaped into the hills. Nobody came to find me. I would return in my own time.

I hoped my father would be expecting the same now.

Thrashing through thick undergrowth towards the rise of the hill, I eventually came out on the track near the shrine.

I needed to talk to my mother. I always felt close to her there.

'She would never agree to me marrying that oaf!' I shouted into the trees. Movement not far ahead caught my eye and a figure emerged onto the path.

'Yodo-san!' Relief at seeing my only ally merged with fury towards my father and tears flooded again.

As a sentinel she stood, her appraising gaze fixed on me, on my bedraggled appearance, my inflamed face. Raising her chin slightly, she invited my explanation.

'Father is marrying me off to Sato Junior,' I shouted, not slowing my pace. 'Trading me like a roll of fabric.' I stomped passed her. 'I'm going to tell Mother.'

I barely stopped to bow at the *tori*, making do with a quick dip of my head as I strode right on up the path. Hurrying through the water-cleansing ritual, I clapped and bowed only once, bypassing the offering box, I lurched for the thick bell ropes, wrapped my arms around them and gripped like a scared child clinging to the legs of a protective parent.

The giant bamboo pipes clattered in discord overhead, eventually settling into harmonious rhythm. My hands slipped down the ropes and my knees pressed into the wooden deck underneath.

'Mother!' I sobbed. 'Can you see what's happening here? Mother? I can't marry Sato Junior. He is a slob. He makes me sick! Do you want me to spend the rest of my life being sick? Every time I look at him, I will throw-up. Is that what you want for me? Mother?'

I waited.

No answer. Had my mother deserted me when I most needed her?

I looked around. Yodo-san stood outside the shrine entrance on guard, as usual, framed by the *tori,* motionless and expressionless, dead-centre like an embodied spirit.

I shouted in her direction. 'Yodo-san.' I paused to pull in a raspy breath. 'You said I can choose who I marry.'

As impassive as the carved god statues in the garden, she showed no response. Had she deserted me too?

I drew breath and continued shouting. 'You said follow your heart feeling. You said make your own destiny. You said traditions are invisible ties. So, tell that to my father. Tell him he can't make me marry Sato Junior.'

I grabbed the bell ropes and struggled to my feet. 'My heart wants to marry…' The hollow clatter of bamboo chimes drowned my words. I steadied the ropes and the ringing slowed to a rhythmic beat. Raising my voice to full, furious volume, I shouted into the silent pause between clangs. 'My – heart – wants – to – marry – Mick-san!'

I shouted it again, this time in English words to alert the worldly gods, in case the spirits here were too steeped in traditional ways.

I steadied on my feet, feeling deeply the ironic freedom of unbridled self-expression.

Nobody – nothing – would over-shadow my wishes. I called out again. 'Mick-san is my destiny and you said…' my voice caught in my parched throat and I slumped over in a fit of coughing, dropping again to my knees.

I heard Yodo-san speak. I turned to grasp her message. But she wasn't facing me. She looked down the track as she spoke again.

A man's voice came in response. Panic raced through me.

Father? Takeda-san?

She had betrayed me. Standing there on guard, not to keep me safe – as she had done so often over the years – but to keep me entrapped within the shrine perimeter. Securely fenced on all sides, the high barrier provided no escape, the *tori* being the only opening.

'Traitor!' I yelled at her. 'It was your idea I could marry Mick-san. You can't take him away now.'

I detected a smile – a smirk – on her face. I was on my own.

What could I do? My mind raced.

Calm down. Pretend to agree with Father. Go along with his repulsive plan. And escape in the dark of night. Yes!

I glared at her, then closed my eyes, dreading and preparing for my jailer to appear. When I forced myself to look again, beside Yodo-san stood, not my father, not Takeda-san, but Mick-san, framed by the flame-coloured *tori.*

He stepped up, paused to bow, and fixing his eyes on me continued up the path, not stopping till he dropped down beside me on the steps.

A smile twitched at the corner of his mouth. My shattered heart leapt, in denial of my impossible situation.

His finger touched under my chin, lifting my gaze to his.

I felt ashamed of my inflamed face, my unchecked tears, my dishevelled clothing. He didn't seem to notice how I looked and I didn't resist his touch.

'So,' his smile widened, 'you want to marry me.'

Chapter Twelve

The future lies before you
like paths of pure white snow.
– Anon

Friday afternoon, nearly two weeks later, Yodo-san pushed open the mess hall door at the Kiwi Base. She entered carrying the large cardboard box I had sent her to uplift from my family's storeroom.

Tomoko-san and Yoshi-san, the kitchen staff, ushered her into the side room they had converted into my dressing room for this occasion.

Yodo-san lowered the box onto the table, its lid held in place with a red ribbon tied in a neat bow.

I stepped forward, loosened the bow, lifting the lid, nervously folding away the wrapping fabric and covering cloths, to reveal the contents – embroidered silk the colour of ripe persimmons.

The women let out a collective sigh.

My wedding kimono – my *uchikake*. In truth, it was my mother's wedding kimono, and maybe her mother's too.

'It needs hanging,' Tomoko-san instructed, 'to let out the creases.'

Yoshi-san brought forwards a bamboo frame on legs, its hanging rods empty.

Many hands lifted the kimono out, breaths held in anticipation as the unfolding garment revealed embroidered cranes in flight and golden chrysanthemums stitched, each motif united yet separated with bright green leafy vines, curling and twisting upwards from the hemline, as if growing.

Yodo-san gave me a smile, a nod, before bowing deeply and leaving the dressing room. She had other tasks to attend to.

Yoshi-san continued hanging all the items, the white under kimono – for purity, the lemon-yellow obi-sash, and various ties and ribbons. Finally, in a box of its own, the hair decoration of silk flowers.

Only once, as a child, had I set eyes on this *uchikake*. With Father away on business, Mother had planned the surprise for me.

I had then observed the unpacking of her wedding outfit, with wide eyes and loss of words, as I did now.

Tomoko-san turned to me and clapped her hands. 'Come, come. You must dress.' I unfastened my *yukata* – the summer robe I had slipped on after bathing.

I stood entranced, as she efficiently fixed layer upon layer, throwing instructions to Yoshi-san to pass this and hold that, smooth this and tie that.

My mother had known I would be wearing this, on my day.

I smoothed my fingers over the stitched feathers of a crane's wing.

Had my mother's fingers touched here? Had her gaze settled on this wing?

I stroked the long stitches of golden petals, smooth and satiny.

Did Mother like the flowers or the cranes best?

I couldn't decide my favourite.

'Stand straight!' instructed Tomoko-san as she wrapped the lemony *obi*-sash.

Did Mother's dressers pull it so tight?

This obi had contained my mother's breath, just as it now contained mine.

'This colour is good on you,' Tomoko-san offered. 'Red suits you.' She pulled on the overlap and adjusted the visible peep of the white under collar.

Did Mother look good in red, too? I decided, she did.

'There,' Tomoko-san announced, standing back to look at me. 'All dressed.'

Yoshi-san added one final clasp to the blossom cluster tucked into the weave of my hair, tendrils of tiny flowers cascading down one side of my face.

She stepped back to look. 'Done!' she announced.

I pressed a hand over my heart, drawing in the essence of my mother, my ancestors. Silently, I called on them. *Traditions are invisible ties,* I told them. *These are new times.*

Tomoko-san and Yoshi-san stepped back to look at me, saying nothing. Their eyes said it all.

Eventually when Yoshi spoke, her voice caught. 'Aw, you beautiful. Mick-san is so lucky.'

'You are lucky too.' Tomoko-san said to me, with her usual directness. 'Mick-san is a good man. You are fortunate girl. Marry Kiwi is good luck.'

'How come you get marry so fast?' Yoshi-san asked, envy in her tone, emotion seeming to have loosened her tongue. 'Mick-san has just arrived.'

It crossed my mind that my good fortune, my Mick-san, might have been her dream too.

Tomoko-san pushed her aside. 'Just happens so. Open that door.'

***

As the evening sun set the western sky aflame, I stepped out wearing my wedding kimono, my mother's *uchikake*. It represented her presence on this day and I offered a silent prayer, knowing she would hear, and watch over me.

Mick-san's Australian friend, Croc, waited beside the staff car at the bottom of the steps, holding the door open for me. He was to drive us to a shrine along the coast, where the modern-thinking priest had happily agreed to marry us.

After settling me and my wedding attire into the jeep, Tomoko-san slipped into the seat beside me and Yoshi-san jumped in the front, their enthusiasm as bridal helpers overshadowing my apprehension at so suddenly and unexpectedly becoming a bride.

An indigo blanket of night settled softly overhead, as Croc drew us to a standstill at the beachside *tori*. A line of twinkling candle lanterns marked the path ahead towards the shrine. I edged off the car seat and found my balance under the heavy layers. Tomoko-san and Yoshi-san fussed around me, checking my readiness for the bridal walk, before they went ahead to join the guests. Yodo-san came to my side.

In the twilight silence, I became aware of the soft swish of waves arriving and leaving the beach nearby. The ocean was breathing.

Senses alert, I drifted forward, towards the future. My future. Mick-san would be waiting at the shrine.

Shinto custom would have him walk the path with me. But he suggested a tradition from his country – the groom waiting and watching as his bride walks to his side. To me, this sounded more romantic.

Where previously rituals had given little room to move, we took the liberty to alter traditional ways.

War had changed many things.

Therefore, in front of the small shrine waited, not one, but two clerics, both robed in white. The *kannushi* – the Shinto priest, the host of the shrine, pressed together his fingertips forming a steeple between his palms. The other, Mick's friend and chaplain, Father Declan, his eyes warm and sparkly.

I found my focus. Mick-san, tall, handsome, in his moss-coloured uniform, eyes fixed on me, drawing me to him, inviting me into his world, his life, his love.

I had not yet met his best friend, Brooks, who stood beside him.

The QM, Croc and others in uniform gathered on one side, joined by Tomoko-san and Yoshi-san.

The bells chimed in the evening breeze – as the distance closed between us.

I stopped before Mick-san and bowed, the thumping in my chest causing my breath to become erratic. He bowed in return and tilted his head forward, looking directly into my eyes.

Did he like what he saw? Was my kimono good enough for him.

'Beautiful,' he mouthed, and I relaxed a little.

The *kannushi* stepped forwards and indicated for us to turn, to stand together, ready for the ceremony to begin.

Mick-san's sleeve pressed against mine, his hand brushed mine, a finger linked through my fingers and squeezed. My knees went weak.

Father Declan stepped up to the raised platform in front of the altar. 'Dearly Beloved,' he began. 'We are gathered here today to join this man and this woman together in holy matrimony.'

The *kannushi* approached the altar, purifying the shrine and pulling on the bell ropes to call the *kami* – the gods to bless our union.

'*San-san-kyu-do* – three, three, nine,' the *kannushi* announced, picking up a tray with three ceremonial saké cups, holding it before us.

We sipped three times from each cup, symbolising the shared joys and sorrows of married life.

'Man, woman and child,' the priest translated. My heart leapt.

Child!

I hadn't thought about a child. I hadn't thought beyond *us*.

The saké caused havoc with my nerves and made me dizzy. I wondered if I could walk, my legs were so heavy. I wondered if I could talk. There were words to say.

Father Declan stepped forward. 'Michael Peter Mitchell, do you take this woman Emiko Tanazawa, to be your lawful, wedded wife?'

Mick-san answered, 'I do.' He turned to me and smiled, an easy, relaxed smile.

I breathed out, let the tension fall from my shoulders, swallowed, but couldn't manage to return his smile.

Father Declan turned to me, his face kind. 'Emiko Tanazawa, do you take this man, Michael Peter Mitchell, to be your lawful wedded husband?'

I looked at Mick-san. He raised his eyebrows and nodded at me. I didn't look away. I looked right into his eyes. 'I do,' I whispered to him.

The kannushi moved to a large vase of Japonica leaves. He lifted out a sprig and held it up for the guests to see. 'Sakaki leaf,' he explained. 'Thank you to spirits for blessing this wedding, this couple.' He passed the greenery over our heads and turned, placing the offering on the altar.

Father Declan came forwards and nodded to Brooks, who reached a hand in his pocket and brought out a small box. He lifted the lid and came to stand by us. Tucked into a tiny cushion of pleated silk were two gold rings.

I looked at Mick-san, my surprise surely obvious. Where did he manage to get gold in such a short time, in such a war-torn country?

Father Declan carefully removed the smaller ring from the cushion, passing it to Mick-san, who reached for my hand.

'With this ring, I thee wed,' he said, sliding the ring smoothly onto my finger.

Next was my turn. Mick-san held out his hand, and I wriggled and pushed, and together we slid the ring on.

'Just one more thing.' He reached into a pocket, removing a small woven pouch, pulling out a jade-green pendant on a long silver chain. 'This is called greenstone or pounamu in my country, jade in yours. The twisted shape is called a *pikorua*.' He took my hand and guided my finger around the smooth curl in the shape of a number eight. 'See,' he said. 'It has no beginning and no end.' He unhooked the clasp and fastened it around my neck, the jade pendant sitting just at the vee of my kimono. 'This is for family connections and eternity. Just like our love, it's never-ending.'

My eyes misted as he bent to me, his lips found mine as I clung to him, never, never wanting to let go.

The bells overhead chimed and our guests clapped, bowed and laughed at us, still holding each other.

He smiled at me. 'We are married now.'

***

As clearly as I remembered the details of our beautiful ceremony, the rest of the evening became a misty dream to me.

The party was back at Kiwi Base in the mess hall.

Mick-san hardly left my side. I felt safe there, tucked under his arm.

I looked around the room at my new friends. The ties of tradition were certainly very flexible. Here, under this roof, people represented many ethnicities, in harmony with each other.

At last I met Brooks and his Japanese wife, Noriko-san. I couldn't ask her enough questions and she couldn't have been more helpful. It was as if they had blazed the trail for us to follow. Noriko-san told me they were going to New Zealand to live when Brooks' year in Japan ended. She asked me if we had the same plan. I was ashamed to admit we hadn't talked about it. All we'd had time to do was plan our wedding.

Tomoko-san had organised others to look after the kitchen this time, although she couldn't keep away, ensuring the trays of cocktail snacks were arranged just so, and served to the guests correctly, respectfully.

Mick-san said the QM had gone to some trouble to get extra food for the supper. His supply of saké was generous and the gathering soon became lively and noisy.

'I would like to thank QM for organising this party.' I said. 'Before I get too tired to remember my manners.'

We wandered over to where he and Croc were having a loud discussion, Father Declan looking on in amusement.

It was strange for me to see a man in a kimono – not a *yukata* like men often wear as a summer robe, but a women's kimono, with bright flowers and patterns and an *obi*-sash.

It didn't seem to bother the others and when I had previously asked Tomoko-san about it, she waved my question away with a sweep of her hand. 'Just happens so,' she'd said.

'Nah, nah, QM,' Croc was saying as we approached. He tugged on the QM's sleeve. 'This isn't a uniform. For a start, you're the only one with this style.' He turned to the chaplain and flicked the long scarf draping down his front. 'This is a uniform, because it's what all chaplains wear. And this,' he reached for Mick-san's sleeve as we arrived beside them. 'This is a military uniform. But you, QM, you're on your own there.'

'Beg to differ,' the QM said, his focus resting on my *uchikake.* 'I have company. This beautiful bride is also wearing kimono.'

'Oh, so you're a bride today,' Croc shot at him.

Laughter erupted from the group and died away as they simultaneously lifted their glasses to their lips and drank.

'Mick,' QM said suddenly. 'Before I forget – my quarters are yours for the next few days – bridal suite. I'm heading off to do the rounds with Chaplain here.' He swung an arm around the cleric's shoulders and leaned rather heavily.

'You're kidding,' Mick-san replied.

'True,' the QM added. 'I need to source some hard-to-find supplies and I just might need God on my side.'

'You two, on the road,' Croc chipped in. 'I hate to think what that'll be like. You won't get past the first distillery!'

'Be that as it may,' the chaplain replied. 'I am to have the questionable company of my old friend, and it won't be half bad, having someone else along to cheer the bumpy roads for a wandering man of God.'

We thanked the QM for his generosity.

I don't know how much later we walked across the compound towards the QM's stand-alone cabin, towards welcoming candlelight flickering from the window.

Mick-san swept me up into his arms and carried me through the door. 'Over the threshold,' he told me, 'as in my country.'

'What else do they do in your country?'

He lowered me slowly to my feet and stepped close, pulling me to him.

'They do this,' he said, brushing his lips over mine. 'And this.' His lips drifted across my face, settling briefly on each closed eye, like a butterfly's kiss. 'And this.' He bent to my ear, his teeth giving a sharp nip to my earlobe.

I squealed, jumped and tried to pull away. No room to move. He held me firmly to him, laughing, moving his mouth towards my other ear.

I stilled, waited, calm on the surface, while my insides were in a crazy turmoil.

My hair decoration dangled in his way, and I laughed as he tried to blow the threads of silk flowers away from his lips.

He turned his focus to my hair, finding hair pins, removing them one by one, and letting them fall where we stood, until the jasmine cluster came free. He put it down beside the candle lamp, the petals glowing like little moons in the light, the tiny butterfly's wings appearing to flutter with the flickers of flame.

The release of my rigid hairstyle came like a soft breeze on a hot night. I shook my head side to side, enjoying the freedom of its flow. Mick-san threaded his fingers through, giving a slow, tantalising massage to my scalp, sliding down the full length of my hair, with a soft tug at the end tipping my head back.

He then leaned in and brushed his lips over mine, exploring, playful and tempting, his tongue finding mine.

I moaned as my legs weakened – giving in to the pressure of his hands on my back, supporting me against him.

His fingers found the cords wrapping around my *obi*-sash, loosening the ties until they fell away, my *obi* sliding to my feet. The white under-robe was revealed as the overlapping edges of my heavy brocade kimono drifted apart and began to slip down my shoulders.

Before I could catch it, Mick-san lifted it away and draped it carefully over the back of a chair.

I felt light-headed, light hearted, and a little scared as he turned to look at me in my under-kimono in the glow of the lamplight.

A smile twitched at the corner of his mouth. 'You look like an angel, pearly and pure,' he whispered.

My fingers found the remaining, securely-wrapped ties and teased apart the knotted ends. A silk cloud drifted around me as the robe broke free, settling tentatively on my shoulders, floating open like a silent sigh of relief.

His expression lost its playfulness and his eyes darkened. He reached for my hand, lifted aside the drape that divided the room, and led me to the other side, to the bed – bigger than any futon I'd seen, with scattered petals over its smooth, fresh sheets.

I couldn't look, then I couldn't look away, as my husband unbuttoned and removed his uniform, dropping each garment where he stood, his gaze on me, holding me, until he stood naked and came to my side.

As his hands guided me onto the bed, I let my robe fall away, my naked body shyly acknowledging his.

His lips found mine, his tongue played hide and seek with mine, encouraging me, leading me and waiting for my response, guiding me to him, until I was overwhelmed.

With an urgency I had never known, I reached for him, pulling him to me, my fingers digging into his back and my legs wrapping him, as I drew him into my body, my mind and my soul.

Now, truly, husband and wife.

Chapter Thirteen

When you do things from your soul
you feel a river moving in you,
a joy.
– *Rumi*

Our married life continued as a dream. I had never known such happiness and such freedom.

We stayed in the QM's quarters for several days after our ceremony, and when the QM returned at the end of the week, Mick-san moved back to the barracks, and I became a lodger with Tomoko-san, making some money by helping her and Yoshi-san in the kitchen at the mess hall.

I didn't think about my father and the life I once had. I thought of myself as a bird, having flown from the nest, not needing my parents and my childhood home, making my way in the world, through good and bad.

Nor did I miss the luxury of the family house and conforming to traditional expectations. I was more than happy to leave behind the shackles associated with living there.

Mick-san and I spent every possible moment together, mostly at the onsen, and when the QM was away on his frequent trips, we stayed in his quarters.

I still travelled on the truck to the hospital as before, the villagers keeping to themselves as they always had. Eyes averted, lips sealed but, no doubt, minds humming with judgements and questions that voiced themselves in gossip when I wasn't around.

Some days I travelled with the QM to translate negotiations with local suppliers.

On those days, Yodo-san came along as my companion. On other days, she did some scouting work, which she never talked about.

As the nights became cooler and the colours of flame blushed the hillsides, it felt so good to sink together into the warmth of the onsen.

Mick and I would get out much later, very reluctantly, dress fast, shivering, and run back to base hand in hand, carrying the heat in our veins and the togetherness in our hearts.

I thought this wonderful world, free of constraint and full of love, would never end. But of course, it did.

***

In the dying days of autumn, Mick-san got the order. He was being transferred to Eta Jima Island in the Inland Sea.

Why? I cried to myself in the dark.

'Why?' I asked him. 'Is it because our marriage isn't legal in the eyes of your army? Is it because my father or Sato-san must have the last say? Is it because you are so good at your job that you are needed elsewhere? Or is it because the gods are punishing us for breaking tradition?'

Mick-san had no answers. Nobody did.

***

'I will apply to be posted back here as soon as I can,' he promised. 'Or I will come for you when I first get leave.'

In silence we said our farewells, the autumn moon looking over the onsen – over us, its late summer glow faded to a frostiness of indifference.

I stayed on with Tomoko-san and continued to help her and Yoshi-san at the mess hall kitchen, which became busier as more personnel arrived in camp.

Riding the truck to the hospital became an unpleasant experience as the new driver was not Mick-san and his driving was rough, making everyone – especially me, feel sick in the stomach.

At the same time, QM wanted to increase the trade of fabrics and my knowledge of homegrown cottons and silks helped him make good trades, buying well and selling at a profit for industry and export.

I liked that work. It was interesting, and took my mind off Mick-san – for a little while.

I was so grateful that Mick-san and I were married and that our wedding had gone smoothly – father had not dashed my plans. Yodo-san and I had managed a very good smoke screen, concealing my whereabouts, although it was unlikely he would search for me.

Father must disown me for my refusal to accept Sato Junior and for marrying someone of my own choosing, for rejecting the traditional way.

A wayward daughter *must* be renounced, otherwise the family name would be tainted.

His priority would be to salvage his business connections with Sato-san, and the only way he could save face over the failed marriage arrangement would be to publicly abandon me and assure Sato Junior I was not worthy.

I would be dead to my father.

***

As each long winter night stretched out before me like an interminable silence, an ache settled into my heart, keeping insidious company with the chill in my bones.

English dictionary at my elbow, making the exercise one of learning as well as love, I passed those evenings writing to my husband.

The postal service was notoriously unreliable. I knew that because Mick-san's first letter, three weeks after his departure, told me of many letters he had posted before.

Like me, he would write something every night.

Our cold hands wrote warm words for each other, while hunched under layers of blankets in our distant rooms, unified by the harsh stare of the same frosty moon.

At least we had that fragile thread of togetherness.

The more I missed my husband, the less I missed my father and the restrictions a woman had to endure in the traditional home. The worm in horseradish knows only about horseradish.

Freedom from that life, even with no husband to share it, opened up a new world for me.

Every day, I discovered new joys as I grew into being myself more fully.

One day, it was an honest conversation with Tomoko-san about the strengths of women, neither of us worrying about saying the 'right' thing in the 'right' way.

The next day, it was my successful negotiations over the value of silk and cotton for the QM.

When I didn't work, I loved the absolute freedom to think – sometimes I thought my head would explode with all the possibilities taking flight. At those times, I would take my journal and pen to a quiet place, sit in the thin wintery sunshine, and write as fast as my thoughts flowed.

Maybe one day I would find a way to make a difference for others – break down the crippling barriers at all levels, and let all women have a say. We already had some women in government.

It seemed to me, women in this country had every reason to look for change. We had followed instructions far too long.

***

At first, I didn't know, but slowly began to realise, I was about to embark on a journey new to me but familiar to many women.

Tomoko-san showed no surprise when I said one morning the smell at the fish market was disgusting – and every morning after that. She nodded, her lips pressed, when I left my green tea untouched. She shook her head with good humour when all the pickles had gone from their jar in the mess hall kitchen.

The next message I wrote to Mick-san came out in shy, formal, little-girl words.

Our wedding had been an escape, glittered with the sparkly optimism of young people in love, dominated with thoughts of nothing but each other. We had not talked about family. We were a couple. Husband and wife.

Now, we were to be three.

Chapter Fourteen

JAPAN 1947

One kind word
can warm three winter months.
– Japanese Proverb

I waited, more anxiously than ever before, for my husband's reply. What would he think about having a baby? Would he love the idea – or hate it?

His letters didn't arrive. I worried. I stopped eating.

Tomoko-san insisted I eat something, so I broke off little bits and pushed them into my mouth, chewing and swallowing, more with forced determination, than any enjoyment of the food.

When Mick-san's next letter arrived, the envelope was marked, not with the familiar Eta Jima postmark, but from another place, an unfamiliar name.

I tore it open and read his words hungrily. There was no response to my letter – to the baby news.

He had been transferred again to a more distant post.

As I had waited so nervously for his response, he hadn't yet received my letter but had moved on before it reached him.

'What is the problem?' Tomoko-san asked, noticing my tears but not waiting for my answer. 'You still have a baby growing, whether Mick-san knows it or not. You don't need his permission or his approval. He has already stirred your pot. It doesn't matter when he finds out. You do what you must for the baby, just as he does what he must for the army.' She raised her eyebrows and added something my mother used to say. 'Unspoken words are the flowers of the future.'

Blurry through my overflowing eyes, I watched her bustling around in the kitchen, knowing she made sense, but still wishing things were different.

'Find something to do,' she instructed. 'Fill your days with things that fill your mind. Stop waiting for the postman.'

When I took my journal and pen to a sunny spot the next day, it was not to write my ideas, but to read them.

I flicked the pages and my journal fell open at an experience I had written about a few weeks earlier, after Yodo-san and I had visited a small farmers' market where families could buy or trade, while food rations were so inadequate.

'One young Japanese mother, head bowed, waited quietly in line at a vegetable stall, her babe in an onbu on her back. The baby opened its sleepy eyes to look around, fixing me in its sights. The wide eyes looked strange to me, the baby's skin a soft, delicate tone – not the harsh, dark skin of most children who lived on the land, or on the street.

Unusual, yet familiar, the baby continued to focus on me, alert and inquisitive beyond its years, holding me in a kind-of spell.

A foreign soldier's baby.

'Hafu!' someone shouted. I jerked around. The woman selling from the stall had picked up a bamboo broom and ran at the young mother. 'Hafu,' she yelled again, advancing, waving the broom in the air as if swatting a giant fly. The young mother turned and ran towards a narrow lane behind me, my lasting memory of the baby bumping on her back, its head still turned in my direction, its face curling up like a crumpled rag, bursting forth with a wail of protest.

I watched until the mother and babe had ducked from sight and the pursuing woman turned with a satisfied smile. 'Hafu!' she snorted. 'Don't want that rubbish around my stall!' She swung the bamboo broom playfully, as if still swiping again at the escaping young woman with her unacceptable baby.'

I clapped my journal shut and jumped to my feet. 'Yodo-san!' I called, heading to the back of the barracks, repeating the call.

The under-floor space, as the land sloped away, provided a retreat where Yodo-san could often be found, in between duties. She got to her feet as I approached, ready for my request.

'Come with me,' I instructed. 'But first I need something from the kitchen.'

I pushed through the mess hall door, quickly filled a bento lunchbox, slipped it into my *kinchaku* – the cloth shoulder bag where I kept my journal and dashed out to where Yodo-san stood.

'The farmers market,' I announced, striding out of the compound and heading down the road, explaining my intentions to Yodo-san as we walked.

This late in the day, the market had been packed away, but I knew the area and quickly found the lane down which the young mother, with the beguiling hafu baby, had scuttled, evading the threat of the bamboo switch.

We came to an area where huts and shacks made of building scraps leaned precariously against each other, some fastened to tree trunks for stability. Dusty children in tatty clothes played in the dirt, stopping to watch us approach. I didn't look into the shelters but was aware people sat in there, whole families huddled into spaces less than the size of a tatami mat, hunched against the chill.

'What will it be like when the snow comes?' I asked, throwing my question to the gods, disgusted that they had turned a blind eye to these people.

In the hope of showing some respect to the families whose backyards we were invading, I let Yodo-san take the lead.

An elderly woman sat on a straw mat in the doorway of a hut, watching us approach.

Yodo-san bowed and asked her a question.

'*Hafu*?' the woman replied. '*Hai* – yes.' She raised a mud-caked hand and pointed further along the lane. 'Foreign soldiers' babies and the mothers down there.'

Yodo-san reached into her sleeve pocket and withdrew a fabric parcel, unwrapping a *satsuma-imo* – a cooked mountain yam. The woman's eyes widened, her mouth falling open as Yodo-san passed the yam to her, bowed quickly and continued along the path.

Soon the lane widened where a cluster of small, dilapidated dwellings and huts gathered together, ghetto-like, as if trying to shut out the world.

Small children, otherworldly with fair skin tones and eyes in shades of the ocean, played in the dusty forecourt, watched by mothers sitting to the side, some with babies on their back or in their arms.

Their conversation stalled as we approached. I scanned the group for the young woman I had seen at the vegetable stall, but realised I had not observed her face well, having focussed mainly on the bright-eyed child at her back.

I reached into my bag, withdrawing the bento box. '*Sumimasen* –

excuse me. I saw the unkind woman at the farmers' market,' I ventured, addressing them all, faces lighting up in recognition of my intention.

I realised it didn't matter which mother I had observed scurrying away from the shrew's broom. They probably all had fled her at some time – maybe repeatedly.

'I have some food for you and the children.' I passed over the small offering, and they nodded uncertain thanks, their eyes reflecting hesitancy and confusion over such a donation.

So inadequate, I was embarrassed I had brought so little. 'I'm sorry, I didn't realise this was such a community. I will bring more food tomorrow.'

I bowed quickly and turned away, heading back into the lane, feeling as if I had given a single drop of water to a parched animal.

As we trudged up the hill, I grappled with the reality of what I had just seen. 'There's so many of them,' I hissed to Yodo-san. 'All hafu babies and their mothers – treated as less-than-human.'

Part of me felt like part of them. I worried about the baby growing inside me and wondered how many of those hafu's mothers were married – like me, but for some reason found themselves abandoned. 'Why have the husbands left them?'

Yodo-san shot a look at me. 'Mostly, no husband,' she said, her voice flat.

'What do you mean? They must have husbands – they have babies.'

She shook her head. 'Do you know about rape?'

'Rape? I have heard some things…' My voice trailed off in disbelief.

'Thousands of babies from rape by soldiers.'

Stopping in my tracks, I glared at her. 'No.'

She nodded. 'And prostitutes – you heard of them? For the soldiers.'

'They don't get babies.'

'Sometimes they do. And if they keep the baby, they can't work any more.'

I looked back down towards the ghetto, faces fixed in my mind. 'Did they get raped? Were they comfort women?'

Yodo-san nodded slowly, her expression softening. 'Maybe some of them had a no-good husband. Or they wanted to marry, but he went away.'

My stomach lurched and I dragged in a determined breath. This was not about me.

The women I knew, although controlled by traditional roles, at least had the support of family, society.

Those young mothers at the ghetto were victims again and again – as they, and then the baby they didn't ask for, became rejected by their families, by everyone, because they had children whose fathers came from elsewhere.

Bile rose and I swallowed hard, tamping down tears. Breathless, I turned to the grassy bank beside the rough road, lowering myself onto its cool softness, willing calm into my racing heart, my churning stomach.

I tried to push aside my anxiety about Mick-san's postings, his infrequent letters and most of all, no reaction about our baby.

I trusted him and believed he loved me. He *would* come back. We *would* be a family.

With positive determination, I got to my feet and continued up the hill, ignoring the niggling thought that maybe those hafu's fathers wanted to come back, but were controlled by the decisions of others.

'Mick-san will come back to me.' My statement came out more like a question.

Walking beside me, Yodo-san smiled. 'You have baby?'

I nodded, letting her see my anxiety.

'You are not like the hafu mothers,' she said, showing uncharacteristic warmth. 'You will not be like that. Until Mick-san comes back, you have Tomoko-san and Yoshi-san and me, QM and Father Declan. You have a job at the mess hall and with the QM. We are all like family.'

I studied her, soaked up her words, wanted to fix them in my heart. 'What about my baby? It will be hafu.'

'The people around you already accept you for marrying a *gaijin* – a foreigner. *You* walk on the bridge between old ideas and new.' She turned to me, giving her words significance. 'That is a very important thing.'

I heaved out a sad sigh, feeling the weight of my future like a heavy shroud. 'Why is that important?'

She smiled, and raised her chin at me as if lifting me up. 'You are destined to make a difference – for them.' She nodded in the direction of the ghetto. 'And any others who can't make it on their own.'

I shuffled the pebbles under my feet. 'What difference can I make? There are so many of them, and the law doesn't care.'

Yodo-san scoffed. 'The law is changing. First, it's the Emperor in charge, and all the young men go to war. Many don't come back. Then it's the foreign occupation in charge. Is it better? I don't know. The face of the enemy…' She shrugged, opening her hands to the heavens. 'But I know this – now women can vote. Times are changing. We have to grab the chance while our country is confused.' She paused, then continued slowly with emphasis. 'You can make a difference.'

I looked at her for some time, my thoughts returning to the *hafu* ghetto, then I looked up to the sky – to my mother. To Mick-san.

'We will go back tomorrow – *ashita*,' I puffed to Yodo-san. 'Take all the spare food we can carry.'

Unquestioning, she nodded.

Arriving back at the mess hall late for dinner preparations, I kept my head down, went straight to the vegetable bench and started peeling.

Tomoko-san watched me from across the kitchen. 'One bento box is missing.' Always the quartermaster of her own stores.

Putting aside my work, I turned to face her, explaining about the farmers' market, the young mother and her *hafu* baby, the cruel vegetable seller and the sadly inadequate bento box of leftovers that I felt ashamed to leave at the ghetto community.

Tomoko-san listened, eyebrows raised, lips pursed. 'How many?' she asked. 'How many mothers?' She nodded, impatient.

'Maybe eight mothers, I saw. But I guess twenty or thirty must live there. And about as many children.' Then I remembered the woman who gave us directions. 'And some others in huts, maybe families, down the lane.' She focussed on me a moment longer before returning to her work.

After dinner, with the mess hall emptied out and quiet again, the door swung open once more. Yodo-san led in the QM and Father Declan.

Tomoko-san turned to me. 'Tell them about the *hafu* ghetto.'

***

After breakfast the following morning, a jeep pulled up to the mess hall steps and Tomoko-san signalled the driver to load the leftover hotpot she had made in double quantity on hearing my story about the ghetto.

And so, it began, my days filling up with a new project – helping the *hafu* community.

Around me grew a ground-swell of support and donations – not just food, but surplus bowls and china spoons from the mess hall, an old tent –

once barracks, and two gasoline cookers, allowing raw food to be donated and the women to do their own cooking.

Tomoko-san was right about not waiting for the postman. I had long passed the stage of being desperate to hear from Mick-san. I was now quietly confident that all would be well.

When my husband's next letter finally arrived, I tucked it into my sleeve and ran along the forest track to the little shrine up the hill from Kiwi base.

Seated in the garden of worship, I peeled open the envelope and savoured every word.

Mick-san was delighted about the baby. He would come back as soon as he had finished the assignment, although that may not be for many weeks yet.

He said he had sent money to me every week so I would not have to work. That explained why so few of his letters arrived, and when they did, they had been damaged so much I was lucky if anything was readable.

He asked me to consider where I would like us to go when his army service finished in June. Did I want to move to New Zealand and start a new life there? Or did I want to stay in Japan and make our home here?

That evening I started my reply, not that I had any answer about where we would live – I said we would have to talk about that. I needed to know more about New Zealand, and he needed to know more about Japan before we could decide what kind of future we would have.

My heart settled. Anxiety around my baby, our baby, ceased. All that mattered was that Mick-san would soon return and we would plan our future – the future for our family. It surprised me how easily I accepted the unknown.

End of year approached, winter's sharp teeth biting into every aspect of life.

The systems of support for the *hafu* village continued to work smoothly. I was grateful that my presence was needed less and less, tiredness claiming my energy. Working in the mess hall kitchen became all I could handle, and often the smell of the food sent me running.

Mick-san surprised me with his return at Christmas. I felt shy, nervous at his touch and anxious about my expanding middle.

My kimono didn't wrap over neatly. Its front edge pulled sideways and stuck out untidily. The wide obi-sash, designed to flatten the front of a woman's shape, did not allow for curves.

I breathed out and tried to hold my stomach taut, but it objected to the restriction and ballooned again as the in-breath came involuntarily.

'When is this going to happen?' he asked, placing his hands on my belly, his smile mischievous.

'Late July,' I whispered, looking down, not ready to voice the reality of our creation.

He took both my hands and led me to sit on the bench in the shrine garden, where I had been when he arrived.

For a long time, he said nothing, just sitting, letting us be, together.

His gaze moved over me. I felt it resting on my face. I couldn't look up. He reached for a stray strand of hair, tucking it behind my ear.

'July,' he repeated. 'Perfect timing. My army year ends in June.' His sideways smile twitched at the corners. 'Maybe we go to New Zealand then.' His eyes danced. 'Would you like to live in New Zealand, Mrs Mitchell?' I gasped, not used to hearing my new name.

He nudged me with his elbow, leaning towards me playfully.

A sudden smile betrayed my reserve. I ducked my head but he missed nothing, wrapping his arm around me.

'We would be in New Zealand before the baby arrives.'

Then he told me he was coming back to the Kiwi base for a few weeks, maybe even months.

My breath rushed out in a sigh and my shoulders relaxed. My husband had returned. It was going to be all right.

Our married life resumed as before. I continued to stay at Tomoko-san's and Mick-san moved back into the barracks. We took every chance to be together, usually at the onsen or the garden shrine. Sometimes at the QM's quarters, when he went away.

Life settled and we almost took for granted our easy existence, full of love for each other and the new life growing.

One day Mick-san received another far-away posting. We took it with resignation and bravery. After all, it would be only a matter of months till his army year ended.

We said goodbye as we had done before, without words.

The days were longer without him. Even the sun went slower, spring needing its warmth to sprout new growth. Trees blossomed, lily leaves sprung out followed quickly by buds, birds chirped louder and people relaxed with a friendliness that was often hard to find in winter.

Everybody, except my baby, welcomed Spring. At the end of a day's work at the mess hall, my legs and back ached so much I couldn't sleep.

Tomoko-san didn't say anything, but I could see her watching me as I moved like an old woman.

'Enough work,' she announced one day. 'You stay home. Feet up.'

A few weeks later, in the middle of the night, I was torn apart with a pain so deep I couldn't breathe. My scream brought Tomoko-san running. A jeep arrived and many hands carried me to lie on the back seat, as we bumped the excruciating road to the hospital.

I had no idea of time – hours, days, weeks, drifting in and out of consciousness, my body nothing but pain, searing sweat, my vision floating into focus then jarred into nightmare images, voices coming and going through a tunnel from far away, echoing – Tomoko-san, Father Declan, QM and uncanny, unfamiliar voices saying, 'Drink this,' as bitter liquid dripped into my mouth. All I wanted was Mick-san to return.

And my father, his voice distant, echoing. Was I dreaming? Then nothing.

I awoke to find cool sheets over me, calm sounds around me. I blinked into brightness, squinting to focus.

Where was I?

Nothing looked familiar. Strange smells, medical, herbal smells assaulted my nostrils.

Where was I?

My hands rushed to my flattened belly. 'My baby!' the voice from my throat harsh, unrecognisable. I swallowed, a bitter taste burning my insides. 'My baby,' I screeched again. I tried sitting up.

Voices floated towards me, then drifted away before I could grasp any meaning.

Singing came from somewhere. Caressing sounds. A slow, gentle song. Maybe a lullaby.

'Your baby is here,' a calm voice answered. 'She's very tiny. She arrived too early.'

'She? Where?' I lurched up, then paralysed by wrenching pain, dropped back. 'Bring her to me please!'

'She's very weak, dear. Be prepared for the will of the gods.'

My dear baby,
I saw you then, wrapped in cloth. I held you, so light in my arms.
I heard you, a murmur, kitten-like.
I smelt you, the aroma of life. I touched you, of my own flesh.
You opened your eyes.
Not my eyes, but your father's, wide and round, all-knowing, all seeing.
We had created you,
The perfect blend of our love.

PART THREE

JAPAN 1947

The seed I would like to plant
in your heart
is a vision
where all our people
live together in harmony
and share the wisdom
from each culture.
– Dame Whina Cooper

Chapter Fifteen

The bamboo that bends
is stronger than the oak that resists.
– Japanese Proverb

Too impatient to wait for a bus, Mick hefted his kitbag and headed off on foot towards the Kiwi base camp. To Emiko.

The last time he had seen his wife was at the end of his short Christmas leave when they had decided on New Zealand as their future home.

Sayonara leave had come at last – the final weekend off-duty before they would sail together to New Zealand.

He set off at a jog, keeping to the main roads, for the chance of catching a ride in an army vehicle.

Despite the rising summer humidity and the weight of his bag, he hurried on. This was the moment he had been dreaming of, the sweet reunion of husband and wife – especially as their time together since marrying had been cut short by his remote postings.

Emiko would be getting on in her pregnancy now. He wanted to be there for her. Now was his chance to prove himself as a husband, to take her to their new homeland and to settle her in before the baby came. He hoped the sea voyage wouldn't be too hard on her.

At the beginning of the hill climb, a farm truck came along, slowing to allow him to clamber onto the stack of straw on its tray.

He jumped off at the top of the hill and hit the ground running for the mess – expecting he would find Emiko on dinner preparations in the kitchen.

Tomoko-san swung around as he burst through the kitchen door, anxiety etched in her face.

'The baby started to come early,' she stammered. 'Too early.'

'Where is she…? Is she okay?' Anxiety tightened its stranglehold when Tomoko didn't answer right away.

'She's at the hospital. We don't know any more. They won't let us visit.'

'How long ago…?'

'Few days.'

Mick dropped his kitbag where he stood, swung around, out the door, down the steps, onto the road, running.

A vehicle approached from behind and slowed. 'Hop in, Mate.' It was Croc in a jeep.

'She's in the hospital…'

'I know, Mate. Hop in. We'll get you there quick.'

'Kick it!' Mick shouted, as he landed in the passenger seat. 'What do you know?'

'Not much, Mate. They took her to hospital in the night.'

'Jeez!' Mick dashed a hand through his hair, his boot pressing into the floor where the accelerator would be if he was behind the wheel. 'Can't this thing go faster?'

'Wanna get you there safe.' Croc threw him a concerned look. 'Understand your anxiety, Mate, but I'm sure she's in good hands.'

'I've seen in those hospitals, heard about the shortages. No such thing as in good hands. Shit!' He slammed a fist into his thigh.

Mind racing, he fought off images of Emiko in pain, calling his name. Was there anyone holding her hand, moping her brow, whispering soothing words? Was anyone with her, giving her sips of tea?

'Nearly there,' Croc assured as they sped around the final corner.

The approach to the hospital Mick knew so well, until now, had been someone else's source of anguish.

He jumped out before the jeep had come to a stop, running for the entrance.

'I'll wait here,' Croc called.

Dashing from room to room, from alcove to alcove he called her name. She'd been moved, someone said, the day before.

'Where did she go?'

Nobody knew. Her father had made the arrangements, they said.

'Her father!' His heart sank. 'No! Why!'

He'd been called, they said, because she was in serious trouble, and the baby was arriving too early. Maybe he went for his own doctor… Maybe he took Emiko home…

Maybe…

Mick rushed out of the building.

He had to find Tanazawa-san. Damn the protocol. Damn everything!

Dashing out towards the waiting jeep, he heard his name called. He swung around to see Kazu emerging from the hospital, followed by his grandmother.

Fleeting relief at seeing familiar faces was shortly swamped with new desperation.

'Emiko-san went to special place,' Kazu translated his grandmother's words. 'Special hospital for mother and baby.'

'Goddamit! Where?'

'On island. I can show you where is boat.' Kazu jumped into the back of the jeep as Croc accelerated away.

The boatman, receptive to Mick's desperate offer of American dollars, made the crossing in a few minutes, delivering him ashore a stony beach, winged on both sides with the rise of rocky cliffs.

High-walled buildings, fortress-like, impenetrable – dominating the land, not resembling a caring institute in any way.

Mick made his way around the outer rim looking for an entrance. Finally, he came across a heavy wooden door which creaked open when he put his weight behind it, letting him into a grey, gloomy corridor.

He moved with stealth. Clearly, visitors were neither expected nor welcome.

The interior reflected nothing of local style. Its surfaces stark, resembling a military bunker, noticeably without the glowing warmth of wood and bamboo. Eerie, empty silence, interrupted only by the occasional distant clang or clatter.

Straining for voices, he heard nothing.

But then – something. Voices from one of the rooms. As he drew nearer, stealthily he pushed the door and looked in. One woman sitting up in a bed, the other sitting on the edge, their heads bent over needlework.

'Emiko-san?' he whispered.

Startled, they both looked up, neither face familiar to him. 'Emiko-san, *doko desu-ka?*'

The woman in the bed widened her eyes and nodded. 'Hai.' She pointed further down the corridor.

'Emiko-san *wa soko ni imasu*' – that way.

Mick waved his thanks as he rushed on.

Pushing open more doors then retreating, he became less careful with his silence and more desperate to find Emiko.

He sensed her before he fully recognised her, taking a moment to be sure. She'd never looked like that – so fragile, so exhausted, so pale. His heart broke.

He closed the door behind him and approached the bed, bare floorboards creaking under his weight.

Her eyes opened heavily then dropped shut before opening again with a jerk, fixing on him. A stifled wailing sound echoed from inside her.

He hushed her, held her softly, caressed her frailness. 'It's going to be all right,' he whispered. 'I'm here now.'

Aware that his presence could be discovered any moment and he would likely be ousted from her bedside, urgency forced him to ask.

'The baby?' he began, wanting and yet not wanting to know the answer.

Emiko tried to speak. A scratchy whisper then a rasping cough stole her words. She swallowed and tried again. 'Too soon. Baby girl.' She dropped back on the stiff mattress and pulled in air.

Mick unhooked the water canteen from his belt and held it to her lips, lifting her head gently so she could take a sip, then another.

'*Muzukashii.*' Her voice barely a whisper. 'Very difficult.'

How long had she been like this?

She took another sip of water. 'The nurses… kind, caring. No medicine. Only herb tea. For sleeping…' She dropped back, breathing heavily. 'Praying,' she said. 'Always praying.'

'Where is the baby?'

'Karina. Her name Karina, means summer jasmine. White for death.' She paused, swallowed and mustered frail strength. 'Our baby gone…'

'Gone? Emi, what happened!'

She pressed her eyes closed. 'Don't worry,' she whispered. 'It's the best way.'

Mick shook his head. 'What do you mean? Emi?'

How could she accept it so easily? Their baby had gone – died?

She drew a raspy breath, gripping Mick's shirt with sudden strength, pulling him into her line of vision as her words came, staccato. 'What they do – is best. *Muzukashii* life – very difficult, for mixed-blood baby. No future…' Her voice faded as Mick's escalated.

'What do you mean!' His desperation was not disguised. 'We are going to New Zealand where our baby would be treasured…'

His voice dropped away as he focussed on her face, beaded with sweat, her breathing now rapid, eyes sunken. He realised suddenly that the loss of their baby was not his greatest concern.

'Emi,' he said softly. 'we've got to get you out of here.'

In his absence, with her difficult delivery, she had become a daughter again. No longer his wife, the mother of their baby, but suddenly under the control of her father.

How could she forget their plans to raise their family in his homeland?

The tea! Makes her sleepy – and compliant. Heavy footsteps thundered in the corridor.

'Emiko!' Mick spat his words with urgency. 'Don't drink the tea.' Her eyelids flickered in confusion.

'The tea,' he repeated as the door flung open. 'The tea is dangerous!'

He grabbed a slip of paper from his pocket and held it in her line of vision, as two heavy guards burst in. 'Our ship leaves in three days. Here are the details. I must get you out of here. I'll come back for you.' He pressed the paper into her hand, wrapping her fingers around it. Her eyes flashed comprehension.

Hard hands gripped his shoulders and wrenched him to his feet.

'Don't drink the tea,' he repeated, raising his voice, as he was spun around and pushed towards the door. 'I love you, Emiko. I will always love you.'

In all his military experience, Mick had never been so physically forced in one direction with his intentions so adamantly fixed in the opposite.

Being frog-marched out the same door he had sneaked in gave him no further understanding of the layout of the building – should he find that door locked on his return.

Mick's struggle to break free resulted in the grip around his arms tightening as he was pushed towards the beach.

The hum of a boat engine growled into the distance. He squinted into the fading light.

The ferry had left for the day.

The two guards shot meaningful looks at each other and Mick's heart sank. This could mean dire circumstances for him. Clearly, it was their job to get rid of him, one way or another.

The noise of another engine kicking to life caught their attention. All three looked along the beach as the rumble escalated, echoing from within a tumble-down boatshed which clung precariously to the rising clay cliff and jutted out on poles into the lapping tide.

Communicating silently the two guards turned suddenly, pivoting Mick between them, and trudged towards the noise.

As they approached, a heavy wooden tug, bobbing in the shallow waves, came into view. One of the guards called to the boatman. The exchange of shouted communication appeared to have been successful, as the grip on Mick's arms loosened and he was shoved forward, followed by grunted instructions.

A blunt object dug into his back, prodding him down the beach. He swung around to see fully their weathered scowls, their muscled bodies and the heavy wooden rods gripped threateningly in their gnarled fists, pushing him towards the throbbing boat.

Why would a maternity hospital employ such heavy-duty security guards? What could be the threat...?

One thing for sure, they meant business and if he was rebellious, he would be no use to Emiko wounded, or worse.

He would leave quietly and find a way to come back to her. Somehow.

Before he could think it through, he was shoved again and stumbled, feet running to keep upright, into the lapping waves. More prods on his back pushed him further, knee deep in the water. He reached up, grabbed the rim of the hull and pulled himself into a chin-up.

He swung his legs to and fro, until a foot caught the top edge of the hull, his hands gripping with determination as he edged his weight over the rim, dropping into the hollow boat landing amid a tangle of ropes.

The engine roared as the boat's underside grated on the stony bottom, then lurched free.

Mick quickly pulled himself upright, determined to observe every detail of the island, the bay, the short route to and from the mainland, to commit it all to memory.

He would come back for Emiko.

The two guards, backs now turned, walked up the beach, sticks over shoulders like fishermen going home – fading figures in a twilight watercolour.

The ugly building beyond them soon became a mere shadow in the gloom.

Mick struggled with the reality of his discoveries. Emiko was so sick; their baby had gone – he'd had no time to console her. His arms ached with emptiness, the memory of her frail body haunting him like a ghostly nightmare.

He could not deal with that now. He must push those thoughts aside. Questions flooded in – questions he'd not had time to ask. Push them aside too. There would be time for answers. Not now.

His heart ripped as the distance between them widened.

He shook himself. He had to be in control. Logic! Planning! Observations!

Refocussing on his surroundings, he looked around the boat from where he had landed, in the middle of the long hull.

He might need to use this boat again.

The driver up front paid him no attention. It seemed to Mick that his relaxed posture was of someone who knew his job well.

For the first time Mick noticed the small, partially-covered cabin at the back. Squinting into the enclosure, he could make out the outlines of other passengers.

Managing to balance, he scrambled to his feet and approached the open doorway.

Sitting inside, on a low bench, were two women wearing something like hospital uniforms. He greeted them. They replied shyly, in English.

He put on a casual manner. 'Where does this boat go?'

'Take babies to orphanage,' the younger one replied, waving a hand to four covered baskets tucked in at their feet.

He shot a glance at the baskets, his mind reeling. 'What? Babies?'

The older woman carefully picked up a basket, placed it on her lap and pulled aside the soft fabric cover to reveal a baby, peaceful in sleep.

He stared at the tiny face. 'Orphanage?'

They nodded, smiling. 'All babies from hospital go orphanage.'

'All? Why?'

'Family pays,' the younger one answered simply. 'Mothers can't keep.'

'Hafu orphanage, good place,' the other added, nodding pleasantly.

'Hang on.' He shifted his stance, struggling with both physical and mental equilibrium. 'Family pays? To send babies to the orphanage?'

The women nodded. 'Island hospital good place,' the older one said. 'Get mothers strong. Go home to family like new and find good husband.'

He shook his head, unable to comprehend what she had just said, fixing his focus on the baskets. 'Do the mothers want their baby to go?'

Head shaking, matter-of-fact. 'They not know, usually. They just know "baby gone".'

Mick's eyes widened in disbelief.

Emiko didn't know the truth.

His thoughts tumbled clumsily, spitting out frantic words. 'When do you take the babies? How often do you go? Is my baby here?'

The women looked at each other in confusion. He pointed to the baskets. 'Whose babies?' They responded with blank stares and shrugs. He quickly rephrased. 'Babies have name?'

'Ah, *hai*.' The younger one lifted the covers, revealing a small card tied inside the foot of the basket. 'Mother name.'

He blurted all possibilities. 'Emiko, Tanazawa, Mitchell…'

She read the name label on each basket. None sounded familiar. The older one looked directly at Mick. 'Tanazawa?' she repeated.

'Yes, Tanazawa. Emiko.'

The women exchanged a few quick words in their own language before looking back to him.

'Another day. Before,' the younger one said brightly. 'Tanazawa baby to orphanage.'

His urgent questions about the orphanage's whereabouts provided no information he could understand. He didn't know the region and failed to decipher the description or the official name of the place.

Their willingness to talk dried up as the boat slowed and gently ran aground on a deserted beach. Not the mainland jetty, but a remote location further along the coast.

The women, a baby basket tucked under each arm, eased past Mick and stepped down a narrow plank to dry ground.

Mick followed them, persisting with his questions. 'Could he travel with them? Could he follow them? How could he find his baby?'

The women walked steadily, for several minutes ignoring his presence, their precious cargo peaceful and silent in the baskets. Stopping at a heavy door in the wall beside a white stone church, the younger woman shouted a greeting to the interior.

The older woman turned to face him. 'This is convent. We stay here this night. No men.' The gate clicked open from the inside and both women stepped through as it swung shut with a metallic clunk behind them.

Mick pushed on it, banged with his fists, called out, then stepped back with a heavy sigh. If there was one thing he had learned in Japan, it was that bad manners and aggressiveness got you nowhere.

A lesson in humility, indeed.

Exhaustion, frustration, helplessness swamped him. His shoulders slumped and a jelly-like sensation rippled through him. Giving way to the buckling of his legs, he slid down the door, sitting as he landed, blocking the exit.

His only chance to reach his daughter was to follow the delivery of those babies to the orphanage the next morning.

With nothing to do but wait, he pulled his beret over his eyes, knowing sleeping would be unlikely, but at least he would be there, ready, when they opened the door and left for the orphanage the next day.

His mind whirled, confusing spirals leaping into the dark, preventing any sense of peace or constructive thought.

Sometime in the middle of the night he jerked upright, startled as something bumped his foot. He looked up to see an orange-robed monk standing before him.

'This door,' the monk said, 'for going in only. If you waiting, other door, over there.' He waved his hand, indicating another side of the enclosure. 'That door for leaving.'

He had not even thought about another opening in the fence. He thanked the monk, scrambled to his feet and they walked together in silence around the corner, following the high wall to another gate, this one with a small porch roof over long bench seats on each side.

The monk studied Mick, his feet grounded. 'A much more suitable place to sleep, I think, if you must sleep outside.'

Over the gate Mick could see some of the building beyond. A light came on in a high window, then another. The outline of a person stood momentarily in sight then moved away. The cry of a baby drifted through the dark. His heart thumped.

But he could not give in to his emotions. He must focus. His work was only beginning – he owed it to Emiko to go through the pain and suffering as she had, to fight for their baby and to save his family. Only then could he let go, give in and release the anguish that smouldered deep inside him.

Remembering that good manners equate to currency, he expressed his thanks to the monk. 'I need to find the hafu orphanage tomorrow.'

The monk gave a single nod.

'My baby is in the orphanage.'

The cleric looked puzzled. 'Why is your baby there?' He took a seat on the bench and indicated for Mick to do the same.

The words fell out of Mick's mouth, as he purged the events of his day, ending where they had met, at the monastery entrance.

The monk pressed his lips. 'Ah, yes. That happens.' He gave a soft laugh but his compassion over-shadowed any pretence of amusement. 'Nobody knows what to do with *hafu* babies.' He waved a hand, indicating the hills beyond. 'Just send to *hafu* orphanage now and think about it later.'

Mick's gaze followed the gesture, the pointing fingers, indicating the highlands at the end of the valley. 'Wait a minute. Do you know where it is? The orphanage?'

The monk tucked his arms across his front and smiled. 'Of course.'

***

Mick arrived to high walls and locked doors, as expected in the dead of night. He slept at the gate for the remaining hours of darkness, and woke alert and ready for action at the first glimmer of daylight.

Before long the gates clicked open and an old woman carrying a cane basket of gardening tools bowed deeply to Mick as he headed her way.

'It's open?'

'Hai,' she replied. '*Irasshaimase*.' Welcome. That was where his welcome began, and ended.

The hum of love emanating around the sanctuary, somehow didn't stretch to him. A foreign soldier, he represented the evil paternity of all those homeless children.

Some of them from rape, some from prostitutes, some forbidden marriages, all of them victims, in a country stretched to breaking point.

His optimism sparked when the attendant looked at the records and confirmed the arrival of the female baby of Tanazawa Emiko a few days earlier – as the nurses on the boat had recalled.

The rejection became complete when his enquiries resulted in scepticism, and the final blow – no man alone can adopt a baby.

'I don't want to adopt. She is my daughter. She came here by mistake a few days ago. Her mother and I are married…'

The same answer. No man can adopt. Come back with the mother.

Again, two guards appeared.

Mick heaved out a sigh. 'What is it with you sumo wrestlers?' he grumbled under his breath.

'Hai, sumo!' one of them answered, planting his feet and widening his stance, creating an impassable barrier.

Boots heavy with reluctance, Mick had no choice but to leave, the two sumo warriors on his tail and one thought on his mind – how could he possibly come back with Emiko?

He had already over-stayed his weekend's leave. With only a few days till the ship's departure, Military police would be scouting for Kiwi personnel stretching out their final farewells. Watch guards would be all over the city and around the port.

Getting back to Emiko would be like running through a mine field. Those going AWOL would be arrested on the spot and delivered promptly to the ship, with no way out. He could not, would not, risk that.

The boat he had arrived on might be his only hope of transport, if it was still on the beach. It seemed to be the hospital boat, stored in the concealed boatshed, and therefore could be waiting to return the two nurses after they had completed their delivery to the orphanage.

He ran, retracing last night's steps, back past the convent and on towards the shore as the sun glided into view over the Pacific Ocean, its golden glow hitting him with taunting warmth and comfort.

It seemed so long ago that his year in Japan had begun with the magical lure of *Hinode-mura*, the sunrise village in the inland hills overlooking the devastation of Hiroshima. He remembered his first ride on the truck with Buster, his first encounter with the flirty grandmother and then the grandson, Kazu, who had become his wingman.

But the vision that held him together all the past months of remote postings, was setting eyes on Emiko for the first time. He conjured up that image again, his knees almost buckling at the emotional rush. Pushing the memory aside, his heart wrenched as he turned his concentration to the seemingly impossible task ahead – getting Emiko off the island.

On reaching the beach, he pushed himself harder at the sight of the boat, lying askew on the gritty sand. Hopefully the boatman would be nearby. If not, it crossed Mick's mind he could steal the boat.

He called out from some distance, and again as he came near. A gruff reply and the boatman appeared from the rear cabin.

The negotiations were eventually settled, with more and then more of Mick's American dollars sealing the deal.

With the help of a long bamboo punting pole skilfully manoeuvred by the boatman's Sinbad-like biceps, the heavy craft inched off the beach, the engine roared to life and they motored into the bay.

Mick attempted to focus on the journey this time. Having been so involved in conversation with the orphanage couriers the previous evening, he didn't recall the route taking them so close to the mainland. His memory was more of an island-to-island trip, taking a wide, offshore arc.

His real focus was how to get to Emiko. He hoped – he prayed – that she had understood his message to avoid drinking the tea, to realise its doping effect. It would be so much easier for them to escape if she was alert and aware of what they needed to do. He hoped the early morning hour would catch the security patrol off-guard.

He'd decided to ask the boatman to remain at the hidden boatshed until they returned.

The promise, and the flash of another bunch of dollars should ensure his cooperation. The plan was taking shape.

He looked out and to his horror, saw they were approaching the mainland jetty, not the island itself but the departure point for it, where Kazu had directed them.

'No!' he called to the boatman. 'Not here.' He slashed his hands through the air, the universal signal to abandon the plan. 'The island!' He gestured wildly out to the bay.

'Quick stop,' the boatman explained. 'More passenger.' He cut the engine and they drifted sideways towards the jetty, the punting pole being used to pull them alongside and hold the boat steady. Someone on the jetty called out a place name and the boatman nodded, inviting them aboard.

The boat was about to push off when a loud shout and a scuffle in the crowd on shore ensued. The boatman paid no attention, trying to dislodge the holding pole where it had become jammed between the jetty boards.

Then Mick saw them. Patrolling military police had spotted him and were heading for his boat. He ducked into the little cabin, hoping his uniform had not been identified. But it was too late. While the boatman struggled to free the pole, two officers jumped aboard and rushed to where

Mick cowered.

'Under arrest!' one of them shouted as they reached for him, pulling him forwards and man-handling him off the boat.

'You're AWOL,' the other informed him. 'All leave ended Sunday midnight.'

'It's Monday already?' Mick doubted that playing dumb was a suitable strategy.

'Accept it, soldier. Your leave is over.' They gripped his arms and forced him to walk, heading onto the road towards the port about half a mile away.

'But my wife is on the island… and my baby is in the orphanage. I need to get them on board too.'

'Left your run a bit late then, didn't you?'

Mick struggled against their grip. 'They're coming to New Zealand with me. We are a family. My baby is half Kiwi. A New Zealand citizen.'

'Ship departs in two days.'

He dug his feet in, struggling against their combined strength.

Was the whole world against him? Were all doors closed?

His dream of their life in New Zealand, their new start, was slipping away. The dream that had kept him going on all those lonely nights.

He would conjure it up whenever things were too much. In his head he would plan it – a little house somewhere, maybe on the farm, but not near the main house, tucked away where they could be private and live their own way. Emiko would want to do the furnishing, she had a way with that. He felt sure floor cushions would replace the sofas and mattresses like futons instead of bed frames. She would be delighted at the selection in the shops and everyone would be delighted with her.

All he could think of was how he had failed her. She would have been better off marrying as her father had planned. He gave himself a mental kick. He had really let her down. Marrying a grump would surely be better than this, for her.

Nothing could be worse than this. He had ruined her life. But his fight was not finished yet.

He had to try everything. 'Give me a chance, I just need to pick them up. It's all arranged. There's enough time.'

'Not as far as I'm concerned. You're on the wanted list.'

'Do you fellas get paid for being unreasonable?'

'Better shut your mouth and get marching, soldier, or you'll have "resisting arrest" added to your charges.'

The other one spoke, his tone less threatening. 'If she's worth it, come back for her. Go home, sign off, and do it right. She'll wait. Japanese women love a Kiwi.'

Mick said nothing. That might be his only option. He had to think things through.

He began to admit his attempt to rescue Emiko was laced with obstacles and uncertainties. But he'd had to try.

What was the chance of her being well enough to leave the island, even to get out of bed and walk? She could barely open her eyes just the day before.

Entering the building unnoticed would be challenging enough. Escaping with Emiko and making it to the boat was another matter, even if the boatman was willing. The next challenge would be at the jetty. What if they'd got that far and he was arrested, forced to desert her there? The results could have been disastrous.

As logic took control, it dawned on him that the urgency to get Emiko out of the hospital was not only about making it to the ship together but about removing her from the influence and control of her father.

Strangely, he had to admit, she was being cared for now in a way he couldn't. He didn't like seeing her sedated, but it allowed her to sleep through the pain and heart ache, to heal and maybe – on some subconscious level – to relax about her destiny.

Her father had paid for that so she could eventually regain her health. Shouldn't he be thankful and not so impatient?

This process was about Emiko, not him.

Pulling in a calming breath, he walked more willingly. His escorts eventually dropped their hold on him.

The officer was right. He must think long-term, plan his return for Emiko. First, he must make sure she was all right and let her know his intentions. 'Can I send a message?' he asked suddenly.

'No special privileges for you, sunshine.'

'Tell you what,' offered the more senior of the two. 'Write a letter and we'll let you send it from the port.'

Dear Croc,

In trying to get my wife and daughter onto the ship, I have overstayed my leave, been arrested and will no doubt be under supervised duty on board 'till departure.

I need to enlist your urgent help.

Can you find Yodo-san and tell her where Emiko is? I don't know the island's name, but you know the jetty where you delivered me. Kazu can give more details.

Tell Yodo-san to explain to Emiko I will come back for her, where-ever she is, even if I must return to New Zealand first to sign off my military term.

My hands are tied, old mate. And so is my heart. With deepest appreciation,

Mick.

With the letter despatched to Kiwi base, Mick did the nearest thing he could to praying, asking the universe to get the letter to Croc quickly and for Yodo-san to speed to Emiko's side.

But for Karina, he could not leave her at the orphanage. His mind raced through a range of possibilities – and he settled on a plan, his only option.

He knew Brooks would be on board already and Noriko would be on shore, preparing to depart with her husband for their life together in New Zealand.

Dodging away before his duties began, he hunted for his mate, hurriedly explaining the situation.

'I must have faith that Emiko will be all right.' His voice caught. 'And you know I'm not that good when it comes to having faith.' He rubbed a hand roughly across his mouth. 'All I can hope is that Yodo-san is on the job and that Emi is soon well enough to speak for herself.' His eyes welled up, he shook himself to regain control. 'But my daughter can't.'

Brooks' lips clamped, showing he had no idea what to say.

'I'm thinking this – and it's a crazy notion, I know.' He turned to Brooks and lowered his voice. 'Noriko, as a woman, could adopt Karina.'

A frown creased Brook's brow. 'Adopt her…'

'I know. I know. It's a huge favour to ask. The only reason I can't get Karina is I'm male.' Mick spun around and began pacing, running a hand over his hair. 'I tried. Believe me, I tried.' He gulped at the memory of how he was escorted from Emiko's bedside, then from the orphanage and finally from the boat. His voice escalated in frustration and he slashed a hand into the air with each word. 'I – got – stopped – at – every – turn.'

Brooks reached out, dropped a hand on Mick's shoulder to steady him. 'Okay. Okay. I see what you're up against. I'll ask Noriko.'

'You will?'

'Of course. What harm can it do?'

'It's only temporary. As soon as we get home, I'll do the official thing. It's just to get her on board…'

'I know,' Brooks assured him. 'Don't worry, Mate.' He slapped his hand repeatedly on Mick's shoulder. 'You'd do it for me, wouldn't you, if the tables were turned?'

Mick looked directly at his friend. 'Without thinking.'

Brooks nodded. 'I'll keep you informed,' his tone suddenly official, as Mick was marched away by his supervisor.

The confinement duties didn't let up and Mick, under twenty-four-hour surveillance, could not put a finger out of place. The busyness of his manual tasks didn't stop his mind from reeling however, tormenting him with possibilities and what-ifs, every minute of the excruciating day.

He hashed and rehashed each heart-breaking possibility.

What could go wrong with the letter to Croc? He knew only too well the failings of the postal system. It might not get there in time – had he addressed it clearly? What if Croc didn't understand the urgency? He had written it under pressure, with his arresters impatient to deliver him to the ship.

What if Yodo-san was not available? What if she had been pulled back into the employment of Tanazawa-san? His heart leapt at the sickening thought of Emi's father taking control over her and her baby, sending them to that God forsaken island! Who would send anyone to such a place? For such a purpose? To have your daughter drugged and your grandchild forcibly removed, to become an orphan – a castaway.

Emi's weak voice echoed in his head. *Baby gone.*

He swiped a hand across his stinging eyes, trying to wipe the memories away at the same time.

Then the mental nightmare would begin all over again – no reprieve for his distressed mind when meticulous scrubbing and polishing kept his hands busy and his mind captive.

Mick barely held himself together the next day, and almost dropped with relief when Croc appeared in an officer's cap, pulling rank.

'Driver Mitchell?' he called as he approached.

Giving nothing away, Mick nodded.

'I'll take over here,' he said, dismissing Mick's supervisor with a wave of his hand.

Croc slung Mick's kitbag onto the floor at his feet, lowering his voice. 'You'll be needing this, Mate.'

Mick breathed out, shoulders slumping, chin wrinkling.

'So,' Croc found something to lean against. 'Here's the progress report. We got the island information from Kazu and the grandmother. Yodo-san went to the island last night. We can rest assured with all her ninja stealth, everything will be under control there.' He nodded, pressing his lips, and added quietly, 'Even if we can't get her out, just yet.'

Mick closed his eyes. 'So close. It's so close to getting them both on board.'

Croc continued. 'I understand Brooks' missus is going to the orphanage. That could happen – for the baby. But Emiko…' he blew out a loud exhale, fixing his stare on Mick. 'Maybe not this sailing, Mate. Gotta be realistic about her health. You know?'

Mick pulled in a shaky breath. He knew.

He had to accept that.

'I tell you,' he said. 'This is the worst bloody time to be doing menial tasks! Give me something to occupy my mind, help the time go by. But this bloody scrubbing and shifting stuff around – it's torture. I just keep rehashing the situation.'

'Don't like the duties, Mate?' Croc adjusted the cap, lifting his chin with a touch of arrogance. 'I'll fix that while I'm here.'

Mick was too tired to laugh but nodded his appreciation.

Their farewell much more formal than it would have been in a different environment, Croc left, telling Mick to get some shut-eye as he headed off to pull strings in adjusting Micks' duties.

Sleep, his first rest in over fifty hours, came in fitful bursts punctuated by dreams of better times and nightmares of possibilities far worse.

Departure day dawned with the haunting shadow of night still pressing on him. Thanks to Croc, Mick had been assigned duties on deck without much supervision, allowing him to join the crowd on the gangway from time to time.

Only the reality of Emiko's health complications held him from running the plank again, in a desperate bid to find her, get her on board. His previous effort had earned him a painful blow to the ribs with the butt of a rifle from the gangway guards, thwarting any further attempt to jump ship.

Croc's advice, becoming a mantra in his head, kept him from going insane with anxiety – *gotta be realistic about her health. Maybe not this sailing, Mate.*

When he did manage to shuffle his way to the railing where he could easily watch the comings and goings on the busy wharf, he strained for recognition in the puzzle of faces, scanning with determined optimism.

It was his only hope. His lifeblood. It kept him breathing.

***

Brooks appeared at his shoulder. 'Mitchell, you're required for duty in the quarters.'

'Tell me,' Mick demanded, his whisper harsh with anxiety as they negotiated the series of narrow passageways. 'Noriko is here.'

'And!'

'She has the baby.'

Raw emotion exploded somewhere inside him as Mick reached for his daughter, the lightweight bundle, so tiny he feared she would drift from his grasp.

His eyes pored over her, taking in every minute detail. He was in awe of this miniature version of Emiko, her expression twitching then smoothing as she slept.

'She's a little Emiko.' His throat choked and his eyes overflowed. 'So beautiful.'

He glanced to his friends, full of gratitude to Noriko for her willingness and success in getting his baby to him. 'I don't know how to thank you.'

Noriko's eyes glistened. 'You are welcome, Mick-san.'

The three of them stood transfixed by the tiny human in his arms.

'There were so many babies,' Noriko was saying. 'I wanted to bring them all!'

Brooks wrapped an arm around his wife. 'How did they identify – I mean, with so many, how do you know?'

'Her name on her basket.'

Brooks held back, not persisting with his question, his doubts.

Mick, knowing too well his mate's tendency to ferret out details, could only think of the positive.

This must be his and Emiko's daughter, Karina.

He could think of her no other way.

He studied the doll-like face, stroking her soft cheek with a fingertip, her skin satin-smooth to his touch. Emiko's skin. His fingers ran over her hair, silk threads the colour of black cherries, like Emiko's. Her sleeping eyes, fringed with long dark lashes, just like her mother. The rosebud mouth, pressed into a pout as she slept, like her mother.

His breath caught. The resemblance to Emiko was, simultaneously, delightful and unbearable.

Mick wrapped the loose folds around her, cocooning her against him, tucking in the long skirt which draped over her tiny feet like a christening gown.

Had Emiko made this gown for their baby?

Running a fingertip around the neckline where a loose bow held the garment closed, a loop of the ribbon caught and the bow came undone. The neckline curled open and just inside, almost invisible, tiny stitches in grey thread spelled out the initials *ETM. Emiko Tanazawa Mitchell.*

Double checking through misty eyes, he focussed on a loose thread. 'Emiko must have finished this in a hurry, with you arriving early,' he said to his daughter. 'It's not like your mama to leave needlework untidy.'

While realising the nonsense of his nervous chatter and the trivia of a loose thread, he rolled it between his fingers.

But it wasn't a thread. It was a fine silver chain, each link almost too tiny to see. He lifted it from where it was tucked inside the nightgown. As it came free, so did the pendant it carried.

The *pounamu* greenstone pendant he had given Emiko on their wedding day. The one his mother had given to him when he left New Zealand.

The baby's eyes drifted open, the gaze at first unsettled. 'Hello, Karina. I'm your daddy.'

She gave a little gasp at his voice, and turned, appearing to focus on him.

The love connection that moment, equal to only one other, pulled Mick forwards into his destiny, mesmerised by those beguiling eyes, dark pools the depth of a midnight onsen.

Chapter Sixteen

NEW ZEALAND 1947

**It is precisely the uncertainty of this world,
that makes life worth living.**
– Japanese Proverb

Two paddocks behind her and one more to go, Dorothy Mitchell glanced at the letter in her hand.

I have to tell Jack!

Her husband wasn't in sight yet, but she heard his tractor behind the row of trees and saw the cows heading that way. He would be feeding out winter hay.

She paused to catch her breath and tuck a spiral of hair behind her ear. It bounced out again. Why was it always that curl, the bit that hung over her eyes? Bad enough looking untidy, but did it have to be that bit, with silver threads. At her age. Far too soon.

Trudging up the creek bank, she pushed on, leaning her weight forward, working her reluctant legs in a way they were not used to any more.

Their farm under the mountain had a series of near-parallel icy streams instead of fences to separate the paddocks. At least Jack had put in planks for bridges, but crossing those required a balancing act.

The tractor came into view through the gate, Jack perched up high on the seat. She waved. He wasn't looking.

How could he miss her in this, her biggest, brightest, floral dress? Although a cotton caftan was not ideal for the New Zealand winter, it was warm enough with cosy under-layers, and allowed her to persist with the style of her Pacific homeland, the Cook Islands.

Holding up the letter, she waved it like a flag, side to side. Jack noticed her and started driving towards her over the rutted ground.

Her boots covered in mud, she stood in place while getting her breath back, so she could talk and read him the letter.

'Jack,' she called, long before he was within hearing, holding out the envelope as if he would get the message just by seeing it. The tractor rumbled towards her, came to a stop and Jack cut the motor.

'What, Dee? What's going on?'

She inhaled deeply, intended to shout the news, but her voice caught somewhere in her motherly chest.

'Mick! It's Mick…' was all she could get out, her face crinkling with the effort.

'Oh God, no!' He clapped a hand over his mouth and stared at her, seeing her tears.

'Not Mick! What, Dee? Tell me.' He jumped down from the seat and in two strides stood before her, grabbing at the envelope she held out.

But she wasn't crying. She was laughing.

'He's coming home!' she managed, her voice strangling with emotion. 'Home.'

She pulled the paper from its envelope and passed it to her husband. He fiddled with unfolding it, his labourer's fingers not used to fine work.

'His ship would have left on the eighth,' Dorothy summed up their son's brief note. 'So, he'll land in Wellington next week.'

The trusty tractor carried them back to the house, Jack taking care to avoid the worst bumps with Dorothy sitting on the tray behind him, cushioned inadequately on the remnants of hay.

Mick's news was enough for Jack to stop work and come back to the house for a cup of tea. Nothing else would warrant such a break in his routine.

The best china teapot came out. 'Just a little celebration,' Dorothy explained, warming it with hot water before spooning in tea leaves.

'Haw! Dee.' Jack was pulling his boots off in the doorway. 'He isn't even in the country yet and you're bringing out the good china.' He crossed the wooden floor in his well-darned socks, taking his usual seat at the dining alcove.

She carried the tray to the table. 'Next Thursday!'

'In Wellington?' He reached for a home-baked afghan biscuit. 'That letter took a while getting here. Just beat him home.'

She poured tea into their cups. 'Always does. You know how the mail is these days.' She pushed the plate of afghans towards him. One was not enough for Jack. 'You know, I thought we could go down. Meet his ship.'

'We wouldn't all fit in the car. Mick will have a bag or two, I'd imagine. And Samuel's so lanky, he takes up the back seat on his own.'

'We don't *all* need to go. Maybe just you and me?'

'What? Leave Samuel home?'

'He's not exactly a kid, Jack. But we could ask Jessica to stay over. Keep an eye on things.'

'You're right. He *is* nearly sixteen!' He pursed his lips and nodded. 'I guess we'd only be gone a day or two. Go down Thursday, meet the ship, find a bed for the night.'

'Let's make it two nights. We hardly ever get away. Would be nice to have some time in Wellington with Mick, before we drive back.'

She cradled the cup to warm her hands. It was over a year since their firstborn had volunteered to serve in the peace-keeping forces in Japan. Now she wanted him to themselves for a while. 'I'll book a place.'

'Somewhere close to the wharf. I don't want to be driving all around Wellington, trying to find my way.'

'Maybe Samuel can go to Jessica's after school on Thursday and they can both come back here Friday night. Jessica hasn't been back to stay since the wedding.' She looked down, pressed her lips, hoping the promise of the new baby would mend things after such a shaky start to their marriage. 'Don't think George's keen to visit us.'

'*Hmm.*' Jack never was one to complain. Dorothy knew he wasn't that thrilled about their son-in-law, but he said nothing rather than criticise.

'Maybe she'll come and stay more when she knows Mick is back – all the family together again.' Something warm glowed inside.

'Don't expect too much, Dee. Gotta let Jess and her husband make their own life now.' He reached across and patted her hand.

Even though he spent his days outdoors, Dorothy's Pacific Island skin tone would always be a few shades darker.

'I know. It would have been so much easier if she hadn't lost the first baby.' She pressed a hand to her mouth and steadied her breathing. 'The wedding – such a rush, and then the miscarriage. And I'm not sure George is that supportive. She still needs her family around.'

She topped up Jack's cup. He was patient with her when she took things to heart. He knew that family was the most important thing to her. It was her life.

'That's all history, Dee. They've got another one on the way now. Something to look forward to.' He smiled that warm, all-encompassing smile.

She knew he loved her and he always would. Time had taken its toll on them both. It didn't matter she had spread out over the years, expanding with each pregnancy, until most days her style of choice was the loose caftan that covered everything.

It was a good few years since sailing away from Rarotonga, yet she'd ended up just like the mothers and aunties she grew up with – always keeping the family together, the home fires burning.

'Something else.' She took a breath and blew it out. 'I think we could keep it a secret, Mick's return.'

'What? Not tell anyone? Not even Samuel?'

'That's what I'm thinking. He's a bit resentful these days, as if Mick's not part of the family any more.' She looked directly at Jack and knew he would defend Samuel.

'He was only fourteen when Mick left. Can understand he felt deserted with his big brother going so far away for so long.'

'It's more than that. And it's got worse recently.' She ran a finger along the gilt rim of the cake plate. 'I know he'll grow out of it, but I just don't want his grumbling to spoil things. So, can we keep Mick to ourselves for a bit?' She didn't wait for his answer because she had already decided. 'We'll just say we are taking a day or two away.'

Jack emptied his cup and carried it to the sink, heading back to work. Then he surprised Dorothy – turning and wrapping his arms around her. He was laughing. For a moment, it seemed he actually lifted her off the ground.

He was usually a controlled man – the strong silent type, as good as his word and not often given to affectionate displays. But when the moment caught him, for Dorothy it meant the world. Time dissolved. She would always be that young girl, in Jack's arms. His little frangipani, he used to call her. Sometimes, when the mood took him, he still did.

***

Dorothy waited till later in the day before calling Jessica, when she would be preparing dinner and not wanting to talk for long. Dorothy already knew what her daughter's response would be.

'What do you mean, you and Dad are going away?'

'Just a couple of days. We have some... business in Wellington.' Dorothy crossed her fingers behind her back. 'Can Samuel come to your place after school on Thursday, then he can go to school as usual on Friday and you can both come out home Friday afternoon? We'll be back on Saturday afternoon.'

'You've never done that before, gone away, you two.'

'That's true. So, don't you think it's time we did? It'll be fun for you and Samuel – and of course George is most welcome too.'

'You know he doesn't like the farm.'

'I'll make up both beds just in case.'

At least it gave her an excuse to be running around with bed linen and tidying the spare room, in case Samuel noticed.

They waited until Wednesday night to break the news and, as expected, Samuel protested. 'I don't need a babysitter!'

'It's not a babysitter,' Dorothy told him. 'It's your sister, and so you won't be stuck here – they have a car, in case you need anything or something goes wrong.'

'Nothing will,' he grumped.

'Good,' his father cut in. 'No harm in spending time with your sister.'

'Like the old days when you two were such good mates,' Dorothy added, not able to hide the tremble of nostalgia.

Samuel rolled his eyes and let out an exaggerated sigh.

Jack gave her a twitch of a smile, meaning *Don't overdo it, Dee.*

'Silly me,' she laughed, pressing a hand to her chest. 'I do miss those times when you were all young and we were one big family.'

'Don't blame me,' Samuel snapped. 'Mick stuffed that up when he pissed off to play soldiers. And Jess marrying that bonehead! Sure, hope he doesn't turn up.'

'It's unlikely,' Dorothy assured him, while hoping one day their son-in-law would fit into the family with less tension.

The next morning Dorothy watched Samuel step aboard the school bus before it roared off down the road towards the High School in town.

Now she could finish getting ready in peace. The dress and coat she'd bought for Jessica's wedding had been hanging in the wardrobe, untouched ever since. She lifted it down and wrapped her arms around its heavy warmth.

Spreading the outfit on the bed, she began undoing the buttons – big as half-crowns, covered in the same fabric as the coat, the colour of cranberry jam. The lady in the shop told her the design was the *swing style* – the latest fashion – with two extra buttons on a half belt at the back, doing nothing but showing off the pleat.

More expensive than any garment she had ever owned, Dorothy had been about to leave it on display in the shop, when Jack said, 'You get it, Dee! This is our daughter's wedding and be blowed if we're going to look like country bumpkins.'

So, she went all out and chose a hat the same colour. Just a rounded crown with no brim but it had a little black net which dipped down over her eyebrows then gathered up under a cluster of pink silk flowers at the side.

'Just the ticket!' Jack had grinned.

She bent over the bed, pulled open the coat and looked at the dress, which hadn't been so easy to choose. The latest dresses with their nipped-in waists were out of the question for a woman her shape, so she'd settled for something softly draping across the bodice with a full skirt falling loosely. A flash of deep pink and teal roses peaked out at the front when the coat flipped open.

Jack was already outside. She could see the car bonnet propped up. He would be checking the oil and water before the journey.

Dorothy stepped out of her housecoat and, forgoing the uncomfortable corset she had endured for the entire wedding day, wriggled into the dress. Coat, shoes, gloves, and finally – the hat, held in place with a pearl hat pin.

A look in the mirror reminded her of her daughter's big day, but swallowing that memory she turned her thoughts to Mick. She wanted to look her best for him. And this outfit was certainly her best.

She gave herself a little smile before picking up her small leather suitcase, locking up the house and heading to the car.

Jack looked out from under the car bonnet. Then he straightened up and grinned at her. 'Just the ticket,' he said.

Once they were on the road, she blew out a sigh. 'At last,' she said, more to herself than to her husband. 'This has been a very long week.'

Now there was no risk of being overheard she wanted to talk about Mick, but couldn't think what to say. What words would sum up this past year without him around?

Jack had not been happy when Mick said he'd signed up, but he was old enough to make his own decisions. Japan, he'd told them. Jayforce. Joining the post-war peace-keeping occupation.

'Japan! That's… a long way away,' she had said, trying to keep her voice steady.

'You did it, Mum. You left Rarotonga to come to New Zealand.'

She had been eighteen then and all she had thought about was her exciting adventure ahead. Not exciting for those left behind, though. Had her mother felt empty when she left, watching the ship leave? All the streamers and hooting and cheering when there was nothing at all to celebrate for those left behind – only a fractured family and breaking hearts.

She'd replied to Mick. 'But this is war, Son.'

'It's not war! They've surrendered. We're going to help them get back on their feet. They've been bombed to smithereens. The country is in ruins.'

Jack had said nothing. His lips were pressed tight. She knew what he was thinking. The propaganda. The rumours. The very real fear of an invasion on their own precious soil. All too recent and too raw to put into the past.

***

Now they could put all that behind them. She looked at her husband, his hands strong on the steering wheel, his eyes narrowed in concentration.

For Dorothy, the road trip to Wellington couldn't go fast enough. As the miles rolled by, she felt the cavern in her heart slowly mending.

Eventually she broke the silence. 'Mick's ship might already be in New Zealand waters.' She felt like a kid awake too early Christmas morning. Jack nodded and smiled at her. 'Maybe he can already see land,' she added.

Chapter Seventeen

Prepare for a thunderclap
from a clear sky.
– Japanese Proverb

Dorothy didn't mind the crush of people on the wharf, the uniting sense of purpose creating high-spirited camaraderie. She peered anxiously through the crowd, expecting to glimpse her son among the hundreds of uniformed soldiers, nurses and other military personnel jostling together along the ship's railings.

The massive, military vessel which had so cold-heartedly taken Mick away over a year ago now appeared benevolent and not at all scary.

She reached up to catch a streamer that fluttered nearby and laughed at herself. Jack laughed too. Hooters and whistles were sounding all around. People were waving flags and handkerchiefs. Somewhere a pipe band started up with *Auld Lang Syne*.

This time there *was* something to celebrate. Mick was coming home.

She continued to search the faces. Sometimes she had to look twice when something caught her attention, when someone called out on recognising their loved ones, but still she couldn't find Mick among the waving, laughing line-up.

For Dorothy it was both agony and ecstasy. Waiting, waiting. They all looked the same in uniform. 'Where's my boy?' she said into the crowd.

The woman beside her gave a smile. 'Hard waiting,' she said. 'My boy, too.'

Dorothy's eyes ached from squinting into the glare, so she looked down into the restful grey at her feet.

Then a shout came from the crowd, and another, and in a moment the whole wharf reverberated with the sound of cheering.

The barrier had been removed and the personnel moved forward, heading down the ramp.

Dorothy searched the faces again and again. No Mick yet.

An Asian-looking woman walked beside her soldier, his arm around her. 'War bride,' someone near them said.

Jack muttered, 'He better bloody not.'

Dorothy shot him a glance. *Don't start.*

More soldiers, more Asian women – some alone, some in groups. Then another line of soldiers. Dorothy strained her eyes, scanning the individual faces for something familiar in the line of identically uniformed young men.

A rally of shouts came from the wharf and a soldier shot out his arm, fingers spread, face laughing as he recognised his welcoming party. Another soldier, waving energetically, blew a kiss to his sweetheart who returned the gesture, tears streaming down her flushed face.

More soldiers, nurses and more welcomers erupted into cheering, laughter, flowing tears and, soon, long-awaited hugs.

Dorothy held up her arm, just in case Mick appeared next. 'He will be looking out for us.'

Jack raised his voice above the cheering. 'He doesn't know we're here.'

Her arm dropped. 'He would know. Surely, he would expect us to come.'

'He doesn't even know we got the letter yet, Dee.'

'That's right – he doesn't!' She pondered the situation then shrugged off any doubt. 'He'll know we'd be here, come hell or high water!'

But now, more anxiously, she squinted at the faces, wondering if Mick could have already arrived and they had missed seeing him.

The queue stalled again. 'Why don't those on the wharf step back – clear the way for them to get down the ramp?' she asked.

Jack looked down at her, his eyes misted. 'Would you, Dee?' He wrapped a heavy arm around her shoulders and gave her a jovial shake. 'Nah! You'll be pushing through the crowd just like them when you first see Mick coming down.'

A never-ending procession – sons and daughters, sweethearts and fiancés – appeared on deck and edged down the ramp, their eyes searching the crowd, their arms shooting up, their shouts ringing out when they recognised familiar faces.

Groups of reunited families – chattering, laughing, hugging – began to move away. The crush on the wharf opened up. Only a dozen or so groups remained.

Dorothy looked around anxiously. *Why were they still waiting?* 'Where is he?' She turned to Jack. He shrugged, his expression giving nothing away.

They moved forward.

The line on the ramp had become a trickle.

Still no Mick.

Dorothy clamped a hand to her chest. 'Where is he?' Her voice failed to hide her growing anxiety. Jack remained staunch but she saw tension in the way his brows knitted.

The ramp was empty when a young man in naval uniform appeared at the top. Stern-faced he scanned those still waiting.

Eying him suspiciously, Dorothy dragged in a shaky breath as a lump formed in her throat. 'What's he doing?' she muttered, her growing anxiety causing nausea to rise.

On reaching the bottom of the ramp he turned directly towards her and Jack. She gripped Jack's arm.

The sailor drew to a stop in front of them, addressing Jack. 'Are you Mr Mitchell?' Dorothy's heart thumped.

The soldier turned to her. 'Mrs Mitchell?' Her mouth went dry.

Jack said something.

The sailor lifted his hand and read from a paper in his palm. 'Parents of Michael Peter Mitchell?'

'Oh my God!' Dorothy grabbed Jack's arm. 'What's wrong? Mick's supposed to be on this ship. Has something happened? He should be on board this ship…'

Jack tapped her hand to halt the frantic outburst.

The sailor, his face expressionless, spoke again. 'Would you come with me please?' He spun on his heel and turned back towards the ship.

Dorothy's heart thumped so loud it pounded in her head.

'Hang on!' Jack reached out and gripped the sailor on the shoulder. 'What's going on?'

'I don't know, sir. Just following instructions to see if you were on the wharf – to bring you on board.'

'Whose instructions?' Dorothy's voice escalated. 'Where's our Mick!'

'I don't know anything, ma'am. Come with me, please.' Ignoring their persistent questions, he set off at a pace. They followed him up the gangway and along a series of dank corridors.

Dorothy, clinging to Jack's arm, struggled to keep up. Breathlessness prevented her speaking – but it didn't still her frantic mind.

Where was Mick – Was he sick – Were they going to see him in a hospital bed – Or had he failed to get on board – Had he fallen overboard! Oh no, not that, please! What had the weather been like lately – not rough at sea? Had Mick done something wrong – Was he being held prisoner? Not Mick, no. He's always so sensible.

They were ushered into a stark office with a bare desk and a semi-circle of upholstered club chairs.

'Take a seat please,' the sailor instructed and promptly left.

Too anxious to sit, Dorothy clamped a hand over her thumping heart and turned to Jack. 'What's going on!' Her frenzied voice rose in pitch. 'Something's wrong – I know something's wrong…'

Silent and grim, Jack began pacing.

Dorothy collapsed into a chair, grabbed her handkerchief, and covered her sobbing face. 'Where – is – our – Mick?'

The door opened. Three uniformed men came in.

Dorothy gulped back her sobs and struggled to her feet, dreading yet desperately needing an explanation.

Solemnly, the officer introduced himself, the chaplain and the young soldier.

'Mr Mitchell, Mrs Mitchell – I'm very sorry. We have bad news.' A guttural sound rose from Dorothy's core – her soul breaking.

Jack found his voice. 'Out with it.' He barked at the Officer.

'I'm afraid Mick… became ill soon after we left Kobe – he had sustained an injury which became infected…'

'Where is he?' Dorothy cried, refusing to accept what he said and fearing his next words more than anything else in the world. 'Take me to him.'

'I'm so sorry, Mrs Mitchell, Mr Mitchell.' He faced each of them as he spoke, then lowered his voice. 'He didn't make it.'

'No!' Dorothy reached for Jack. 'That can't be true!'

He wrapped his arm around her, pulling her in with a breath-taking force.

'No! Not Mick!' Her words disintegrated into desperate keening. Her knees buckled and she slumped against Jack.

The chaplain pushed up a chair as she collapsed into it.

Mick! Her firstborn. Her strong, brave boy. How could he… how…?

Suddenly she found her voice. Glaring at the officer, she spat her accusations. 'It's not possible! How come he got so sick?'

Her Mick!

Choking on her words, she pushed on. 'Did you give him the right medicine? Did you try? Did you sit up day and night and nurse him, like I did? Did you know how special he was? Did it even matter to you…?' Then her voice took on a strange tone – unearthly and desperate. 'Was it just another war casualty to you? Just another statistic?'

The chaplain spoke next. 'We're so very sorry, Mrs Mitchell, Mr Mitchell. We do understand your pain.' He pressed his fingertips together as if he was about to pray. 'But, if there could ever be a silver lining for such a tragedy, I can tell you – there is a little silver lining.'

'Don't tell me this is the way of God,' her voice rumbled. 'There is no God who would take our Mick.'

The Chaplain ushered the soldier forward. 'Let me introduce you to Ben Brooks. He was a very good friend of your son.'

The soldier shook hands with them both, solemnly offering condolences. 'Brooks has some… special… information for you.'

His voice thick with emotion, Brooks began. 'When Mick was ill, and when he started to think… that it was really serious, he asked me to write down what he said.' Brooks passed Jack the envelope he had been clutching.

'This may explain something,' The chaplain added gently, almost in a whisper, 'It was his dying wish…'

Pressing both hands over her mouth, Dorothy choked back rising sobs.

His face twisting, Jack opened the envelope and pulled out a single page. The chaplain offered to read.

Dear Mum and Dad,

I can't accept what the doctor tells me, but I agree that I am in a bad state, and not getting any better.

Today, I can't sit up and my fingers are too weak to grip the pen, so my best mate, Brooks, is writing what I am managing to say.

In case I don't make it home, there is something very dear to my heart, something I wanted to tell you in person.

I know this will come as a shock to you, that I was married in Japan to the woman I love, and that at the last minute her confinement delayed our dream coming true – that we would travel to New Zealand together and settle there. I plan to return to Japan and bring her home.

I wanted to tell you about it all in person, to explain the reasons for the path I chose, and if I don't get to, I am so sorry you are finding it out like this.

Also, on this ship, in the care of Brooks' wife, is our baby daughter. At least I managed to get her on board, and in my desperate attempts to get my wife on board, I received an injury which I'm told has turned septic.

The only consolation is I have thought many times how I would willingly die for my beloved wife. Maybe fate is taking that course – I can't tell you how much I wish it were not the case.

I'm running out of steam now, so will finish by giving you my only legacy – My daughter's name is Karina. I'm told she looks like me.

Will you take her home and bring her up as your own? I can think of no greater life than the one I have had. I want the same for my child.

I'm sorry, Mum and Dad. I have no other way... Your loving son, always,

Mick

Dorothy reached for Jack, his image swirling through her tears as she gripped his hand. He dropped into the chair next to her.

She called their son's name. Again, and again. 'Why…?' she demanded.

'How…? Mick… Mick! Why did he have to…?'

Jack mumbled wordless responses.

Hearing the pain in Mick's carefully chosen words, his fears, his brave acceptance of what might happen – made the harsh truth so real… so very, very raw.

Jack held her while she cried, gasped and blurted out questions, assumptions, any thoughts that ran through her scrambled mind, struggling – but failing miserably – as she tried to make sense of anything in Mick's letter.

Through her grief, through the black cloud, in the far reaches of her consciousness, she sensed a little glimmer of hope.

What was that?

Within the heartbreak, strangely, she felt it and struggled to recall the words – Mick's words, Mick's goodbye.

The fog of sadness overwhelmed her again. '… Didn't see him… didn't say goodbye… didn't… couldn't… no goodbye.'

Jack's hands moved over her back, the rhythm strangely comforting, soothing. '… should have been there… with him… take care of him… tell him…'

Her sobs exploded, filling the room, 'To say, we love him.'

She forced the fog aside, looked up at the chaplain. 'I – I don't understand – Mick has a wife? And a – child?'

Slowly Jack pulled away from her to stare at the floor, his expression a kaleidoscope of confused emotion. 'It's not true!' he rumbled. 'Mick would not get married… over there. Without telling us.'

Brooks spoke. 'It is true, Mr Mitchell.'

Dorothy shook her head. 'But why didn't he tell us? Why didn't he say in his letters home?'

'He wanted to tell you himself – to explain – to help you understand his reasons…' Brooks' voice faded, then he rallied and stated, 'He wanted you to know it was a proper church wedding.'

Dorothy nodded, her tears flowing again. She spoke through her handkerchief. 'He knew that would matter to us.'

'Doesn't make any difference,' Jack barked.

Dorothy felt a divide opening between herself and her husband. In grief, she already knew they coped very differently. He refused to accept and she needed to find the light.

'Is his wife… a kiwi girl, from the forces?' Dorothy ventured. Brooks shook his head. 'Japanese.'

Jack let out a low growl.

Brooks continued. 'Like my wife, Noriko,'.

'J-Japanese?' Dorothy's voice sounded thin. 'Mick married a Japanese girl?' She shot a look at Jack, his expression twisted and dark.

The chaplain stepped in. 'Would you like to see your grandchild?'

Dorothy shot a look at Jack, her voice fading to a whisper. 'So, the baby is…?'

'She's a beautiful wee girl,' the chaplain assured her.

Brooks nodded. 'She sure is. Noriko has become very fond of her – and taken really good care of her – she's a natural mother.' A softness crossed his face. 'I think it won't be long before we have our own.'

Jack jumped to his feet. 'Well, keep that one!' he barked. All eyes shot to him.

'Take the bloody half-caste,' he added. 'No use to us. Mick's not here...' He turned and strode across the room, his voice reverberating off the wall. 'How do we even know it's his?'

'Jack! Jack, no Jack!' Dorothy struggled to her feet, following him. 'She's Mick's baby.' Lowering her voice, wishing for privacy, she pressed on. 'It's all we have left of... him. It's his request...' She rallied and her voice found a tone of authority. 'We have no choice, Jack. We must take care of Mick's baby.' She rounded to face him. 'She's our grandchild.'

'You need some time to talk this through.' The chaplain signalled to Brooks. 'We'll leave you for a moment.'

The door clicked behind them.

'Bring it up as our own?' Jack spat out the words from Mick's letter. 'What? Pretend it's ours? How can we do that? Impossible, Dee.'

'No,' she pulled up to her full height. 'Not impossible.' She looked down at the voluminous folds of her dress. 'Only last week a shop assistant asked when I was due!'

He turned to her. 'What are you saying? Pretend you were expecting? All this time – and never told anyone?'

'It wouldn't be the first time. Women my age often conceal till the very last. There's so much at stake...'

Her mind raced and the room swirled. She reached for a chair and sat heavily, clamping a hand to her chest and dragging air into her lungs.

Eventually she spoke, allowing her grief and exhaustion to come through. 'I can't do all this alone, Jack. I can't deal with the news we've been given – Mick... and the baby... while arguing with you. I can't handle your narrowmindedness right now.' She let that settle. 'We can't change what has happened, Jack. You have to change your attitude. There's more to this than your feelings. You are not supporting me and you are not considering what Mick has asked us to do.'

Jack fixed his narrowed eyes on her for some time before heaving an exaggerated sigh, pulling another chair around to face her and lowering into it.

'We've lost so much.' She began, allowing tears to flow unchecked. 'The chaplain is right. This is a silver lining.'

Each consumed by their personal myriad of feelings and possibilities, they sat, until Dorothy's thoughts spilled out. 'We didn't tell them – Jessica and Samuel – why we've gone away. We didn't say anything about... Mick... coming back. We just said we'll bring back a surprise.'

Jack shot her a look, then retreated into his own world. She knew how he processed things. As a man of the land, he took his time – a day or two, a week, a month, a season... the next rain or the next dry spell. There was always a reason to wait and see.

There was a short knock and Brooks appeared. 'Can we come in?' He carried a large canvas bag which he placed against the wall, then turned to hold the door.

A diminutive woman walked in and stood at his side.

'This is my wife, Noriko.' Brooks introduced them. 'Mr and Mrs Mitchell.'

Dorothy got to her feet, attempting to smile. '*No-ri-ko?*' Immediately she noticed the tiny bundle cradled in Noriko's arms, a little body cocooned against her.

She was aware that behind her Jack remained staunch. She felt his tension, his conflict, his rejection of the entire situation.

Noriko's eyes filled as she focussed on the doll-like face. Her voice like tinkling bells, she spoke. 'I will miss her.'

She walked towards Dorothy, shifting her hold to pass the baby over as Dorothy's arms came out to receive, mother to mother.

Dorothy settled the featherweight bundle in her arms, overwhelmed by the delicate features, the dark lashes, the mouth curved into an up-side-down smile, so tranquil amid the life-changing event taking place around her this very minute.

Looking up at the young couple, Dorothy realised it could have been Mick and his Japanese wife she was facing, while holding her granddaughter for the first time.

She struggled to find her voice. 'Thank you for taking such good care of her.'

Noriko looked up at her husband, who put his arm around her shoulders and dropped a kiss on the top of her head.

Brooks pointed to the khaki kitbag. 'There's the baby things – milk formula, bottles, clothes – everything you'll need.' He seemed about to say something else until he caught Jack's moody expression, then quickly wished them well as he ushered his wife out the door.

The baby murmured and stretched in her sleep. Dorothy repositioned her hold, not taking her eyes off the tiny face, so engrossed she forgot about Jack in his black mood.

My first grandchild! Our granddaughter! Mick's baby – does she look like Mick? He said she does in his letter...

Her breath caught and she swallowed hard. 'If there's anything that will help us get over the loss of Mick,' – she astounded herself at being able to say those words – 'it's this dear little baby. Come and look at her, Jack!'

PART FOUR

1965

You were born with potential.
You were born with goodness and trust.
You were born with ideals and dreams.
You were born with greatness.
You were born with wings.
You are not meant for crawling, so don't.
You have wings.
Learn to use them and fly.
– Rumi

Chapter Eighteen

Eighteen Years Later
NEW ZEALAND 1965

Turn your face towards the sun
and the shadows
will fall behind you.
– Maori Proverb

Dorothy sat at the big family dining table in the recently extended farmhouse kitchen, peering out through the new bay window to the empty driveway.

Karina was coming home for the summer holidays – the end of her first year at teachers training college.

Dorothy couldn't wait!

Karina had been the best possible medicine to help heal their loss of Mick. His request that they raise her 'as their own' had been initially bundled up with their grief, but the busy life with a baby soon became a godsend. That secret had remained fast with her and Jack. While weighing heavily on her mind from time to time, Dorothy had managed to push it aside and eventually, Karina felt like her own child. Just as Mick wanted.

The baby's dark colouring and exotic features appeared very similar to their own South Pacific offspring, boosting their confidence that they could get away with the deception.

Jack had been particularly keen to keep Karina's true background hidden – that she was Mick's daughter from a match they knew nothing about and from a marriage that was not official in their eyes. Not to mention his, and nearly everyone else's, avoidance of anything Japanese after the war. Time had mellowed his prejudice, as global attitudes became more inclusive.

Surprised family and friends readily accepted the story of a deliberately concealed pregnancy, easily done by a woman with a mature figure, in a time when it was not socially appropriate to comment on any woman's shape. Dorothy had the added advantage of having always favoured the loose-fitting mumu-style caftans of her Pacific homeland.

They had contrived that on doctor's advice it made good sense to opt for a city hospital, better equipped than a local maternity hospital for a delivery considered more likely to have complications.

An elderly mother! Dorothy had quoted indignantly when telling the made-up story, using the maternity term for a woman over thirty.

That story had long since become their reality, the truth about Mick and his Japanese wife tucked away safely in their hearts.

The years had flown, and now Karina, already eighteen, had been away for a year, following her dream to train as a school teacher.

Her elder daughter Jessica and son-in-law George would be arriving any minute, after meeting Karina's bus.

Dorothy checked the driveway again – still no car.

At the kitchen bench, her second son, Samuel, added the finishing touch of mint leaves to a large bowl of fruit punch, his always-popular contribution to family gatherings.

Dorothy pressed a hand to her chest. 'Jessica said they'd be here about four.'

Samuel knew his mother's impatience when family was expected. 'Maybe Kari's bus from Palmerston North arrived late.'

She turned to look at her son, marvelling that he'd become such a family man, as his twin sons burst into the kitchen, falling at his feet in a tussle of arms and legs. Having grown up in the middle between sisters, one just a bit older and one much younger, he'd had his fair share of the complications of family life. Especially when Mick, his big brother and hero, joined the army and left for good – a rejection Samuel had taken personally.

Suddenly, Dorothy threw her hands in the air. 'Here they are!' She edged off the seat. 'At last.' She started across the kitchen, trying to pick her way through the flailing limbs and writhing bodies of the wrestling six-year-olds.

'Hey, boys!' Sam raised his voice to be heard over their racket. 'Boys! If you must wrestle inside, go into the next room where nobody will trip over you.'

The two froze, locked eyes, silent communication, agreement. They jumped up simultaneously and headed into the sitting room.

‘Mind my china cabinet,’ Dorothy called, reaching the back door. Mick’s photo and a few precious mementoes always had pride of place on the cabinet. ‘Don’t knock anything over,’ she added, heading down the steps, knowing she wouldn’t be heard.

Their four kids were so different, each to his own. Karina was the only one to leave home for further education. Different times now from when the others had finished school.

It had been hard having her go away to Teachers’ College, seeing the baby of the family leave. In some ways, in a sad way, it echoed Mick’s departure when he left for Japan. The oldest and the youngest moving away. Dorothy patted an embroidered handkerchief to her mouth and tucked it back in her apron pocket.

At least their middle two lived nearby, providing all the grandchildren she and Jack could handle. Jessica and George had Sarah the same year Karina had arrived, and a few years later Kevin came along. Samuel and Emma had the twins and now three-year-old Rosie.

Smiling to herself, Dorothy made her way along the path. There was nothing that filled her heart more than the family getting together. And here they were, bringing Karina home for the long summer break.

At the car, Jessica hefted a large carboard box from the boot. Her contribution, as usual, the dessert. ‘Hi, Mum,’ she said, bending sideways around her load to plant a kiss on her mother’s cheek.

‘Hello, Darling,’ Dorothy gave her daughter a one-arm hug.

‘Sarah’s coming a bit later, when she finishes work,’ Jessica explained, before Dorothy could ask why her granddaughter was not in the family car.

‘She’s driving by herself?’ Dorothy’s mouth twisted with concern.

‘She’s had her license over a year now, Mum. And her father made sure she got a reliable car. She drives herself everywhere.’

George carried a box of beer bottles. ‘Mum!’ he said, giving her a cheeky smile. ‘The bus came in late,’ he added, knowing Dorothy would have been waiting for them, anxious to see Karina.

Kevin, Jessica’s and George’s second child, bounced out of the back seat.

‘Give your aunt a hand with her case,’ Jessica instructed. He bounded around the car to the other side and began pulling on the handle of the suitcase, now wedged between Karina’s lap and the car roof.

‘There you are, Darling,’ Dorothy exclaimed, trying to see Karina in the jumble.

Karina let out a hiss of air. 'Ouch, Kevin! That won't work. It needs to go out the other side.' She pushed the case off her lap onto the seat beside her as Kevin spun around to face his grandmother.

'Hi, Gran,' he said, good naturedly, pausing to plant a kiss on her cheek. 'You're getting shorter, Gran.'

'You're getting bouncier, Tigger,' she responded.

He gave her a twisted smile. 'Really, Gran? Don't you think I've outgrown Pooh Bear yet?'

She managed a friendly pat on his back as he brushed past. 'Never too old for Pooh Bear.'

'*I'm* not too old,' Karina called, emerging from the car. 'I've joined a Pooh Bear Book Club at college.'

'Have you, Darling.' Dorothy reached for her baby, pulled her in, held her tight. 'At last, you're ho-,' her voice caught. She drew a steadying breath. 'Home.'

Arm in arm, they followed the others along the path to the house, Dorothy hardly taking her eyes off her girl, her heart swelling. 'You've got taller,' she couldn't help saying. 'Grown up a bit.'

They piled into the kitchen; boxes, bowls and bags covering every inch of the bench, every corner of the floor.

Samuel greeted his younger sister with a huge hug and exchanged play-punches to shoulders with his older one.

For once Dorothy didn't supervise where things should be put and who of her grandchildren hadn't yet greeted their cousins, aunts and uncles. She was focussing on her youngest, watching her being welcomed back into the arms of the family.

It was almost overwhelming to have her home again. She grabbed the handkerchief again and pressed it to her mouth.

Jessica took over the organisation while ladling herself a cup of punch. 'Kevin, don't put Karina's suitcase there in the middle of the kitchen. Carry it to her room.'

'Which is her room?' he asked.

"Really?' Jess made a stand, hands on hips, glaring at him. 'Think about it, Kevin.'

'I'll take it,' Karina offered. 'I need to unpack some things and get changed.'

'Then, go and get your Poppa,' Jessica instructed her son. 'Go anywhere out of the kitchen. And take your cousins with you. Seems they have some energy to spend, too.' The twins had returned to wrestling, having paused momentarily to say hello.

'Good idea,' Dorothy added, ushering them outside. 'Poppa's probably near the hay shed. Go and find him. Tell him nearly everybody's here.'

Samuel carried the punch bowl to the tea trolley parked against the wall, pushing his big sister aside as she reached over him to refill her cup.

'I'll pop over home to see if Emma needs a hand,' he said. 'Rosie's been digging in her toes a bit lately. Won't get dressed, won't have her hair brushed, won't stand up. Thinks she's a cat, crawling around the floor, meowing.'

'Never mind,' his mother said. 'We could do with a cat. Even a scruffy one. We'll love her just the same.'

He gave a half laugh. 'I thought the twos were terrible enough. Now we've progressed to the thrilling threes. Can't wait for the fabulous fours.'

When Samuel and Emma had become engaged, they'd built a house on the farm, so Sam could keep working with Jack and eventually take over the farm when he retired. That time had come, although they all laughed at the suggestion of Jack retiring. They knew that would never happen. It was more a case of switching roles, with Sam on management and Jack being the right-hand man, no doubt still having a good deal of say about the way things should be done.

When Karina reappeared in the kitchen, Dorothy wrapped an arm around her, guiding her to a chair at the table, like an honoured dinner guest. Jessica ladled out three cups of punch and they joined Karina at the big table.

'Where's George?' Dorothy asked.

'You know him. Found a quiet place for himself and his bottle of beer, no doubt.'

'Do you know what I love about coming home?' Karina said suddenly. 'It's predictable! The twins will be wrestling, Dad will need fetching from the farm, Sam will make punch. You Jess, bring a load of dessert, and Mum has a big roast in the oven.'

'Kevin's energy doesn't reach his brain,' Jessica added, 'and George is the smartest of us all, hiding somewhere with a drink until the meal is ready,' she added with a laugh.

Dorothy held up her glass cup for a toast. 'Here's to our wonderful family! We love them all!'

'Family,' Jessica said.

'To you, Mum and Dad,' Karina said.

'And here's to Mick,' Dorothy added quietly. 'Bless him.' She took another sip.

Jessica reached across, rested her arm around her mother's shoulders. 'There's always that missing piece, isn't there?'

Dorothy swallowed hard. *Mick.* She took a heavy breath and blew it out. Over the years she had rationalised it. Mick had gone, Karina had come. Lost one, gained one. Not the same, but better than nothing.

'How's teachers' college?' Jessica asked Karina.

'Great! I love it. Miss home though.' She gave her mother a screwed-up smile. 'But I think that will get easier in the second year. And since I've got a part-time job, keeps me busy weekends and term holidays. Saving my money.'

'And you've got good friends?' Dorothy voiced her main concern.

Karina smiled, nodded. 'It's so sociable. Like being in a big family – huge family.'

'And now you're home, with your real family,' Dorothy added, resting her hand over Karina's. 'How long is your summer break?'

'About two months. And I have a plan!' She gave a mischievous smile. 'But I'll wait till Dad is here.'

Excited jabbering voices came into hearing as the grandsons escorted Jack back to the house, all talking at once.

'Speak of the devil,' Dorothy joked, as she heard her husband's voice.

'Is that so?' Jack was saying, in reply to any and all comments fired by the boys. 'Go on, there! You don't say!'

Karina got to her feet, as the familiar thump, thump thumping sound reverberated from the back steps, Jack kicking off his boots in preparation to enter the house.

'Where's my little girl?' he called out, with Karina only a step in front of him. 'Come here, you!'

He held out his arms and she fell into his huge embrace. She, laughing, he looking a bit choked up. Dorothy joined them, wrapping arms around both and calling on Jessica to complete the huddle.

The four of them had only a moment of nostalgia before the twins caught on. Seeing an opportunity to cause chaos, they came running, connecting with the group and pushing like a rugby scrum, the grown-ups not resisting too much. All six of them were soon scuttling sideways across the kitchen floor like a giant crab.

'That's enough,' Jack called out, before they were squashed against the wall. Samuel arrived just in time to peel his sons away. The cluster disassembled, laughing, crying happy tears and gasping for air.

'Oh, dear me,' Dorothy said, fanning her face with one hand and tousling the twins' hair with the other.

George turned up, looking pleased with himself. Jack sent him to retrieve and replace a couple of bottles from his beer chiller in the creek – a tin tub wedged between rocks, kept perpetually cool by the swirl and swish of the mountain stream.

'I'll go and clean up,' Jack said, which would involve washing his hands right up to the elbows with substantial lather, running a comb through his dark crop of hair and changing his shirt to a clean one, still with a plaid pattern or stripes no doubt, but a finer cotton, ironed smooth and crisp by Dorothy.

Emma, Samuel's wife, arrived carrying a large casserole, followed by a crawling, meowing Rosie. 'Don't walk on your sister,' she called to her sons as they scrambled past, heading outside to avoid the playful threat of their father's hand.

Greetings complete, the grown-ups settled around the table, the women with topped-up cups of punch, meowing Rosie at their feet. Jack flipped the cap off a large bottle of beer, still dripping with creek water, icy cold. He poured glasses for the three men.

'Welcome home, Kari!' Jack said, raising his glass to their youngest, his smile saying it all.

They echoed the toast in various versions, smiling, drinking.

'Ah, that's good,' Jack said, smacking his lips, as he always did. 'Nothing like a cold beer to quench your thirst.'

'See what I mean?' Karina burst out, pointing to her bewildered father. 'Predictable! I love it.' She raised her glass. 'There's no place like home.'

'What? What did I do?' Jack looked affronted.

Dorothy laughed and reached her hand to his. 'Nothing, Dear. It's just Karina was saying before how she loves coming home – it's so… comforting – that our family is so… predictable.' She looked at her younger daughter. 'That's what you said, isn't it?'

Jessica jumped in. 'Yes, well summed-up, Mum.'

'How long's your summer break, Kari?' Samuel asked.

'About two months…'

'Oh, and,' Dorothy interrupted. 'She's got some exciting plans.'

Jack put his glass down. 'What's that, Kari?'

'We-ell,' Karina began, deliberately building the suspense, everyone now looking her way, waiting. 'You know how I'm studying childhood development?'

The response was a mixture of nods, shrugs and blank stares.

She continued. 'One of the things we're looking at is nature and nurture.' Many more blank stares.

'We've been talking about family backgrounds and why we are like we are.' Samuel was getting impatient. 'What are you trying to say, Kari?'

'I know about nature nurture,' Jess joined in. 'It's about what you learn growing up and what's in your family genes. Like family strengths and traits and weirdness and nutcases.'

'Hah,' Samuel laughed. 'Like the black sheep of the family.'

Karina called the attention back to herself. 'I – was – saying…' She turned to her mother. 'Mum, have you ever wanted to go back to the Cook Islands?'

Dorothy looked blank.

Karina continued in a rush. 'All I'm learning about heritage and ancestry has made me curious. I want to know more about my extended family, and I want to go to Rarotonga – with you. Find my grandparents, learn about my heritage.'

Dorothy shot a look at Jack, his eyes already fixed on her.

The twins burst in the door laughing. 'Ke-vin's dru-unk, Ke-vin's dru-unk,' they chanted.

'What? Better bloody not be.' Jessica jumped to her feet, sending the chair flying back, then suddenly gripping the edge of the table. 'Shit, Sam, what's in that punch? It's gone straight to my knees.'

'Yeah, sorry,' Samuel replied with a grin. 'I was a bit heavy handed with the sherry.'

'Take it easy,' George said, waving for his wife to sit down again. 'I'll go.'

She remained standing, leaning on the table, eyeballing him. 'Did *you* give him beer?' she accused.

'Nah,' he laughed. 'But he's fifteen. Not surprised if he found some.'

Jack looked amused. 'Has he found my chiller in the stream?'

'Yup,' one of the twins said. 'He's down the creekbank.'

'Singing,' the other continued.

'Badly,' the first added.

'I'll go,' Jack said, getting to his feet.

'I'll come too,' Dorothy said, grateful for an excuse to escape, buying herself some time to process Karina's suggestion.

'Sit down you two,' she said to Jessica and George. 'Neither of you would pass as a good role model, right now.'

Samuel followed with a quip, Jessica retaliated, George let out a whoop and Rosie the cat crawled off her mother's lap onto a vacated chair, meowing again.

The twins started to lead the way down the creekbank track until Jack called them back, sensing his wife's need to talk in private. 'Go up to the house paddock,' he directed the boys. 'See if the chooks are all in the henhouse. If not, get them in, before it starts getting dark.' The boys changed direction, charging up the track past them and out of sight.

'What am I going to say?' Dorothy hissed, '– to Karina.'

Jack huffed out a long breath, slowing his pace so they could talk before they reached Kevin. 'Remind her you don't like flying. That explains why you've never been back there.'

'Then she'll go by herself. I can see that look in her eyes. When she gets an idea, nothing will stop her. Like going to teachers' college, when it was the last thing *we* wanted.'

'She does make up her own mind,' he agreed.

'I'm afraid if she goes to Raro,' Dorothy persisted, 'she'll find out more than she should. What if it doesn't stop there – her search for family connections? What if she doesn't get the answers she wants, what if…' her words trailed off. She'd never voiced her greatest fear – that Karina accidentally finds out the truth about her parents.

'They won't notice a thing. We've got this far – eighteen years and no-one has suspected.'

'I think I've always been a bit anxious someone might, though. And sometimes I wonder if maybe we should have done it differently. Told everyone the truth.' She pulled in a shaky breath and huffed it out, needing to calm her thumping heart. 'But then, Karina has always been ours.'

Dorothy reached out for Jack's hand. 'I'm just not sure I want to keep lying to her.'

'It's not a lie, Dee. It's solid gold. Nothing will change that. Ever.'

'But, you know, Jack. It's different these days. People can find out about their real parents. Adopted people can. I read in my magazine about a girl who knows both her mothers, and it's all right with them all. There's even an agency where you can search family records. What if Karina did that?'

'Why would she, Dee? She's got no reason to suspect anything. No-one has.' Jack turned and continued down the track, the conversation over, as far as he was concerned.

'I suppose you're right,' she agreed, coming close behind him as he reached the bottom of the slope.

Turning along the edge of the creek, they could see Kevin just ahead, perched on the grassy creekbank, partially concealed in the scrub.

'There you are, boy,' Jack called in a friendly tone.

Camouflaged by his khaki gear, their grandson hunkered down, looking flushed and sheepish, arms wrapped around his drawn-up lanky legs. The story *Toad of Toad Hall* flashed through Dorothy's mind, a wayward but likeable giant frog.

'I do worry though,' she continued, in loud whisper. 'I've thought a thousand times, what have we taken away from Mick, from his memory? And while she was growing up, Karina not knowing the truth.'

A scuttling sound from behind caused Dorothy to freeze.

'Truth about what?' Karina said, materialising from the undergrowth.

Dorothy swung around. 'Where did you come from?' she exclaimed, giving vent to her shock, clamping a hand over her racing heart.

'Down the shortcut,' Karina said, pointing directly up the steep incline. 'The Truth about what?' she repeated.

Oh my God! She heard! How much did she hear?

Dorothy called out, needing an ally to subdue her panic. 'What were you saying, Jack?' *Change the subject!*

Jack swung around at the tone in her voice, saw his wife looking distraught, Karina standing directly behind her on the narrow track, curiosity written all over her face.

'Err,' he began, scanning the situation. 'Kevin's right here,' he called. He turned to his grandson, raising his voice another notch. 'You right there, mate?' He held out a hand and Kevin grabbed it, awkwardly getting to his feet.

'There you are, Kevin,' Dorothy said with forced gaiety. 'Soon be dinner time.' Leaving no room for a repeat of the question, she spun to face Karina, immediately ushering her ahead. 'You lead the way,' she said briskly. 'It's follow-the-leader on this track.' Hanging back until Karina gained some distance, she started off slowly, hoping beyond hope that her daughter would forget whatever she had overheard.

The other two came scrambling along behind, Jack giving Kevin cheerful encouragement, bloke to bloke.

Dorothy struggled to think up a different answer, should Karina ask again what they were talking about, but her scrambled emotions prevented clarity of thought.

The twins came running to meet them at the top of the track, shouting to their grandfather that they had got the last of the chooks shut in for the night. Then grabbing Karina by the arms, they pulled her to visit their treehouse.

Dorothy hurried back to the kitchen, intent on getting the dinner on the table.

Jack, having sat Kevin down on the back steps with a large glass of water in his hand, retrieved the folding camp table from storage, and passed it to George and Sam, giving them the task of setting it up in the corner of the kitchen for the kids.

Jessica washed and dried the punch cups and glasses, returning them to the table for mealtime toasts. Emma set the big table and Jack rummaged for his carving tools, taking his place at the head of the big table, ready to go to work on the roast Dorothy had removed from the oven.

'Which plates?' Emma asked.

'Already in the warmer.' Dorothy had got Jack to lift down the best china from the top shelf before he went out to the farm that morning. 'Leave them there for a bit.'

'Mint sauce?' Jessica asked.

'In the fridge,' Dorothy answered. 'We've been getting ants, lately.'

'Why would they want mint sauce?' George had already claimed his place at the table. 'It's not sweet.'

'Yes, it is,' his wife replied. 'Look at the label.' She held it annoyingly close to his face. 'Sugaaar.'

'Get out of it.' He pushed her hand away. 'I don't care if it's got ants. Don't like the stuff anyway.'

‘Ready for plates,’ Jack called. Emma grabbed the oven cloth, wrapped it around the gold-rimmed dishes, and placed the pile on the table beside the roast. Jack layered large slices of mutton onto each plate, Emma and Dorothy distributing them to the place settings. For the kids it was plastic plates from the picnic set and the meat cut smaller.

‘Get the kids,’ Dorothy instructed. ‘From the treehouse.’

‘I’m onto it,’ Samuel replied, heading out the door to track down his sons.

Rosie, now walking and no longer meowing, was given the job of setting plastic tumblers at each place on the camp table and distributing the cutlery.

‘Where’s Kevin going to sit?’ Dorothy asked. ‘He’s too tall for the kids table.’

‘Think he might be good on the back steps,’ Jessica answered, with a twisted smile. ‘I’ll take his out to him.’ She lifted the lid off Emma’s casserole dish, at the centre of the big table, ladling out a good scoop of vegetable hotpot for her ever-hungry son. Emma followed with smaller portions for the kids’ plates.

Samuel arrived back, ushering his boys to their table where their sister had appointed herself in charge.

‘Sarah has arrived,’ Jessica announced, returning from delivering Kevin’s meal outside.

‘Just in time,’ Dorothy called, pausing to exchange cheek kisses with her granddaughter. ‘Hello Sweetheart! Come in, find a seat.’

Greetings exchanged, they all shimmied around the table.

Under normal circumstances Dorothy would be determined to sit beside her youngest but she wanted to avoid encouraging any further conversation about family history.

Jack seemed to read his wife’s anxiety, as she shuffled the seating arrangements. ‘Kari, over here,’ he called. ‘Head of the table for the guest of honour!’ Karina made her way around and took the seat beside him.

‘Mum, you can be at this head,’ Sam said, pulling out the chair at the other end, playing right into her hand. Dorothy paused, making sure everyone had a place, before taking the seat beside him.

‘Before we start,’ Jack called out, getting to his feet.

The twins groaned and dropped their poised cutlery with a clatter. ‘Hey!’ Sam called across the room to his sons. ‘Mind your manners.’

Jack started, ‘While we’re all here together…’

'Oh God, Dad,' Jessica interrupted. 'You're not going to say grace, are you?'

'Oi!' Sam pulled her up. 'No more punch for you!'

'Mind your own beeswax,' she retaliated.

'You two!' Dorothy hissed. 'Manners! Both of you.'

Jack waited patiently, his air of authority eventually silencing the rabble. 'This is a special occasion for a few reasons. Of course, Karina is home for the break.'

Samuel lead the cheers. 'Hip-hip-hooray.'

'And me,' he paused. 'You all know I've been under a lot of pressure from certain members of my family this year.'

Dorothy feigned concern. Samuel laughed. Others enjoyed the pantomime.

'They tell me I'm getting too old! But I don't want your pity… it's not all bad.'

More laughter and heckling.

Jack continued. 'So, this old man is stepping back and Samuel is taking over the farm management. While I have severe concerns about his ability…'

'Yeah, right!' Samuel laughed.

'I'm going to be in the enviable position of complaining about everything *he* decides – for a change.'

They all laughed. The cheers were repeated.

'And, on a little more serious note.' He paused, looking to his wife. The room hushed. Dorothy held his gaze.

'We usually say something to include Mick.' Heads nodded, eyes downcast.

'There is something we will talk about later, to do with Mick. But that's for later. Now, let's eat!'

Chattering filled the room. Requests for things to be passed across the table, instructions to the children to sit down, eat up and leave their siblings alone – general dinnertime mayhem prevailed. Dorothy began to relax and revel in her most favourite event of all time – the family gathering.

After the main course finished, she organised the clearing away and making table room for the dessert.

'Kevin didn't eat anything,' Jessica announced, returning to the kitchen. 'He must have sneaked in through the front door and is now sleeping like a baby in the boys room. George's taken up the other bed to keep an eye on him.'

After the meal Jack and Samuel gave in to pressure from the boys for a game of cricket on the lawn.

'They say women talk a lot,' Dorothy said. 'It's certainly a lot quieter with those men and boys outside!'

'Karina and Sarah sidestepped the cricket invitation and took themselves away for the sort of catch-up girlfriends need to do in privacy.

What's Dad going to say about Mick?' Jessica asked, as she and Dorothy stood before the sink, a mountain of dishes on both sides.

Dorothy let out a heavy breath. 'We've just redone his photo and freshened up the cabinet top.'

Emma appeared beside Dorothy. 'Gran, can we swap places? Rosie wants you to show her your old dolls. I can take over here.' Her daughter-in-law undid Dorothy's apron ties, pulling it off and re-tying it on herself.

Dorothy took Rosie by the hand, happy to leave the stack of dishes to the younger women. 'Now, where are those dolls?' she asked her youngest granddaughter.

'In the cupboard, Silly,' Rosie giggled.

'Don't talk to your grandmother like that,' Emma reprimanded.

'Well, she is silly.'

'Yes, I am! Can you show me, Rosie? I should know where they are. They've been there for so many years…'

After half an hour of dressing and undressing the dolls, and finally tucking them into the boxes that became beds, Rosie returned to her mother, ready for her own bed.

Emma scooping up her daughter – now too tired for meowing, called to her husband as she stepped outside. 'Those boys can jump in the bath before they go to bed. They'll be covered in grass and mud.'

'I'm onto it,' Sam agreed. 'Then I'll come back for a cuppa,' he called to his mother, who stood at the doorstep watching them go.

The kitchen was tidy when Jack and Sam drifted in from outside.

Karina and Sarah emerged from the bedroom, their conspiratorial connection renewed.

It was adult time – the slower, gentler end of day as the family gathered in the sitting room, the day's work done and the youngest in bed.

Cups of tea passed around, Dorothy and Jack settled into their adjoining armchairs. As always, Karina perched on her mother's armrest, Sarah squishing in beside her mother and uncle on the sofa.

'What did you change with Mick's photo? Is that a new frame?' Jessica asked, turning to the display on the china cabinet.

Dorothy nodded. 'The other one was twenty years old.'

Jessica shook her head. 'Can't believe it's twenty years since he left.'

Jack got to his feet. 'Now you're all comfortable – as your mum said, it's twenty years since our Mick left home.' He paused. 'We wanted to recognise that with a little memorial. Dee reframed Mick's photo, as you see, and I made a display case for his matchbox cars collection.' His throat caught but he continued. 'Gave them all a touch of paint.'

Dorothy couldn't look up, her fingers pressed to trembling lips.

Sam moved to examine the display. 'That's great, you two.' He studied the face of his big brother about ten years younger than his own age now. 'I saw you doing this, Dad,' he said, examining the glass-lidded display box of miniature vehicles. 'They look like new, each in their own little compartment. Funny how the army truck was his favourite.'

Dorothy nodded, the room now a blur through her misting eyes.

'I made something too.' Sam reached under the sofa, retrieving a varnished wooden box. 'I made this – as a case for all Mick's letters.' He turned to his mother. 'I know you kept everything he wrote home, Mum. I've always known his letters were in that old shoe box hidden under the floorboards of the wardrobe.'

Dorothy clamped a hand to her chest. Eyes widening, she pulled in a shaky breath.

Sam continued. 'I knew they must be deteriorating there. So, I made this, to keep them safe.'

He tipped the box to her, showing '*Mick'* artfully engraved on the top, framed within the curl of a leafy vine. A tiny brass padlock held the lid fast.

Sam reached in his pocket, retrieving two carved wooden shapes, one a heart, the other a diamond, each dangling a small brass key on a fine chain. 'This is yours, Mum.' He bent over to kiss her cheek, placing the heart keyring in her trembling hand. 'And yours, Dad.' He turned to his father, passing him the diamond one.

The men's hands met in a strong grip which held fast long after the handshaking ended. Their eyes locked, reflecting the emotional exchange, their silence saying much more than any words ever would.

Samuel turned back to his mother, placing the wooden box in her lap. She gripped it. 'Are my letters… in here?' She looked up to see him nod, her voice breaking away. 'Did you look at them…'

'No, Mum. I know how personal they are.'

Jessica reached up to pat her brother's arm as he returned to the sofa. 'Why didn't you tell me you were all doing something? I would have too.'

'We didn't plan it, Dear,' Dorothy said, her voice frail. 'I had no idea Samuel was up to this.' She held the box tight, her fingers tracing the etched lettering and following the vine.

'You can still do something if you want,' Samuel suggested. 'There's no right time.'

'And it doesn't have to go on the china cabinet,' Dorothy added quietly. 'We could do something together, as a family. Like a garden bed or an outside memorial.' Her voice faded, but she rallied and continued. 'After all, we don't have a grave…' – her words dissolved as she pressed her handkerchief to her mouth.

Karina leant over, wrapping arms around her mother. 'That's a good idea, Mum,' she said, sounding upbeat. 'Let's think about what we could do in the garden.' She rubbed her fingers over the box lid. 'Mick,' she read. 'Sometimes I feel really sad that I never knew him. And he was my big brother.'

'Hey, hey!' Samuel interjected, faking offense. 'What about me? This big brother?' He raised both fists, pointing his thumbs towards himself.

'Thank God,' Jessica exhaled. 'Someone's adding a little light to the situation. The way I see it, we can all be morbid or we can get on with life.'

Faces turned to her. 'What are you all looking at me for?' she protested.

Jack spoke. 'I think there's a place for both.' He held up his keyring. 'Samuel, thank you for this. It's very special, and I know your mother already loves having those letters in a safe place.'

'Open it, Mum,' Karina said. 'See if the key works.'

'Not now, Dear.' Dorothy locked her arms around the box. 'His last letter is… too much, at times. He was coming ho –,' her voice broke up before she finished the word. It always got her, the word *home.* He never made it, so she couldn't say it.

Jack moved back to his armchair beside his wife. Sinking in, he reached for her hand, brought it to his lips and pressed it there.

Jessica persisted. 'Did you plan to go to Wellington to meet him?'

'We did want to,' Jack said eventually.

'Let's play cards,' Dorothy intercepted, getting to her feet, holding the wooden case to her chest and tucking the heart-shaped keyring into her apron pocket.

'Thank you, Samuel.' She bent over him, dropping a kiss on the top of his head. 'This is so special.' She turned away and headed out the door.

'Where are you going, Dee?' Jack called to her. 'Put it on the cabinet with the other things. Samuel made a real good job of that. It should be on display too.'

Dorothy turned in the doorway, answering slowly. 'I – I want to keep it safe in the wardrobe, like before.'

Jack shook his head. 'Should be on display. It's Samuel's contribution to Mick.'

Dorothy hesitated, blew out a tired breath and carried the case to the cabinet, rearranging the other mementos to make room.

Then she rummaged in the cabinet's top drawer, holding up a double pack of cards. 'Anyone for five hundred?'

Chapter Nineteen

Three things cannot be long hidden –
the sun, the moon, and the truth.
– *Buddha*

Jessica's competitive edge won over as usual, and she and her father were declared outright winners of the card game against their mother and Samuel.

Karina and Sarah had been privy to many such adult gatherings from their very early years, tucked up on the sofa until slumber enveloped them. Obviously happy to be the 'big kids' again, they huddled together under a blanket, pawing over their high school yearbooks in whispered conversations, reliving their days as schoolmates until a year ago – aunt and niece, similar in age, more like cousins.

Sleepovers were frequent and tonight would be no exception, Sarah having already claimed the twin bed she had always referred to as *my bed* in Karina's room.

George and Kevin were sound asleep in the boys' room, there to stay.

Returning from the linen cupboard with an armful of blankets, Jessica announced her claim of the sofa, large and cushiony – a popular place for overnight extras to doss down.

Their parents bid goodnight with hugs and kisses.

Samuel, before heading home, decided to put on the kettle for one last cup of tea.

'I'll have a cuppa too,' Jessica called to her brother in the kitchen as she settled onto the sofa with the girls, pulling a blanket over her feet.

Sarah nodded towards the display cabinet. 'So, what's in that case Uncle Sam made? Is it just Uncle Mick's letters?'

Jessica pulled in a breath, tensing her neck muscles. 'I don't know. You'll have to ask him.'

'And why is Gran so weepy, after a whole what, twenty years?'

Karina answered. 'She's always like that – it's just her. She cries even when she's happy.'

Sam returned passing Jessica her tea then settled into their father's armchair.

She blew into the cup. 'Think it's getting worse, not better, as the years go by.'

Sam looked up. 'What is?'

'Mum, all weepy. And the secrecy about those letters.'

'Yeah. It's hard to know what to do. I knew making the box would set her off but I'm sure she's happy to have her letters in a safer place.'

'*Her* letters!' Jessica shot a look at her brother.

Sarah persisted. 'Why are those papers so secret? Did you see the shocked look on her face when you said you'd found them in her wardrobe. I thought she would explode.'

Sam shrugged. 'I guess it's just that his letters are all she has, especially the last one… and the one before – saying he was coming home.'

'You know, that gets me.' Jessica cut the air with her hand. 'They had a letter saying he was on his way home, and we knew nothing about it.'

'Wasn't it all about the time I was born?' Karina looked from her sister to her brother.

Jessica nodded. 'And we knew nothing about that, either.'

Karina laughed. 'Yeah, I was a big surprise to you all.'

'Strange.' Sam twisted his mouth, looking at Jessica. 'You know, I never thought about it like that – the secrets. But then I was fourteen – not thinking about much but myself.' He gave a short laugh.

'Yeah, and I was pregnant. So, I wasn't thinking about much else, either.' Jessica swung around to face her brother, impatience surging. 'But you had the letters in your hand. Didn't it occur to you to read what your brother had written before you locked them away again?'

He shrugged. 'Not really. They're all in envelopes, tied up. Just thought it was private. You know – for Mum.'

Jessica jerked upright. 'Do we really believe Mick was writing just to Mum? What about Dad? And the rest of us? Wouldn't his letters have been for us all?' She pointed at the locked case, her face screwing up. 'Aren't those *our* letters, too?'

Samuel rubbed a thumb across his chin. 'Good point.'

'And you locked them away without even looking at them?' Jessica raised her eyebrows to him. 'Not even a peek?'

Samuel shrugged. 'Was running out of time to get the carving finished.'

'Got another key for that padlock?' Sarah fired.

They all eyed the locked box, as if it might spring open under their stare.

'Mum put her key in her pocket,' Karina said.

Jessica sprung up to where their father had been standing beside the fireplace. She dived a hand onto the mantlepiece and spun around, the wooden diamond dangling from her fingers. 'Ta dah!'

Samuel fixed his eyes on her while shaking his head slowly from side to side. 'You wouldn't. It's Dad's.'

In two steps Jessica was at the cabinet, picking up the box and carrying it to the sofa. She shot a look at Samuel. 'Just remember, these letters are from *our* brother.'

The girls watched intently as Jessica fitted the key into the padlock. Turn. Click. The lid eased open on its hinges.

Inside the envelopes were tied together with coloured ribbons.

Jessica picked up a bundle, studying the hand-written address, the unfamiliar postage stamps and the foreign postmark.

Karina leaned across to look. 'That's his writing? Strange seeing the writing of the brother; I never knew.'

Jessica studied the date stamp on the envelope. 'This one's May, Nineteen forty-seven. This might be his last letter.' She glanced at her brother, then slid the envelope free from the ribbon, pulling out a single, handwritten page. 'Dear Mum, Dad, Jess and Sam.' She clamped the letter to her heart and looked up at Samuel, her eyes blurring. 'These letters *are* for us all. I knew it. Why haven't we been able to read them before now?'

Sam got up and moved behind her, looking on.

Jessica scanned the writing, then read aloud. '… my ship is due in Wellington on Thursday the twelfth of June.'

'Hang on,' Karina said, looking over at the letter. 'He was due back on my birthday! The actual day of my birth!'

Jessica flicked through the other envelopes in her bundle, reading the postmarked date on each. 'It was all a jumble, I remember. Their sudden trip away, then the unexpected baby and the sad news about Mick. It all happened at once.'

Jessica returned her focus to another letter, reading to herself, soaking up the words of her long-lost brother, trying to imagine the life he had there, the life she knew so little about. 'God! This is Mick!' She turned to Sam. 'I can't believe we haven't had a share of these letters – all those years. He just disappeared from our lives and – left a huge void.'

'What did he die of?' Sarah's curiosity disregarded her mother's nostalgia.

Karina pulled the blanket up to her chin. 'He got an infection; Mum told me once. Some sort of injury when he was leaving Japan, they reckoned.'

Sarah shimmied across the floor to the bookshelf, reaching for the giant atlas that had always fascinated her with its huge maps and, at the back, lists of countries and their colourful flags. 'Whereabouts was he in Japan?' She carefully lowered the book to the floor, as she had done since she was small.

Karina joined her. 'Hiroshima. You know. The city that was bombed.'

Jessica picked up another bundle and loosened the ribbon. She flicked through the envelopes. One caught her eye – a different size and shape to the others, just *Mr and Mrs Mitchell* in unfamiliar writing, with no address and no postage stamp.

She took out the single page and began reading. 'This is it.' She pulled in a shaky breath. 'His final letter…' Her eyes widened as she read further. She shot a look of alarm at her brother, darted a glance at the girls engrossed in the map of Japan, and returned her attention to the page in her hand, pulling it secretively close. Suddenly she gulped, folded it, returned it to the envelope and, fixing Samuel with an intense stare, slid the envelope into her pocket.

'What?' he mouthed.

She clamped a hand over her mouth, flaring her nostrils in panic. Her eyes darted a look of horror, leaving Samuel in no doubt they needed to discuss something in private. She jumped up from the sofa.

'Okay, that's enough for one day. Better lock these away, Sam.' She waved a hand to the disarray of letters on the sofa and turned to the girls. 'Off to bed, you two. Didn't realise the time.'

Karina and Sarah looked up, expressions puzzled.

'This is my bedroom and I need some sleep,' Jessica added.

'Already?' her daughter protested.

'Nearly midnight.' Jessica hurried them to their feet and shooed them out of the room. The need for quiet in the sleeping household prevented the girls objecting as they were ousted into the hallway, whispering protests as they felt the way to their bedroom in the dark.

Jessica closed the door with a secure click and frantically signalled Samuel towards the safer distance of the kitchen.

She pulled the letter from her pocket and thrust it at her brother. 'Read this!'

Chapter Twenty

The saddest thing about betrayal
is that it comes not only from your enemies.
– Ancient Wisdom

Sarah's breathing had settled quickly into the even rhythm of sleep, leaving Karina to struggle alone with her homecoming thoughts.

She felt irritated about the way Jessica had bundled them out of the living room – Karina's living room – this was still her home.

Yet her childhood bed, once her cosy retreat, felt oddly unwelcoming.

The family – heart and soul of the home – seemed somehow at odds with itself.

The evening hadn't ended with the usual jovial warmth and togetherness, but with jarring hints of long-held secrets, discontent, confusion, and a breach of privacy.

Is this what it's like to be an adult? She curled up, pulling the covers over her ears, wanting none of it.

Why had they opened the letter case? It almost felt like invading a tomb. As curious as she was about Mick, she would have preferred to ask her parents outright.

But Jessica could not wait, so had forged the betrayal.

Karina couldn't recall a time of discord within the family. This wasn't the homecoming she had been looking forward to.

Her throat constricted and mouth parched, she swung her feet around and found the floor. Edging her way across the room she reached out in the dark to identify the doorframe.

Easing the door open, she followed the glow spreading along the hallway floor, flowing from the gap under the kitchen door. Someone must have left the light on.

As she approached, she heard Jessica's harsh whispers. Then Sam's deeper tones, only a word or two. And Jessica, sharp, again.

She'd had enough tension for one night so decided to forgo the glass of water and avoid walking into their on-going dispute.

Turning slowly, she instinctively stepped around the creaky, tell-tale floorboard that had been her enemy when she came home too late after high school parties.

Sam's voice came through again. '... But poor Karina! Shit!'

She froze at her name, ears straining to hear.

'We think *we've* been lied to, tricked.' Sam continued, 'But what about Kari? This is her whole world, turned upside down... turned to shit!'

Chills ran through her.

In one move Karina wrenched the door open and charged into the room. 'What the hell?' she hissed. 'What are you talking about?'

Jessica froze.

Sam whipped a sheet of paper behind his back. 'What is that?' Karina snatched at a it.

He held it at arm's length, his eyes wide and mouth gaping, speechless.

She grabbed at him, jagged words and fractured meanings ricocheting around in her head. 'Give me that!' she snapped.

Jessica intervened. 'It's too late. I think she heard. Let her read it.'

Sam shook his head violently. 'Not like this.'

Karina leapt at him. He lost his footing and overbalanced against the cupboards. The paper he was holding fluttered from his grip.

In one scoop Karina snatched it up. She tried to focus on the writing but her hands shook so furiously it was impossible to decipher anything.

'Who's it from?' She demanded. 'Who wrote this? What does it say about me?' she shot at her brother.

His mouth moved, no words came out.

Jessica reached out. 'I'll tell you,' she offered. 'I'll explain...'

Through flooding eyes and exploding panic, Karina thrust the letter at her sister.

Jessica turned to face Karina. 'It's from Mick. On the ship,' she began carefully. 'But it's not his writing. It's dictated to his best mate. Mick was really sick by then... and he didn't know if he'd make it home... if he'd still be – okay – when the ship arrived.'

Karina nodded repeatedly, trying to hurry the explanation. 'What does it say?' she demanded, 'about me?'

'It says –,' Jessica shook her head as if in disbelief. 'I can't...' she swallowed hard and tried again. 'It says –,' her voice dropped to a whisper and she gripped Karina's shoulders, pulling her close. 'It's from Mick – he says – it says – he's your father.'

The words echoed, reverberated in Karina's head.

'No! No!' Mick could not be her father! She shoved Jessica aside, her pitch escalating. 'That's not true. How could he be? – you're lying.'

Sam reached for her but she evaded his arms. 'We don't know, Kari…'

Karina headed for the door. 'I know who does, and I'll prove you wrong,' she shot back at them. 'Mum!' she yelled. 'Dad!' Racing down the hallway, she burst through their closed bedroom door. Her hand slammed against the wall switch. Stark, harsh light engulfed the room, as if demanding the truth.

Startled from sleep, her father sat bolt upright. 'What's going on?' he barked, blinking, focussing on her. 'What's wrong, Kari?'

Facing her parents, Karina couldn't find the words. Frustration erupted into a voiceless scream.

Jessica and Samuel arrived in the doorway.

Her father squinted from one to the other. 'What's up? What's going on?' His infuriatingly neutral voice gave away little hint of concern.

Alarmed, her mother pulled herself up to sitting, eyes flicking from one to the other before settling on Karina. 'What is it, Dear?' Her voice breathless, her lips trembling.

'Is this true?' Karina screeched, brandishing the letter, shaking it furiously in the air. 'Is it?'

Her mother's eyes focussed on the paper and bulged in recognition. Her hand clamped over her mouth.

'What's that, Kari?' her father asked.

'A letter – about me! About Mick… Is it true?' Silence hung in the air like a hangman's noose.

Her father reached out to his robe slung over a chair, slipped into the sleeves and stood, tying the belt firmly around his middle. 'What's it say, Kari?'

'You know what it says,' she shot, her eyes darting from one parent to the other. 'It's addressed to *you*! Tell me it's not true!'

Her mother turned to face the other two standing stock-still inside the doorway. 'You opened my letters? And you involved Karina?' Her tone accusing, threatening, damning. 'How dare you interfere!'

'That's not the issue now, is it, Mum?' Jessica shot. 'That's not the *real* betrayal here.'

Her father's expression gave nothing away as he firmly ushered the three of them out. 'Come on now. Let your mother get her robe on. We can talk about it together around the table.'

Karina attempted to break free from his guiding arms, but he was ready. 'No, Kari.' His strong hand clamped on her elbow. 'Everybody out.' He pulled the door closed behind them.

Sarah appeared, roused from slumber. 'Back to bed, Sarah,' he instructed. 'This doesn't concern you.'

'Like hell,' she responded. 'The shouting woke me up. I'm already concerned.' Jessica reached out to draw her daughter into the shuffling group.

Sarah looked at each of them. 'What on earth is it? What's happened?'

Jack maintained control, ushering them to the kitchen. 'We're going to talk about it when your Gran is here. Everybody, take a seat. We'll get nowhere running around like headless chooks.'

Karina had never disobeyed his voice of authority. Until now.

'I can't wait!' She spun around to confront him. 'Tell me!' She waved the crumpled notepaper in his face. 'Is this true?'

He appeared not to hear, turning his back to fill the kettle.

'She has a right to know,' Jessica countered from his other side. 'We all do.'

Sarah stared at the letter. 'Know what?'

'Something about – Mick,' Jessica answered.

The door opened and her mother appeared. She'd put on her best velour dressing gown and matching slippers trimmed with woolly sheepskin, her hair freshly combed, her complexion ashen, lips trembling. There was even a waft of flowery perfume – or was it the talcum powder she often sprinkled on her toes?

Jack reached out and took the letter from Karina's hand, ushering his wife to the table, infuriatingly calm, indicating for them all to sit. Placing the letter on the table, he flattened it beneath his weathered hand and faced Karina.

He took a deep breath. And began. 'Remember when you were little, Kari, you wanted to know where the cattle and sheep were going when the truck arrived to take them away?'

'You said they were off to another farm, to eat new grass.' She wished he would deal with the letter, but knowing from past experience he would handle it his way, in his own time, left her powerless to change his pedantic process.

'You know now they were going to the meat works, but when you were little, I didn't think you needed to know the real truth. A little white lie served well until you could handle it.'

Jessica cut in, impatience edging her voice. 'Dad! This is not a *little white lie*!'

He turned to Jessica, his expression stern. 'Maybe not. But the reasoning is the same.'

Their mother shifted in her seat. 'It's just that – there never was the right time. At first, we thought the right time would come, but it didn't. And then it didn't matter.' She dabbed a handkerchief to each eye. 'But now, it does.'

Chapter Twenty-One

Hope is seeing light
in spite of being
surrounded by darkness.
– *Ancient Wisdom*

Barricaded in her bedroom Karina attempted to process the new and ugly shape of her world.

Solitude and silence. Time alone to breathe, think, shout and cry.

In response to the intermittent knocking and repeated enquiries about her wellbeing, she barked, 'GO AWAY.'

Fading footsteps echoed in retreat, followed by muffled voices in tones of concern and disappointment.

She still won't open the door. She needs more time…

How much time?

Is twelve hours enough? Twenty-four?

How long does it take to heal a nineteen-year lie?

A lifetime.

Sometime after daybreak, it wasn't a gentle knock or an anxious enquiry that breached her isolation but a strong pushing on her obstructed door, sliding the blanket box blockade aside.

Sarah's head squeezed through the gap. 'Okay,' she said with determination. 'I'm coming in.'

And she did. Backwards. Pushing the door with her behind, carrying two steaming mugs. 'I'm on your side,' she added, placing the cups on the bedside table and going back to the door to restore the barrier.

They sipped in silence, Karina feeling resuscitated by the comforting warmth of her milky tea, gurgling and settling heavily, soothing her empty stomach.

Eventually, she spoke. 'Funny thing,' she began flatly. 'Nothing has actually changed.' Sarah looked up, creases furrowing her brow.

'This is still my home. I can come back here every holiday if I want.

Mum and Dad–' she paused, giving a nod towards the living room. '…them, are still my legal parents. They brought me up. That will always be the case. Treated me as theirs, and gave me all the love I could ask for. Probably always will. So, what has really changed?'

Sarah shrugged, and gave no answer.

'I'll tell you.' Karina drew in a steadying breath. 'Trust.' She pressed her lips and shook her head slowly. 'The people I trusted most in this world have lied to me. Been lying to me all my life.' She looked up, focusing on Sarah's reaction, wondering how to sum up her own jagged feelings. 'I just – I can't figure out how to cope with that.' Her breath caught.

Sarah's voice came soft and gentle. 'Not everyone lied. Not everyone in the family knew. I didn't. Had no idea. And I'm pretty sure Mum didn't. Nor Uncle Sam.'

Karina looked into her cup, letting the steam drift over her face, inhaling the damp warmth.

Sarah reached out, resting a hand tentatively on Karina's shoulder. 'It's not all bad. The best thing is – we're actually cousins. You've been my best friend all my life and now we're the same generation.' She leaned her face towards Karina. 'Remember how we use to pass ourselves off as cousins at school, when we couldn't be bothered explaining the aunty-niece connection?' She gave Karina a playful nudge. 'It's a dream come true.'

***

About midmorning they emerged from her room and Karina faced her family in the living room. They turned to look, their washed-out expressions reflecting the sleepless night. Familiar faces, today appeared as strangers, family ties stretched to breaking point.

Determination setting her jaw, she announced, 'I'm going to Japan!'

Sarah came up from behind, slinging an arm around her. 'I'm going too.'

'What do you mean?' Jessica's voice rasped.

Karina lifted her chin 'We're going together.'

Dorothy's complexion bleached. 'Japan?' She swallowed visibly. 'Why?'

'Like I said last night – I want to trace my family origins. And as the Cook Islands is not such a strong connection,' she shot a look at the woman who raised her, 'it'll be Japan.'

Dorothy let out a shaky sigh, her eyes filling and overflowing again. 'We *are* your family.' Her voice reduced to a weary whisper.

'I mean where I was born. My homeland.'

Karina knew that would cut deep. She didn't care. Anger made her lash out, made her tongue sharp. She turned and left the room.

How could she trust them? Ever?

***

Looking out Sarah's car window at the blur of countryside sliding by, Karina's body and mind felt like two separate entities, with no connection. 'I feel like shit.'

'Of course, you do.' Sarah slowed, changed gears and checked for traffic before turning onto the Main South Road. 'I feel pretty crappy, too. And it's not even about me.'

'My legs are numb. My gut has dissolved. My head pounds. I'm hungry as hell, but I'm determined not to throw up again.'

Her cousin took a hand-off the steering wheel to give Karina's knee a quick pat. 'You'll come right. We've got things to look forward to. We're off to the travel agent. We're going to book our flights!'

'Strange. I couldn't wait to get in the car and leave the place. I thought that would end the pain. But now we are on the road, I see the bloody pain has come too.'

Sarah blew out a slow breath. 'Maybe it'll get easier in time.' Karina swallowed, nodded.

Overflowing eyes betrayed her determination not to cry again. 'I feel so bad that I was angry at them – Mum and Dad. I wish I could tell them that now.' She spun to face her cousin at the wheel, voice rising in desperation. 'Can we go back? I just want to say goodbye properly. I feel so bad that I was rude to them, gave them more pain.' She wiped the back of her hand across her face.

Sarah raised her eyebrows. 'We're nearly in town – the travel agency is only five minutes from here. We'll be back home in an hour.' She shot a glance at Karina, waiting for that to sink in. 'What about you ring them? We'll stop at the phone box.'

Karina nodded and pulled in a shaky breath. 'Okay.'

'And it's going to be so exciting – booking tickets. I always wanted to travel. There just wasn't a good enough reason. Now there is.'

Karina couldn't match Sarah's enthusiasm. In the middle of the night, when she and Sarah talked about it, she would have accepted any plan that would get her away from home. Now, in the light of day, she wasn't sure.

After all, what did she expect to find? Mick was dead.

'You know,' Sarah began. 'None of this is their fault.' She threw a glance at Karina. 'They did what Mick asked – they brought you up as their own. With him dying, and all they were dealing with, what else could they have done?'

Karina tried to think what it must have been like for them – losing their first son and gaining an unexpected baby, all at once. 'I was all there was left of Mick.'

'But they couldn't talk about that, because of the secret. They were suddenly faced with being your parents – permanently. No hope of Mick coming back to take over. They had to live with the lie.' Sarah shot a look at Karina, her face anxious, as if she feared she'd said too much.

'You know, I'm starting to understand what they went through – pretending I was their baby because Mick asked them to. But having to keep on lying because he wasn't going to return…' Karina shook her head slowly, trying to comprehend the enormity of their commitment.

'What if Mick had come back? I wonder how different your life would have been with him and your Japanese mother.'

'You know, I still can't believe that – I have a Japanese mother! I'm half Japanese! How come I didn't realise that? Why didn't I twig? Do I look Japanese?'

'No! You look like the rest of us – like a Cook Island Kiwi. Like Gran. She's got kinda Asian eyes.'

'That's because her grandfather was from Taiwan.' Karina pulled down the sun visor and examined herself in the mirror, before flicking it back with a shrug. 'You know, all this stuff we're studying at college, about the strength of family ties and the importance of ethnicity, how it's *integral to our identity.* All this time, I had no idea about my real origins.' She turned to face her cousin. 'So how integral is that? I've been fine without knowing.'

'Yeah! Heck, you didn't even want to take Japanese language at school, even when I was telling you how good it was.'

Karina thought about that for a while, wondering why she hadn't felt the pull to learn Japanese, when it was in her blood. 'Will you teach me some Japanese?' she asked suddenly.

Sarah nodded. 'Sure, I will. When we get back home, I'll hunt out my old text books.'

***

Karina folded clothes into her suitcase, then pulled them out in a bundle, dropping them on her bed, mumbling to herself.

The sense of adventure, mingled with anxiety, was magnified by the wait, the awkwardness in the household over things unsaid, the perpetual elephant in the room.

Dorothy hovered in the doorway from time to time, then busied herself in the kitchen, only to return a few minutes later, with something she needed to say.

Jack had left the house at daybreak. He would be out on the farm, his lips pressed tight to keep his thoughts captive, pretending his mind was not fixed on family matters while he attended to agricultural practicalities.

Finally, on the day of departure, Sarah arrived and not a moment too soon. Jack lifted Karina's suitcase into the tiny boot.

Not one for formalities, Karina launched forward, hugging her mother, then her father.

'I just want to say,' she began, brushing the back of her hand across her eyes, 'you will always be my parents. What I've found out about Mick, his Japanese wife, – it doesn't change anything. It's like I've just discovered a new branch on the family tree.'

Dorothy nodded, struggling to find her voice. 'And it's sprouting cherry blossom.' She reached into her apron pocket, retrieving a small woven pouch. 'This is for you, Kari.'

'What is it?'

'It was with Mick's things the day we… met you in Wellington.'

Karina reached into the tiny bag and withdrew a silver chain suspending a pendant, a smooth twist of greenstone. She studied it, the only thing she had from her actual father. 'It was his?'

Dorothy nodded. 'We gave it to him when he left home for Japan. This twisted shape is called the *pikorua* in Maori.' Dorothy reached out, holding the smooth jade curl between her fingers. 'It stands for a bond between people and cultures, across time and space. I lost faith in it for many years. But now I see it might work in unexpected ways.' She crinkled a smile at Karina.

'Mick wore this?'

'I believe so. His friend, Brooks, said he gave it to her… your… Emiko, at their wedding. When you were born, she put it around your neck. That's how Mick knew he had the right baby from the orphanage.'

'Thank you.' Karina pressed it between her hands, eyes misting again. 'This is so special.'

Dorothy helped fasten it around Karina's neck. 'There you are, my darling. From one mother to another. And back again.' Her voice caught. 'Full circle.'

'Come along now,' Jack said, opening the passenger door to interrupt the prolonged hugging. 'You're only going for two weeks.'

They all waved until out of sight.

'Thank heavens we're on our way.' Karina's voice choked as she pressed the smooth greenstone to her lips. 'I was dreading the goodbyes.'

Chapter Twenty-Two

JAPAN 1967

Freedom is nothing
but a chance to do better.
– Dame Whina Cooper

Mid-January, only three weeks since Karina and Sarah had decided to visit Japan, they waited – on a rollercoaster of nerves and excitement – for their boarding call.

The first leg to Sydney, busy with mealtime and a little too much wine, passed in a festive whirl.

Waiting in the airport for the connection to Osaka was a sobering experience. It was now midnight. The party was over and a long night stretched before them.

The seats in the terminal were rigid and upright.

Other flights arrived and departed.

All attempts at conversation failed, so they slumped into gritty-eyed silence.

As the soft lemon glow of dawn spread across the eastern horizon, they got the call.

Energised with relief, they hefted their cabin bags and trudged to the boarding gate.

On finding their seats lushly padded, they sank down, wriggled into a heads-on-shoulders arrangement, and slept fitfully for the first half of the flight.

'Where – where are we?' Karina's voice croaked.

Sarah groaned. 'In the sky.' She struggled to sit upright. 'My neck is stuck sideways.'

From the heavens, a stewardess approached with a trolley. 'Tea? Coffee?'

Fingers gripping warm cups, they sipped in grateful silence until brain function began to return.

'Do we have a plan of attack?' Sarah asked finally.

Karina pursed her lips as if hatching a clever plan. 'I guess not. It's more like a reconnaissance mission. Go there, find out stuff.'

Sarah stared into her cup. 'Can't believe that's all you've worked out.'

'I couldn't think about going – about actually being in Japan – until I'd left home. Saying goodbye was such an emotional block for me.' Karina took another sip.

'Yeah, I get that.'

'Now we're on the way – really on the way – like there's no turning back!'

'You mean we can't just go up to the pilot and say, "Excuse me, I've changed my mind. Can you return us to Auckland?"'

Karina laughed. 'No turning back.' She thrust a fist in the air. 'Onward!'

'At least we've got a guesthouse booked, and we know we get to Hiroshima by train. What next?'

'You know, I thought about a settling-in time.'

Sarah turned to her. 'What? Like an orientation programme?'

'Not formally so, but take some time to get the feel of the place. Then I won't seem such a novice when we start asking around.'

Sarah blew out a slow breath. 'What have you got in mind?'

'That book I got from the library – it says there's hot pools, and that would be nice since it's winter there. Probably snowing.'

'True. We'll be feeling the cold, coming from our summer.'

'And the temples. You know there's Shinto and Buddhism? And there's wonderful gardens where they do tea ceremonies.'

'Look, we've only got two weeks. You don't want to spend a week sightseeing, then run out of time for what we're really here for.'

Karina lowered her voice. 'I didn't mean a whole week. Just a day trip or two.'

Sarah put her cup down on the tray table and swivelled in her seat to face her cousin. 'I see this as delay tactics. And I totally get that. You're nervous about what we might find. But I think we need to get into looking right away – on the first day. We can take a break from time to time, but we need to make a start.'

Karina puffed her cheeks and blew out a forceful breath. She said nothing.

'Am I right?' Sarah nudged her.

A sneaky smile played at the corners of Karina's mouth. 'Maybe,' she said slowly.

'How about this? We have a good sleep on arrival, get something to eat, then go to the tourist office.'

Karina frowned. 'Tourist office? What for?'

'Information. They might know about the Kiwi Camp where Mick was based.'

Karina shrugged. Something was making her pull back. The reality of her quest suddenly felt overwhelming. 'He's dead,' she said flatly. 'I'm not sure what I'm wanting to find out.'

'Her!' Sarah smiled gently. 'Your birth mother. Look, I know it's a bit scary. But put aside your apprehensions for now. Don't think about that. Think about her – what it will mean for her to find you, after all this time.'

***

A day and a half after leaving Auckland, having crossed the equator and therefore swapped seasons, an invigorating chill snatched their breath as they stepped out to a fresh and frosty morning in the land of Karina's birth.

Leaving Osaka terminal, shuffling along the crowded walkway, Karina searched the faces for a surge of unspoken kinship. 'I feel nothing.'

Sarah slumped her shoulders. 'I feel tall.'

'Are we going the right way? What were the directions to the train?' Karina rummaged in her shoulder bag. 'I've got the map here somewhere.'

'No need.' Her cousin pointed to the sign up ahead.

Karina let out an impatient sigh. 'I can't read that! It's written in noodles.'

'Look at the symbol after the writing.'

'What is it? Looks like the nose of a plane.' Karina groaned. 'I don't want to fly any more. I'm done with planes.'

Sarah pointed again. 'It's a train. That's the railway symbol.'

'Really?' Karina squinted at it. 'Bad enough not reading the writing, but the pictures are a foreign language too.'

Her cousin draped a heavy arm across her shoulders, adding more weight to her already laboured steps. 'Don't worry. We've got all day to get to Hiroshima.'

'Can't wait for that guesthouse.' Karina blew out a heavy breath, tiredness and tension bringing her close to tears. 'Two days without a decent sleep, I'm not at my best.'

'You'll be fine. Don't forget, you're dealing with quite a lot.' The arm around her shoulders tightened. 'Don't push the river.'

Karina spun to face her cousin. 'Dad used to say that. I thought it had something to do with farming.'

'Mum says it too – has something to do with patience.'

Karina huffed, a persistent smile edged across her lips. 'That river must run in the family.'

Her thoughts drifted around family connections and she realised that he, Mick, was again at the forefront. 'Wonder if he used to say that – don't push the river. Wonder if he told himself that here – when he was in Japan.'

Would he have used that idea to help him cope with the disaster he faced? 'He would have been only five years older than we are now. What would it have been like, walking into such a scene? It must have been a culture shock.'

'A shock in every way. We know he thought the women were pretty, though. Or at least one of them.'

Karina smiled, raised her eyebrows and nodded slowly. 'Wonder what she was like.'

***

The softly upholstered seats and the smooth motion of the train lulled Karina into an easier state of mind.

Leaning her head against the window, she focussed on every detail of the strange new world just beyond the glass.

'Can't believe I've been here before.' Her breath clouded the glass and she wiped it with her sleeve. 'Born here. This would have been my life, if he hadn't got me from the orphanage.'

'You could be like those girls.' Sarah nodded to a group of female students in pleated navy skirts and blazers, standing together in silent companionship at the front of the carriage; not taking the few individual vacant seats which would separate them.

'I would understand the language and read the signs, know the customs…'

Her heart pounded and a sickening pulse of disconnection brewed in her belly. A flick of fate had changed her direction.

Changed her life. Changed her.

By birth, she was of this land.

By upbringing she was foreign. Estranged. Divided.

The acceptance of her true parents sometimes settled easy, fascinating her. At other times, like now, the confusion whirled so fast that her mind lost its grip on reality and she felt dizzy.

Sarah leaned into her. 'It's going to be okay.'

Karina twisted her mouth and an apprehensive smile broke through.

Soon they were out of the city, leaving behind the tall, grey buildings, laundry hanging to dry on bamboo poles suspended off miniature balconies. Leaving behind the puzzle of streets appearing just wide enough for motorbikes, where two cars would meet and squeeze past each other, under a tangle of power wires looking like a discarded mistake of giant macramé.

In the towns, one after the other with no distinct start and stop, small houses pressed up against identical neighbours, whole blocks sharing the same front path. Narrow lanes sandwiched between neat vegetable plots growing parallel rows of winter crops. Every now and then a bigger plot with a bare, sunken surface looked like a disused tennis court.

Here and there locals in padded jackets, going about their business, ignored the long train sliding by.

Karina lifted her gaze to the mountains in the distance, too steep for a village, draped in deep green velvet, the highest peaks fingering the low, misty sky.

And suddenly a narrow road snaked alongside the train and curled around a cluster of anonymous, windowless buildings. Factories manufacturing secrets.

Then a highway, smooth and straight, compact cars racing each other into the distance.

The whirr of the train deepened and echoed when they crossed a stony river, the water below rushing like a stampede. And soon, another river, wider and slower. Then a tunnel, hushed and dark.

Karina closed her eyes, her gritty tiredness welcoming the relief. She pulled her jacket up to her chin and let her head lull against the padded headrest, the meditative rhythm rocking her like a baby.

Like the baby she once was. In this place.

She accepted the blur of thought, the stage of fuzzy consciousness that settles on you like a closing curtain, just before sleep.

As the movement slowed, she stirred into bright daylight. They were among city buildings again. Right beside their window other trains rushed away as theirs clicked to a standstill at the long platform. Hiroshima Station.

Swept up in a wave of people, some lugging suitcases, they found themselves at the exit.

'Look, taxis right here.'

The back doors swung open and the boot lid clicked up as a white-gloved driver emerged from behind the wheel, bowing quickly before stowing their bags. They slid into the plastic-covered back seat and the doors closed smoothly, automatically, after them.

Karina knew Mick's arrival here nearly twenty years ago would have been very different. She'd read about how quickly Japan bounced back after the war. Trams were operating within a few days of the bombing, many buildings replaced in a few months, and now Japan was an economic example for the global economy.

Sarah passed the guesthouse address to the driver.

He studied it a moment and handed it back. 'Hai, domo.'

'What did he say?'

'Yes, thanks. Okay.'

They took off into multi-lane traffic, weaving smoothly in and out.

'It just seems like a dream.' Karina looked around, unable to accept the magnitude of their adventure.

After endless motorways, the streets narrowed, the taxi slowed.

'You know what scares me the most?' Karina threw a look at Sarah. 'If she's – you know – dead.' She swallowed hard. 'It would just seem such a tragedy. If she'd died without us meeting, I wonder if I could forgive them – Mum and Dad – for keeping the secret so long.'

'So many things are up in the air.' Sarah reached across and grabbed her hand. 'What do you want to do first?'

'Sleep. I can't even think straight.'

Sarah nodded. 'Me too, and stretch out. Been curled up for days.'

The taxi turned and turned again, and they appeared to double back on themselves, only to enter a narrower street, then a one-way lane, and finally a driveway that looked barely wide enough for a car.

They edged in and stopped. Sarah took care of the fee and their doors sprung open. The suitcases unloaded, the driver bowed and drove off.

Karina looked around. 'Where are we?'

Sarah studied the address in her hand 'Sakura Inn,' she read. 'Means cherry blossom.'

'Well that's usually easy to spot. But I don't see any.'

'And you won't. It's winter. Cherry blossoms are in spring.'

'Oh, goodie. I can't wait!' Karina blew out a despondent breath. Sarah approached a finely carved plaque fixed to a high fence.

Karina followed her, reaching up to run a finger over the etched decoration on the sign. 'It's a blossom. This must be it.'

A bell tinkled as a section of the fence swung open at their touch, revealing a small stone-paved courtyard. Tall spindly plants alongside the fence reached for the wintery sun. A knee-high rock with a hollow top forming a water basin no bigger than a soup bowl was filled with a trickle from a bamboo spout. Mossy rocks alongside feathery plants thrived in the basin's overflow – a perfect miniature depiction of untamed nature.

Karina felt an emotional rush – instinctively she knew why Mick had fallen in love with this place, why he had fallen in love with her mother. Her heart leapt as she felt the essence of this adventure.

Low verandas edged the courtyard on two sides, leading into rooms behind sliding screens.

'Is this someone's home?' It felt too private to be guest accommodation.

A shuffle of sound came from one of the rooms, followed by the screen sliding open as a woman emerged onto the veranda, stooping towards them into a low bow.

Sarah said their names and started to explain the booking arrangement when the woman nodded and ushered them onto the adjoining veranda. Sliding open the screen, she invited them to look in.

The room, empty except for a vase on a low stand containing a single leafy stem of bamboo, had no furniture. Straw matting covered the floor in a basket-weave pattern and a single scroll with a painted, snowy scene hung on the wall above the vase.

The woman slipped off her scuffs and entered in her socks, sliding open a wardrobe door to reveal, not hanging space, but shelves holding neatly folded mattresses and quilts – their bedding.

'Okay?' she asked.

'Okay.' They nodded.

She produced two pairs of fabric scuffs and waited for them to change their footwear before leading them down a narrow corridor between the rooms.

Pausing at the bathroom, she demonstrated her instructions to shower first before sinking into the short, deep bathtub.

'Okay?' she asked again.

Sarah tried her Japanese. 'Hai, arigato.' Karina nodded her thanks.

They returned to the courtyard, carried the suitcases into their room, and looked around, wondering how to settle in to such a confined space.

'Makes sense,' Karina observed. 'Sitting room in the day, bedroom at night. You don't need to sleep when you're sitting around, and vice versa.'

'Chairs would be helpful, though.'

'*Sumi-masen*,' came the hostess's tinkling voice from outside. She slid the screen open and stepped in, placing a tray with short legs in the centre of the room. On the tray, sat a teapot with a leafy design and handle-less cups to match. Some types of food – walnut-sized white balls decorated with intricately cut-out leaf and flower shapes, were placed on a square, black plate.

They thanked her as she backed from the room and Karina turned her attention to the delicate offerings.

Sarah looked down. 'We won't fit our legs under that. I've seen pictures of people sitting at a table like that to eat, but never tried it myself.'

They tried various ways to sit on the floor, tucking legs under and folding them to the side.

'I feel like Alice in Wonderland,' Karina added. 'Suddenly I'm a giant, and that,' she pointed to the tray, 'is the smallest tea set I've seen, except for in a dolls house.'

The tea looked and tasted grassy and the morsels, as they nibbled tentatively, were not savoury, not sweet, just doughy.

'I can't make it out.' Karina studied the soft ball between her fingers. 'I have no idea what this is. It looks like jam in the middle. But it doesn't taste like it.' She screwed up her mouth and ran her tongue around her lips, trying to identify the taste.

In the periphery of her mind, she knew this food, this décor, this culture

– so strange and new to her – would be second nature to her mother.

'Maybe red bean paste,' Sarah suggested. 'I've heard about that as a filling, but it's not sweet. Don't expect things to be sweet like we're used to. Sugar isn't used much here.'

'It's not cooked,' Karina deducted. 'It's like raw dough. They forgot to cook the buns!'

Sarah laughed, nodded agreement and tried to wash the gooey texture away with more green tea. 'Just as well we ate on the train.'

'You know what?' Sarah dropped her voice and squinted at the cupboard door. 'I could do with a nap. It's so nice to have a motionless floor underfoot and room to stretch out.' She stretched her legs long and scanned the tiny space.

Karina clamped her hands to her head. 'I agree. My ears are still ringing from engine noises. We can go out for dinner later. From the taxi I saw some intriguing little restaurants nearby.'

Dropping her hands, she rested her gaze in her palms. Eventually, adding, 'I feel like I have landed at last, physically and emotionally. There's something very calming, welcoming – about this place.'

'Well,' Sarah stumbled to her feet and slid open the screen door. 'I'm going to put this tiny table outside the door and make use of the bathroom facilities.'

Leaning back against the wall, Karina breathed into the silence. Her fingertips stroked the smooth, woven surface where she sat, inhaling its fresh, straw-like aroma.

Her gaze encompassed the room. The simplicity was not unwelcoming. Rather, it allowed space for its occupants to fill in their own gaps – a clean slate. A complete turn-around from the homely clutter of her upbringing.

Now, because of the overwhelming flick of fate – her chance rescue from the orphanage, giving her a childhood there and not here, she could find no words, not even a logical thought, to rationalise the magnitude of that fork in the road.

She crawled across the floor, opened her suitcase, pulled out some sleepwear and changed.

When Sarah returned, together they hauled the thick mattresses from the cupboard, arranged them on the floor, grabbed a quilt each and stretched out full-length for the first time in nearly fifty hours.

Words not possible, they let out sighs and groans, nonverbal expressions of appreciation for the comfort and peace, before much-needed slumber engulfed them.

Chapter Twenty-Three

JAPAN

Every morning we are born again.
What we do today is what matters most.
– Buddha

It was dark when Karina woke, scrambling for her wristwatch. 'Seven!'

Sarah emerged from beneath her quilt. 'What?'

'Seven. In the morning. We slept through the evening and the night.'

'Really? No wonder I'm starving.'

Wobbly and confused, they struggled to their feet like new-born foals.

Karina's voice betrayed the nervousness which jumped inside her. 'I'm going to manage that shower, without a soak in the tub.'

'Me too. And then I'll pack a day bag so we can keep on the move right after breakfast.'

When they returned from the bathroom a tray of steaming tea and lidded bowls waited on their deck and the room had been restored to the serene and simple space it had been on arrival.

Suspiciously, they picked at the breakfast tray, managing only a spoon or two of the salty broth, a few scoops of the plain rice and a tiny cup of green tea which still tasted like grass – avoiding the uncooked egg, something smelling very fishy and some slimy green vegetable slivers.

The nibbles left them even more in need of a hearty breakfast.

Karina dressed with more care than usual, her greenstone pendant showing just above her neckline. 'I've been thinking. I don't want to go asking around for her – for Emiko. What if someone does know her and guesses what we're here for – guesses who I am? I don't want her to find out like that – Chinese whispers.'

Sarah nodded.

'Nor do I want to find out anything – bad – about her like that. I've decided to ask about Mick first, about Kiwi base. That will be a safer line of questioning to start with.'

Sarah picked up her carry bag. 'Okay. As long as we don't run out of time. You know a lot about Mick. But we have to start from scratch to find her.'

'I think we will find her, through his connections. I think he will lead us to her.' She turned to Sarah, eyes misting. 'I *feel* his presence – he's leading me.'

Karina took a deep breath and slipped into the mulberry swing coat Dorothy had lent her. The style had not gone out of fashion although it was almost twenty years old. Karina draped her high school scarf around her shoulders. The grey tartan weave with its thin maroon stripes was a perfect match.

Sarah, transfixed, had been watching the finishing touches. 'Sweetheart, you look like a model. A film star! Audrey Hepburn! Turn around, look at me.'

Sarah's eyes ran over her as a look of disbelief crossed her face. 'You *really* look like her – dark hair, high cheekbones, doe eyes. I can't believe I haven't noticed that before.'

Suddenly Karina did feel rather grown-up. 'Probably because I haven't dressed up before.'

They stepped onto the deck and slipped on their shoes.

Their misting breath mingled with traffic fumes as they picked their way between the bumper-to-bumper vehicles. They crossed into a small arcade where a cluster of tiny shops and restaurants advertised their fare with colourful street signs and plastic food in window displays.

Karina pointed at a familiar dish. 'That looks like a bowl of noodles'.

Sarah looked over her shoulder, remembering the once familiar characters. '*Ud-on.* I reckon we could ask for that.'

'Noodles? For breakfast?'

'It's warm and we can say the name. Beggars can't be choosers.'

They pushed on the heavy door and entered a tiny, toasty-warm restaurant not much bigger than the family dining room. The only two tables were already taken so they edged between them to a couple of high stools at an eating bar against the wall, pulling off hats and scarves. An older woman tapped Karina on the arm, beamed a gold-flecked smile and pointed to the basket on the floor beside them. Karina looked around and saw similar baskets piled up with discarded woollies. She nodded, smiled and did the same.

A chef behind the counter called out over his flaming hotplate.

Sarah looked around and quickly deducted he was addressing them. She gulped. 'Here I go,' she whispered to Karina, and answered him. '*Udon. Kudasai.*' Then she held up two fingers. The chef responded with another shout and a flurry of leaping flames.

'That's it? You ordered noodles for us? I'm impressed.' Karina patted her cousin on the back.

'*Hmm*, not sure. I ordered *something*. Two of them.'

Karina closed her eyes and inhaled the myriad of unfamiliar yet mouth-watering aromas. 'Well, as long as it's edible.'

'Don't get your hopes up.'

Soon a waitress appeared at their elbows, carrying a black lacquer tray with two bowls of steaming, fat noodles floating in pungent broth. She nodded, and placed the bowls in front of them, with large china spoons and chopsticks.

Sarah picked up the chopsticks, arranging them between her fingers. 'Right. I can do this. We practiced this in school. Japanese class.'

Karina looked at her sideways. 'How do you eat soup with them?'

A dripping noodle dangled like a fat, white worm from one of Sarah's chopsticks as she struggled to make the other stick work in tandem. Finally, the two came together like scissors, the noodle sliced in half and dropped into the bowl with a splash.

'Maybe use the spoon.'

With an inelegant combination of spoons and chopsticks, they scooped and slurped their way through the tasty, satisfying dish. Sarah took care of the payment and they stepped out, pulling on hats and wrapping scarves against the chill.

Reaching the main street Karina fumbled in her bag and opened out the map.

Sarah ran a finger around where their guesthouse was circled in red ink 'Are tourist offices marked? What symbol would they be likely to have?'

'Excuse me.' A man in a dark uniform and cap approached. 'Can I help you?'

'Ah, yes.' Sarah held the map towards him. 'We're looking for the nearest tourist office.'

He nodded. 'Not far.' He stepped forwards and pointed on the map to a location about six blocks away. 'I can take you.' He indicated his taxi at the curb.

'Great,' Karina said. 'Too cold to walk.'

'Hai, domo arigato,' Sarah responded, then muttered under her breath, 'Got to practice the language when I can so I remember it when we really need it.'

The taxi doors swung open, they slid in onto the glossy seat and sped away.

A moment later they pulled up, Sarah handed over the relevant yen, and they stepped out in front of a modern, concrete building, its ample windows covered with posters of spectacular scenes – trees of cherry blossom like giant candyfloss, Fuji – of course – with its snowy peak of marshmallowy topping against the dusky sky, manicured gardens, majestic temples... Karina's mouth fell open in awe.

Sarah broke the spell. 'This way,' she called, heading impatiently to the entrance.

They shuffled into the heated foyer, again removing hats and scarves as they headed to a reception counter covered with stands of brochures.

The woman behind looked up and smiled. 'Good morning. Can I be of assistance?'

Karina blew out a breath and stepped forward. 'Good morning. We are hoping for information about the Kiwi Army Base that used to be near here.'

The receptionist considered the request carefully. 'Would you please take a seat.' She indicated the upholstered bench behind them. 'I will ask.' She turned and walked into an inner office.

Karina fiddled with the scarf in her lap and looked around the floor. 'No basket here?' She gave a nervous laugh.

Sarah patted her cousin's fumbling hand. 'It's going to be all right. Breathe. This is just the beginning.'

'I don't know what to think – I'm both impatient and reluctant.'

'I can understand that. Me too, a bit.'

Ongoing conversation between the receptionist and a male drifted indistinctly from the inner office.

Karina tapped her toes on the floor. 'What's taking so long?'

'Probably thinking of the best way to answer. The Kiwi base buildings may not even be there any more. They may have been just temporary constructions.'

'Wouldn't that be a quick and easy answer, then?'

'You're right. So, I'm guessing they have something to tell us. Maybe he's telling her what to say. You know the Japanese – they will make sure they do it right.'

Karina considered and concluded. 'That's a good characteristic – generally. But I wish they would hurry up.'

The receptionist returned. 'Will you come with me please.' She led them through another door to the inner office where a man in a dark suit sat behind a large, tidy desk.

'This is Mr Shimizu. He will help with your enquiries.'

He stood and bowed. They returned the gesture and accepted the two chairs placed side by side in front of his desk. 'I understand you are asking about the Kiwi base.' He took his seat. 'May I ask – what is the reason for your interest?'

Karina's nerves allowed no place for polite formalities. 'My father used to work there,' she answered quickly.

'Your father… a Kiwi?'

'Yes. We're both from New Zealand,' Sarah replied. 'We're wondering if we could find somebody who might have known him.'

'He died,' Karina added, hoping to qualify their inquiries.

Mr Shimizu nodded. 'Finding records is quite difficult. Of course, military information always remains a secret.'

Karina fidgeted in her seat. 'What about the buildings?'

'The buildings do still exist but, of course, there is a different purpose now. It is an English college for young people who want to work in tourism – an important industry now.'

'We are just wanting to find someone who might remember when it was the Kiwi base, someone who might have known some of the Kiwis there.'

'It is quite possible you will find that. Mr Hashimoto who runs the school might know some of the history, but you understand, there is no military connection there now. Some of the people who live in that area could have worked there. The Kiwi soldiers were very popular with our people, very helpful. Many local residents found work at the base. The number twenty-eight bus will take you there.' He stood and reached out his hand. 'I hope you find what you need to know. Good luck, Miss?'

‘Karina.’ She accepted the handshake.

He nodded. ‘Miss Karina.’

He turned to Sarah. ‘And Miss…?’

‘Sarah.’

‘Please come and see me again if I can help further.’

They thanked him as he ushered them to the foyer.

He pointed across the street. ‘There’s the twenty-eight bus. I think at this time you will find it full of students who are very keen to practice their English on you.’

He was right. They were bombarded with questions. ‘Hello, what is your name?’ ‘Do you know Paul McCartney?’ ‘Where do you come from?’ ‘What is it like in your country?’ ‘Do you like Japan?’ ‘Who is your favourite movie star?’ ‘Do you have a boyfriend?’ ‘How tall is he?’…

The bus made its way through narrow streets edged with tiny homes and shops side-by-side, turned into a country lane and struggled up a steep hill where buildings stood on poles to offset the slope.

They came to a stop in a large carpark. Everyone clambered out and several chatty students accompanied them as far as the office, where a receptionist listened to their request and suggested they speak to Mr Hashimoto, the Headmaster. She ushered them to wait in a small room with a simple desk and a row of chairs against the wall.

A moment later a man entered and greeted them cordially with handshakes as they all introduced themselves.

He was small of stature but carried a powerful presence, his eyes alert and curious through his dark-framed spectacles. ‘What brings you to our college?’

Karina shifted in her chair. ‘We hope you know something about this place when it was the Kiwi Base Camp. My father was a soldier here.’

Mr Hashimoto pressed his glasses onto his nose. ‘That was a long time ago – but I do remember back then. I grew up nearby. As a teenager I was involved in some work with the Occupation Forces.’ He focussed on Karina, the greenstone twist at her throat appearing to catch his eye. ‘I knew some of the Kiwi soldiers. Who is your father?’

‘His name is Mick Mitchell.’

His sudden intake of breath and the widening of his eyes told Karina more than any words could. He removed his glasses and pressed his forefinger and thumb against the bridge of his nose. His voice became soft and distant. 'Mick-san. *Hai*, I know him.'

Karina's heart thumped. She jumped to her feet. Her mouth went dry. 'You knew him!' Her eyes misted.

He stood and approached her, bowing deeply. 'Your father was my best friend – in my whole life. He taught me so much – so very much.' His face twisted momentarily, then he returned to formality. 'I am Kazuya Hashimoto. I am very honoured to meet Mick-san's daughter. I can't believe it…' He paused then continued in a solemn tone. 'I was very sad to learn about Mick-san's illness. So tragic. He did not want to leave Emiko-san here. He hoped so much to take her to New Zealand, with you.'

'Wait! You know about me? You knew my mother?' Karina's breath became erratic, her voice panicky. 'Is she… is she…? Do you… still… know her?'

Vice-like, Sarah's arm clamped around her shoulders.

He nodded. 'She used to live near here. She worked at the women's university. Now she works in many places. Even U.S.A. sometimes.'

Karina's hands cupped her mouth as she processed the extremes of information. Her birth mother was alive.

'How can I find out where she is now?'

'*Hmm*, let me think about that.' An expression of concentration crossed his face, a finger tapping the tip of his nose. 'I think the university can tell you. They will know her schedule.'

'Where is that university?'

'I will write it for you.' Reaching in his pocket, he retrieved a small silver case that could hold four or five cigarettes but when clicked open, it revealed a small stack of business cards. He wrote on the back of one, turned it over and carefully passed it to Karina. 'Here are my details, and over is the university. Not far from here. Maybe ten minutes by taxi.'

Karina thanked him and wanted to ask him more. *What was my father like? What were the many things he taught you? What was my mother like? What is she like now…*

But the receptionist appeared silently at the door.

He glanced at her. 'I am very sorry, I must go. My students are waiting. However, I think we have much more to discuss. Can I take you both to dinner? Does this evening suit?'

Karina and Sarah exchanged nods of agreement and thanked him. They made quick plans. He would come by Sakura Inn at seven.

Chapter Twenty-Four

JAPAN

Everything you've always wanted
Is on the other side of fear.
– Anon

Sarah's initial attempts to draw out Karina's feelings resulted in distracted one-word answers, so the taxi ride to the university continued in silence for some time.

Eventually Karina's thoughts floated to the surface. 'I hope he doesn't tell anyone, especially not her – Emiko.'

'He won't. He seemed really thoughtful. And really pleased to meet you.'

'I don't know what I'll say to her, but I don't want anyone else telling her.'

'I'm sure it'll be fine.'

'What if she's away, like he said? She goes to America.'

'Let's wait and see. If that is the case – we might just have to wait a bit longer…'

'I don't know how long I can wait – now I know it's really going to happen. Probably.'

'It'll be easier when we find out her schedule.'

The taxi turned into a narrow side street which wound up a steep hill, pulling to a stop before a modern building.

Large glass doors slid open to reveal an indoor garden with white sand sculptured into ripples like the sea lapping around rock islands. They picked their way carefully across stepping stones, over an arched bridge and onto the polished tiles of a modern foyer where hundreds of portrait photos hung on the walls.

'Woah!' Sarah laughed. 'The female Hall of Fame.'

They approached the first few, attempted to read the name plates and glanced at the biographies printed in Japanese and, surprisingly, English too, on silky scrolls hanging beside each portrait.

Silently Karina read some of the qualifications and achievements. 'They seem to be the faculty over the years. I wonder if she's here?'

A white-gloved assistant approached and asked if they needed help.

'We're wondering if there's a photo of Emiko…' Karina began, then paused, not sure what her official name would be. 'Emiko Tanazawa.'

'Emiko Tanazawa Mitchell?' the assistant suggested. 'This way, please.'

Karina couldn't answer – it hit her – for the first time she was about to see the likeness of her natural mother – who still used Mick's surname – Karina's family name.

They followed the assistant and stopped before the photo he indicated.

'Oh my God! There she is!' Sarah blurted.

Karina could find no words. Her eyes feasted on the face, so similar to her own, yet so different. In one way she felt like she was looking into a mirror. In another way she was looking into an alternative world.

Sarah squeezed Karina's hand. 'She's – just – beautiful.' Stepping up to the scroll she squinted at the finely printed translation. 'Emiko Tanazawa Mitchell began her academic life at this university. As a sociology graduate, she won a scholarship to the United States of America where she completed her masters. On her return to Japan, she quickly became an authority on the development and management of social equality. In addition to her extensive speaking schedule throughout this country and overseas, she is an advocate for women and children in poverty, promotes women's education and is active with several charities, including an orphanage and a women's employment organisation.' Sarah turned to Karina. 'She is one amazing woman.'

Karina took a beat, and gave a single, determined nod. 'Let's see if we can find out her schedule.'

The assistant, still nearby, directed them to an information counter where the attendant asked them to wait and returned a moment later. 'She is away at present,' they were told. 'Her next lecture here is on Thursday, eleven a.m.'

Karina turned to Sarah. 'What's today?'

'Tuesday.'

The attendant continued. 'It's an open lecture on women in leadership. Do you want to put your names down?'

They both did a spontaneous little dance of joy.

Karina pushed Sarah forward. 'Say your name.'

'Sarah Roberts.'

Karina stepped up. 'Jessica Roberts.'

They thanked the attendant and turned back to the foyer.

'What was that for?' Sarah asked. 'Why did you use my mum's name?'

'Why do you think? If I'd put my name down, she might see it or someone might make the connection.'

Karina steered them back to Emiko's portrait, pulling out her camera. 'I've got to get a photo of her.'

***

They walked back towards Sakura Inn; after checking the map and guessing, it would take about half an hour. In fact, it took more than two hours including a stop at a vending machine to work out how to buy two cans of Coca Cola.

After peeling off coats and woollies, they pulled out their futons from the cupboard and flopped onto them. 'Is this what they call jetlag?' Karina said, focussing on the woven ceiling panels. 'It's early afternoon, and I just want to sleep.'

'Probably. Add to that it's been an action-packed morning, not to mention emotionally charged.'

Karina thought about all they had discovered. 'I'm surprised. It has happened so easily – so far. And there's a lot more to come. I wonder what Mr Hashimoto will tell us over dinner tonight.'

'Perhaps that's a good reason to have a little nap now. I want to be alert for all that. I can't wait.'

'I'll set my alarm so we don't sleep through the night again.'

***

Dressed in what they hoped would be appropriate for the restaurant, Karina and Sarah stepped out onto the street at seven, just as a taxi pulled up.

Mr Hashimoto jumped out and greeted them warmly, bowing followed by handshakes. 'Karina-san. Sarah-san,' he addressed them. 'Please, call me Kazu, as your father did.' He ushered them into the back seat as he took the front, giving directions to the driver.

They headed into the city wonderland of colourful lights and neon signs, each structure looking like a Christmas tree, each building a Santa's grotto.

The taxi came to a stop and the back doors swung open, the festivity of flame-coloured lights outside the restaurant giving a welcoming glow in the chilly evening. They stepped in and were seated at a long narrow bench edging a hotplate the size of a large dining table. On the other side a red-faced chef wielded a large, steel spatula, skilfully sliding pancakes piled high with toppings across the griddle.

'This restaurant is okonomiyaki,' Kazu explained. 'It's a specialty food to this area of Japan. When rice was scarce after the war this meal became very popular – it uses ingredients people could find easily – from the gardens. I think now we add a lot more than the original recipe. It varies from place to place. You will see what this chef does.'

Kazu ordered the house specialty for each of them and the chef poured three dinner plate-sized circles of batter.

'Did you go to the university today?' Kazu asked them. They told him about the hall of fame, seeing Emiko's photo, reading her biography and putting their names down for her next lecture on Thursday.

He nodded as if he already knew.

The chef, with a flip of his wrist, sent pancakes sliding across the hotplate to stop directly in front of other patrons.

Karina turned to Kazu, bursting with the questions that had been bottling up all day. 'Did you go to Mick and Emiko's wedding?'

He explained how he had sneaked there, having been banned by his grandmother, because of her loyalty to Emiko's father, Tanazawa-san, her employer.

'What was it like?'

Kazu took a moment, swallowed hard. 'It was the most beautiful ceremony. I can never forget, as long as I live.' He told them about the shrine by the coast at twilight, the flame torches along the path and the sun setting over the hills. He marvelled how the two priests, Shinto and Christian, shared the service so seamlessly. He told them about all the friends who attended, mostly from Kiwi Base. The best man was Brooks,

Mick's friend from his early army days, who had also married a Japanese woman, Noriko. He named Croc the Australian carpenter, QM the quartermaster who was notorious for his moonshine saké and kimono-costumes, Tomoko-san and Yoshi-san who worked at the mess hall and became Emiko's 'family' when Mick was stationed elsewhere. And, of course, Yodo-san the woman samurai who had been Emiko's companion and bodyguard most of her life, in lieu of her mother.

'I didn't know women could be samurai.' Karina wanted to know more, but that had to wait until later.

His voice became a whisper when he mentioned the handsome couple and their obvious love for each other. 'It was so beautiful.' He raised a hand to the heavens. 'Out of this world.'

Karina sat in deep thought, visualising the glorious wedding, while overcome by sadness that their life together was cut so short.

A welcome distraction came from the chef, his spatula clattering on the hotplate as he scooped errant shreds of vegetables back onto each pancake, the utensil moving so fast it was merely a blur. A cup of noodles and paper-thin slices of meat were added, left to heat through then sprinkled with seasoning and a zig-zag drizzle of sauces.

Completing each work of art with a delicate garnish the chef spun them around on the griddle with a flick of his wrist, sending each one sliding across the steel surface to arrive precisely in front of each patron.

Chopsticks in hand, conversation ceased as they followed Kazu's lead, separating bite-size portions, marvelling at the unbelievably delicious combination of flavours. Their appetites were not satisfied until the hotplate had been cleared of the last morsels.

They sat back with sighs of contentment.

Kazu rested his chopsticks. 'I have a suggestion for tomorrow,' he said. 'I've cleared my schedule for the day. I'm hoping I can take you to some places of interest.'

Karina nodded enthusiastically. 'Where do you plan to take us?'

'For a start, I think, to my village where I first met Mick-san in his army truck and maybe some other places of importance.'

'That sounds good. There is one thing. I don't want Emiko to find out about me from someone else – I think it would be a shock – if she heard someone claiming to be her long-lost daughter was looking for her.'

Kazu gave a slow nod. 'I have thought of that. It is your place to tell her. Don't worry. I have told no-one and if somebody guesses, they will not be seeing her before you. Emiko-san is overseas until tomorrow.'

'She is overseas? They didn't tell us that.'

***

With their bellies full of delicious food and their heads full of new information, they stepped out of the taxi at Sakura Inn.

Plans in place for the next morning, they thanked Kazu for the dinner and said good night.

Chapter Twenty-Five

JAPAN

No amount of regret will change the past.
No amount of anxiety will change the future.
Any amount of gratitude will change the present.
– Ancient Wisdom

The bedding had been set out neatly in their room. They quickly washed, changed and sank into the depths of their futons.

'There's something about having a bed on the floor,' Karina said to the ceiling. 'It's feels so solid and secure.'

'You mean there's no room for monsters and spooks underneath?'

'That too,' Karina said eventually, as her thoughts drifted away and settled on the discussion of the evening – her parents. They weren't just a young couple who fell in love and had a quick and secret wedding. They were strong, mature people who wanted a better world for all. They were optimistic and well-meaning and hard-working. They went above and beyond their call of duty, to question and strive. They didn't look for an easy life.

The more she learned about Mick, the sadder she became about his untimely death – right when the world was opening up for him. Realising he was seriously ill, she could feel the pain of knowing that he may have to leave his wife and baby in a world without him. Her heart ached as she imagined how heart-breaking that would have been. He would have battled to survive. She switched her thinking away from that – it was overwhelming.

Turning to her mother's life, she analysed the theory that Emiko's work – her drive and her successes – were powered by her losses. Karina liked to think that Emiko would have gained strength from having known Mick, that she had learned from him and sensed his presence as she carried on in a life without him. Just as Karina had felt his presence today, maybe guiding them to find Kazu.

Gulping back a sob, she buried her face in the pillow.

Sarah stirred, reached across, and flopped a heavy hand on Karina's shoulder. 'What?'

Karina pulled in a calming breath. 'It's strange. How can I feel overwhelmingly sad about the loss of Mick yet, at the same time, joyful about finding Kazu? He's the very best guardian I could imagine to bring the past alive. Just knowing him makes me feel closer to Mick.'

'I get that. They were really good mates.'

'Something about him carries something of Mick – it's weird. As if he's got bits of Mick reincarnated in him.'

'Mick did give him a new life, in a way. Helped him overcome his destroyed world – to dream big.'

'*Hmm* – Follow your dreams,' Karina mumbled, as sleep enveloped her.

***

The almost inaudible tinkle of chinaware outside the door caught Karina's attention.

Their hostess had delivered the breakfast trays.

She pulled herself upright and checked the time on her watch. Eight o'clock. Kazu-san would be coming about nine. Plenty of time.

She pushed her quilt aside, and got to her feet, tiptoed to the door and slid the screen open. Two tray tables sat side-by-side, lidded bowls and tiny tea sets. She carried them one at a time, and placed them on the tatami mat in the narrow space between their futons.

'*Ohayoo!*' she called chirpily to her cousin, trying out some of the vocabulary she had been practising.

Sarah emerged from the covers, her tangled hair like a wind-blown haystack.

Karina laughed, then sat on her bed and pulled the tray table onto her lap. 'I'm determined to try more of this stuff today,' she said. 'That dinner last night was delicious, that *okono-yam…*'

'*Okonomiyaki,*' Sarah finished for her.

'Yeah, that. So, this can't be too bad.' She lifted lids to peek at the contents. 'It's different today. There's rice again, but the egg is cooked.'

She lifted another lid. 'And there's little toast, in triangles.'

They ate hungrily, enjoying the luxury of breakfast in bed and appreciating the efforts of their hostess to provide more familiar food for them.

'Still haven't had a soak in that deep bath,' Sarah commented as she put her near-empty tray aside and scrambled to her feet. 'Maybe tonight.'

They dressed quickly, Karina foregoing the heavy coat for a quilted jacket. Pulling on hats, wrapping scarves and grabbing gloves, they headed out to meet Kazu.

Standing outside the gate of Sakura Inn, he smiled broadly when they appeared and they exchanged greetings like old friends.

'We have just a little walk,' he said, starting off on foot. 'No taxi today. We will go in my car.'

They made their way across the busy street and down a few blocks, over a small bridge in the footpath where a tiny stream was channelled into a concrete ditch, around a tall apartment building, and into a public car park where Kazu located his car.

'My village is called Hinode-mura,' he explained, as they left the city streets behind and drove along a narrow causeway, empty low-lying fields at each side. 'It means Sunrise Village, because it is on the hilltop.'

They stretched their necks to look up where he pointed, but could see only lush forest.

'Mick-san used to drive the army truck on this road up to my village to take the volunteers into the hospital every day. That's where he met Emiko-san – on his truck.'

'My mother came from that village too? She was a volunteer?'

'Yes, like my grandmother and most of the women from the village. They took food from the gardens and helped look after the patients. Resources were very scarce and so many people had bad injuries after the war.'

Karina shuddered. It was a time in history she knew little about.

'Mick-san was very kind. He made the truck better for the villagers. He made a ladder for the back of the truck, so the people could climb up and down safely.'

Karina nodded and smiled. 'Sounds like my father – I mean my grandfather, Jack, he is always fixing things.'

'Yes. Mick-san said on the farm, he learnt everything.' His voice became thin. 'And then he taught me, the farming way. He was my teacher and my best friend. He opened up the world for me, after the war had shut it down.' He sniffed and wiped the back of his hand across his cheek. His voice brightened. 'Then Mick-san got tatami mats made for the seats in the truck.'

'Tatami mats?'

'Yes. We found a tatami maker who had damage to his house from the bomb. Mick-san had some wood in the truck, left over from the ladder, so we fixed Tatami-san's house while he made seat mats for the truck.' Kazu breathed in short puffs, pressed his lips and whispered, 'So proud to help Mick-san.'

At the edge of the valley the road wound up steeply.

'Tatami-san and his wife were very happy. They gave us delicious meals every day. Back then it was hard to find good food.'

Karina couldn't imagine what that would be like. Yet that was the world she had been born into. Again, she felt the blur between her two worlds – her life could so easily have been here, her childhood so very different.

At the top, the land flattened out and beside the road, vegetable plots juxtaposed together like a giant puzzle.

Just ahead, a cluster of small houses huddled together alongside a narrow lane.

'This is my village.' Kazu parked in a turnaround beside the road. 'We can walk from here.'

They got out, Kazu stood beside the car and turned to them. 'Mick-san's truck stopped here for the villagers. He called it the bus stop. That's where I met him on the first day. Grandmother said the new driver needs someone to show him the way to the hospital, or we'll get lost and we'll be late. She told me to do it. I could speak a little English. I rode in the passenger seat and I was his navigator.' He smiled. 'Good memories. We talked all the way – he learned Japanese, and I learned English.'

Karina stood firm. Mick was here. In this very place. She turned and looked down the village lane, the smell of wood smoke filling her with childhood nostalgia. The houses here had individual character, not like the city apartment buildings with anonymous occupants. She wanted to go inside those cottages, to meet the families. She felt something of their lifestyle – strangely akin to her own county upbringing.

Two children, a boy and a girl, stood shyly on the porch as they approached the first house. Kazu stopped and spoke to them, and they responded only with solemn expressions.

'That is my house. These are my children.'

Karina felt a sudden pang of guilt that she knew nothing of his life. All conversations had centred around her family members.

'This is my daughter, Rumi. And my son, Mikio.'

Karina and Sarah said 'Hello.'

'How old are you?' Karina ventured, wondering if they would understand her.

After some hesitancy, Rumi said she was nine and Mikio was seven.

'Kazu-san, they are delightful.'

He smiled proudly then ushered them on along the lane. 'I named my son Mikio, like Mick.'

Karina clamped a hand over her mouth and turned back to look at her father's namesake. She waved. They waved back and ran inside giggling.

Kazu led them further into the village; Karina fixing her attention on the houses, some were in need of repair and others seemed to be deserted. 'Are these houses empty? Were they damaged in the war too?'

'Luckily, this village is far enough away to have not been damaged in the war. But in the last few years, many people moved away. It's better to live in the city for work. Old people die and no one wants to live here. I am lucky. My home and my work are just across the valley from each other.'

Karina stepped onto an empty verandah and peeped through the tattered shoji screen. 'I would live here,' she said, turning back to Sarah and Kazu. 'I would fix this place up and definitely live in this village,' she added.

Kazu laughed and shook his head. 'Just like your father.'

She faced him directly. 'Am I? How am I like him?'

'He loved this village. He loved Japan. He wanted to live here too.' Kazu continued walking and they kept pace.

'Could he have lived here?' Karina persisted. 'If they had not decided to go to New Zealand, could my parents have lived in one of these houses – with me, like the other villagers?'

Kazu's mouth twisted. 'I think not.'

'Why not? Can't foreigners live here?'

'It's more like – Emiko-san could not live here, in this village.'

Karina frowned. 'I don't understand.'

'How do I say it? Maybe because her family property is nearby, she would have to live there. Or move away to another place.'

Unable to make sense of that, Karina returned her focus to their surroundings.

The houses became more wide-spread and garden plots gave way to forest, as the path narrowed and they left the village behind.

'Where are we going?' Sarah asked, intrigue tingeing her voice. 'Is there a shrine down here?'

Kazu just smiled and walked on. 'You will see.'

Along the bush track they came to a high point in the path looking down on a cluster of buildings, the full vista of an expansive property with magnificent gardens spread out before them.

Karina saw children running across the grass, playing in the trees, the tinkle of their excited voices carrying over the treetops as if on the wings of a bird.

Kazu continued around a corner where the path dipped and opened into a clearing.

Before them, steep stone steps led down to a paved terrace where a high entrance gate stood between two small huts, topped with a long, narrow roof.

'Let's sit here.' He sat on the top step, taking in the grounds.

They followed, scanning the expansive property of scattered buildings and gardens as far as the eye could see.

'What is this place?' Karina asked.

'This is Emiko-san's childhood home.'

Karina's mouth fell open. Her eyes widened. She looked around at the acreage befitting an emperor's palace.

'Your grandfather, Tanazawa-san lived here for many years, and his ancestors before him.'

'My grandfather?' That felt strange to say – she had grown up without knowing grandparents.

Questions ran rampant in Karina's mind, weaving themselves into confusing tangles.

Does my grandfather still live here? Does Emiko live here? Who are the children over there? Why didn't you tell me before we came?

Kazu continued. 'But the people here now aren't Emiko's family. When this property came into Emiko's hands, she established an orphanage.'

In disbelief, Karina turned to him. 'It's an orphanage? She set up an orphanage?'

'That's what we read on the wall at the university,' Sarah reminded her.

Kazu nodded. 'That's right. It's one of Emiko-san's enterprises. Initially, she wanted hafu babies and their mothers to have a safe place to live so she added dormitories…'

Karina interrupted him. 'What are hafu babies?'

He blew out a breath and his voice became soft. 'It means "half". Babies with one foreign parent and one Japanese parent – usually the mother is Japanese.'

'What? Like me? Hafu?' Karina cupped her hands each side of her face.

Kazu smiled. 'Yes. At one time it was a big shame to be hafu. But since the work of tutors like Emiko-san, people understand better that everyone is the same no matter where the parents are from.'

'So, the orphanage was for hafu babies and mothers.'

'It was at first. Since then it has opened up to include women and children from many circumstances.'

Karina turned to Kazu. 'You said this is one of her enterprises. She has others?'

He nodded. 'Many of the mothers as well as women from the villages around here work in the clothing factory that was her father's business. Now it is called 'Yofuku Kiwi'. Western style garments for women. It's very successful, and the profits cover the running costs of this.' He made a sweeping gesture, encompassing the buildings and grounds. Then he pointed to the long building surrounded by verandahs on all sides, one corner overhanging a large pond. 'That's the original homestead where Emiko-san grew up.'

'Who looks after this when she is away?'

'Emiko-san doesn't usually work here. Many of the staff she has known for many years. Last night at dinner, I told you about Yodo-san, Emiko-san's childhood guardian and bodyguard.'

Karina nodded, remembering she wanted to know more about female samurai.

'Yodo-san is the manager here. And Tomoko-san, from the mess hall, manages Yofuku Kiwi clothing. She was like a big sister for Emiko-san when she got married.'

'Yes, I remember. You said there were two women who were like family to Emiko when Mick went away. What about the other one?'

'The other one,' he paused, 'Yoshi-san. She is the clothing designer at Yofuku Kiwi. And I am very fortunate. She is also my wife.'

They shared their congratulations.

'I hope you will meet her but today she is working. Her mother is looking after our children.'

He stood and suggested they head back.

On the way through the village, Karina and Sarah peeked into more of the empty houses, their conversation running away with possibilities.

Kazu, entertained by their interest, slowed his pace to keep in step, answering their questions about the families who had moved on.

With nobody home at his place, he suggested they go to an udon house in town for a late lunch.

Feeling more confident using chopsticks now, they tucked in with enthusiasm, thankful that slurping noises were acceptable and showed appreciation.

Dabbing their mouths with embroidered napkins, the conversation shifted to meeting Emiko the next day.

'What do you want to do?' Sarah asked. 'Attend the lecture, and then what?'

Karina contemplated. 'You know, I haven't thought that far ahead. It felt like such an achievement just to know she will be there then.'

'You can't just bowl up to her in a public place. *Hi, remember me?*'

Karina sniggered, then sobered. 'I thought I would wait till the lecture is over and ask to see her privately.'

'What if she doesn't hang around? What if she's got another meeting somewhere and gets whisked away in a taxi?'

'*Hmm.*' Karina didn't have an answer.

Kazu stepped in. 'May I suggest something?' They turned to him, urging him to continue.

'I sometimes organise a business group which Emiko-san attends when she is in town. The group meets every month and sometimes a few of us meet in between to plan upcoming events.'

Karina nodded, keen for him to continue.

'I could send a message to her saying I want to meet with her tomorrow afternoon.'

'And then what?' Sarah asked. 'How would that work?'

Kazu turned to Karina. 'We would plan it however you want. What do you think?'

'Of course, it all depends on Emiko being available and willing to meet you.'

'If not tomorrow, then maybe another day soon,' Kazu suggested. 'Unless she's going out of town again.'

They discussed various ways of facilitating the process and agreed on the plan that Kazu would meet Emiko alone first, break the news gently that her daughter had turned up.

'We'll wait nearby,' Sarah added. 'You call us or wave to us if she's ready to meet.'

Karina slumped. 'I'm not handling all the maybes very well. It's exhausting.'

'Me too,' Sarah agreed.

'I suspect you still have some jetlag,' Kazu suggested. 'Would you like me to drive you back to the inn. It's the Japanese way to sleep whenever you need to.'

'I like that idea,' Sarah jumped in. 'At home, only babies and nanas are allowed to nap during the day. Otherwise it's considered lazy.'

'Here the reverse is true. A short sleep is likely to give you more energy for the rest of the day. You will work better.'

Outside Sakura Inn, Kazu said he would send them a message as soon as he had made contact with Emiko-san.

They thanked him for the outing, said goodbye and returned to the sanctuary of their immaculate room, pulling out the futons and collapsing down with groans of gratitude.

'I could get to like this napping thing,' Sarah mumbled into her pillow.

'I'm falling in love with this place…' Karina's voice drifted away.

Chapter Twenty-Six

JAPAN

Fall down seven times,
Get up eight.
– Japanese Proverb

The afternoon nap had been fitful and disturbed. Rather than waking energised, as Kazu had predicted, they felt fuzzy-headed and at odds with each other.

The hot tub was the only thing they could agree on.

***

Karina moved suddenly and more water sloshed over the side. 'I don't think I can do it.'

'Stay still! You're emptying the tub!' Sarah sank lower until the warmth covered her shoulders again. 'What can't you do?'

'See her. Emiko.'

'You're kidding. We've come all this way to find her, and now you're a chicken?'

Karina draped the washcloth over her face and mumbled through it. 'I didn't really expect to find her. I just thought I would find out *about* her.'

'Why? What's the point if you don't meet her – and bridge the gap?'

'I just think… she might not want to see me.' Dropping the cloth, she fixed her gaze on the shadowy branches bathed in moonlight just beyond the opaque window. 'She's a successful woman. Even famous – here and overseas. And she's managed all that because she… had no other responsibilities. Do you think she wants to be shackled with a long-lost child?'

'Don't be ridiculous. You're not a child. You are also an independent woman.'

'She still might not want to see me.' Karina slapped a hand onto the surface of water. 'I'm so stupid. What made me think she would be okay with us meeting up?'

Sarah struggled to her feet. 'I'm getting out.' She stood on the duckboard, wriggled into her robe and tied the belt with an impatient tug. 'You can stay there until you come to your senses.'

Karina's spirits as damp as her environment, her thoughts drifted aimlessly. The whole revelation of who her real parents were had been so consuming that she had thought of nothing but herself since then.

What if Emiko had actually rejected her, the hafu baby she had given birth to? What if that was the reason Mick had taken her back to New Zealand with him, alone? It all made sense now – why Dorothy and Jack had brought her up as their daughter.

All her life until now, nobody had mentioned her real mother, nobody had attempted to tell Emiko where her baby had gone. Why? Clearly, because she had rejected the hafu daughter.

That was why Jack and Dorothy had kept the secret all those years. They didn't want her to find out her real mother had not wanted her. They were trying to save her from the painful truth.

With a sudden lurch, she was out of the tub, dripping onto the slatted floor, pulling on her robe and leaving wet footprints along the corridor to the room.

'She didn't want me,' she announced to Sarah.

'What!'

'She didn't want me. I'm so dumb. Why didn't I see that?' She pulled the screen door closed behind her. 'If Mick knew he was dying – and clearly, he did, from his letter, why would he ask his parents to raise me? Why would he not tell them who my mother was and ask them to get hold of her?' She dropped onto her futon. 'Or Brooks – his best mate, there with him in his last days – why did he not get Brooks to arrange my return to my real mother? It's obvious! She didn't want me!'

Sarah's mouth hung open, the likely truth leaving her speechless.

Silence hung in the air, suffocating and ugly.

The night passed as a sleepless nightmare, the demons of reality tightening their stranglehold on Karina's childish dreams.

***

They received the breakfast trays with even less enthusiasm than on the first morning.

Kazu's note was delivered soon after. He wrote that Emiko had flown in overnight and had already accepted his request to meet following her lecture. He named a teahouse adjoining the university as the meeting place.

'I'm not going.' Karina said flatly.

'Fine.' Sarah slammed the lid down on her toast bowl, and stood. 'I'm not going to argue with you any more. If you change your mind, I'll see you there.' She rifled through her suitcase and pulled out an outfit for the day.

Karina watched her get dressed. 'You're still going?' she asked, hoping the answer was "No". She needed an ally in her misery.

'Of course. I want to see my aunt. I want to hear that lecture. And I want to figure things out.'

'I can't believe you're going – without me.'

Sarah grabbed up her shoulder bag and turned to face her cousin. 'I'm just sticking to the plan – our plan. So, the problem is not that I'm going. It's that you're not going.' She slid open the door and slipped into her shoes on the deck. 'I'm certainly not going to waste the time and money I've spent getting here. If you change your mind, you know where I'll be.' Without a backward glance, Sarah turned and headed across the little courtyard and through the high gate to the street.

Karina's bones felt like concrete, her muscles like ancient leather, and her mind belonged to someone else. She eventually dressed, walked down the street someway and into a large green area of mowed grass and giant trees.

What had happened yesterday? On arriving home from the day out with Kazu, she'd fallen into her futon saying something about loving this country.

On waking from the nap, she seemed to have had a personality transplant, with the world becoming dark and sinister.

To make sense of her change of heart, she could only attribute it to Mick – as she had done with all her inspirations and revelations since she'd arrived.

'I can feel it – he's leading me,' she had frequently confessed to Sarah.

He'd led her to Kazu, to Emiko's photo at the university, and then to register for her lecture. He'd been with her at the village and again as they looked over Emiko's family home, now the orphanage.

Why had Emiko established the orphanage? Was it guilt for having deserted her own child?

What did Mick have to say about that? Where was he, now that she was in despair?

Where was his influence, his guiding spirit?

She stopped and looked up to the tree tops, their fingers tickling the clouds sliding by.

In the distance the alluring sound of wooden windchimes piqued her curiosity, the soft melodious percussion drawing her forward. Down the pathway and through a clearing between the trees she saw a wooden gateway the colour of chilli paste. Two tall poles topped with heavy crossbeams. A path meandered underneath to a small building beyond.

Arm in arm, two women walked her way, one of them wiping tears. 'That was amazing!' her companion was saying, her accent American.

'Excuse me,' Karina interrupted them. 'What is this place?'

'Oh, it's a shrine. You've got to go and see,' the companion replied. 'The fortune telling is right on the money!'

The other woman tucked away her handkerchief and managed a smile. 'That's right. That's the best news I've ever had. I'm going to be a grandmother. And my daughter's been married five years. I can't wait to get home to tell them.'

'You go up the steps,' the companion informed her. 'Clap three times and say a prayer, then pick up a bamboo cup and shake it till the first stick falls out. The number on it corresponds to a paper slip in the tiny wooden drawers on the wall. It's called *omikuri*, I think.'

'*Omikuji*,' her friend corrected.

'Oh, that's it. *Omikuji*. I don't understand how it works, but it sure does,' the companion continued. 'It's just amazing.'

They walked on, deep in discussion.

Karina let out a loud sigh and continued through the gateway. 'Omikuji,' she repeated to herself. 'I might as well.'

She climbed the steps, clapped three times then pressed her hands together to pray. Pray? What would she – could she – pray for? There certainly wasn't any reason to give thanks. Could she express hope? What for? A hope that her life would make sense. 'My life doesn't make sense,' she whispered. Feelings welled up inside. 'Yesterday I had hope. Today I don't know who I am.' She sat down heavily on the top step, dropped her head into her hands and let time float by, unchecked.

'Shake the cup.'

Karina looked up.

A girl, about twelve years of age, stood before her, the sleeve of her elaborate kimono draping from her arm like a festival banner, her hand holding out a bamboo container. 'Shake the cup,' she repeated. 'Find your number. My grandmother says it will help.'

Some distance away stood a diminutive woman in a thick, navy kimono, her greying hair pulled back neatly. She gave a subtle smile, a nod.

A number of bamboo sticks about the length of chopsticks protruded from the cup.

Karina guessed, from what the American women had said, numbers would be written at the other end.

The girl thrust the cup closer, her expression patient, unmoving. Karina heaved a sigh and reluctantly took the cup.

'This way,' the girl said, heading into the building and turning to wait.

Karina launched to her feet and followed, stopping beside a table covered in red felt.

'Shake,' the girl instructed, vibrating her hand above the table.

Karina's heart wasn't in the mood for games, but she had the feeling this was the only way to reclaim her peace. She shook the container. Nothing fell out.

The girl demonstrated again, more vigorously. Karina obeyed and one stick dropped onto the red cloth.

'Come.' the girl danced away to the cabinet of tiny drawers. 'This way.'

Karina picked up the stick and looked at the writing on the rounded end. It was in Japanese characters. She walked over and showed it to the girl, who spun around and opened the relevant drawer.

'Take one.'

Karina reached into the drawer, withdrew a small slip of paper covered in unfamiliar script. She held it out for the girl to read.

'*Hmm.*' She took it, studied it, shrugged and ran outside to show the grandmother. Curiosity overcoming reluctance, Karina's mood began to lift.

As she went to follow, a young priest appeared, his paprika robes reflecting the hue of the woodwork.

'May I translate?' he asked.

Karina shrugged. 'They have my paper.' She indicated the grandmother and child outside.

'Ah.' The priest smiled and nodded. 'That is good. Listen to the wisdom of age through the words of a child.'

As Karina approached them the girl said, 'Grandmother says Number three is *Han-kichi* – means half blessing. Half blessing is good.'

Karina's mood slumped. 'How can a half blessing be good?'

The woman looked up at Karina, her gaze appraising and profound, like an x-ray of the soul. It was some time before she spoke again. The girl translated. 'Grandmother says bad luck gone. Good luck is coming.'

Then the girl concentrated as her grandmother spoke at length. 'Good luck for travel, good luck for your heart, luck for study and learning new things…'

She prompted her grandmother to repeat something. *'Tenkyo,'* the woman said, then added, '*Usemono.*'

The girl turned to Karina. 'Maybe a new place to live and good luck finding something lost long time ago.'

'Machibito,' the grandmother added finally.

'Good luck for an important person being waited for.'

Karina stared from one to the other, her heart beginning to thump, her mouth running dry.

The girl handed back the fortune paper.

'Thank you. *Arigato.*' Karina bowed to them both, wanting to say more, cursing herself for being tongue-tied with the few Japanese words she knew.

The grandmother and child bowed and turned to walk away.

'Wait! What's your name?' The words came to her. '*Onamae wa?*'

The girl swung around, a smile lighting up her face. 'Emiko,' she said.

Chapter Twenty-Seven

JAPAN

Expect the unexpected,
Believe in the unbelievable,
Achieve the unachievable.
– Ancient Wisdom

Karina's eyes fixed on the girl and her grandmother as they walked away, their image eventually forming a misty memory.

'Okay, Mick-san,' she looked up at the treetops, their branches waving to her in the chilly breeze. 'I guess you're on my side again.'

She must get to the meeting on time.

Looking at her wrist, she realised she'd forgotten her watch so had no idea of the time.

Her heart began thumping.

Frantically Karina looked around. The park was bordered densely by trees on all sides.

She strained her ears to pick up traffic noise and set off at a run hoping to find a taxi.

She might have already missed the meeting. What if Sarah had gone to the teahouse and met Emiko – without her? She kicked herself for being so stubborn and not going with Sarah to the lecture.

Her cousin had been a great companion on this venture and Karina couldn't have done the trip without her, but she didn't know if it would be possible to forgive Sarah if she stepped into the breach in her absence.

Out of breath, she reached the street and waved her hand. Within seconds a lemon-coloured taxi swung to the kerb, the back door opening in an anonymous welcome.

'The women's university,' she said to the driver, getting in.

'*Hai*,' the driver replied. The doors clicked closed and they pulled out into the stream of traffic.

Nothing outside the cab looked familiar and she prayed they were going the right way, hoping she had said the name correctly. There was nothing to do but sit tight and expect the universe to take care of her.

'Mick,' she whispered. 'Stay with me.'

Eventually the taxi turned into a narrow side street, edged up a steep incline and pulled to a stop when an advancing crowd made it impossible to drive further.

Karina paid the driver and got out.

Dozens of women, excited, laughing, chattering pressed towards her. Were they all coming from Emiko's presentation?

'Excuse me, *Sumimasen*,' she said to the group in front of her. 'Hai, yes?' one of them said.

'Did you see Emiko Tanazawa?'

'Oh yes!' she replied. 'Emiko Tanazawa Mitchell.' The others nodded enthusiastically.

Another clapped a hand dramatically on her chest. 'She's my hero.'

'You know the hardest part?' A third one added, holding a handkerchief to her cheek. 'About her baby, how she had to give her up. That was so sad.'

'But it inspired her to help others,' the first woman jumped in again. 'That's what kept her going. She's so brave.'

Karina found her voice. 'Why did she have to give her baby up?'

'She was really sick when the baby was born,' the third one said.

'Her husband was away so her father sent her to an island hospital where they took the babies to an orphanage.'

Karina swallowed hard. 'Did she… did she try to find the baby – later – when she was well again?'

'Oh yes,' the dramatic one replied. 'But the baby had been adopted to another couple and they were going to America.'

Karina frowned. 'America?'

'That's where most adopted hafu went. She still looks for her when she's there,' the handkerchief one said. 'I so hope she finds her.'

'Oh, there's our bus.' They waved goodbye and hurried on.

America!

An unasked question had been answered – why Emiko had not looked for her in New Zealand.

Karina blew out a breath. The most important thing was – *she had been looking.*

Elation mingled uncomfortably with new anxiety, as Karina realised she had yet to find the teahouse. Sarah had Kazu's note with the teahouse name. Looking around she saw nothing – nobody – familiar.

Changing direction, she crossed into a side lane to go with, not against, the foot traffic. 'Sumimasen,' she said to a woman walking nearby. 'Is there a teahouse around here?

'I think so.' She turned to her companion. They discussed as they walked, gesturing in various directions. She turned back to Karina. 'We think this way.' She pointed ahead. 'Just a little more. After the university garden.'

Karina hurried on, the rollercoaster of emotions sweeping over her as she wondered how many more ups and downs were yet to come.

'Karina!' She swung around to see Sarah picking her way through the throng.

'Thank god you came,' she said, enveloping her in a strong hug. 'I don't want you to miss this – miss her – for the world.'

'How was it? – How was she?'

'Amazing! Of course, I couldn't understand much of what she said, but I got bits, and I saw how others reacted.'

Karina nodded. 'What does she look like?

Sarah locked eyes with her and gave a little smile. 'Like Jackie Kennedy.'

The pedestrian flow urged them forward.

'I talked with some others back there,' Karina said. 'They said she spoke about the baby – about me. How she *had* to give me up.' She wiped the back of her hand across a cheek. 'She's been looking for me… but she thought I had been adopted and taken to America.'

'Really? But she's been wanting to find you – that's the important thing.'

'I'm getting impatient, now I know. Where's that teahouse?'

'It's too soon to go there. Kazu needs to talk to her first.'

Karina grabbed her cousin's sleeve. 'That doesn't need to happen now. I know she wants to find me and you know what she looks like.'

'*Hmm*. Don't you think it's still a good idea for Kazu to meet her first?

Kind of prepare her?'

'No. It's not like it's bad news. The real reason I wanted him to check with her first was in case she didn't want to see me. That's not the case now.'

Sarah pointed some way ahead. 'Look, there's a teahouse. I wonder if it's the one.' She rummaged in her bag for Kazu's message. 'Mizuki Teahouse,' she read.

As they got closer, Karina noticed a banner sign hanging from a pole at the entrance. 'Got no idea what it says but I'm pretty sure the picture is a tree. That mean anything?'

Sarah shot Karina a look. 'It does actually. For some strange reason I remember *mizuki* means a dogwood tree.'

'Dogwood? We had dogwood trees at school.'

'Well that's how I know it. This must be the place.'

They stopped for breath at the entrance steps.

'Karina-san! Sarah-san!'

They looked up to see Kazu standing on the verandah.

Karina froze. 'She didn't come.'

Sarah grabbed her arm and pulled her forward. 'We don't know that. Let's see.'

Kazu bowed his greetings.

'Well?' Karina's nervousness rendered her incapable of formalities.

Kazu held up a reassuring hand. 'She's not here yet but I expect her soon.'

Karina told him what she had learned about Emiko – about herself – from the group.

Kazu looked surprised. 'America! I didn't know she believed that. But then we have never discussed it.'

'You have been friends all that time and you didn't tell her Mick took me to New Zealand?'

A thoughtful expression crossed his face and eventually he answered. 'Emiko-san was away for a long time, firstly at the island hospital, and because of the bad news about Mick-san she eventually returned to her father's home to recover. After a year or so I saw her again.' He paused and drew breath. 'There was a big divide between the Emiko-san I had known and the new Emiko. She could go on, she told me, only by putting the past behind her – by trying to forget. That was how she made a new life. For me to tell her about you would have been opening wounds. She did not ask so it was not my place to say.'

In one-way Karina understood. In another she found his reasons for secrecy so frustrating.

Sarah expressed it clearly. 'You really do follow protocol!'

He gave an understanding smile. 'People have their reasons. As your grandparents did for keeping secret what they knew. We must always use our own judgement about how best to serve others.'

Karina pondered her response. Kazu can't have been the only one who knew Mick had taken her to New Zealand. What about Emiko's other friends?

She was about to ask him when something caught Kazu's eye.

'I think I see Emiko-san now.'

They spun around to look into the crowd. 'Where?'

'Yes, it's her. Do you want to wait here while I bring her to you?' Karina's insides leapt and twisted.

Kazu placed a reassuring hand on her arm. 'It's all right, Karina-san. I will say nothing about you – but maybe,' his eyes levelled with hers, 'I should say there is someone here to meet her?'

Karina gulped and gave a single nod.

He held her gaze a moment longer to be sure, turned and headed down the teahouse steps.

Chapter Twenty-Eight

JAPAN

Emiko

One joy can drive away a thousand sorrows.
– Japanese Proverb

Hoping my legs would hold me up until I was out of view, I gave a final bow and stepped off the stage, with my audience still applauding.

'Why do I do this?' I asked my assistant, sinking into the chair she had ready for me in the side room.

Hana-san clicked the door closed. 'Do what, Emiko-san?'

I picked up a fine china cup from the tray she had prepared, rubbed my finger across the abstract design and sipped, thankful for the taste of familiar tea after ten days in America. 'Two things – firstly, accept a booking to speak straight after a long flight.' I sipped slowly, thoughtfully.

'And the second thing?'

I blew out a breath and dropped my head back, as if looking for an answer from the skies. 'Talk about… her.'

Hana-san sat down on the stool, facing me. 'You talk about your baby because it makes you real. It means so much to your audience – they relate to you over those personal connections. They know – or need to know – how important it is to override such challenges.'

I groaned. 'I don't want to tell it again. And again. I think it gets more painful every time.'

She studied my face, her expression showing wisdom beyond her thirty years, her voice carrying the soft understanding of a grandmother. 'Is it because you are disappointed again? Not finding anything more about her on this trip?'

I nodded and wrapped two hands around my cup like a child.

'Sometimes I want to stop these speaking tours.' My voice brightened. 'I will one day.'

Hana-san shifted her position. 'What will you do then?'

'Ha!' I forced a short laugh. 'What will I do! I have no idea. Maybe I will go back to designing at my factory or fill my time at the orphanage. Maybe I'll retire – retreat. Get a home base instead of living in hotels. I might even buy one of those empty little cottages I love in Hinode-Mura. Do it up. Anything that means I don't have to think.' I finished my tea and placed the cup on the tray. 'Or talk.'

'Another?' She lifted the teapot ready to pour.

I shook my head. 'I'm meeting Kazuya-san at Mizuki Teahouse in a few minutes.'

'You need to rest,' she said sternly. 'Enough meetings! You just said – no talk, no think, no people.'

I blew out a sigh. 'Just this one. Then I'll rest.'

'What does he want so soon after you arrive back?'

'Something about the business association, I guess.'

'Thirty minutes! That's all I allow. Then I will come and get you.'

I struggled to my feet, resting a hand on her shoulder while I found my equilibrium. 'That'll be good,' I said, realising how little energy I had.

The lane was still busy so I took the path through the university gardens, feasting my senses on the indicators of home. The damp earth – always a grounding aroma, the bare dogwood trees – strong and stark, the peaceful serenity of the gardens in contrast to the lively chatter along the lane just over the high bamboo fence, and the fresh chill in the air making me wrap my arms tighter and anticipate the teahouse fireplace. I took in a breath and let it flow out. 'At last,' I whispered. 'Home.'

My steps settled into a meditative rhythm while my head swam with the ongoing aftereffects of too many hours in an airplane seat.

How many more times would I do that? When would it be enough? When would the chase – the hunt for her – stop pulling on me? I had no answers and the brain work wearied me so I changed the subject in my head.

What could Kazuya-san want so urgently? It vexed me a little to accept his request but he was a good friend so I didn't have the heart to turn him down. He had something lined up for me, he'd said. An idea, a new direction. What could be so important?

Only one way to find out.

I took a side path towards the lane, pushed open a gate in the fence and turned towards Mizuki Teahouse.

Kazuya-san saw me approaching, waved and came down to greet me. His usually calm expression sparkled with excitement, his shining eyes darting from me to the teahouse as he walked beside me, barely concealing a hint of intrigue.

'What are you up to?'

He didn't answer, but looked up at two young women, arms tightly linked, waiting on the verandah. The taller one I had seen in the auditorium, her blonde head conspicuous above all the others.

'What's this about?' I asked as we mounted the steps, having no energy for more students, more work, more talk.

Then my focus was drawn to the other – her dark hair not straight like mine but wavy – like another.

The nervous twist of her mouth growing into an off-centre smile wrenched my heart. I pressed a hand to my chest. *Could it be...? Could she be...?*

But I've thought that so many times before – and been disappointed.

Still, I searched her face, her eyes – deep, beguiling – yet enigmatic – guarding secrets. My gaze flicked over her, frantically taking in every detail.

Did the twist of her mouth really look like his teasing smile?

So many years ago... yet, it seemed like yesterday – he was always fresh in my mind.

I'd filled up my life well enough, but not managed to fill my heart. Then I saw it – *the jade spiral at her throat –*

Dare I hope?

Her hand rushed to it. Long fingers caressed the smooth curls.

'It... it was... originally my father's,' she said, her eyes fixed on my reaction.

Her father's!

I pulled in a breath and forced my internal calm. 'I had one once – a *pikorua*. So very precious.'

Her eyes widened when I said the Maori word and she nodded.

'In my country... this stands for family connections.' Her voice thick with emotion. 'Eternity.'

Her fingers traced the outline of the greenstone pendant. A figure eight. Infinity.

I found my voice again. 'I remember… bringing loved ones together again in some way, one day.'

Her eyes glistened, her words punctuated by little snatches of breath. 'Did you give yours… to someone… you love?'

My voice now a whisper, 'I gave it… to… my baby daughter.' I swallowed hard. 'It entwined my heart.'

A single tear ran down her cheek. 'Because of this… my father found me.'

I had no voice. My lips mouthed his name. 'Mick-san.'

She gasped, her eyes overflowing. 'Mick-san,' she repeated.

My baby?

My daughter?

'Karina?' I asked, still not daring to believe.

'Karina!' She nodded, tears flowing.

I stepped forward, reaching for her through the haze of my own flooding eyes. 'My baby! Karina!' I tried to calm my thumping heart. Irrelevant words fell nervously from my mouth. 'You've grown so tall!'

She laughed, her hands grasping mine. 'I have just… recently learned… the truth,' she whispered.

'So, have I,' I managed. 'This very moment… been looking… so long.'

My eyes drank in everything about her. My hands clutched hers. *Would I ever be able to let go?*

She spoke through her tears. 'I'm sorry… it took so long… so much… time lost.'

I took her beautiful face in my hands, drawing her into my heart – as I had before. 'Just one joy can drive away a thousand sorrows.'